The Smoke of Summer

by I. YEVISH

Author of
Cape Island

In Memory of
My Mother and My Father

Published by
I. Yevish Books
Box 366
Cape May Point, New Jersey 08212

Manufactured in the United States of America

"Are you under thirty, Miss Harrah?"

Willacassa did not know what to make of the question. Nor did she want to be intimidated by the sixty-year-old virgin.

"I'm twenty-three, Miss Dix."

"And very pretty."

"Is that bad?"

Dorothea Dix ignored the question. "With a wasp waist and crinoline," she continued with birdlike observation, her blue-gray eyes flashing defiantly. "I cannot use you, Miss Harrah."

"Why not?"

"Because you cannot turn a full-grown man around in a bed."

"Try me."

"And because you have never done menial work."

"I most assuredly have!"

"Where?"

"In a hotel. My father's hotel."

"Your father's?"

"In Cape Island." Willacassa did not mention the name, Trescott House, for fear that its reputation for luxury might do her in here. "I made beds side by side with Harriet Tubman."

While this was not exactly true, it was not entirely false either. Harriet Tubman had worked for her father, and when Nathaniel Harrah was shorthanded, Willacassa had made beds, too.

"Harriet Tubman, was it? Next you'll be telling me you worked for the Underground Railroad. All right, I'll try you, young lady. Much against my better judgment. You're far too pretty to be much good around here. You'll be assigned to one of the hospitals. If the surgeons or doctors want you out of there, you stay and you do your job. No matter what. Those are my orders."

"Yes, Miss Dix."

"Remember, you stay no matter what. I can't have the hospitals understaffed because of some deep-seated prejudice against women. Women are better cut out for this kind of thing anyway. Men have taken over the profession more by default than by design. The important thing is that our boys do not suffer too much. The women I assign will do what they can to ease pain and make them comfortable."

"I understand."

"What did you say your name was?"

"Harrah. Willacassa Harrah."

"I'll put you down as thirty, although nobody will believe it.

Can't have them think I'm changing my standards."

Though Willacassa took particular satisfaction in winning out over the stern, newly-appointed Superintendent of Women Nurses, she was not as successful with the nurses and stewards. These men regarded the hospital—a makeshift infirmary that had formerly been a run-down church—as a male bailiwick and Superintendent Dix's nurses as interlopers. The only work they assigned was of the most menial kind, the dirty jobs and tedious tasks that no one wanted. Nor did Willacassa look forward to tending the bedridden. There had been precious little fighting in the two months since the rebellion broke out. Most of the hospitalized were men unaccustomed to camp life, stricken with fever or inflammation of the lungs. There were no really battle-wounded among them. And though she certainly was not looking for casualties, Willacassa liked to think she was part of the nobler side of the war, the dedicated struggle to bring secession to an abrupt end.

One day while she was changing soiled linen, a young recruit, slight of build and not yet given to shaving, was carried in so fever-ridden that a male attendant immediately went to work. Unbuttoning the heavy flannel shirt of the recruit, he reached for a sponge. Halfway he stopped. Almost as an afterthought he peered at the young recruit's body, and peered again. He scratched his head, then smiled a silly smile as he signalled two other nurses to the bed.

"Here, look at this. Do you see what I see?"

The nurses approached. "I'll be shot for a horsethief!"

Whatever it was that prompted the remark piqued Willacassa's curiosity. As soon as the male nurses and stewards gathered round and began whispering among themselves, she put down her fresh bedsheets and pillow cases and moved to see for herself. This was not easy. A mass of male bodies blocked her view, and it was only between undulating shoulders and elbows that she caught a glimpse of what was going on.

Stretched out on the bed and moaning in a high fever lay the young recruit. The face seemed boyish enough, with its high cheekbones and parched lips. But below the shoulders, naked to the world, pointed red nipples and a woman's breasts.

"Tried to pass for a man," snickered one of the male nurses. "Got exposed, I guess."

"No doubt about it."

"Can't you see she's sick," interjected Willacassa, outraged by the conspiratorial inactivity of the men. "The least you could do is cover her up!"

The mood among the nurses and stewards, which had been

4

one of curious surprise and quiet amusement, changed with Willacassa's outburst. A few felt awkward and embarrassed by her presence. They were inclined to let her make her way through the circle of onlookers to the half-naked invalid's side. But the others resented the sudden interruption of what had become a compelling spectacle, and refused to give ground.

"It's not our fault she's here," said one of the nurses. "Or that she passed for a soldier. Besides, covering her up won't do her fever any good."

Willacassa tried to squeeze her way through to the young woman. But the press of male bodies in her path proved too much for her. "Let me pass!" she demanded. She even stamped hard on a nurse's foot, hoping to shock him into stepping aside. But the man only laughed and did not budge from his vantage point.

"Too bad she wasn't in my tent," he said, pointing towards the invalid. "Could have helped pass the time."

"Idiot!" cried Willacassa. "If you don't let me through, I'll report you to the chief surgeon!"

"He'll only want to see for himself, Ma'am."

The mock response infuriated Willacassa. She grabbed the man by the arm and tried to pull him aside. Without much trouble the nurse held fast. The more he ignored her, the angrier Willacassa became.

But their struggle was brought to an abrupt end by Dorothea Dix. Flanked by two plain-faced female aides, the dour superintendent had unexpectedly appeared. "Prying and poking around," as was her custom, with no authorization over anyone but her own nurses, she was determined somehow to weed out idlers and incompetents, whatever their sex.

"What's going on?" she demanded, forcing a path through the male nurses. Though she was petite and near sixty, no one was prepared to do battle with the woman whose brown hair was combed back flat over the ears and coiled at the back of her head like a wagon spring.

When she spied the young "recruit," her breasts exposed for all to see, Superintendent Dix turned ashen and pulled a sheet over the woman, firing hostile glances in all directions.

"What animals you are!"

Turning to Willacassa, she lamented, "These poor souls! When will they learn to leave soldiering to the men? Every day we're finding stowaways in the camps! War is no adventure, no romance. Why don't they understand that? It's a grim business and, from the looks of this one, could be a deadly one."

She ordered the woman removed to a tent outside, and left

one of her aides in attendance while she sought out a surgeon.

"Are you in charge here?" she asked a breveted major whose eyes were baggy and bloodshot and darting out of focus. Before he could reply, Superintendent Dix fired a few broadsides. "You're short of tents and cooking utensils. The diet of these young men is deplorable. You need more green vegetables and fruits and less meat. Otherwise there'll be an outbreak of scurvy. Isn't someone attending to these matters?"

"Madam, I'll thank you to attend to your business. And I'll attend to mine." The major's face was heat red and blotchy.

"Then attend to it! Or I'll file a complaint with Surgeon-General Wood!"

"As you wish, madam!" the major shouted. "Now please allow me to get back to my work!"

"And why aren't the windows open? Are you trying to suffocate the poor lads—those who still have lung enough to breathe? The place smells foul. The air is vile." Superintendent Dix sniffed suspiciously and stepped back horror-struck. "And you—you, sir—have whiskey on your breath!"

The major flushed even redder than before.

"How could you, doctor! How could you! I'm going straight to the Surgeon-General to demand your discharge!" And with a look that could wither a brigade, the diminutive superintendent scurried from the room.

The superintendent's visit had a sobering effect on the hospital. Within minutes all bottles of whiskey were confiscated or at least hidden away. And the tents that had not yet been unpacked were unfolded and set in place. Without a woman's breasts to fasten their eyes upon, the male nurses and stewards went back to attending the sick and the dying.

But Willacassa was disappointed. Though the superintendent had eyes for everyone and everything—the "raw" recruit, the ogling nurses, the drunken surgeon, the poor ventilation, the deficiency of food and supplies—Dorothea Dix had barely noticed her. The sixty-year-old spinster had selected her for work in the hospitals. Yet in her visit the superintendent had left no indication that Willacassa would be among the first hundred women chosen for special training as nurses. Without this training, Willacassa's present role would not be markedly different from that of hundreds of other women who were pouring into Washington, sent by local aid societies or state agencies to do what they could to ease the lot of the newly-recruited soldiers. Or the scores of wives, sweethearts, and sisters who came to visit their ailing loved ones and stayed to make them comfortable, ministering not only to their own but to the other men in the wards who had no one to look after them.

Still, Willacassa had to be grateful. At least now she had something to do, something of an official nature, unlike her first two months in the capital. Those turbulent, unsettling times had convinced her that far from ending the war in ninety days, the Federal government would be fortunate to end the rebellion at all.

When Willacassa first arrived in Washington, her blonde hair blowing in a stiff Potomac breeze, the place was living with a siege mentality. Nothing was organized, everything was makeshift, the streets were uneasy with rumors. Though regular army troops patrolled the city, volunteers called for by the president in his proclamation of April 15 had not yet arrived. In fact, there were reports later that five hundred Pennsylvania troops and a Massachusetts regiment had been stopped and stoned in Baltimore by Southern sympathizers and that the New York Seventh, a well-drilled outfit, was proceeding with unbelievable difficulty towards the capital by way of a circuitous route, avoiding the city of Baltimore altogether.

The feeling, the talk in the crowded streets, pulsating with movement but with no apparent direction, was that the Rebels would invade. And if they invaded, the capital would fall. Later everyone was quoting freely from the *Richmond Examiner* of April 23, which maintained that the capture of Washington City was perfectly within the power of Virginia and Maryland. All that was needed was one wild shout of fierce resolve and Washington, "the filthy cage of unclean birds" would "assuredly be purified by fire."

This closeness to the Rebels, this propinquity to the Confederate forces on the Peninsula, had an element of excitement for Willacassa which she could not entirely account for. Though she knew that the army of Virginia quite naturally consisted of natives of that state, she had it in back of her mind that a certain South Carolinian, who was once deep in her affections, had somehow become part of that army. And if the Rebels invaded Washington, Willacassa had no doubt that she would come across him again. Wild speculation, ridiculous fancy? Perhaps. But it was a notion she could not shake loose. And for an instant she understood why the young "recruit" had chosen to pass as a soldier. Anything to draw closer to a loved one.

Just why the idea of meeting Francis Grandee again had become such an obsession with her, Willacassa could not fully comprehend. She knew their romps in the surf and their horseback rides on the strand of Cape Island belonged to another, carefree time. She knew

7

that they had allegiance to two different worlds, his a fiefdom in South Carolina built on sweat and the black man's toil, hers the frantic guesthouse world of Cape Island's ten-week "visitors' season." She knew that the war had driven them further apart, into opposite camps, and that their view of things would never truly be reconciled. And she knew that their last meeting at Trescott House had all the finality of a third-act curtain and love's demise.

She knew all this, and yet she could not remove the sting of love from her memory. Perhaps it wasn't love so much as the feeling of emptiness that the absence of love induced. Perhaps it was the idea that her first love did not prove to be as sacred or lasting as first love encountered in romantic novels. Whatever it was, Willacassa felt compelled to search out Francis Grandee, to learn what he was doing and how he was managing his life without her. It was as if in looking for Francis Grandee, she would somehow be able to sort out and separate the piled-up baggage of feelings their parting had left behind.

Willacassa had spent her first few weeks in Washington at the Evangelical Residence for Young Christian Women. She shared a bed with a girl who munched crackers and in the morning left the bed full of crumbs to run off and roll bandages and knit socks at a local war relief society. It was only when her roomate spent the night out with one of soldier friends that Willacassa had the bed to herself.

"Why don't you come too?" her roommate would suggest with a silly smile. "They are the nicest boys. And from all over— Pennsylvania, New York, Massachusetts. They're just looking for female companionship."

"I think not."

"If you're afraid of becoming pregnant, you needn't be. The army teaches withdrawal. Besides, it's one way to contribute to the war effort."

"Is it?" She let it go at that.

Willacassa did not at this time have the faintest idea what she herself would do for the war. She looked for an answer to Joseph Leach's letter of introduction to *Harper's Magazine,* recommending "W. Harrah" as a sketch artist. As W. Harrah, she hoped to preserve the anonymity of her sex. But she had no word yet from *Harper's* or from Cape Island where Joseph Leach was writing brilliant editorials in the *Ocean Wave*. Determined to help in any way she could, Willacassa had decided to aid in the sorting and unloading of boxes of food and clothing that ladies' relief societies in towns and villages around the country were sending by train to Washington. This was a tedious and thankless job, made no less thankless by the knowledge that half the food sent had become moldy, sidetracked as it was to make way for the movement of troops and military supplies, and half the clothing was too frilly and unsuitable for soldiers at the front.

It was only when Willacassa got up enough courage to face the tiny but formidable Dorothea Dix that things began to change. Having taken the Superintendent of Women Nurses by storm and secured an assignment in a hospital, she was determined to find her own living quarters. Whether it was because of a change in her fortunes or this new aggressive attitude on her part, Willacassa managed to find an apartment in the heart of the city where everyone had said none was to be had. And it was at this apartment on Sixteenth Street that she received her first letter from her father.

"My Dear Willacassa,

"I have had a letter from Eliot Irons. His regiment, the Second Rhode Island, is on its way to Washington and should be arriving shortly. He is most anxious to see you. Apparently he did not know you had left Cape Island.

"There is a quality about the letter that is very high-spirited for Eliot, as though he had finally found something to throw himself into with whole-hearted abandon.

"I wish I could be as enthusiastic about the war as he appears. But despite our victories at Philippi and Bethel Church, Virginia, small triumphs indeed, no more than skirmishes, I have the awful feeling that the rebellion, probably avoidable from the outset, is going to drag on and on.

"These Southerners, I am afraid, are a military caste and, if perhaps outnumbered, are well-trained and highly purposed.

"Did you you know that Major-General Robert E. Lee, commandant of the Army of Virginia, spent a couple of summers on Hughes Street in Cape Island? They say Lincoln offered him command of the Federal troops but he chose his home state instead.

"The summer season is almost underway. It will probably be a disaster because of the war, but the hotel owners are vying with one another for patronage in their usual competitive way. The problem is that Atlantic City has been spreading calumnious sentiments about Cape Island. On the one hand, Philadelphia newspapers have carried stories saying that our businessmen are abolitionists and coercionists. Then, in a reversal of form, they have alluded to the fact that a piece of muslin with a palmetto tree painted on it was hoisted on a pole at one of our hotels. Advertisements have been placed in all the Philadelphia and Baltimore papers to give the lie to these stories. If the season is a failure, it will not be for lack of effort.

"I do miss you, Willacassa. And, though you are a grown woman now, I cannot help worrying about your health and general welfare. If there is anything I can do to make your stay in Washington any easier, please send me word by the Cape Island Telegraph, whose line I understand has been repaired.

"Don't forget to look up Eliot Irons. And don't forget to write to your father and let him know what you are doing.

"With all my love,
Dad"

The next day, as soon as she was free from work, Willacassa made her way to the U. S. Arsenal at Greenleafs Point where she planned to make inquiries about Eliot. It was fast growing dark; and the streets were filled with Baltimore plug-uglies, Washington toughs, and wild Zouaves who had been recruited from volunteer fire departments in New York. The Zouaves were a sight in their scarlet and blue costumes with baggy pantaloons and little red caps. Armed with bowie knives and rifles, they were spoiling for trouble.

Willacassa was already regretting that she had come out at night when a gang of Zouaves on horseback galloped past, shouting obscenities, overturning carts, and throwing rocks through shop windows. One of the Zouaves drew up his horse and mounted the sidewalk at the corner where Willacassa was trying to cross.

Firing his rifle to gain her attention, the Zouave, a rough-looking hooligan with a broken nose, offered her a swallow from his short-necked flagon. When Willacassa refused the drink, he clumsily dismounted and started towards her. "When I drink, you drink," he slurred as he reached out to grab her.

Willacassa, who did not frighten easily, felt her legs give way. She backed up against the wall of a building and watched the Zouave careen towards her. She saw him wildly wave the flagon in his hand as he staggered, then stumbled forward. But the Zouave never did reach her. A guardsman in sergeant's stripes, with a soldier's moustache and a pointed chin beard, came between them. Roughly he shoved the Zouave aside. "Get out of here. Or I'll have you arrested and thrown in jail!"

The Zouave backed off. Vainly he struggled to get back on his horse, but he was so drunk he had to settle for walking beside it. Finally he led the animal away. The guardsman now turned his attention to Willacassa and in the glare of a street lamp he let out a cry of recognition. "Willacassa! Oh, my god! What are you doing in Washington? Don't you know the streets aren't fit for walking?"

"Henry Sawyer! Is it really you, Henry?" She embraced him. "I've never been so glad to see anyone!"

Broad-shouldered and muscular as ever, Sawyer responded to her embrace, then gently released her. "You shouldn't be here, Willacassa. You should be back on Cape Island. These Zouaves are crazy! They're wild enough when they aren't training. But when they drill all day, they're impossible. Once the evening dress parade is over, they go berserk. I'd go berserk myself. But it's my turn to stand twenty-four-hour guard duty."

Willacassa smiled at his assessment of the situation.

"What thay need is action," said Sawyer. "And there's precious little of that around."

"Have you seen action, Henry!"

Sawyer shook his head. "No one has yet. But our heavy artillery is pointed towards Alexandria. So maybe we'll move out soon. Meanwhile I'm assigned to an outfit some Kentucky abolitionist put together. The Cassius Clay Battalion. When we're not protecting government buildings or storehouses, we're escorting bigwigs from one bureau to another. But I'm expecting a transfer out."

"A transfer?"

"It's the cavalry I'm itching for. A seventy-year-old lawyer is trying to get a regiment under way in Jersey. I hope he's better at briefs than he is at organizing. He hasn't fielded a single company yet. But as soon as the First Cavalry reports for training, I'll be there." Suddenly he broke into laughter. "Why should a man fight on foot when he could ride a horse?"

Willacassa beamed at her fellow Cape Islander. What a joy he was! Henry Sawyer did not have the intellect of Eliot Irons or the impeccable manners of Francis Grandee. But he was the salt of the earth. No, the earth itself, strong, deep-rooted, enduring, his honest face brimming over with good cheer and a lust for the rough and tumble. She remembered the old days on Cape Island. After a full day's work as a carpenter, he would ride a borrowed horse to the beach and wave a Mexican War sabre at imagined foes, thrusting, parrying, then dashing off into the gathering mist along the ocean. What delight there was in just watching him! In the full bloom of physical manhood, yet ever the fun-loving boy, whether tossing horseshoes or splashing fully dressed into the sea or unceremoniously dumping a pile of lumber into a yard where a porch was to be built, Henry Sawyer was raw American youth waiting to take on the challenge of life itself.

And now about thirty years of age, married and the father of children, he was prepared to do his bit in the war. No ninety-day enlistment for him, no waiting for a bounty before offering his services. Henry Sawyer saw his duty clearly. His country needed him. The sooner he packed his sabre, the sooner the war would be over. All he wanted was a spirited horse and a brace of pistols. He would supply the rest. It was as simple as that.

"Have you by chance run into Eliot Irons?" she asked.

"Eliot? Is he in Washington?"

"Yes, he's part of the Second Rhode Island."

"Don't know where they're situated. They may be quartered in the Senate chamber, like I was when I first got here. This is a funny war."

"No matter. I'll find him." She squeezed Sawyer's arm and moved to go. "I'm so glad you were on hand tonight, Henry. Don't know what I would have done without you. Please send my love to Harriet—and the children."

"I will. But be careful, Willacassa. Sure you don't want an escort?" When she shook her head, Henry Sawyer smiled a warm smile, then, tipping his guardsman's cap, reluctantly sauntered away.

After several weeks of scrubbing floors and making beds, Willacassa was promoted.

"You have two primary duties," she was told by the steward in charge, a man with one blue and one gray eye, both drooping. "Check out the medical supplies on the storage shelves and fill the panniers."

"Panniers?"

"Yes, those twin medicine boxes carried into the field by horseback. Apparently some of your Miss Dix's stalwarts—those plain old maids of hers—aren't too thorough about replacing the medicines used."

"I suppose I should thank you," she said.

"Don't thank me. Anything to get Miss Dix off my back."

For her work with panniers Willacassa was given a list of numbers, and she filled the bottles and vials with such medicines as silver chloride, iodine, tartar emetic, chloroform, linimint, tincture of opium, ipecac, rochelle salt, tannic acid, and camphor pills. There were fifty-two numbers in all in the list of medicines for the panniers, the containers themselves bearing no identification. Only the tops of the corks were numbered, and Willacassa wondered how such a loose system could be adopted for such a precise business. And so she double-checked her markings, worrying that one mistake could cause grave consequences later on.

Packing the panniers so that all the vials and bottles could be comfortably squeezed in was another task she did not much enjoy. No matter how she arranged things, one or two bottles were left standing outside. These Willacassa placed in the panniers sideways, pushing the corks in as hard as she could.

Willacassa was a bit more comfortable with the storage of supplies in the hospital. Once the drugs were shelved—ammonia water, acacia, cantharides, ether, morphine, olive oil, castor oil, sulfuric acid, mercury pills, and the like—she stocked the hospital stores. And as she put away the nutmegs, sugar, black tea, condensed milk, corn starch, farina, jellies, beef stock, lemons, candles, and dried fruit, she was reminded of home, of the huge pantry at Trescott House on whose clean shelves many of the same things were housed.

One of the other women, a spare old maid from Salem County, New Jersey, insisted on supervising the dressings and other equipment, and set aside her own little corner for them. So Willacassa gladly turned over the adhesive plasters, the cotton wadding, the splints, the sponges, the basins, the buckets, the hospital knapsacks, the muslin, and the surgeon's silk to her, along with responsibility for the same, and for the first time in weeks had time to go out into the streets of Washington before dark.

Though the doctors and surgeons were generally annoyed at the intrusion of women into the hospitals, often ignoring or bypassing Superintendent Dix's ladies for male nurses, the younger doctors were not unaware of Willacassa's youth and good looks. Several of them asked her to dinner. With no major skirmishes being fought, things were slow at the hospital and they had time to frolic.

Willacassa turned them down, all except a man called LeClerc. Lieutenant LeClerc was an assistant surgeon with wavy red hair who had a pleasant face and any easygoing drawl. From his accent Willacassa guessed correctly that he was from South Carolina—Port Royal in fact. And she was burning curious to know if he counted Francis Grandee among his acquaintances.

She agreed to have some wine with him at a small tavern in Georgetown, which was thriving now that the Union Hotel and Tavern on M and 30th Street had been shut down to be taken over as a hospital. But all she could learn from LeClerc as they sat table where a sign clearly indicated no spirits would be served to military personnel was his disappointment over his commission.

"I should have been made a captain," he said, "drawing $115 a month. After all, I took my degree at the University of Pennsylvania. I could have gone to the Medical College at South Carolina. But I wanted the best training available. Had I signed up with the

Rebels, I would have been commissioned a captain for sure."

"Why did you stay with the Union, Lieutenant?" Willacassa saw no harm in asking him this, especially as LeClerc spoke freely and easily.

"Can't see the war lasting but a few months. Why jeopardize my career for a gesture?"

"Gesture? It seems to me your state is in the forefront of the rebellion. Would have seceded even if the rest didn't."

"That's true. But no one expected the North to take us seriously. Just wanted to rattle things up a bit, so Washington'd be less likely to interfere with what we do back home."

"I see," said Willacassa.

And so the evening went, leaving Willacassa at a loss to understand LeClerc's convictions about the war. More important, she was no more enlightened about Francis Grandee—where he was, what he was doing—than she had been before the assistant surgeon had consumed two carafes of burgundy. Nevertheless she agreed to meet with LeClerc again the following week, and made up her mind to query him directly about Francis Grandee at that time.

But LeClerc stood her up. He never appeared at the chapel next door to the hospital, where they had arranged to meet.

Willacassa returned to the hospital and asked one of the senior surgeons if he had seen Lieutenant LeClerc anywhere in the building.

"LeClerc? He should be back in South Carolina by now."

"South Carolina?"

"He left the service. Monday was the last we saw of him."

Willacassa recalled that Monday was the last she had seen of him, too.

"The Lieutenant's gone over to the Rebs, I'll wager. Stayed just long enough to carry off some panniers and medicine cases with him. Too bad. He was a good surgeon. Had a diploma and passed his examination. That's more than I can say for some of the others."

Yes, too bad, thought Willacassa. Now she'd never know about Francis Grandee. She could pinch herself for not asking about him when she had the chance. What a waste of a golden opportunity!

Willacassa finally met Eliot Irons outside the patent office where the First Rhode Island had found quarters. He wore a dark blue flannel tunic and an army hat pinned up at the side. His gray pants seemed plain enough, almost a concession to the Confederacy.

"You look fit, Eliot. Ready for combat. How do you like

soldiering?''

Irons, who never looked handsomer than when in uniform, his dark eyes and finely chiselled features rendering him a clean-cut look that was as precise as a crisp salute, greeted Willacassa with a kiss.

"I like it fine. It gives me a chance to mingle with my social uppers."

"What do you mean?"

"The First Rhode Island is made up of scions of wealth and breeding. Graduates of Brown University. Heirs of Newport fortunes. Horsemen. Connoisseurs of wine. Don't let their coarse uniforms and blanket rolls fool you."

Willacassa smiled at his genial manner, not quite in character with the Eliot Irons she had known during her summers on Cape Island.

"I expect that when the Second Rhode Island arrives I'll be transferred to that regiment. Meanwhile I'm one of Colonel Burnside's liaison officers. Burnside's an impressive figure. Big, imposing, he not only looks like a military man, he is a professional soldier, a rare breed among the volunteers. I'm thinking of growing jowl whiskers like his."

"I like you clean-shaven, Eliot."

"In that case—"

He reached over and kissed her again but only succeeded in moistening her cheek.

"Did I tell you that I met Henry Sawyer?"

"No."

"He's with the First Jersey Cavalry. He's made Sergeant already, and is yearning for combat."

"Henry will make a good soldier. He has no doubts like me. About the war. About himself. He exudes courage. Given the opportunity, he'll acquit himself better than most. With men like Henry on our side, we have a fighting chance in this conflict."

"You sound as though we're no match for the rebels."

"We're not. Nor are we half ready for them. Francis Grandee—you remember Francis—was in training for years before the war broke out."

At the mention of Grandee's name, Willacassa found herself blushing but she did her best to hide the fact, nodding where she would have preferred to turn completely away.

"You still think of him, don't you?" asked Irons. He was not being off-handed this time.

But when Irons saw the disturbing effect his question had on Willacassa, he apologized.

"Sorry. It was not the gentlemanly thing to ask. It's just that the war has shaken things up a bit. Scattered us to the four winds. Makes one wonder sometime."

"I do think of him, Eliot. He meant a great deal to me at one time. More than I care to admit. But that's all over now. Francis has gone to reclaim his privileged station in life. Despite what he said about being a changed man—about his guilt and his new attitude towards slavery—he responded to the first call of the Confederacy and joined his regiment. If he did have a change of heart, it was the shortest transformation on record."

"It's more than we had a right to expect, I suppose," said Irons. "Coming from South Carolina is not an accident of birth, you see. It's more like a religion."

Willacassa smiled at this new audacity of Eliot's. His uniform had definitely brought out a new jauntiness in him. And it was most becoming. She hoped they would have time to become reacquainted, to recreate the old days on Cape Island. And she expressed this hope.

Irons took her arm. "I'd love to, Willacassa. But I've got a dispatch to deliver. Several in fact. How about tomorrow? Can you get away?"

Willacassa nodded. "Not in the evening. I'm on duty at the hospital. But my day is free."

"Good. Then meet me at People's. Yes, there's a People's in Washington, too," he said, referring to People's Ice Cream Saloon back home. "But there's no connection with Cape Island."

"I know the place," said Willacassa.

"At one o'clock then?"

"I'll be there."

When Eliot met her the next day he brought flowers with him, a small bouquet conservative in their pastel blues and pinks. Francis Grandee would have selected a riot of colors, more in keeping with his passionate Southern temperament. But Willacassa was happy to clutch the flowers nonetheless. She took Eliot's arm and they went inside.

They chatted feverishly at their table, repeating the latest rumors: a reported Rebel movement, a shuffling of personnel in the War Department, and Mrs. Lincoln's reputed allegiance to the South—Eliot's topics of interest rather than her own. And it was just as well, for the chicken was not too good and the service rather slovenly.

"I believe we'll be moving up the peninsula soon," volunteered Irons, putting his fork down.

"You're expecting a battle?"

"The ninety-day enlistments will be up shortly. Lincoln will want the men to see combat before letting them go home. They've seen precious little action to date."

Willacassa frowned at Eliot's cynicism.

"What do you think of the President?" she asked.

"Oh, he's popular enough with the troops," said Irons, putting down his napkin. "But mighty unpopular with the politicians. I've heard it said he jokes too much when he should be serious. And he bristles when the jokes are at his expense."

"Some of the cartoons in the press have been most unkind, even cruel," noted Willacassa.

"The Southern press?"

"No, our own newspapers. Though they reprint much that has been said in Richmond. He's been called everything from a vulture to a baboon."

"Well, it is a free press. Guess we should be thankful for that. Wars have a way of making dictators, you know. So long as the newspapers stick pins into them, our leaders aren't likely to become too arrogant."

Willacassa studied Eliot Irons, so wise in his perceptions, so handsome in his officer's uniform. Why wasn't she able to fall in love with the man? To translate her affection into passion? After all, Eliot was the one who had introduced her to Hinton Helper and *The Impending Crisis of the South*. And while other men were making abolitionist speeches, he had been a silent conductor in the Underground Railroad. She remembered when he first arrived at Cape Island. How taken she was with him then! Eliot was a strikingly handsome man. And there was a mystery about his comings and goings that added to the mystique. But then the bank panic and his sudden departure, and Francis Grandee came into her life. By the time Eliot returned to Cape Island, even though they became partners in abolition, she could not rekindle her interest in the man. Oh, she liked him well enough, even admired him, but any possibility that she could become Eliot's wife vanished in the face of Francis Grandee's claim on her.

Yet it would have made her life so much simpler if Eliot had been the suitor of her choice. Here was someone available to her, someone to heap her affections on instead of having always to long for Francis Grandee who was dug in on the wrong side of the war. Even as she watched Irons speak, with an animation that was new for him, Willacassa sighed. Maybe it was paradox, maybe human perversity. But the spark, the kindling spirit simply wasn't there. Everything was in readiness for the fire of passion—twigs, paper, the log of love itself. The only thing lacking was the match.

Harrah arrived in Washington on July 20. He had taken time off from the rigors of Trescott House and the demands of summer visitors to journey to the capital. Never one to leave Cape Island at the height of the tourist season, Harrah was determined to see Stockton Stanhope, a South Jersey congressman who enjoyed a reputation as a peacemaker even as the war dragged on past the ninety days most men thought it would last.

Much to his surprise he found a room available at the crowded Willard Hotel. Here through an aide he learned that the congressman would meet with him sometime that evening. In the interim Harrah planned to locate his daughter's apartment and spend some time with Willacassa whose absence had created a terrible void in his life.

As he made his way to Sixteenth Street, Harrah saw hordes of men in uniform. To his dismay they were begging money to buy whiskey. Just as well they hadn't yet been called on to fight. Oh, there had been a few skirmishes between North and South. Bethel Church in eastern Virginia and Philippi in the western part of the state came to mind, and an action in Boonville, Missouri. But fortunately no major confrontation had yet taken place despite the clamor of the press on both sides for decisive military action.

Harrah was convinced that it was too early for a decisive victory. The Confederate armies, though staffed by better trained officers and men, were smaller in number. And Federal troops, it appeared, were more motley than mobilized, their dandified leadership spending more time marching their soldiers back and forth than getting them poised for battle.

For this, Harrah was grateful. So long as the North was unprepared or unwilling to test the South in combat, no real clash would materialize. And the chance for peace would still be at hand. As in all beginnings, the situation was fluid. And Harrah was determined to do something while this state of affairs existed.

He found his daughter's apartment in a little house not far from St. John's Church.

"It's so good to see you, Daddy!" Willacassa exclaimed, throwing her arms around him. "Unfortunately I'm due at the hospital in a little while. Can I make you some coffee?"

"No, dear. Just tell me how things are."

"Well enough, I suppose. While there's a lot of movement in town, nothing much seems to be happening. Every day a new regiment arrives. There's the inevitable parade down Pennsylvania Avenue. Then all the excitement dies down."

"All spruced up but no place to go?"

"Exactly. But they'll be going soon enough, Father. Yet all for different reasons. Henry Sawyer to end secession. Eliot Irons to end slavery—"

"And Francis Grandee to perpetuate a way of life?"

Willacassa flinched at Harrah's mention of Grandee. Francis was the one person to be left unspoken between them, she thought. But she let it pass.

"Yes, Father. One war. But different justifications. It's astonishing the differences."

"Doesn't matter, Willacassa. Once the bullets fly, all the differences disappear."

"How is Rachel?" she asked, seeking news from home.

"Busier than ever. Not only cooks but, when I'm away, supervises the chambermaids. May be a bit much for her. That's why I'll have to start back tomorrow."

"So soon?"

"Afraid so."

When Harrah returned to the Willard Hotel, he was happy that he had seen his daughter but weary from the day's exertions. He lay down on a sofa to rest, and had almost fallen asleep when Congressman Stanhope knocked at his door.

"Mr. Harrah, I came as soon as I heard you were here. I received your letter and am much obliged for your support."

"Come in," said Harrah. He uncorked a bottle of cognac. "Something to drink?"

Stanhope was not one to refuse a libation, at least not from a fellow Jerseyite. He sank his lean body into a chair and set his white hat on the table.

"There's talk of a major battle brewing."

"Is there?" asked Harrah. "Where?"

"Near Manassas Junction. I understand that some of the dignitaries and their ladies will drive out to see the goings-on."

"At a safe distance, I presume."

"Always at a safe distance."

"I was hoping there wouldn't be a battle," said Harrah. "Battles create a poor climate for peace proposals."

"Peace proposals?" Congressman Stanhope displayed impatience. "With all due respect, Mr. Harrah. What we need at this time is negotiations, not proposals. We've had peace proposals before."

"Crittenden?"

"Exactly. And you saw how far the old man got."

"I wasn't particularly enamored of Crittenden's proposals," said Harrah.

"Why not?"

"In effect, it divided the country in half. Half-slave and half-free—at the 36th Parallel, I believe."

"But as the old man said, it was better than allowing the government to fall in ruins. Better than having a civil war."

"It would only prolong the inevitable."

"To be realistic," ventured Stanhope, wiping his brow with a handkerchief and pouring himself another cognac. "any compromise is going to have to deal with slavery. It's a fact of life."

"There's only one way to deal with slavery," said Harrah, "and that's get rid of it."

"But how? How can we do that and avoid bloodshed?"

"There are several ways."

"Cite one."

"All right. Buy the slaves free. Indemnify their owners. And then prohibit slavery."

"But that would cost a fortune, man!"

"It's cheaper than fighting a war."

"May be so. But you'd never get Congress to go along."

"Then we've got to let the slave states go, let them secede. We can't be a party to slavery any longer. To preserve such a union would be to sanction the barbarity. No civilized nation can do that."

"That's a pretty radical solution, Harrah. I'm glad you're not president. Besides, how would that help the slaves?"

"Once the slave states leave, once we recognize Secession, we can emancipate the slaves. The voting opposition will be gone."

"But that would have no force in the South!"

"Wouldn't it? Think for a moment. Until now we've returned fugitive slaves to their owners. We're still doing it in some places, I hear. After all, it's still the law of the land. But once we stop returning them, once word gets out the runaways can be free, there'll be mass defections. Every slave will be looking to work his way North. At first it'll be only a trickle. But in time it'll be a flood. And there's no way the owners will be able to stanch the flow. For the Blacks, it'll be like crossing the River Jordan."

"You really believe that?"

"There's no doubt in my mind. The only doubt I have is over the timid souls in Washington. They don't have the courage to do what must be done. Oh, it takes no courage for politicians to go to war. They beat the drums and brave young men are ready to die for them. So they take the easy way out."

Stanhope put away his glass, picked up his hat, and slowly rose to his feet. "You may be right," he conceded. "But we'll never know. As you say, the timid souls in Washington will never buy it."

Stanhope stopped at the door. "Are you sure you won't join

us tomorrow. The military promises a great show. Congressman Ely and I would be pleased to have you."

"Thank you. But I think I'll return to Cape Island."

"You'll be missing a good thing, you know. There's been a tremendous rush for passes. And though transportation's almost impossible to get, Ely's wangled a double carriage. For our friends, of course. There'll be picnic lunches and wine and, most of all, women. Should make for a fine day's outing."

"Sounds festive enough," said Harrah. "But you may find that no battle's a picnic."

"You're too gloomy, Harrah. Victory is still the shortest path to peace, you know. And we're ripe for victory. Too bad you won't be there to see it."

FIRST BLOOD

The Second Rhode Island, to which he was now attached, had dispatched Lieutenant Irons on a reconnoitering mission. He and a few other staffers scouted the upper fords of Bull Run which a few days earlier had turned into a rout for General Daniel Tyler's advance guard.

Irons was not in his best frame of mind. Dispirited by the disorderly retreat of Tyler's men and the feeling that green troops on the Union side would be no match for the Confederates if they chose a frontal attack, Lieutenant Irons finished off a bottle of sutler's whiskey before setting out.

His mission was to familiarize himself with the terrain, particularly the crossings above Stone Bridge. But after a full day of crossing and criss-crossing the area he was no more certain of what he saw than his commanding officer was of General McDowell's instructions. It seemed to Lieutenant Irons that the Confederate left was concentrated at Sudley Springs Ford. In fact, it appeared that their forces were swelling by the hour. But he could not be sure, and rather then bring back a false report to his superiors he thought best to risk another look. There was a little-used track which Irons thought led to Sudley Springs, but he had no idea how long this route was, nor time enough to find this out. And the countryside was getting thick with Rebel pickets.

What troubled Eliot Irons even more was the realization that he was a rank amateur at what he was doing. He had no training for this type of operation. He knew nothing of the Lower Shenandoah Valley or its surrounding environs. That he had accepted his assignment without in any way protesting his inadequacy astounded him now that he was in the midst of things and out of reach of his brigade. He resolved to get back before sundown and make his report, confessing at the same time that he had not effectively fulfilled his mission.

He had proceeded along a scrubby thicket of pine when he bumped into another scout from Heintzelman's Brigade. Both men had drawn pistols and were within a second of shooting one another when Irons, seeing a blue coat, identified himself as Lieutenant Irons of the Second Rhode Island.

"Lieutenant Morton," replied the other man, "General Heintzelman's Division, Colonel Franklin's Brigade."

"What do you make of the Rebels? Have you been to Blackburn's Ford?"

"Don't know where I was. The road to Manassas Junction was

the last place I could identify. The area was so full of Rebs I decided to clear out. If McDowell doesn't move soon, there'll be more Rebels come to Beauregard's aid. There are new troops arriving every day.''

Lieutenant Morton pulled his horse about, then, saluting, galloped away.

Irons was now convinced that he'd better share whatever intelligence he had with Colonel Burnside, and this as soon as possible. The quicker the battle got under way, the quicker he would see Willacassa again.

Yes, he had to admit Willacassa was uppermost in his mind. Everything he did as a soldier, as an officer, as a man, was done to win her approval. Even his enlistment was as much a gesture to please Willacassa as to honor long-standing convictions about slavery and the war. He would, of course, have preferred to spend the period of insurrection in her company, reading the same books, sharing the same table, exchanging fond looks with the young woman, although he had to admit that at the moment the fondness was one-sided. But Irons was hopeful that all that would change, that with the passage of time Willacassa would come to see that he could rise above his weaknesses, his self-doubts, and make of himself a dependable companion and an adoring husband. He recognized that the war might prove an ally to this personal campaign of his. The pressure of the conflict to foreshorten normal waiting periods might act in his behalf. Time was no longer measured by the long days of the summer calendar. Time was rationed in precious grains of sand, or counted like Cape May diamonds plucked from the beach and stuffed into a handy jar.

And Eliot Irons knew that in his officer's uniform he presented a more dashing figure than he did as the guilt-ridden son of a slave-runner who had been rescued on Cape Island. In uniform, even if he were struck by a ball, he could lay claim to Willacassa's respect and admiration, if not her affection. Affection would come later.

When he arrived in camp, Irons was told by Colonel Burnside to report immediately to General McDowell. In the General's tent other scouts and a handful of staffers were gathered to report their findings. By the time Irons was called on to share his intelligence, a picture of confusion and imprecision had emerged.

"I'm afraid I can add little to what you've already heard. I think the track to Sudley Springs Ford is little used. How long it runs or how long it would take a brigade to reach the place I cannot say. And I am not sure that the track leads to Sudley Springs Ford, but it is close enough I should think. As to numbers, I can only say that troops are arriving by the hour. The only thing I can say with certainty is that the road to Stone Bridge would be a straight march.''

General McDowell thanked Lieutenant Irons and the other scouts for the information they had brought back, though Eliot had the distinct feeling he thought their work was amateurish. Dismissing his staff officers, McDowell summoned his field officers for a staff meeting.

Eliot Irons returned to his brigade, had a supper of salt pork and rice, and went to sleep in the expectation that the Second Division at least, General Hunter's Division, would be moving out in the morning. He was awakened before three A. M. and learned that Hunter and Heintzelman's Divisions would follow Tyler's First Division out, leaving Centreville in the direction of Stone Bridge by way of the Warrenton Turnpike.

They started at a good clip, but any hope of arriving at their destination quickly was soon dissipated. For some reason General Tyler's progress was painfully slow. Word was passed back that one of the monstrous guns in Carlisle's battery had periodically bogged down. This turned the march into a push and shove operation, delaying things interminably.

At about 5:30 A. M., having covered little more than three miles in two hours, Hunter and Heintzelman's Divisions veered off the turnpike and headed towards Sudley Springs. About an hour later they heard the guns of Tyler's battery booming forth. And this kept up sporadically.

Eliot Irons listened to the thunder of the big guns and considered it a good sign. So long as they were pounding the Rebels, the blue shirts had the upper hand. Colonel Burnside's Brigade, the Second Rhode Island, now pushed through the woods in what appeared to be a flanking movement. Eliot was certain as he threaded his way among the trees that the next few moments would erupt into battle. He stepped gingerly over broken twigs and protruding branches. He carried his rifle close to his chest. He felt the cool sweat of the morning's exertion on his face. And he slid his lip under his front teeth, unable to decide whether to bite it or to moisten it with his tongue.

Suddenly the brigade emerged from the woods and broke into a clearing. The men advanced across the rolling fields towards the enemy, or at least where they imagined the enemy to be. A burst of fire assured Eliot they had not been mistaken. The Rebels had excellent cover and their volley hit the brigade hard, dropping men an all sides.

Eliot faltered for a moment. In an instant he saw his mortality standing in the path of a chance bullet. It was a blind, cold fear, terrible in its imminence. But the fear was short-lived as men of other brigades joined in, supporting the Rhode Islanders. Their fire forced the Rebels to give ground and break up into smaller groups.

The Rhode Islanders kept up the barrage. Eliot Irons did not know how long he had been loading and firing at the Rebels. It seemed the better part of an hour. And he was fast running short of ammunition. He was amazed that in the face of all that gunfire the small pockets of gray were still able to hold their positions. Yet he knew that if the Rebels weren't put to rout soon, they would be reinforced and once again provide a formidable wall of resistance. His fears were soon realized. Through the heavy smoke of discharging rifles he could see large numbers of grayjackets slipping into position alongside their comrades. The tide of battle had turned. It was now Burnside's regiment taking the heat. Under a heavy barrage of fire the Rhode Islanders were forced to fall back into the trees. His men out of ammunition, Colonel Burnside allowed his regiment to file towards the rear.

Lieutenant Irons led his company through the woods towards the main road. It was a grim retreat. Bullets whistled overhead and shells from a six-pounder tore up the trees. In one instant a dozen men fell to the ground. Then a dozen more.

But it wasn't until he came upon an open meadow that Eliot realized how bad things were. This wasn't war. Wars were fought on a battlefield swept clean of the wounded and the maimed. No, this was carnage. An unbelievable tearing of flesh, of blood squirting in all directions, of bits and human pieces torn asunder and scattered wide and far. Here a youth was lying with his uniform blown away and his entrails exposed. With bloody hands he tried to squeeze them back into his body. In a ditch a womb-like figure was curled, its head half-severed from its neck. On a nearby hillock a man on folded legs was unable to dislodge the bayonet a Rebel had stuck in his chest. No regimental flag was ever planted more firmly in the ground. No gargoyle ever smiled in more hideous agony.

At another rise two horses lay on their sides, their legs stretched out in grotesque rigor mortis. And up ahead men were running, screaming in fright and panic, trying to keep one step ahead of death and screeching bullets. There was no turning now to take aim and bring down their pursuers. There was no heeding pleading officers to stop and stand. The object was to run clear of the gunfire, to find shelter in the swarming crowd of moving bodies up ahead, to flee, to hide, to escape.

As Eliot turned to exhort his men to keep together, to avoid panic, something ripped into his shoulder. It threw him backward.

He looked for something to break his fall and almost laughed at the weird sensation of having nothing to hold on to. Hitting the ground, he struck the back of his head on an outcropping. And then everything darkened.

When he came to, Eliot did not know how long he had been lying on the ground. For some time he had felt the vibrations of men and vehicles in movement, but did not have the strength to pick himself up. His head throbbed, but there was only a dull pain in his shoulder. Lying near the edge of the road, just beyond a ditch, he made out the figures of blue jackets racing madly by. He wanted to stop them or at least ask what was happening. But no one took the trouble to look his way. He called out a few times but soon gave that up as futile. Irons then forced himself to sit up. When he found he could do that without getting dizzy, he reached for a rifle lying nearby and, using it to bolster him, struggled to his feet.

He could now see that the road was covered with discarded weapons and debris. Rifles, bayonets, haversacks, knapsacks, coffee pots, tunics—every conceivable piece of equipment had been abandoned along the way. Even caissons and limbers lay ditched along the road's edge. Following a well-trod path, Irons shuffled unsteadily at first, but managed to stay on his feet. Though he was not bleeding heavily from his wound, he could not stanch the slow steady ooze that trickled from his shoulder. The bump at the back of his head continued to throb. But as soon as the confusion of the passing scene lost its blur, Eliot was able to piece together what was happening. Men in blue were not retreating, they were in full flight. The look of panic, of cold fear was on their faces. No one had fighting in mind, only escape. Anything in their path would ruthlessly be thrust aside.

If they were fleeing, Eliot decided, they had their reasons. It seemed a good idea for him to abandon the area too. But walking might be difficult; running was out of the question. Raising his arm, he tried to flag down an ambulance wagon, a two-wheeled vehicle that careened and spun wildly. But the frozen-faced driver only whipped his horse as the wagon flew past and near knocked Eliot over.

Lieutenant Irons now used his rifle as a walking stick and doggedly moved along. He covered a few miles this way, constantly aware that he was being passed by men, wagons, and horses in flight. A number of animals that sped by were riderless, their nostrils wide with terror or pain. And none of the ambulance wagons that he saw, tipped as they were at the back, carried any wounded.

As he approached Cub Run, a stream that Eliot recognized from one of his scouting missions, he saw an incredible assemblage. Piled up at the other end of the bridge on a narrow road was an assortment of vehicles: caissons, wagons, limbers, and festooned carriages. The carriages had apparently come from the opposite direction, loaded with gentlemen in top hats and women with parasols and festive bonnets, all bent on seeing soldiers at play. But instead of victorious legions marching back with prisoners in tow, they had come upon an army in rout. And their vehicles collided. Wheels broke off. Horses reared. Civilians were thrown into the road. Shouts, screams, and shrieks split the air.

In the midst of this wild impasse, a shell exploded, overturning a wagon crossing the small bridge at Cub Run. A moment later two more shells hit. This time the bridge itself collapsed, throwing men and vehicles into the stream below. What had been confusion and terror before was now rampant panic. Guns and rifles were cast away; blankets and equipment flung aside. On the near bank, men clung to their horses to ford the stream. On the other side of Cub Run, soldiers cut horses from wagons and used them as mounts. In a frenzy they whipped their animals and pushed them through the screaming throng or drove them up the steep wooded hill to the north of the clogged road in order to escape.

What Eliot Irons saw was worse than any battle he had ever imagined, worse than any nightmare he had ever experienced. It was a wild, tumultuous, ear-splitting spectacle, a tangle of wreckage and violent disorder. It savaged the senses. It destroyed one's humanity. And all he wanted was to be free of it.

The wounded from Bull Run were pouring into the hospitals. Hour after hour, day after day, they staggered in, shattered arms hanging limp, face wounds oozing with blood; some in shock, others in the throes of impending death. All had the same story. They had trudged for hours, for miles, all the way from the battlefield. A few lucky ones had been dumped into farmers' wagons and wheeled in. But no ambulance had picked the others up. The ambulance drivers, civilians for the most part, had fled at the first shot. What ambulance drivers they had seen had been searching among the dead for personal belongings, their pockets bulging with gold watches and other valuables. One had even stripped a corpse of its leather boots!

And when they arrived most of the wounded had to wait interminably for medical treatment. The few hospitals were crammed with casualties. The walking wounded had to wander the streets in search of a hospital or a makeshift way station that would let them in. Those inside stood on endless lines or sat against a wall, waiting to have an arm or a leg sawed off. Male nurses sorted out the rest. Men with bullet wounds in the head or spine were expendable. No help for them. Pile them on planks and leave them to die. Those with minor wounds were given a shot of whiskey, a bandage, and shown the backyard. The rest were put to bed, where beds were available, or under a tree or on a bed of straw in a nearby church or barn.

The surgeons worked non-stop. As soon as one amputation was disposed of, another soldier was carried in and placed on the table. While chloroform was pressed in a rag to a patient's nose, the surgeon wiped his long, bloody knife on a red-smeared apron and went to work severing the next afflicted limb. What was cut off was immediately carried away and tossed into a wagon waiting outside the back door, a wagon piled high with severed legs and arms. Orderlies tried to mop the blood from the floor but, despite the tourniquets, the blood ran so fast and so thick that the surgeons and the blood-spattered nurses slipped on the slick floor until ashes were poured to soak up the mess.

When Willacassa, who had been dispatched by Superintendent Dix to Alexandria in anticipation of the wounded, arrived at the temporary hospital, she found it to be in absolute chaos. Unable to find anyone in authority who was free to talk to her, she set herself up at the front door to assist the male nurse who acted both as traffic manager and watchdog. No sooner did she open the door to the vestibule than she was exposed to a crush of men, ripped by shrapnel, who were hemorrhaging from the mouth, who were missing eyes, noses, or ears, and who had large, gaping holes where lips and teeth used to be. Willacassa tried to steel herself to what she saw. But it was not long before she felt chilled and faint, and had to brush by the men to go outside for air. She found a bench and sat down (she would have fallen if she hadn't) and tried to calm herself. She had never expected anything resembling this. A wounded soldier was supposed to cut a romantic figure. If wounded, his head would be neatly bandaged or his arm in a silk sling. Mutilation of this sort simply didn't happen, else why didn't she hear about it? Yet there was no denying what she saw, no pretending the men didn't exist. As they stood in the vestibule, they were a terrible fact of life, part of the dreadful reality of combat not mentioned in the newspaper dispatches.

As Willacassa sat on her crude wooden bench, which was shaded by a beech tree, she watched a pair of farmer's wagons roll in. They were filled with bleeding wounded, men who looked as if they had been dumped inside like slaughtered cattle. What moans she heard were quiet, stifled moans. The young soldiers were either a stoic lot or were too much in shock to give way to cries of anguish.

But as the tailgates of the wagon were lowered and the wounded were helped off by male nurses, one sight so seared her consciousness that she would never forget it. A tousle-headed drummer boy, no more than fifteen, was clinging to his severed leg, unable to bear the thought of parting with it. He hugged it close to his chest—his boot, blood, and all—as though by holding it he would in some way be able to reattach it. Even as they carried him off the wagon, his face ghostly from loss of blood, he couldn't be persuaded to let go of his dead limb.

"No," he whimpered, "let me have it. Don't take it away from me. Not yet. Not yet."

It was at least a half hour before Willacassa could cope with the image. Then somehow she managed to go back inside the hospital. She inquired after the drummer boy, and learned from a surgeon that he had succumbed from loss of blood. Not once, she was told, not even after death, did he relinquish his hold on the severed leg.

Willacassa had assisted in the hospital only a day and a half, but by her own reckoning it seemed a week. The numbing repetition of the wounded crowding in, of amputations, of blood on the floor, of the dying carried out so filled her mind that she no longer measured time, or thought about sleep or craved food. Instead she untiringly threaded her way among the beds and stretchers and tables that were piled high with men in stained uniforms and bloody tunics. To some she gave brandy. To those with stomach wounds she denied water, frantically seeking advice from the handful of surgeons rushing madly about the place.

Among the seriously wounded were several Southerners. These men were treated no differently from the Federal wounded. They lay on cots, waiting for the harried surgeons to look at them. Willacassa had no idea what regiment they came from, whether they were Virginians, Georgians, or South Carolinians. She thought she heard one of them say something about Wade Hampton's cavalry troop, but she could not be sure. As she wended her way among them she stopped. A form lying on one of the cots suggested Francis Grandee. There was no doubt about it. There was something about the slight build but muscular back that reminded her of Francis, that conjured up images on the Cape Island strand. And though she could not see the face, there was enough in the undercurve of the jaw and the ridged adam's apple to bring to mind how Francis swallowed when he talked as though his words were morsels of food.

She crossed over to the other side of the room to gain a better look at him. Only now, with his face in view, could Willacassa see that she had only been indulging in wishful thinking. The wounded young man looked nothing like Francis Grandee. He appeared little more than a half-starved mountain boy from the Western part of Virginia. If anything, it was poverty that was etched in his face. There was no trace of wealth or hint of the plantation life.

But when she stumbled upon Eliot Irons, she recognized him at once. Eliot lay on his back, weak from loss of blood. He held a red-soaked bandage against his shoulder, his coarse blue tunic ripped away at the sleeve.

"Eliot! Oh, Eliot, what happened to you?"

"No more than to the others. It was a rout, Willacassa. A pitiful, shameful rout. And after the men had fought so gallantly. Do you have some brandy for me?"

"Of course."

She poured him a cup and brought it to his lips.

"The bridge at Cub Run, it was a bottleneck. People rushing in both directions. Soldiers, spectators, wagons. It's a wonder anyone got through. Why would anybody outside the army visit the battlefield? Yet the bridge was thronged with carriages and dignitaries and their ladies. What did they hope to see? It's a bloody war going on, not a theatre show!"

"Forget about that, Eliot. You must care for yourself now. As soon as the doctor dresses your wound, I'll get you a cup of soup."

Willacassa left Eliot just long enough to find a young physician who cursorily examined his wound.

"Except for the loss of blood, it's not serious. Put some clean bandages on it. And get him something to eat. Meat if you can find any."

"Yes, Doctor. And thank you."

Willacassa gave Eliot a reassuring grip on the arm and went for some bandages. When she returned, he had dozed off, his dark lashes screening like a portcullis the lids of his eyes. Even while Willacassa removed his tunic and washed and bandaged his wound, Eliot slept. Only once did he open his eyes and then with the faintest of smiles he went back to sleep again.

Later Willacassa found a piece of beef which she braised for him at one end of a huge black stove. She also brought Eliot a cup of barley soup which he drank down almost at a gulp.

Willacassa looked in on Eliot for the next few days. He seemed to be showing improvement but not as rapidly as she had hoped. He had, of course, lost much blood and so it was not surprising he was pale, even for Eliot, and was dark under the eyes. When she took his hand, his touch was moist and somewhat feeble.

Once she brought in a bouquet of flowers from the field. He took them but not without embarrassment.

"It's I should be bringing flowers to you," he said weakly.

"To me?"

"If I were feeling better, that's what I would have done." He coughed slightly as he said this and propped up his pillow.

"I know that," smiled Willacassa. "And you will be feeling better soon."

She wanted to chat with him, but crowded as the hospital was with other wounded and sick men she was needed elsewhere.

"I'll look in on you again before I leave."

"Leave? You said that as if you were going away."

Willacassa sat down for a moment. "I've been assigned elsewhere for a few days. A new hospital is being opened up in one of the churches. As soon as things are set up, I'll be back."

"I suppose the doctors have their hands full these days."

"I'm afraid they do."

"What a waste," said Eliot. "What a terrible waste! These Southerners will do anything but let the slaves go. I don't think we have any idea how determined they are to preserve their 'way of life.' We're going to have our hands full with them before this is over."

Willacassa could not disagree with him. But having delayed too long already, she merely rearranged the sheet that covered Eliot and waved him goodbye. What a sorrowful face he presented as she looked back at him while she moved past the rows of cots that stretched towards the western wing of the building, like shrouded pews in a vast whitewashed tabernacle. Then she could see him no more.

It was almost a week before Willacassa was able to return to Alexandria. Setting up the new hospital had been an exhausting and frustrating task. The delivery of beds and operating tables was delayed because of a mix-up in orders, the beds and tables first being delivered to a hospital already equipped and in operation. Medicines and bandages also arrived late and had to be sorted out and separated because the wagons carrying the crates had collided with a runaway ambulance, capsizing the vehicle and spilling its contents on the muddy road. And the night it rained on the old church, revealing a roof more holey than holy, a crew of workers had to be dispatched with shingles and tar buckets to repair the damage.

During this time the City of Washington, which was always hot at night, was hotter than usual, making sleep difficult for a weary Willacassa, if not impossible. She decided one evening to forego her room and walk the streets which were crowded with men in motley uniforms. A gang of toughs dressed in scarlet and blue Zouave costumes, fit more for a masquerade than a war, pounded on the doors of restaurants that were closing up for the night, smashed windows, fired their rifles, and chased after harlots who would have been more than willing to consort with them if they hadn't been so wild and uproarious. Exhausted by the outing and remembering her own frightening encounter with a Zouave, Willacassa returned to her room where she immediately fell asleep on the couch.

That night she dreamt of Francis Grandee. It was a strange dream, full of unfamiliar habitats and mingled images. First she saw Francis brutally flogging a big buck Negro in what appeared to be a slave market at the edge of a wharf. She was not sure, but she thought the Negro's name, scrawled on a board attached to the whipping post, was Noah. Later she found herself ministering not to Noah but, in a twist of roles, to the torn flesh of Francis Grandee, applying to his back salves, tinctures, and lotions from a pannier that she herself had packed at the hospital. In the next instant she saw herself dancing with Francis at a grand ball in Jefferson Davis's presidential mansion, a Francis that was unscathed and decked out in a Confederate cavalry uniform. Her father was standing to a side, watching them. And Eliot Irons too. Willacassa could not tell whether her father approved or disapproved of her dancing with Francis. But Eliot vehemently disapproved, and he was slowly changing his uniform from blue to gray while his face rapidly turned from scarlet to purple. Henry Sawyer was also in the dream. Recklessly perched on a podium, he one moment waved the orchestra on with a naked Mexican War sabre and the next moment turned to smile at the utterly confused cotillion. Suddenly everyone stopped dancing, and Willacassa remembered only that she wanted to go on. But diminutive Dorothea Dix stood smack in the middle of the ballroom floor, ordering an end to the festivities. And no one dared contradict the spinster Superintendent, not even President Lincoln who had been standing side by side with Jefferson Davis, exchanging political jokes with him.

It was an extraordinary dream, exhausting to the extreme, one that left her body aching with fatigue and her mind distressingly unsettled. But it had a reality and a sense of immediacy that Willacassa could not dismiss. She did not know what to make of it. And an hour after waking up and struggling with the dream, she gave up trying.

The person, then, who had returned from Washington and entered the crowded wards, looking for Eliot in the makeshift hospital in Alexandria, was tired, anxious, and a little cranky.

"Where is Lieutenant Irons?" she asked when she found Eliot's bed occupied by a heavy-set liveryman with a red beard and a lingering smell of horses.

A male nurse who made a project of pushing a mop replied, "Taken to one of the tents where he could breathe better. He's got pneumonia."

She searched through a score of tents, most of them small and unattended, except for an occasional woman in a poke-bonnet, before she found him. A tin cup hung on the tent pole, and a jug of water sat on the ground outside his tent.

"Eliot, what's happened to you?"

Irons turned a feverish eye and parched lips towards her.

"I don't know, Willacassa. All I know is I have difficulty breathing. It's been several days now." His voice was rasp and strained.

"What do the surgeons say?"

"What surgeons? I haven't seen a surgeon in days."

Willacassa sat down beside him and put a hand on his forehead.

"You're burning up," she said. Pouring some water on a handkerchief, she lay it across his brow.

Eliot Irons soon lapsed into a restless sleep, broken first by a profusion of sweat and then, whenever he coughed, by a pain in his side. Willacasssa stayed close to his tent. When the confinement proved too much for her, she briefly looked in at other tents, adjusting pillows for the wounded, pouring water into tin cups, and filling out endless forms requested by the surgeon-general. When a surgeon's assistant finally looked in, he shook his head, left her with a vial of medicine, and departed.

The next day there was some improvement in Eliot. Though still weak, he managed to sit up, bolstered by a discarded knapsack.

"I'm glad you're here," he said. "It's like old times on Cape Island."

He waited until he found enough air in his lungs to go on. "Remember our long talks on slavery? Remember the discussions we had on the books and speeches of the abolitionists? The road seemed so clear then."

"It's still clear, isn't it?" Willacassa squeezed his hand.

"Clear? Yes. But I don't think we had any idea what was really involved." He drew on the little strength he had left. "Oh, there was the Underground Railroad. And that was difficult enough.

33

But we had no idea of the cost in blood and pain."

"Wasn't it John Brown said the crimes of this land would never be purged away except with blood?"

"I know that, Willacassa. But saying it is one thing. Paying it is another." Eliot broke out in a fit of coughing, and the effort was so exhausting that it left him more enfeebled than before.

I'm sorry," he gasped in shorter and shorter breaths. "I didn't mean to go on this way. It's just that until now I saw what an abomination slavery was. Now I see what an abomination war is. Why must one abomination purify another? Why can't we purify our sins without war, fire, and blood?"

Willacassa had no answer for Eliot. And when he dozed off again, more from fatigue than a desire to sleep, she struggled with her own feelings. Eliot was dying. This good, noble, decent young man had abruptly come to the end of his path. And there was nothing she could do about it. Even the love she bore her friend could not delay the end one brief moment. Eliot was dying. And what made things worse, he knew he was dying. And in the face of his impending death she saw his preoccupation with the two evils, war and slavery, as a desperate attempt to give meaning to his short life. In much the same way that John Brown tried to give meaning to his death when he faced the scaffold, Eliot too tried to project a vision. Only Eliot's impassioned vision had more to do with the avenging fury of war than with the longtime evil of slavery. And it was all the more prophetic because Eliot Irons had always harbored a deep personal vendetta against slavery. The son of a Newport, Rhode Island sea captain, he had always borne a double firkin of guilt. It did not matter that Eliot Irons was not the Captain Irons of the slave schooner, *Carolina.*

The end came early the next day. The once healthy body, the once handsome face were totally wasted. The black stubble on the cheeks and chin stood out like tiny metal nails. And the dark, heavily circled eyes were wide and stark. All efforts to talk were futile, but a bony hand clung to Willacassa. And then as though he found a sudden rush of strength, Irons cried out in a cavernous voice. "Why this? It's so ignominious to die in bed! Francis Grandee would have died in battle. Why couldn't I have died at Sudley Springs!"

These last words were his last breaths. And they left Willacassa stunned and mortified. Eliot was dead. The war had taken on a new meaning.

PEACE DEMOCRATS

When he had read the accounts in the newspapers of the Battle At Manassas or Bull Run, as some called it, Harrah was mortified more by the extent of the slaughter than by the rout. According to the dispatches that he read, losses by the Federal forces were estimated at almost 500 killed with about 1,300 men captured or missing while losses by Confederate troops were figured at almost 400 killed or missing. Worse than that, reports he had received from Joseph Leach, whose son Granville had written *The Ocean Wave* immediately upon the conclusion of the rout, said the numbers of sick and wounded in hospitals, and makeshift operating rooms in field tents, churches, schools, and public buildings were incalculable.

It was now clear to Harrah, who had his misgivings before the terrible encounter, that this would be a long and bloody war. The South, though outnumbered, had come to fight. The North, whose military preparedness could be described as nil, would have to do more than wave flags, sing patriotic songs, and raise regiments of raw volunteers if it was to hold its own, much less achieve victory.

The romantic bloom of war, as a result of this first devastating encounter, had quickly faded. The fever pitch of enlistment was giving way to quick departure—sometimes in the middle of a skirmish—by men who had reached the end of their ninety-day hitch. And bounties and other inducements had to be increased by county and state to fill government quotas and attract more young men to the colors.

After living for a few days with the nightmare of the battle's aftermath so that in the morning he thought he saw the ocean roll red upon the strand, Harrah could not drive the image of war from his mind. He tried to think of other things, to occupy his day with Trescott House's clientele, to wait till the end of the tourist season. Nothing worked. The young men that he did see, splendid in their duck pants and colorful jackets and tanned faces, only reminded him of those who would never again attend a "hop" or splash into a swelling surf.

He decided at last that he could wait no longer. He would join the ranks of the "Peace" Democrats and engage in a search for a just solution to the war. Not once did Harrah think that common ground could be found that would satisfy both sides. He knew only that the slaughter had to be stopped and that away from the hysteria of armed men and shrieking patriots, some plan, some approach, some solution would have to be hammered out. Peace no less than war had its anvil, and if its noise could be heard above the din of gunfire it might yet shape the future.

Harrah had heard of such men as Colonel James B. Wall of Burlington and Clement L. Vallandigham of Ohio. Wall was a frequent contributor to the Newark *Journal* and the New York *Daily News*, virulently anti-war newspapers. And Vallandigham, a Congressman from the Midwest, had delivered many speeches on the floor of the House, advocating peace, declaring his mistrust of extremists, both North and South, and attacking Lincoln for selling his soul to New York capitalists and New England factory owners.

Harrah was not particularly enamored of either of these men. He suspected that at heart they were sympathetic to the South, if not to slavery itself. Maybe they were "Copperheads" as the *Tribune* described them. But he felt he must throw himself in league with those who opposed the war, whatever their philosophies or sympathies. Once the war was over, he would settle his differences with them.

He had heard of a peace conference to take place in Northern New Jersey. Though he had no idea who would be in attendance or what the agenda would consider, Harrah made up his mind to attend the affair.

He stopped in the kitchen to see Rachel.

"It's time you took a direct hand in managing the place. I may be gone for several days."

"I've enough to do in the kitchen."

"But we've hardly been overwhelmed with guests," said Harrah.

"Cooking for twenty's no worse than fifty."

This was as talkative as Rachel would get, he thought. But he was wrong.

"Willacassa's no longer here. Chambermaids are hard to get with the girls running off to Washington."

"Washington?"

"Every girl claims a man in uniform. And she wants to be close to him—just when you need her most."

"But what about the young men on Cape Island?"

"The young men on Cape Island are suspect. Visitors and residents alike. Thought to be cowards or shirkers. Can't say as they are. But that's the thinking."

"And what do you think?"

"I think you're expecting too much."

"Too much?"

She nodded. "If you're thinking I'm going to handle this

alone."

"You can get your friend to help you," said Harrah quietly.

Rachel reddened. "My friend?"

"That retired old gentleman. The one who visits you in the kitchen from time to time."

"Mr. Planks? What does he know about the hotel business!" She was flustered and flattered at the same time.

"I'll teach him what he has to know."

"Fiddlesticks!"

"I'm serious. I'll speak to him this afternoon."

"Oh, go on then. I'll manage somehow."

Harrah arrived at Schraalenbergh in Bergen County at the end of July. An immense and enthusiastic crowd of Dutch farmers and Democratic peace-seekers, some wearing in their lapels Indian heads cut from copper pennies, had gathered to demand that the North seek a truce. Bull Run was still in their minds. The shocking setback to Union troops and the heavy loss of life had created an urgency and an indignation that no government statement from Washington could dispel. Here in Bergen County the champions of peace would be heard. And though similar meetings were being held in other sections of the state, all the way down to Cumberland County, Bergen would still lead the way.

Men and not a few women jammed the town hall where chairs and benches were tightly arranged to accommodate the overflow crowd. Harrah himself, conservative and reserved by nature, did not share the enthusiasm and the carnival-like atmosphere of the place. Nor did he join in the torchlight parade preceding the meeting. But once the meeting was called to order, he found himself a seat down front. He waited patiently for the milling around by delegates from Trenton, Newark, and Princeton to end. And more than once had the uneasy feeling he did not belong.

The opening address was made by a man from the Midwest, the editor of a newspaper in Ohio, who wanted to broaden his base of influence by speaking in New Jersey. Rupert Hasbrouck did not look like a Midwesterner. He was not particularly tall. He was not in the least rugged. He did not speak with a twang or a drawl. In appearance he struck Harrah as more like a Philadelphia banker making money out of the war than a member of the Peace Movement. The only thing pacific about his speech was the lengthy introduction. Then he got warmed up, flailing his arms and pounding on the lectern.

"The war, my friends, has degenerated into a murderous crusade for cotton and niggers.

"The North says it is fighting to preserve the Union, but disunion is its motto and Satan is its guide. What the North wants is to subjugate the South and the Middle West to Pennsylvania iron mongers and New England textile manufacturers.

"The Lincoln Administration has no other purpose but to free the negroes and enslave the whites. The free states will soon be overrun by negroes who will place all who work for a living on an equal footing with them. Already an army of contrabands has spilled into our Northern and Midwestern towns, living together under the same roof, holding everything in common including their women and subsisting on whatever they can beg, borrow, or steal. Is this what we are fighting for? Is this what casualty lists are all about? No wonder soldiers are deserting every day. No wonder we are losing our friends abroad.

"The people, I say, do not want this war. The working man and the farmer are burdened with taxes and tariffs. Homes and property have been wantonly destroyed. Widows and orphans have been deprived of their loved ones. There is no glory to be won in a civil war, no more than in a family quarrel.

"Reasonable men feel there is still time to call an end to bloodshed. We have had an ignoble crusade for war, led by abolitionists and political fanatics. Look where it has gotten us. Let us now, then, prosecute a vigorous crusade for peace. Let's enlist all men and women of good will, North and South, East and West. Let us seize the state house and the House of Representatives. Let us throw the scoundrels out, Lincoln and the whole caboodle of them. The party hacks and the job seekers, those Black Republicans with their mulatto mistresses.

"For so long as stupid men govern and tyrants rule the day, the war will drag on and the waste of men, blood, and precious resources will continue."

Rupert Hasbrouck·sat down to a standing ovation.

Harrah was astonished by what he heard. It occurred to him, almost for the first time, that there were those whose chief effect on political movements was to sabotage them. He was not sure it was the deliberate intent of anyone to undermine the peace movement, as he understood it. But the way some of its "champions" behaved, the irresponsibility of their public pronouncements, the tarnished reputations which they dragged into the fray could not help but undo the little good that was being done.

While not giving much credence to gossip, Harrah understood that at least a couple of the "Peace" Democrats had enjoyed something less than unblemished lives. He had heard one man described as an opportunist who had married a widow, mismanaged her estate, and then entered into a second marriage without bothering to dissolve the first.

Another had by turns been an amorous clergyman, a theatrical press agent, a medicine man, and a moonshiner before coming to New Jersey to protest the war. Neither man was moderate in his views, each becoming a virulent advocate of peace, a "nigger hater," and a bitter opponent of Mr. Lincoln.

But Harrah swallowed his displeasure. He tried to find some good in them. At least they wanted an end to the fighting. And he found in others the breath of fresh air on the subject that the miasma of war had all but poisoned.

"My friends," began the final speaker whose name Harrah was not able to catch, "I am not going to argue the merits of emancipation or slavery. There are others more eloquent than I who can make out a better case than I can. And I'm not going to inflame the passions, as others have, by making such irresponsible statements as, 'We are cutting each other's throats for the sake of a few worthless Negroes.' I think we can best argue the cause of peace by putting such rhetoric behind us. Nor is it my intention to foment dissatisfaction in the ranks or give comfort to traitors and rebels.

"But in all honesty I must declare that this war was unnecessary in its origin, and is fraught with horror and the prospect of endless suffering. It is a matter of regret and shame that as we endure the perils and sufferings of war, we lose sight of any principles or convictions in whose behalf the war is supposedly being fought. Those who continue to push this war are wicked, weak, and cowardly men. They neither want the war to end nor have the courage and strength to bring it to an end. They are caught up in the fever of partisanship and will outstrip themselves in their haste to throw others into the smoky cauldron while they at great cost build defenses and impregnable fortifications to protect themselves. Aren't the walls being built around Richmond nothing but a citadel for the protection of Jefferson Davis? Aren't the earthworks strung about Washington nothing but fortresses to protect Abraham Lincoln? How many men must die in order to satisfy the vanities of those who proclaim themselves our leaders? How many battles must be fought to prove them right, when right is only a matter of expediency? Mr. Lincoln has said he has neither the power nor the wish to end slavery in the South. Mr. Davis has said he does not wish to extend slavery in the North. So what are we fighting about? Let the government immediately appoint a commission to meet with the South to end hostilities.

"If, on the other hand, slavery is the issue—whether to abolish it or keep it—then let both sides say so. Let's not have any evasion or deceit on this score. And if once and for all a war must be fought to resolve this issue, then let it be fought—to the bitter end.

"But, for Heaven's Sake, let's not don the mantle of hypocrisy. Let's not for one moment pretend the war has to do with Union or Secession, with States' Rights or the right of a government to remain indissoluble. Lawyers canquibble over the constitutionality of these issues from now until doomsday. But there is no moral imperative here. Certainly no justification for the death of a single soldier—let alone the slaughter of thousands of innocent young men on both sides. What we have in this land of ours is not a struggle for freedom but a license for butchery. What we must mount is a crusade to repeal that license—once and for all, now and forever!"

Harrah shared what he had learned with Joseph Leach. He had known the wiry editor of the *Ocean Wave,* a former teacher, city recorder, Baptist preacher, and father of eight surviving children, almost from the time he came to Cape Island in 1848 and purchased two lots on Hughes Street, building a home on one and selling the other for a handsome profit five years later.

"Yes, Joseph," said Harrah. "The peace movement is very much alive. And it crosses party lines."

Joseph Leach was not impressed. "It's built on quicksand," he replied. "It's bound to sink."

There had, of course, been a definite "cooling off" between the two men. Leach was a fervent supporter of the war, writing his partisan editorials and printing letters from young men who had donned the blue uniform of New Jersey's volunteer regiments or publishing dispatches sent by his son, J. Granville Leach, from military camps. And when he was not editing, he was speaking from political platforms or attending "war meetings."

Harrah, though as ardent an abolitionist as Leach, had not shown any enthusiasm for the war. In fact, as the early campaigns faltered and the casualty lists grew and Mr. Lincoln began to juggle his armies and his generals, Harrah became downright antagonistic to the way the whole business was being conducted. He likened the war effort to the bogs of South Jersey's Pinelands. And he saw the Union armies getting in deeper and deeper with little chance of climbing out unscathed and intact. A quagmire, that was it! And the worst casualty of the war, after the maimed and mutilated bodies of the soldiers, was the issue of slavery or at least its abolition.

"No peace movement can succeed without compromise," said Harrah.

"Meaning?"

"The South wants freedom from the North *and* slavery. The North wants union *and* abolition. If there's to be peace, we must bend. Give the South her freedom if she first abandons slavery. (The Southern women don't like it anyway. They'd just as soon get rid of the black harems.) The North would then have abolition. And with slavery gone, the chances of reunion would be greatly enhanced."

"The Harrah Compromise?" suggested Leach.

"Exactly."

"Neither side will buy it."

"Why?"

"Because what they both want is a contradiction in terms. There can be no freedom with slavery. And there can be no union with abolition. And so war is inevitable."

"But the bleeding and the dying?"

"They will have a sobering effect. Neither side is sober now. They are both tipsy with principle. Once blood is spilled, there will be less pressure to spill more."

"No, Joseph," replied Harrah. "Once blood is spilled, there can be no end to the bloodletting. Not until one side or the other is drained dry."

"We'll see," said Leach, swinging round in his chair to his rolltop desk. "By the way," he added, not without a touch of pride. "I've gotten word from *Harper's Weekly*. They're interested in Willacassa and will take her on. Of course, they know her only as 'W. Harrah.'" He handed Harrah the letter. "You might want to forward this to her."

Just like Leach to hold back on the news. Always the editor. Always saving something for dramatic effect. Well, Harrah wasn't going to criticize the man. He had done his part. The important consideration now was Willacassa.

"Thank you, Joseph. She'll be delighted, poor girl. Since Eliot Irons's death, she's lost all interest in nursing. She needs a change. Something to get her out of the doldrums. This may be just the thing."

WINTER QUARTERS

Willacassa arrived at Camp "Hoosier" in November, finding a room in a small farmhouse nearby where she could stay. Actually the camp had been named for an Indiana Colonel who had been an early casualty of the war. But nobody could pronounce the name, which was German or Bohemian, so it became and remained Camp Hoosier.

She carried with her a letter of introduction from *Harper's Magazine*, countersigned by a senior officer in the War Department. This was supposed to be her entree into the military life of the Army of the Potomac. But from the first she had difficulty getting to see the various company commanders. And when she managed to see them she was invariably turned down.

"I'm sorry, Miss Harrah. But we can't have a woman running about camp unattended. We're at war, you know. And this is enemy territory. And though it looks like we'll be bedded down here in winter quarters, the camp is no place for a lady."

Though the choice of words varied from person to person, the message was always the same.

"But there are other war correspondents and sketch artists attached to the regiment. Why am I excluded?"

"I just told you. It's bad enough having civilians all over the place—government officials, suppliers, horse traders, hucksters, you name it—but at least they're men and won't be offended by what they see. You'll only create problems for us."

"You can at least allow me to try it for a few weeks. If I cause you any trouble, you can ask me to leave."

"Can't take the chance."

"Why not?"

"We've just been over that. I'm sorry. I suggest you return to Washington."

"I don't want to go back to Washington. I want to work here."

"I'm afraid you'll have to look elsewhere."

And so Willacassa did look elsewhere, seeking out the companies in alphabetical order until she had just about exhausted her list.

What made things worse for Willacassa was the incessant thud of axes and the crash of falling trees. She saw all about her a desecration of the land. Magnificent oaks and huge pine trees were being felled by soldiers, their branches and foliage pointing toward the enemy to form abatis. This had been going on to such an extent that what once had been lovely countryside with woods and boskage was now being reduced to a stump-filled, earth-scarred staging area. This troubled Willacassa almost as much as the reports of loss of life that appeared regularly in the newspapers.

"You'd better not stand around, young lady. Or you'll get hit by one of those falling trees."

The officer who uttered these words had just dismounted to move her out of the way.

"Maybe then someone'll take pity on me."

"Pity? You don't look like someone to be pitied." He said this pointedly but with such a kind face that Willacassa could not help laughing at herself.

"That's better. For a moment there I thought you might be one of those unnecessary casualties of the war. And we have enough of those already."

The officer had light brown hair under his kepi—almost blond. His eyes were light too. And his face, clean-shaven, sported a fair complexion. He could have passed for a Scandinavian or a Slav, but his accent betrayed him as a Midwesterner albeit an educated one.

"I'm Captain Shiloh of J Company. If I can be of assistance to you—"

"J Company?"

"Yes."

"You won't believe it, Captain. I was just going to see you."

"About what?"

She handed the captain her letter of introduction. Allowing him time to read it, she added, "I won't be getting in your way. All I want is a chance to do some drawings. Nothing earth-shaking. Just a few sketches of army camp life. Something that readers of *Harper's Magazine* would enjoy seeing."

"That should be no problem."

Willacassa was so taken back with surprise that she dropped the letter the officer had returned to her.

"Is something wrong?" asked Captain Shiloh.

"No. Nothing. To be honest, I thought you would give me a difficult time."

"As a matter of fact, I like *Harper's Magazine*. Nothing would give me more pleasure than seeing how a young woman depicts camp life. I'm afraid it's rather boring at times. Police Call, Surgeon's Call, Drill, Mounting Guard. All in all, it's a tedious business. It can put you to sleep long before Taps. Come to my tent and I'll write you a pass."

Captain Shiloh led the way on foot, tugging his horse's bridle with his left hand so that he could return the salutes of passing enlisted men with his right.

At his tent, a Sibley with a central pole and an adjustable vent, Captain Shiloh invited her to sit down. The Sibley was large enough for a stove, and Willacassa saw a teapot on it, blowing steam.

"Care for a cup? My orderly makes a good brew," said Shiloh.

"Yes, thank you." Willacassa could do with something hot.

Captain Shiloh pulled a sheet of paper from the table drawer and wrote out a pass.

"I could caution you about any number of things," he said in that curiously offhanded way of his. "But you're a grown woman. And I'm sure you could do without my advice."

"All I want is freedom to move about the place. I'll not disrupt anything or disturb the peace of the camp. As soon as I've filled my sketchbook, I'll move on."

"No hurry. We'll be here all winter. Summer's the season for fighting, you know. At least the way our generals see it."

"Then I'll have a free hand?"

"You have my word on it."

She finished her tea and rose to go. "Captain Shiloh, it's been a pleasure. I'm happy to meet at least one officer who doesn't see a woman as the enemy."

"The pleasure is all mine."

Formally attached to J Company, Willacassa was now free to do her sketches. And the sketches she loved to do most were soldiers at leisure. After morning muster and drill, the recruits had plenty of time on their hands and they found an assortment of activities to keep them busy. They made coffee in the crude pots the sutlers sold them. They placed open-ended barrels on stone chimneys to better the drafts. They carved outrageous-looking pipes which they smoked with unabashed pride of accomplishment. They arranged cockfights which they promptly placed bets on. They also bought New York and Philadelphia newspapers at the vendors' carts, and read them aloud for the edification of those who could not read. And they performed for one another on fiddles and banjos. But in-between they found time to write letters and to open the mail that kept pouring in.

Willacassa's favorite subjects were the young recruits. Anxious to emulate the veterans in camp, they wore their jackets looser than loose, they grew whiskers, they smoked smelly cigars, and they slung their kepis rakishly over their eyes. Yet their youthfulness shone through no matter how briskly they went about acting "seasoned." They taunted one another with mindless jokes. They jostled each other at every turn. They postured and posed incredible stances whenever they saw a photographer struggling with his equipment or a sketch artist close at hand.

Only Zeb Yount lent dignity to his age, which couldn't be more than sixteen. When Willacassa asked "Zebulon" to pose for her, the young corporal willingly obliged and in sitting answered fully all her questions.

"Come from Virginia, the western part of the state. My uncle was an abolitionist."

"Really? I didn't know they had any in Virginia."

"Oh, there were abolitionists in the hills long before they sprang up in the North. In fact, the first abolitionist newspaper was printed by 'hillbillies.' Least, that's what my uncle told me. And he also told me that Francis Marion, the old 'Swamp Fox,' said—way back when—that the South had only two classes, the rich and the poor. And the rich had no use for the poor 'cause slaves'd do their bidding."

All this was a revelation to Willacassa who waited for Zeb to go on.

"Yep, the feudin' goes back a long way. The dirt farmers hated the tidewater bigwigs. And the slaveholders had no use for them. Called them white trash and kept them off the ballot. Drove my uncle from the hills and closed down his press. And when he and his friends tried to return, they were whipped and carried out on rails. Other mountain men were shot or hung. But the slaveholders didn't stop there. They took to the stump and scared the living daylights out of us. They talked about buck-niggers mixing with our sisters. And they said that freed slaves would murder us in our beds. So we let them run things. And they're running things still. They hold the land, the vote, and the sheriff's office.

"So when the war broke out I tried to enlist. 'Cause I was only fifteen, the Feds would't take me. The Rebs didn't care, so I signed up with them."

"The Rebels?" Though surprised, Willacassa did not interrupt her work, carefully sketching the kepi that he wore so jauntily over his forehead.

"I didn't know any better. Began to believe what they said about the abolitionists. And it didn't really matter what side I was on so long as I was fightin'. One of my cousins went Confederate. And my brother flip-flopped until he went Union. Trouble is, the Rebel officers were all plantation owners' sons. And I was only a hill-country boy. They treated me no better'n dirt. So I skedaddled and finally hooked up with this Indiana outfit. Captain Shiloh took me in. Helps me with my readin'. Made me a corporal so I could be one of his orderlies. And now that West Virginia is pushing for statehood, I think I made the right move."

"And when the war's over?"

"When the war's over, I'll get an education. Then study law, like Captain Shiloh. He said he'll help me."

When she had accumulated a portfolio full of drawings, Willacassa was anxious to show her sketches off. And the likely person to show them to appeared to be Captain Shiloh. He had not insisted that he "pass" on what she had done. There was nothing of the censor about him. So it was not a question of necessity here. But like Zeb Yount, who did nothing without taking into account how the captain would react, not even the small purchases he made at the sutler's tent, Willacassa wanted his approval.

"What do you think?" she asked.

"I think they're very good. Outstanding, in fact. You have a marvelous way with significant detail."

Willacassa basked in his praise, though she was not sure the faces in the photograph that sat on his shelf were equally approving.

"Your family?" she asked, pointing to the framed picture.

"Yes, my wife and children. Don't let the serious expressions fool you. My offspring can be full of mischief."

"She's a fine-looking woman." And indeed the woman in the photograph was quite handsome, her dark hair severely combed back to reveal a classic, determined face.

"Thank you."

"But where'd you get the towheads from?"

"I was a towhead as a child. My father's side of the family was fair."

"I see."

"Which ones are you sending to *Harper's*?" he asked.

"The first ten. I think they're the best of the lot."

Captain Shiloh nodded in agreement. "I look forward to seeing them in print. Especially the one of Zeb. It's so much like the boy."

"Which ones do you think they'll take?" asked Willacassa.

"All of them."

"That's nothing but flattery."

"Flattery? No, the truth. I'd take them all if I were *Harper's*. You see, you've captured a side of the war not generally appreciated. The drab, the ordinary side. The real side. Too often we romanticize the bloody business. Make it seem as if every day is a page out of Sir Walter Scott."

"When actually it's a page out of Hardee's manual?"

"Exactly."

Willacassa included in her sketches portraits of Negroes at work in the camp. She did not know how many of these blacks were freedmen, pressed into service as laborers, and how many were "contrabands," General Ben Butler's name for them, according to Captain Shiloh. As General Butler reasoned, if slaves could be regarded by the Rebels as personal property, fugitive slaves could be regarded as contraband of war.

In any case, freedmen or contrabands, Willacassa found large numbers of black men working in the stables, on hospital wagons, or as teamsters bringing in an ever-increasing supply of food, clothing, and weapons. Others drew work details or fatigue duty, carrying picks and shovels wherever they went, digging ditches and latrines, building log huts and stone chimneys. Still others got out the "mess," doing not only the peeling and cooking but the scrubbing and cleaning up. Seeing them engaged in such a broad range of tasks, all indispensable, Willacassa could not imagine the Union Army, or the Rebel Army for that matter, functioning without them.

One afternoon, when she was sketching some of the Negroes at mess, a soup ladler accidentally spilled some broth. The soldier on line who had caught the soup on his pants broke into a frenzy.

"You stupid coon! What'd you do that for! I'd whip your ass if I had a cat o' nine."

"Sorry, suh."

"Don't tell me you're sorry. Just get the hell out of here!" And with that he kicked the retreating man in the hindquarters.

"What do you think you're doing!" broke in Willacassa, her face inflamed with outrage.

"And who in heck are you!"

"Never mind. That's a free man you're talking to. And even if he were a slave—"

"I'm for freeing the slaves," said a Yank who had been standing by. "But I don't want them coming North. I'd just as soon ship them back to Africa."

"You can't free the slaves," insisted the soldier with the wet pants' leg. "Anyone can see they're subhuman. Where the army takes over, they should snatch the slaves from the Rebels and turn them over to loyal slaveowners. If I thought this war was to free the slaves, I'd pack up and go home tomorrow!"

This sentiment so shocked Willacassa that she crushed the paper she had sketched on.

"Then pack up!" she said. "The Union doesn't need the likes of you!"

Willacassa immediately reported what she had seen to

Captain Shiloh. "Why, these boys are just as bad as the Rebels. Maybe worse. I had no idea how much they hate the Blacks. The whole thing has been a revelation to me!"

"It's been a shock to me too," said Shiloh.

"But who's responsible for this?"

"The newspapers, for one. There's an anti-Negro daily out of Newark and another bitterly hostile press in Washington that are sold here. The boys read them, then spread their poison."

"How can they be so naive!"

"It's not hard to be naive when you're not yet twenty. And some remain twenty forever."

"Then why enlist?"

"Why? Because they were told by our leaders this is the thing to do. Everyone gets caught up in flag and country."

"I don't understand," said Willacassa. "I believed—I thought this was a just war. Once the South fired on Fort Sumter I thought the course was clear."

"Clear? Well, it isn't clear," said Captain Shiloh. "This is a war that never should have been fought—over an institution that never should have been tolerated."

Willacassa did not respond at once and when she did she was somewhat tentative. "Then you too are saying that the war is being fought over slavery?"

"At least as far as I'm concerned."

"But what about preserving the Union?" she asked.

"If the war were being fought over secession, I wouldn't be here. Let the states secede. We can live without them. They're only making a mockery out of democracy anyway. We don't need an aristocracy to tell the rest of us how to live. Especially as it's to make possible a life of ease and exploitation."

"Then you're saying this is a rich man's war?"

"Of course it is. Not only for the planters in the South, for the industrialists in the North as well. But the rich have another name for it—to make it more palatable to the poor. And the poor are too stupid to know better. At least in the North there's an added inducement."

"What do you mean?"

"Men are getting three or four-hundred-dollar bounties to enlist. In some places as much as seven hundred dollars. That's a good deal of money for someone who couldn't rub two pennies together before."

"And you, Captain? Why did you enlist?"

"Why?" Shiloh abandoned his camp chair. "I told you. I think it was out of patriotic fervor. Though I suspect there were other reasons.''

"Other reasons?''

"Wanting to get away. That's one.''

"From what?''

"What men generally want to get away from. Their wives, their children, the tedium of their profession. In my case, I suppose I wanted to get away from lawbooks for a while. From courtrooms and the petty grievances of petty men. Don't mistake what I'm saying. I made a handsome living at what I did. Not so good a living as President Lincoln. But then again, Indiana is not Illinois. Still, I wanted a respite, a break. When I was offered a commission, I didn't turn it down.''

He chuckled quietly as if he had yet to decide on the wisdom of his action. "And here I am.''

Yes, here he was. A most complicated, contradictory man. Willacassa would have preferred that Shiloh was willing to risk life and limb solely to free the slaves. To her way of thinking, that was what the war was all about. But Shiloh made no such pretense. And if she did not admire him for his "other reasons,'' she at least respected him for his honesty. It was hard not to respect him.

What Willacassa wanted now that she had found a place for herself in camp was to be able to take her sketchbook into the field. On three occasions J Company was ordered out of camp to reconnoiter or probe enemy defenses. It had engaged in a couple of brief skirmishes but nothing that resembled a battle. Willacassa saw no reason why she could not go along at a safe distance.

But on this score Captain Shiloh was adamant.

"It's too dangerous. Can't afford having you stop a ball.''

Never did he say it was no place for a woman, but she knew what he was thinking.

"Other artists go out into the field.''

"Yes, after the battle's been fought and the position secured. What we've seen have been only skirmishes. Snipers and pickets are a constant threat out there. The camp's the only ground we're reasonably sure of.''

"But I need to vary my subject matter. *Harper's* will want some battle scenes.''

"Then *Harper's* will have to get the generals off their camp stools. There's been precious little fighting since Bull Run.''

"Maybe McClellan will turn things around,'' ventured Willacassa, aware that Winfield Scott had stepped down and anxious to show that she knew a thing or two.

"'Little Napolean'? It's possible. But Washington's afraid to leave the capital unprotected. The politicians worry about their own necks first. So long as they are at risk the army won't be marching on Richmond.''

Captain Shiloh would have liked to leave it at that. But when he saw how downcast his refusal had left Willacassa, he said he would try to work something out.

''I've got to ride into town to requisition some wagons. You're welcome to the use of my tent if the weather acts up. If I think of anything along the way, I'll let you know when I get back.''

In Captain Shiloh's absence Willacassa found herself waxing restless. She wandered about the camp looking for subjects, but nothing caught her interest. She tried to start a few sketches but found her thoughts drifting elsewhere.

Willacassa had heard reports of the navy's occupation of Port Royal Sound, South Carolina. She had glanced through the newspapers for details which were sketchy at best. A Union squadron of fifteen warships and gunboats under Captain Dupont and twelve thousand troops under General Thomas W. Sherman had managed to take Forts Walker and Beauregard after a bombardment of only four hours and thirty minutes. That was the broad picture. There was no indication, however, of the kind of resistance offered nor identification of the units involved in defending the forts.

It seemed to Willacassa at first that Francis Grandee might have been among the defenders. His family plantation was not that far from the coast. And he could be expected to fight for home and hearth when they were threatened. But the better part of wisdom soon convinced her that the Union navy, as the newspapers reported, only wanted a depot for strengthening its blockade and that Francis most likely would be a member of some cavalry regiment assigned to Virginia, the principal theater of the war.

Still, the name Port Royal Sound conjured up memories of her short but painful stay in South Carolina—oh, how many years ago? And she could not completely shake the idea that Francis might have had an active role in the fighting.

''Do maps interest you?'' Captain Shiloh asked when he found her leaning over the table in his tent.

Willacassa was startled by his sudden entry. But she quickly recovered.

''I wanted to see where Port Royal was.''

Captain Shiloh approached the table and leaned over. After studying the map, he moved his finger to the left, then slightly upward. ''Here it is,'' he said softly. ''Do you have relatives there?''

''No. Just friends. People who used to summer on Cape Island.

I was wondering how the occupation affected them.''

"Very little, I'd say. It's confined to the forts. I was surprised at how quickly they gave way. Not like the South to knuckle under so soon.''

Unaccountably Willacassa found the nearness of the captain disturbing to her. "Thank you," she said, moving away from the table. "I never would have found it without you. Maps have always been a problem for me."

"Would you like some tea?" asked Captain Shiloh, removing his kepi.

"I think not. Now that the rain has stopped, I'll be going outside again." She paused at the tent door. "I hope you didn't think I was too forward about the map. I guess I should have asked your permission before looking at it."

"Nothing of the kind. Any schoolboy can get hold of it."

But as soon as she had left, Willacassa forgot their little encounter. Her mind turned South once more and her preoccupation with where and when dominated her thoughts.

Willacassa did not know what fighting unit claimed Francis Grandee for its own. All she could remember that last day she saw him on Cape Island was his saying that he would report to his regiment. Willacassa assumed that this would be a cavalry regiment, given Grandee's love of horses and riding. And given his family connections, she had no doubt he had secured a suitable commission for himself, at a rank no less than a lieutenant or captain. As far as she could determine there had come into being several cavalry brigades in South Carolina. But the only true-blooded one was Wade Hampton's legion, recruited and outfitted by Wade Hampton at his own expense. She had heard the 650-man legion was drawn from the scions of the wealthiest and most prominent families in South Carolina. She could not imagine Francis Grandee not being among them.

Later she learned that the legion had played a substantial role at the Battle of Bull Run, losing almost one out of every five men in a furious encounter near the Robinson House. This raised all kinds of possibilities. Like Eliot Irons, Francis Grandee had also been wounded in battle. If wounded, he had been carried off by his comrades to a Confederate hospital or had been taken prisoner by the retreating Union army. The latter possibility seemed less likely in the chaos and confusion of a retreat that was characterized by even the Federals as a complete rout. The second prospect was that Francis had been killed. But Willacassa believed that had such an event taken place she would have received some incorporeal sign, a flash of internal light or a feeling in the pit of her stomach, that confirmed this. And no such feeling possessed her. The only other possibility was that Francis Grandee had emerged from battle unscathed and had returned with the rest of Wade Hampton's legion to a Virginia encampment to await the next engagement. If this were so, the time for meeting him again was not yet at hand. She would have to wait a little longer.

Not that Willacassa had any idea what she would do if ever they came face to face again. Nothing had changed in her attitude toward him. He was still Francis Grandee of South Carolina. There was nothing of the slave-owning aristocracy that had been knocked out of him. Despite his repeated declarations that he was a changed man, that he sincerely repented his past actions with respect to slavery and the exploitation of black women, he had enlisted at the first shot in behalf of the slave states, had become the standard-bearer of the palmetto flag and the tainted banner of the Confederacy. Could she be expected to embrace someone who stood for everything that was repugnant to her? Could she really bring herself to declare her love for a man in whom she mixed admiration with contempt?

She did not know. Willacassa knew only that she had to learn more about Francis Grandee, his place in the scheme of things, a scheme that was becoming incredibly entangled by the war and the unpredictable turns it was taking.

But she had to be careful. In doing this she had to be sure she did not alienate Captain Shiloh. The captain had not made much of the map incident. But he could have. And the one thing Willacassa did not want was a confrontation. The captain after all was her entree to the military, the one person that kept her close to the theater of war. Without him she would still be looking for a place to camp and subjects to sketch. Willacassa needed Shiloh's support and it appeared that she had it. It would be folly to put their relationship and her access to camp in jeopardy.

Several of Willacassa's sketches appeared in *Harper's Weekly* in January and February. Neither was prominently featured, but Willacassa derived the satisfaction of the newly published. She sat for twenty or thirty minutes each time admiring her handiwork and the signature ''W. Harrah'' which appeared in the lower righthand corner of her drawings. And there was still enough of the little girl in her to want to shout, ''Look what I did!''

But except for her father (and Rachel), whom she telegraphed to be sure he did not miss the ''landmark'' copies, the only one she chose to show the magazine to was Captain Shiloh.

''You must be pleased as punch,'' said the officer as he

admired the publication. "Only the other day I realized I had forgotten to buy the latest issue. And sure enough, you're in it."

"I'm pleased with the publication but not with the money they send. I expected to be paid on a regular basis. Instead it's by the picture."

"Are you in need of money?"

"No, my father sends me bank drafts from time to time. But I prefer being independent."

"Why don't you do portraits?" suggested Captain Shiloh. "There are any number of officers and men in camp who would want to send a likeness home. If your portrait of Zeb Yount is any indication, you'd do quite well."

"I've thought of that. But—"

"But what?"

"Most would prefer to have their portraits done at a photographer's studio. I've even seen photographers' wagons in camp. They're exceedingly popular."

"True," said Shiloh. "But you can always be competitive. And there's one thing a photograph can't capture."

"And what's that?"

"The eye of the artist. The camera's eye is only a piece of glass. It has the objectivity of a lottery. There's always a chance it will capture something special. But with the artist that chance is increased a hundredfold."

"I never thought of it that way," reflected Willacassa. "That was well put."

"I hope I'm as eloquent when I plead my cases next week." Willacassa looked puzzled.

"I've been transferred West for a time. They need lawyers there for court martials. Justice must be served, you see, even if it's a swift justice."

"But why you?"

"I'm a lawyer. With nothing doing here—thanks to General McClellan—my superiors thought I could be spared for a while.

Captain Shiloh read the disappointment on Willacassa's face and was pleased by what he saw.

"I'll be back," he said almost with a paternal tenderness. "Meanwhile Lieutenant Farnsworth will take over."

"That silly man!"

"Oh, he's a mite rigid, but not a bad fellow. When he forgets that his father-in-law's a banker, he can be—"

"Almost human?"

Captain Shiloh smiled. "In a war it takes all kinds. Besides, he knows he's only temporary. And I've told him you're to have free rein of the place." As an afterthought, he picked up a pen and some paper. "I'll leave instructions about the portraits, too. They come under the heading of morale building, you see. Just avoid the man as much as you can."

"Don't worry, I will."

"And when I see you again, you should be independently wealthy." This was in lieu of goodbye, so Willacassa took her leave.

But when she was outside Willacassa realized that she did not want to go just yet. Their goodbye had been too abrupt, too military-like. It did not seem right somehow. She stepped back into the tent.

"I left without thanking you," she said. "I didn't mean to do that."

Captain Shiloh looked up from his table where his eyes had been fixed in a vacant stare.

"There's nothing to thank me for."

"Oh, but there is. You were the only one willing to give me a chance. The only one. I'll never forget that."

She noted a sadness in his gray eyes that she had not seen before. But she felt compelled to go on.

"You've been more than I had a right to expect. With all your responsibilities here, I've just been one more burden for you. Yet you've always been kind. You've always had time for me. From the beginning I felt I had a friend."

Still Captain Shiloh sat quietly, his eyes now fixed on the floor.

"Do you understand what I'm trying to say?"

"Yes, Willacassa," he said softly. "I understand."

She rose feeling peculiarly light-headed. She had said what she wanted to say. She had turned it into a proper goodbye. Now she could leave. She stepped outside again. And then it occurred to her that Captain Shiloh had never called her Willacassa before. Strange that she had not noticed this right off. He had said Willacassa, hadn't he? Was her mind playing tricks on her? No, she was certain he had called her Willacassa. There could be no doubt of that. Her skin tingled at the thought. Captain Shiloh had indeed called her Willacassa.

February and March were dismal months for Willacassa. There wasn't that much snow on the ground. But it was raw and cold in camp, and the chief occupation of the soldiers when they were free of drill and guard duty was finding kindling wood for their stoves and outdoor fires. Sometimes the soldiers were overzealous in their passion to keep warm, and a few of the log huts that had been constructed caught fire during the night and burned down.

Actually the excitement and commotion caused by these fires aroused the military out of its lethargy. And Willacassa, who rode in from the outlying farmhouse where she stayed, could read in the faces of the men a welcome change from the monotonous, grinding routine of everyday camp life. Eyes sparkled, honest sweat poured in the struggle to contain the fires, and a good camaraderie developed when the flames and burning cinders were gotten under control. Even shrill laughter filled the air, a strange sound for the quiet, solemn nights of Virginia winter.

But this did not prove to be a propitious time for Willacassa to launch her portrait sketching venture. No one was willing to pose for long out of doors and, short of hiring a tent of her own or a wagon for that purpose, Willacassa had no ready access to a shelter. Even if something lent itself to house her little operation, she had not yet devised a way to provide the kind of light she needed, light that would not cast distorting or disfiguring shadows.

On those relatively warm or springlike days when she did persuade someone to sit for a portrait and managed to draw a crowd to watch her work, Willacassa found that she had Lieutenant Farnsworth to deal with. Despite Captain Shiloh's directive allowing the activity, Farnsworth had serious reservations.

"Doesn't do much for discipline," he said when he called her into his tent.

"Can't see how it hurts."

"Draws a crowd. And crowds lead to squabbles."

"There hasn't been one incident yet."

"But there will be, and then it'll be too late. Besides—"

"Besides what, Lieutenant?"

"It seems to me that a share of your earnings should go into the pot."

"What pot?"

"Each company has a common pot for fines and that sort of thing. When the pot is full we buy things at the sutler's tent."

"I don't think I should be fined for doing portraits, the few that I do. And I think enough money is being wasted in the sutler's tent already."

"That's a matter of opinion. In any case, I'm going to insist on twenty percent of whatever you take in."

"Twenty percent! Captain Shiloh never said anything about paying a commission."

"He never said anything to the contrary either. What's more, I've been directed to review all sketches being made at camp. We don't want to release anything that will be useful to the enemy."

"That's pure rubbish! There's nothing I sketch that can be useful to the enemy."

"I'll decide that—if you don't mind, Miss Harrah."

"But I do mind. And—" She was tempted to break off her connection with the company, here and now, without further ado. But the possibility that Captain Shiloh would return soon kept her from taking an action she might later regret.

"Then you won't agree to the commission?"

"I'll agree only if you put it in escrow—until Captain Shiloh returns. We'll let him resolve the matter."

"But I could stop the portrait painting altogether."

"Not really. That would be countermanding Captain Shiloh's orders. And you wouldn't want to do that."

Lieutenant Farnsworth could see that in her own way Willacassa knew how to wage war.

"All right," he said. "We'll hold it in escrow."

On the first day of spring Willacassa was sitting with her sketchbook on her lap when almost as an apparition Captain Shiloh came riding in on a buckboard, Zeb Yount at his side. The sight of the man so unnerved her that Willacassa dropped her sketchbook and in trying to recover it lost her drawing pencils.

Willacassa sprang to her feet, her face throbbing. She could see that Captain Shiloh was tired from his long journey, and gaunt. This did not distress her. What she feared—of all things—was that he would once more address her as Miss Harrah.

"How are you, Captain?"

"Weary. But glad to be back. If I see another court-martial, Willacassa, I'll turn in my law degree."

He jumped down to pick up her sketchbook while Zeb Yount struggled to hold the buckboard horse in check.

"You were missed, Captain. I can't begin to tell you how much."

This pleased Harrah and drew a faint smile.

"Did Farnsworth give you any trouble?"

"The lieutenant was his usual uncompromising self."

"Some people never learn." He handed the sketchbook back to her. "Do you want to talk about it?"

Willacassa nodded.

"Then why don't you drop by later this afternoon?"

And so at four Willacassa arrived with an apple pie that she had bought at the sutler's tent. After Zeb Yount brewed the coffee, the three crowded round the camp table with their tin cups and Zeb brought the captain up to date on the gossip around camp.

"General McClellan's out in the field now. Got something

going. No more dillydallying. Anyway, that's the talk. And we may be going with him.''

"The weather's warm enough for fighting," observed Shiloh. "Things may be quiet here. But out West the war's been hot and heavy.''

"What were the court-martials all about?" asked Willacassa. "Can you talk about them?"

"Desertions mainly. Desertion, insubordination, and cases of violence against women. I have to say that I can't see trying a man for desertion when all he does is drift back to the homestead to see how things are going. Sometimes they're just homesick. Sometimes there's plowing to do. Almost always the men report back again.''

"Then whey the court-martials?"

"To set an example, I suppose."

"Were they all convicted?"

"Most of them. Those that committed rape and mayhem got what they deserved. But none received a fair trial. And several of the deserters were hung. That's pretty harsh punishment for something that goes on North and South, and is often winked at.''

"What would you do?"

"With deserters? Look the other way."

"Then in effect you'd do nothing."

"Well, war or no war," said Shiloh. "Families have to eat. If soldiers didn't go home for harvest, there'd be no one to bring in the crops. Besides, the men eventually straggle back.''

Shiloh lit his cigar and went on.

"One of the regular army generals wants the volunteer outfits to shoot deserters. I told him if he wanted them shot he'd have to do the shooting himself. I also told him I didn't think he had bullets enough to do the job. Do you have any idea how many deserters there are in this army?''

Willacassa shook her head. "No."

"Enough to make five or six divisions. Anyway, they're not all deserters. Just have to go home from time to time—especially when things get slow around here. That's something the generals don't understand.''

At this Zeb Yount rose to leave. " 'Fraid I'll be desertin' too. Got some horses to look after." He turned to Willacassa. "Thanks for the pie, Miss Harrah.''

"And thank you, Zeb. The coffee was just right."

The West Virginian smiled his portrait smile and stepped outside.

"How bad were things with Lieutenant Farnsworth?" asked

Shiloh when they were alone.

"Not all that bad, really. Suddenly I see no need to talk about it. I realize that my problems pale with insignificance when compared with the war."

"Everything pales with insignificance once the fighting starts."

"Yet the men in camp look forward to the fighting. I think they'd prefer almost anything to drill and work details."

"They deem it all a waste of time," agreed Shiloh. "And maybe it is."

"You still don't approve of the war, do you?" Willacassa knew she was treading on uncertain ground here but was not about to step back.

"If I knew what the war was about, I might approve."

"Then you no longer see slavery as the issue?"

"I thought it was at first. That's why I volunteered. Now I'm not so sure."

Willacassa was beginning to realize she would not get the usual answers here. She did not really know Captain Shiloh. But she sensed something unorthodox about him, even heretical. And she was keen to hear him out.

"You've heard that General Fremont was in the West?" he asked. "In Missouri?"

"I don't follow the war that closely," she replied. All she knew of Fremont was that he ran as the presidential candidate for the new Republican Party in 1856.

"Well, he was there for a while," reiterated Captain Shiloh. "In August of last year he issued a proclamation. He freed all the slaves in Missouri whose owners were partial to the South."

"That sounds commendable," said Willacassa.

"It was commendable. For me, it was what the war was all about. I abhor slavery. I hate aristocracy. I—"

Willacassa had never seen him so intense.

"But President Lincoln countermanded the order," continued Shiloh. "And when Fremont refused to rescind the proclamation, he had Fremont removed."

"I didn't know that."

"So—to go back to your question—I no longer know what the war is about. I thought it was being fought for humanitarian reasons—only to find it is being fought to preserve the status quo. In short, to preserve slavery at this point, not to abolish it."

Willacassa did not know what to make of Captain Shiloh's peculiar logic, peculiar because it went against the grain of all conventional thinking. What she did know was that she found what Captain Shiloh said to be unsettling, disturbing, and, in an inexplicable way, stimulating, much as Eliot Irons had been stimulating in the old days on Cape Island.

But there was a difference. Eliot Irons had come across as someone's disciple. William Lloyd Garrison, Elijah Lovejoy, Wendell Phillips, it did not matter which. Captain Shiloh was his own apostle, his blue uniform notwithstanding.

The next day Willacassa found Shiloh in a rage.

What's wrong?'' she asked.

"I guess it's catching. What they're doing in the West, they want to do here. The regimental commander wants to make an example of skulkers. He's ordered two men court-martialed for desertion. And Lieutenant Farnsworth added one of our own to the list.''

"Does he have the authority to do that?''

"He did while I was away. But I'm trying to countermand the order.''

Somewhat calmed by Willacassa's presence, Captain Shiloh stopped pacing and sat down at his table. "I've offered to defend the deserters. In fact, I'm waiting for an answer now.''

Just then the regimental colonel appeared. He was a heavy-set man with red sidewhiskers and a pulpy, florid face. Impatient to say what was on his mind, he did not ask Willacassa to leave.

"What's this about your wanting to defend deserters, Captain?''

Shiloh rose to explain himself.

"One of the men is in my company, Sir.''

"So much the worse for it.''

"But he went home only because it was harvest time.''

"Makes no difference when he left. Desertion is desertion.''

"But all three of these men came back to their units, Sir.''

"What difference does that make?''

"It hardly seems fair that we court-martial those that come back and let the others go free.''

"But we can't lay hands on the others, Captain!''

"And then there's the matter of the death penalty. Shouldn't we be shooting at the enemy instead of our own men? The death penalty is almost never inflicted in these cases.''

"Well, then, it's time it was! This desertion problem was a steady trickle at first. Now it's a hemorrhage. Strong measures must be taken or the problem will never be solved.''

"It'll never be solved anyway, Sir.''

"What's that?''

"With all due respect, Sir. These men were volunteers. If they can volunteer in, they should be allowed to volunteer out.''

"Are you serious, Captain? Where would we be if everyone did as he chose! The army'd be decimated in a week!"

"But it's decimated already. If you punish those who choose to come back, the others will never return! We've either got to liberalize our leave policy—or look the other way when they take off for a spell."

"Nonsense, Captain. Utter nonsense! Now I'm certain you won't be permitted to represent them. But be sure to be present when the execution takes place."

"They haven't been court-martialed yet, Sir."

"They will be. And the verdict's a mere formality." He turned to leave and then noticed Willacassa. "I'm sorry, Mrs. Shiloh. I didn't mean to give your husband a dressing down in your presence. But I have no time for bleeding hearts!"

The colonel stalked out of the tent as suddenly as he had arrived.

"So you see where it's at," said Shiloh as Willacassa made ready to leave. Willacassa could find no words of comfort. She was already outside the tent when she heard the captain mutter, "That bastard. That goddam son of a bitch!"

But Captain Shiloh wasn't through yet. He wrote a letter to the family of the soldier in his outfit, giving them the grim news. And after the verdict was rendered, he cabled President Lincoln for leniency. Then, according to Zeb Yount, there was a battle between Shiloh and Lieutenant Farnsworth at the shooting range.

"Captain Shiloh learned that Lieutenant Farnsworth was assemblin' the firing squad himself. Every day he was teachin' the dirty dozen, as the captain called them, how to position themselves and fire."

" 'No dummy bullets for this group,' says Farnsworth. 'All bullets real so the men can share the guilt.'

"Captain Shiloh comes ridin' in to the shootin' range and a shoutin' match ensues.

" 'Who the hell told you to do this!' Captain Shiloh wants to know.

" 'I volunteered for the assignment,' replies Farnsworth.

" 'Can't you surfeit your taste for blood elsewhere!'

" 'I'm just doing my duty. There's no place for shirkers in the army.'

" 'But the Johnson boy's from your home state. Practically a neighbor!'

" 'Makes no difference!'

" 'Farnsworth, you're the sow that eats her own sucklings!'

" 'Don't call me a sow!'

" 'I'll call you what I damn please!' And Captain jumps off his horse to have a go at him. They come to blows, Captain Shiloh punchin' hard. But other officers step between 'em. Captain Shiloh is still hot when he leaves the range and Farnsworth is left shakin'."

Willacassa later learned that all Captain Shiloh succeeded in getting for his efforts was a reprimand, signed by Burnside and countersigned by the regimental colonel. And the day for the execution was summarily set.

"I want you to do a sketch of the execution. Several sketches if necessary," said Shiloh who had just returned from a visit with the doomed soldier, Private Johnson. "I know it's a grisly business. But if it appears in *Harper's*, there may be an outcry against such punishment. The idea doesn't trouble you, does it?"

"I'll be there," Willacassa said.

And on the day of the execution they were both there, Shiloh in protest, having temporarily stepped down from his command, and Willacassa not three feet from his side.

On the drill field about a thousand soldiers were gathered to witness the execution. In front of them, on three sides of the square, the condemned men's regiment was lined at attention. The officers and staff were all mounted and in dress uniform, their usually restless horses strangely quiet. At a signal a company of slowly marching men began the proceedings. This was followed by a military band, playing a mournful tune. With the start of a drumroll they brought the condemned men out, followed by their coffins, each coffin shouldered by four soldiers whose white faces marked the solemnity of the occasion. When the condemned men were brought to a stop, they were blindfolded, turned round, and made to sit on the edge of their open coffins which had been set down on the ground behind them.

Willacassa sketched furiously, telling herself that while her pencil moved the execution would not be carried out. At the last moment someone would step forward and call an end to it. Someone did step forward, but only to check the blindfolds and to see that the hands of the condemned men were tied securely across their belt buckles. When Lieutenant Farnsworth was satisfied with what he saw, he stepped back out of the way.

The drum roll now stopped and a naked silence fell on the camp grounds. Then at an order rifles were raised and the clank of trigger guard levers being pulled down and snapped back again was heard. A long pause followed. Willacassa involuntarily stopped to watch. A moment later a dozen shots rang out and the three men tumbled back into their coffins.

When Willacassa began to swoon and fall forward, Captain Shiloh who had moved to her side caught hold of her.

"Steady," he said softly. "It's all over."

"But these poor men—"

"The army's made its point. Nothing can be done for them now."

Willacassa fell ill. For two days she climbed out of bed in the morning, dressed, and made a valiant effort to ride into camp. But each time she grew so weak sitting on her horse that she had to turn back. The old woman at the farmhouse put her to bed, brought her some tea or chicken broth and encouraged her to sleep the day through.

Willacassa had no reason to push herself. She had put the execution out of her mind. She had no schedule to meet, no urgent appointments, no promises to keep. Yet sick as she was, she chided herself that time was wasting. When finally she was up and around, she pushed her horse into camp and tied in at Captain Shiloh's tent.

"I'm glad you stopped by," he said "I didn't know where to get in touch with you. I'm leaving again."

"Leaving?"

"Yes, I'm on a scouting assignment this time. The maps we have—even the maps we've captured—show precious little detail in them. The Rebs at least know the terrain. We don't. Zeb and a handful of others will accompany me."

"I feel cheated," protested Willacassa.

"Cheated?"

"You've been here scarcely a month and now you're leaving—"

"I know. I'm sorry. Farnsworth is the culprit, I'm afraid."

Willacassa wore a look of unmitigated displeasure.

"He wants my command. It will help him further his political ambitions. You know, a military record and all that. Of course, the assignment is only 'temporary.'"

"How 'temporary'?"

"Three months in the field, then two or three months at the War Department in Washington. By then they may find him another company to command. It has to be from Indiana, you see. And right now the state has more captains than companies in the field."

"I didn't know you were an expert on maps," remarked Willacassa.

"I'm not. I can read them, of course. But that's as far as it goes. You're not suggesting the War Department be logical, are you?"

Willacassa became alarmed. "They're not sending you out there to—"

"Get rid of me? Hardly. Virginia is probably the safest place in the war right now. If McClellan has his way, we'll conquer the enemy by waiting them out."

"But Zeb said the General's in the field this time."

"We'll see." He reached into his tunic and pulled out a slip of paper. "Look, this is where we'll be in July. If you're in Washington, look us up. And I'll take you to dinner at Willard's." He hesitated as though not wishing to be meddlesome. "What will you be doing in the meantime?"

"Well, I can't stay here. Probably go back to Cape Island. Unless—"

"Unless what?"

"Unless you can secure a pass for me."

"A pass?"

"To the Sea Islands of South Carolina."

Shiloh was startled out of his normal composure. And Willacassa had the awful feeling he could read her mind.

"The Sea Islands?"

"Yes. You pointed them out yourself. I have friends in the area that I must see. Friendships don't end just because a war's going on."

"I don't think I can do that," said Shiloh.

"Why not?"

"You'd be crossing enemy lines."

"But Port Royal is occupied territory now, isn't it?"

"That's right."

"Then my going there should present no problem."

"I suppose not. Except that you're a civilian. And a woman."

"Other non-military personnel are there, I hear. Ministers. Teachers."

"That's true."

"Then let me go too."

"I know very few people authorized to grant such a pass."

"One is enough."

Shiloh laughed his quiet laugh. "You're a persistent young lady, aren't you? Are all Cape Islanders like that?"

When Willacassa did not answer him, he donned his kepi and rose to leave. Then at last, somewhat reluctantly, he said, "I'll see what I can do. But I make no promises."

Overjoyed, Willacassa was tempted to kiss him, a peck on the cheek, but resisted even that display of emotion. Instead she squeezed the captain's hand.

"And you meant what you said about Willard's?"
"I'll even order a bottle of wine."

THE SEA ISLANDS

Just as Fort Sumter sparked the beginning of the rebellion of the states, the Sea Islands of South Carolina marked the beginning of a revolution. For blacks were everywhere and Southern whites gone. With the fall of Fort Walker and Fort Beauregard, the Confederates had left with undue haste, abandoning tents, muskets, bayonets, cartridge boxes, blankets, knapsacks, carriages, and dead mules, taking time to set fire to hundreds of bales of cotton and cotton barns in a scorched earth policy.

And wherever they had vacated, former slaves moved in, holding high carnival in the deserted mansions, smashing doors, mirrors, furniture, and appropriating all that took their fancy. After this they reveled in idleness and luxury, returning to their home plantations until a bunch of missionary superintendents arrived, fresh out of Yale and Harvard, and took the place of their overseers.

The superintendents rounded up the contraband cotton that had not been burned and set about raising new cotton for the North. And, of course, they attempted to convert their "poor black wretches" to rudimentary book learning and Christianity. But they did something else which hadn't been done before. They set aside a few parcels of land the slaves could work for themselves. And they hoped this experiment would serve as a model for emancipation at large.

In the midst of all this Willacassa arrived. She showed her pass to the commander, but steered clear of the commander's staff and the officers and men who patrolled the island, and "Gideon's army" as well. She sketched quickly, almost feverishly, to convince those around her that her sole business on the islands was for *Harper's Weekly* and to allay any suspicions to the contrary.

One of Willacassa's drawings was of the foretop of the U. S. war steamer *Mohican,*, which lay with its crew in the harbor, its guns pointed west. Another was a group picture portraying in different attitudes of repose a band of slaves who had been left behind when their masters fled the islands. A third was a black woman still dressed in the silks and white lace curtains which she had looted when the Yankees took over. These drawings were not Willacassa's best work but they were good enough to enable her to pass as a legitimate sketch artist and to wait until such time as an opportunity to move on presented itself.

"What's a Cape Island girl doin' in South Carolina?" she heard someone say one day. She turned to find Harriet Tubman, short, strong, rotund, and red turbaned.

"Oh, Harriet! I thought I'd never see you again." The two women embraced and then, standing apart, tried to bridge the years with a quick accounting of appearances. But only Willacassa had changed that much, the years having transformed her from a love-sick girl at a seashore resort into a self-contained young woman of the war.

"I didn't mean to run off," said Harriet, "leavin' you and your father during the busy season. But the authorities were closin' in. There was no time to say goodbye."

"We understood that, Harriet. No one ever reproached you for leaving. But what are you doing here?"

"I'm a nurse now and a laundress. And now and then the army finds things for me to do. Scoutin', sailin' up rivers, checkin' things out. I do what I can." She laughed. "Don't tell me you're scoutin' too, Miss Harrah."

"No," smiled Willacassa. "I'm doing sketches for *Harper's Weekly*. On assignment, you might say."

"Fiddle-faddle! You can't tell me that all you're here for is sketchin'. I know you're working hard at it. And the pictures are fine to look at. But the Sea Islands are no better than Cape Island this time of year. So you must have something else in mind."

"Is that what you think?"

"I do. And I'm 'minded how love-sick you were some years back. He was from South Carolina, wasn't he? That young man you were all broke up about. You're still pinin' away for that white boy. That's why you're here. You can't fool me!"

"I have to see him, Harriet," admitted Willacassa softly. "At least where he lives. I've got to see if he still means something to me. Do you understand?"

"Yes, I understand. I remember when my husband took up with another woman. My heart was poundin' like a cannon. No one understands better'n I do the pain and the torment. But what about the war, Miss Harrah? There's fightin' and bleedin' and dyin' goin' on. It ain't like Cape Island. There's no time for sentiment anymore. No time for chasin' after loved ones."

"Are you scolding me, Harriet? Do you think I'm selfish for wanting to see him?"

"I'm not scoldin' you, girl. And I'm not judgin' you. That's for the Lord Himself to do. All I know is that there's work to be done. And while the Good Lord gives me the strength, I'm openin' up the freedom road. So long as one black man is in bondage, I'm goin' to be leadin' the way out. Understand me, child. I'm not preachin' to you. If the colored people don't do for themselves, no one else will. And no one else should. Besides, you've done

66

your share—long before this. You've done conductin' in the Underground Railroad.''

Willacassa could see where Harriet was leading her, but she was not following this time. This time she had another calling, an unfaltering singlemindedness of purpose. She could not breathe for thinking about it. Nothing else counted. So long as her feelings for Francis were unresolved she had in some way to deal with them.

"I'm sorry, Harriet, I've got to put this thing to rest. I can't go on wondering and speculating. I can't pretend I don't care. I've got to see for myself."

"Think no more on it, Miss Harrah. You owe nobody nothin'. Besides, there's promise and prospects here. An experiment, they call it. Some of our people been given their own land to work on. And they been plantin' corn and cotton. Got a few schools goin' too. And maybe some day the government'll sell us the plantations that the 'massas' run away from. Seems there's a new world acomin', slow but sure. And I aims to be part of it."

"What would you do with the plantations?"

"Cut 'em up, I expect. And passel them out to the colored people." She paused. "Sometimes, though, I have a funny dream."

"What's that?"

"These Sea Islands, they remind me of Cape Island in the summer. I dream we make the plantations into big hotels. Just like Columbia House and Congress Hall and the New Atlantic. Only this time the old 'massas' wait them tables and their wives be the chambermaids and do the cookin' and the washin'. And the young scions clean the stables and the outhouses. 'Course it's only a dream. They ain't no justice. So nobody need to worry."

"Then you won't help me?" resumed Willacassa, albeit tentatively.

"Help you?"

"You'd have no trouble slipping in and out of the mainland. You know your way around. You've been passing through for years and years."

"There's still a reward out for me, Miss Harrah. The war hadn't changed that, so far's I know. Besides, I have my own special chores to tend to."

For Willacassa this represented a subtle shift in loyalties. Because of their closeness in the past, Willacassa never doubted that Harriet would be willing, even eager, to help her. Yet this was not so. And the idea pained Willacassa. Oh, she realized that theirs was no longer an employer-chambermaid relationship. The war had changed all that. And other changes were in the making. And

Willacassa had no quarrel with this. But there was the memory of their work together in the Underground Railroad. Willacassa's loyalty had been tested again and again and never found wanting. Could she expect any less from Harriet? True, hers was a personal matter—nothing on a scale with helping slaves escape. And she recognized the difference, even with a sense of self-indulgence, if that's what it was. But there was such a thing as personal existence too. Indeed, the whole question of whether or not someone could put personal considerations before the war itself had long troubled Willacassa. In a sense the war was being fought by both sides for personal gain. All this fuss over cotton had not gone by unnoticed. Slavery as a moral issue was as yet no real issue despite the strident stand of the abolitionists and the pre-war disputes between the slave states and the free-soilers. But Harriet stood for more than personal gain. Hers was a selfless dedication. And if she wanted to put the horse of war on a different footing, more power to her. The question for Willacassa was not whether Harriet was right or wrong. She knew in her heart she was right. The question was, Did Willacassa have a right to her own existence as well? And was there such a thing as personal loyalties? The least Willacassa had expected from Harriet was a helping hand.

Harriet read the disappointment on Willacassa's face and softened somewhat.

"No, honey, I can't help you. But I know someone who can—if you don't mind sailin' the waters at night. Are you sure you want to do this?"

Willacassa nodded.

"Then tomorrow I'll have Obadiah take you where you want to go. He's an old darkie knows these parts. He'll go cheap too. I'll see to that."

This was better. This was something. A strain had been put on their friendship. But a surrogate for Harriet was better than nothing.

Willacassa embraced the woman. "You're a good soul, Harriet."

The black woman, who had held strong, gave way to her emotions. "Couldn't let a Cape Islander down. Leastways, not a railroad conductor like you. I ain't forgot what you done, girl. And the others, they remember too. If they're still alive."

Obadiah was a shrivelled old black man with grizzled, sunken cheeks. He met Willacassa on a desolate part of the beach and uncovered a skiff that had been hidden in an abandoned fishing shack. Not once during the whole operation did he say a word to her.

Willacassa wore a gray cloak (she left her blue one behind with her artist's paraphernalia) and carried a small bag of possessions. She knew enough to travel light. She was less likely to be stopped this way. Obadiah carried nothing.

They set out on a moonless night heavy with cloud. With the wind blowing hard, they crossed the sound in what seemed like an hour's time. Two miles inland, along a side road, Obadiah made his way to a darkened hut or stable and returned with a mule and a small oxcart. Without a word he set Willacassa's bag in it and she understood that she was to find a place beside it.

"You can sleep now," he finally said. "Be more'n half a day 'fore we get dere."

Willacassa did sleep during the night, but only fitfully as the oxcart rolled from side to side and rumbled over ruts and bumps and stones. But by morning she had gotten the fatigue of travel out of her system. Through the side slats of the cart she saw a generally marshy terrain thick with moss-hung oaks and crossed by a network of creeks and small rivers. Over each body of water lay small roughhewn bridges which the cart crossed with more or less monotonous clatter. Along the roads—back roads, they seemed—sat numerous cypress swamps steaming in the morning sun. Though here and there, on higher ground, were the entrances to large plantations, the inevitable "big house" white and pillared and visible from the road, it surprised Willacassa how many poor whites inhabited the region along the fringes of the plantations, their dilapidated huts and scrubby pieces of ground little better than slave quarters.

Becoming hot and uncomfortable in the humid morning air, Willacassa called to Obadiah who had stopped the cart and appeared to be resting as he had been inclined several times before during their long journey.

"We have come a good distance. Do we have much farther to go?" She could not keep her heart from pounding at the prospect of seeing the Grandee place again. Who would she find in the big house? Hazon Grandee? That would hardly do. A hateful, vituperative man, rabid on the issue of slavery before the war, he could scarcely have mellowed in the interim. Mrs. Grandee? Though Willacassa had nothing against the woman, the chance of seeing the mistress of the house once more put no joy in her soul. And it was hardly likely she would find Francis at home. But on the chance she did, on the chance Francis in his gray uniform was given a few days leave from his regiment, how would he receive her? Like a long-lost love? Like a damn Yankee sympathizer? Like a—

No, this was a stupid thing she was doing. How did she ever cook up such a scheme? What drove her to come this far? It was a thoughtless, senseless, idiotic idea. She felt weak just thinking about it. Her stomach churned, her legs shivered, her hands trembled. She was completely unnerved by it all. Feeling distraught, utterly wretched, she berated herself for ever coming to the Sea Islands. She must have been out her mind!

"Obadiah, let's turn back!" she almost shouted.

When she received no reply from the taciturn black man, she looked at the ruin and utter devastation of the landscape about her. How ravaged everything appeared! It was as though the whole world had been caught up in the war—even where no war was being fought.

"Can't go back now," replied Obadiah at last. "Get down. Somebody comin'."

Willacassa crouched down again and had to settle for a view of things by looking out the side slats of the cart. What she saw was a small party of black renegades on horseback. They were well-armed, and behind them marched a wretched band of plantation Negroes who looked as if they had been roused from their beds. The Blacks carried bags on their shoulders, baskets on their heads, and squealing pigs and chickens under their arms.

"Let's get movin'," she heard someone say. "Do you want them Southern soldiers to catch up with us?"

Most of the slaves shuffled forward. But a few refused to go any farther.

A spokesman for the recalcitrant Blacks cried out his reasons. "When dey catch us, dey kill us. Ah's goin' back 'fo it's too late!"

"You ain't goin' nowhere," a woman's voice announced. "We settin' you free. Least you can do is come along quick. Once we reach the river and board the Union boat, no one can stop us."

"Ah ain't goin'," said the spokesman. "An dat's dat!" He sat down on the road.

"Listen, house boy! When I say go, you go." She pointed a pistol at his head. "We movin' out. Understand?"

Willacassa's mouth dropped open. Why, it couldn't be! But it was. The woman sitting her horse like a half-barrel and pointing the gun was no other than Harriet Tubman. And hers was no idle threat. Harriet was in dead earnest as she cocked her pistol.

The reluctant man was reluctant no more. He rose from the ground, dusted himself off, and fell in with the others.

Noticing the cart, Harriet turned her horse about and galloped over to it.

"Why so soon, old man?" She glared at Obadiah but stuffed

her pistol into her gunbelt. "I told you to keep her away from us, didn't I?"

"Ah figger yo' be finish by now. Ah kep' stoppin' an' restin' to kill time. It's daylight a'ready. Didn' know yo' still be heah."

Harriet Tubman turned to Willacassa. "I didn't want you to see what we're doin'. This 'scoutin' party' must be kept a secret. And now it's out."

"I won't give you away, Harriet."

The black woman studied her for a moment, then broke into a broad smile, missing teeth and all. "I trust you, Willacassa. I know you'll keep the secret. Jus' had to be sure."

"Can Obadiah still take me to the Grandee plantation? It can't be far from here."

"The Grandee plantation? Look around you, honey. What do you see?"

Willacassa looked about her. "Nothing but ruins."

"No, girl. You're lookin' at the Grandee plantation. Done burn to the ground. Obadiah'll tell you all about it. I'd best be goin' now."

Disbelief, astonishment crossed Willacassa's face. She didn't have the presence of mind to bid Harriet Tubman goodbye. She turned to Obadiah for enlightenment.

"Is this really the Grandee plantation?"

Obadiah nodded.

"What happened?"

"Someone done put de torch to it. Can't yo' see de foundation stones of de big house?"

"But I thought—"

"You said to take yo' here. I done dat. I nebber say yo' find de big house lak it was."

Willacassa sat numb for a moment, stunned by what she heard. Involuntarily she clung to her small bag of possessions. Then, in spite of the collapse of her expectations and the depression she found herself in, she began to laugh. The absurdity of the situation, the raw spectacle of what lay devastated before her—charred timbers, the foundation stones of the big house, the ruins of five chimneys—all provoked a bizarre nervous hysteria.

"This cannot be," she kept repeating. "No, this cannot be! It's too ridiculous, too ludicrous!" Then, covering her face, she gave way to stifled, choking sobs and an uncontrollable surge of tears. Willacassa hated herself for breaking down, especially in the presence of the old man. But her disappointment was so bitter, her hopes so madly dashed, her dreams so shattered that she could no longer hold back the walls of her bulging storehouse of pain.

"But nobody done get hurt." Obadiah announced, trying to calm her. "De Grandees—dey all git out safe enough. Den couple weeks later Massa Francis come home."

Willacassa stirred. She looked up and wiped away the tears. "Francis?"

"Dat's right. He done come from his cav'ry unit in Virginny. Ah was tenden' horses on de nex' plantation when he come. De Grandees done hired me out."

Willacassa grabbed the old man's arm. "What did he say? Tell me. What did he do? Please tell me everything!"

"Massa Francis jump off his horse to see de rubble. He pick among de ruins but foun' nuttin' wuth savin'. De poor whites took everythin' they find an' hide it in de woods. Massa Francis cuss an' fume an' swore *re*-venge. He were madder dan a hot poker when he rode off. Dat's de las' Ah see o' him."

Francis here! Willacassa was on the verge of breaking down again. Why couldn't she have been there to meet him? If only she had caught a glimpse of the man! That's all. Then she'd know what her deeper feelings meant. It was important that she know. She could not go on with her life until her feelings had been brought to the surface, put to rest. Oh, it was more than unfinished business. At stake was the whole thrust of her existence. War or no war, secession or cessation—it was all part of the turmoil within her. And as the war dragged on without her seeing him, there was as little likelihood of a resolution of her private conflict as there was of the conflict at large.

And yet there lingered a feeling of hurt avenged. Still longing for love, the love of Francis Grandee, she harbored at the same time a dark disposition to despise him. This constant duel within her gave her no peace. It left her wounded and apprehensive. But there was one consolation. The place she despised, the scene of her unbearable unhappiness, had been burned to the ground. There would be no more thinking about it, no more wondering what kind of life went on there. Francis Grandee was now a lord without a castle—if not in retreat against the Union forces in Virginia, in total and abject retreat from the place he had once called home.

A sudden thought took hold of her.

"How did Harriet learn about this?"

The old man nodded. "She wid de raidin' party dat burn de place down."

"Harriet?"

"Dat's right. De fire were accident. It start in de big house, den spread to de stables. Harriet roun' up an' took'n de slaves wid her. She lak a man, dat Miss Tubman. When a house nigger din

wan' to go, she point dat gun at his head an' say. 'We movin' out.'
Jus' lak wid dat man jus' now. He come along after dat.''

Willacassa sank back in the oxcart. A raiding party? Then
Harriet knew. She knew all along what had happened to the
Grandees. No wonder she was reluctant to be Willacassa's guide.
Now all the pieces fit together. It was never a question of loyalty.
It was a question of expediency. The deed had been done. There
was no help for it. There was nothing to do but go through the
motions and let Willacassa see for herself. Except that the timing
of her expedition had been inopportune.

A cynical piece of playacting on Harriet's part? Perhaps. But
Willacassa couldn't fault the black woman. She was fighting the
war in her own fashion, the only way she knew how. In the larger
scheme of things, what happened to the Grandees was not her
problem. It was theirs, of their own making. The pity was,
Willacassa had been caught in the middle of it all. And who knew
how long it would be before another opportunity presented itself,
an opportunity to see Francis Grandee once more?

IN HOSTILE TERRITORY

On the same day that Willacassa bade goodbye to Captain Shiloh, Harrah came home to find his son Jonathan waiting for him on the porch step of Trescott House. He had stacked his gear at the front door of the house and was puffing on a pipe. Though now near twenty-seven years of age, his son looked little more than nineteen. He rose when he saw Harrah and, dropping his pipe, threw his arms around him.

"It's good to see you, Dad!"

Harrah hugged the young man, not yet sure that he wasn't embracing a figment of his imagination. Then he stood back to examine him.

What he saw was still a stripling, tall and gawky, with much of the adolescent—the shooting galleries, the archery tents, the amusement halls of Cape Island—still clinging to him.

"Why, Jonathan, I couldn't believe my eyes! Almost a year now! And no word from you. I've about given you up for dead!"

"Been meaning to write, Dad. But could never find the time." He pulled on his seaman's cap and slapped the pocket of his peacoat. "Been to sea most of the time. And I've made a fair amount of money. The British pay handsomely to run the blockade. And that's what I've been doing."

"So you've chosen sides," said Harrah, not without profound disappointment.

"Not really. We don't run arms. We buy cotton and sell manufactured goods. Perfectly respectable and perfectly neutral. Sometimes we sell the cotton in Northern ports. It's really not all that complicated. And everybody looks the other way."

"Come inside," said Harrah, putting his arm around him. "You must be famished."

"Already had some ham and eggs at Mrs. Corgie's. But I'll be glad to have some sherry." Picking up his gear, Jonathan followed his father inside.

His story was a complicated one. And Harrah was not sure how much of it was truth and how much had been salted up a bit. But as far as he could determine, Jonathan had signed up with a British schooner. At first he was taken on as a common seaman. Later he convinced the purser and then the first mate that he had engaged in trade on Cape Island, a business that had been terminated by fire. He hinted that he had broad experience in merchandising and could be useful in making commercial transactions in the South. He had dealt with Southerners all his life and spoke their language.

As an agent, he asked for only a small percentage of whatever deals he could pull off, above and beyond his earnings as a seaman. According to Jonathan, the captain was skeptical at first. But he gave the young man a shot in Savannah where so much cotton was sitting on the wharves that Jonathan had no trouble buying it at half the going rate. Instead of returning to England, the ship's captain was persuaded to dispose of the cargo in Boston and then return to Savannah for another load of cotton, this time for shipment to England.

Harrah could not follow all the intricacies of his son's narrative but he gleaned enough from it to determine that Jonathan was now his own man, very sure of himself, if not a mite cocksure, and that he enjoyed uninterrupted passage behind Southern lines, leaving the ship for weeks at a time to stop at the Tredegar Ironworks in and about Richmond or to deliver supplies to the Chimborazo Hospital.

"How's that possible?" asked Harrah. "Don't they check people crossing the lines?"

"Most of the time there are no lines. And security is lax. So long as you come in by boat or on a railroad they ask few questions. Besides, I have a pass signed by General Winder himself. And I always wear my British seaman's cap. Oh, I've been detained once or twice. But when the authorities learn I'm arranging for the shipment of badly needed medicines or supplies, they quickly release me. Let's face it, even Union parolees freely walk the streets of Richmond. Why should they worry about the likes of me?"

Harrah was astounded. First by what he heard. Then by the fact that his own son was the author of it. He drank not one glass of sherry but two.

"I tell you, Dad, there's nothing I can't arrange down there. After all, I'm only a common seaman. It's not as if I'm someone the authorities have to fear. All I do is pull out my letters of introduction and the doors swing open."

Though first abashed by what his son was doing, Harrah now warmed to the idea. After all, even if Jonathan was no more than a glorified courier, he wasn't dealing in contraband, at least as Harrah understood it. Medicines and supplies, that's all. He saw no problem with medicines for either side. And then his already weakened defenses were invaded by an idea. "What if—"

"What if what, Dad?"

They were both slightly tipsy by now.

"Never mind, we'll talk about it tomorrow."

But in the morning Harrah could not wait until his son got

out of bed. He rattled about outside his room and even knocked at his door. But Jonathan slept like dead and it wasn't until noon that the smell of bacon in the house awakened him.

"All that talk last night," said Harrah in the kitchen, "how much of it was the truth and how much just scrimshaw?"

"You don't believe me?"

"It's not that. But sailors do get carried away at times. And you were never one for playing a story down."

"It's all there, I tell you. Well—mostly. And I have made a lot of money."

"It's important that I know."

"Know what?"

"Just how good your credentials are. Just how freely you move about in the South."

"I have no trouble with that." Jonathan swallowed an egg whole. "Why are you asking?"

"Why? Because I have a letter I want you to deliver. Two letters in fact."

"What kind of letters?"

"Nothing that will cause you any trouble. They're for people in Richmond. It's difficult getting anything delivered through the lines these days—unless it's by way of Canada. And that takes much too long."

"Richmond? You're in luck. It so happens I have to be there on Monday. I'm trying to arrange for a shipment of medical supplies to the Chimborazo Hospital."

"Are you travelling alone?"

"No, the first mate will accompany me. That is , I'll accompany the first mate. I don't know how to explain it. But the Rebels would sooner stop one man for questioning than two. A man travelling alone always looks more suspicious."

"I suppose you know what you're talking about."

"Besides, we have General Winder's passes. So there's no problem if we're stopped. If you want some letters delivered, I'm the man to do it."

Harrah looked long and searchingly at his son. He did not for a moment dismiss any of the reservations he had about him. He saw that he was anxious to impress. He knew that he sometimes flirted with the truth. He suspected that he liked looking larger than life. Yet, at the core, he saw a young man who was certainly not afraid of taking chances and, in taking these chances, was neither foolhardy nor reckless.

"I'm going to trust you," he said to Jonathan. "If a man can't trust his own son, things have reached a sorry turn."

Harrah dashed off a letter to Madeleine Craddishaw, and when he finished, he sealed it with his mark, the horseshoe crab.

All the while that he was furiously writing, Jonathan stood by watching his father, reveling in the fact that he was now part of what he regarded as an out-and-out conspiracy. Not that he knew what the conspiracy was about. Not that he dared imagine what would happen to Madeleine Craddishaw or his father or himself if the letter somehow fell into the wrong hands. No, the important, the exhilarating thing was that he now played a crucial role in what he saw as a kind of theatrical dumbshow, a drama where dialogue was ruled out and only action, subversive, secretive, symbolic action, fraught with all kinds of national significance, had any claim on the observer's attention.

Suddenly he was no longer a scoundrel. He was no longer the black sheep of a very white family. As a courier, as a runner of the blockade, Jonathan Harrah was in the enviable position of being able to complete a vital communication. If the message or messages he was delivering carried any weight at all, his self-esteem had to be enhanced, a phenomenon that had all but escaped him these past few years.

Jonathan not only delivered the letters but returned to Cape Island to tell his father so.

"We're heading for Boston," he said. "But I persuaded the captain to put up at Cape Island. Just wanted to tell you what was done. You see, I'm as good as my word."

Harrah could not have been more pleased.

"And I've got a present for you. A pass from General Winder. All signed, sealed, and delivered."

"For me?"

Jonathan nodded. "Now you can visit Richmond yourself. If that's what you want. I'd offer you passage. But we're heading in the opposite direction."

Harrah examined the pass. He could not conceal his admiration for his son's achievement.

"I've also got a message from Judge Arrows. Just one word, 'Anytime.' He said you'd understand."

"Jonathan, I'm astonished. I don't know what to say."

"Just say you love me, and I'll be gone."

Harrah embraced the young man and bade him farewell. And then as quickly as he had come, Jonathan was gone.

The Judge Arrows that Harrah had contacted had only become a Richmond magistrate in the past few years. When Harrah knew him as one of his guests at Trescott House in the early fifties, he was a distinguished attorney who had little use for slavery. Though he had servants to run his fine Georgian house, they were freed slaves who were paid good wages. One of these servants announced Harrah, and Judge Arrows was delighted that the hotel owner he knew on Cape Island had at long last paid him a visit.

"It took a war," said Harrah. "But I'm here."

"And just in time for dinner."

"I feel guilty," said Harrah after a tasty repast of roast pork and yams. "You were always a paying guest at Trescott House. And here I'm enjoying your hospitality without cost."

"It's not the same thing, my friend. On Cape Island everything's for hire. You have but a short season. In May or November I'd be the beneficiary of your hospitality."

"Then visit soon," said Harrah.

"I will—immediately as this unnecessary war is over."

Harrah cast a discerning look at his friend. "Then you too see it as unnecessary? I was beginning to think I was virtually alone."

Judge Arrows clasped Harrah's shoulder. "Come into my study. We can speak freely there. No use letting the servants hear what they might only be tempted to repeat."

Judge Arrows pulled apart the white sliding doors and Harrah entered his host's sanctuary. What he saw filled him with envy. Though he had his own "office" at Trescott House, it was a small room with barely enough space for a desk and a couple of chairs. What books he owned he kept on shelves he had installed in his bedroom. In the judge's capacious study he found the library of his dreams. Every white wall had floor-to-ceiling walnut bookcases. And whole sets of Scott and Smollett and Fielding novels filled the shelves. Apart from the usual classics, Aristotle, Plato, Chaucer, Shakespeare, Milton, Byron, and Wordsworth, stood such recent works as *Great Expectations*, *David Copperfield*, and *Nicholas Nickelby* by Dickens; *Pendennis*, *Henry Esmond*, and *Vanity Fair* by Thackeray; *Barchester Towers* and *Doctor Thorne* by Trollope; George Eliot's *The Mill on the Floss* and *Romola*; and Charles Kingsley's *Alton Locke*. Nor were the French ignored. Along with Lamartine's *Geneviéve*, *histoire d'une servante*, George Sand's *L'Homme de neige*, Hugo's *Les Miserables*, and Merimee's *Carmen* appeared Balzac's *La Cousine Bette* and *Eugenie Grandet*. And on the table, next to the chair Harrah finally slid into, he found copies of David Hume's *History of England* and Edward Shepherd Creasy's *The Fifteen Decisive Battles of the World*.

"You're a book lover, I see."

"Mostly from afar. I've never read most of the books I wanted to own. Never seemed to have the space for them—or the time."

"Well," mused the judge, "I find I have too much time on my hands. Especially these days. So I spend a good many hours in here. It's rather a refuge from the incessant hoots and shouts of conflict. It'd be a shame if this house, this room, one day became a casualty of war."

A shame indeed, thought Harrah. Much as he wanted slavery to end and the society which rested on it to fall, he did not want to be a witness to wanton destruction. Yes, he wanted the "peculiar institution" blown to smithereens, the former slaveowners themselves reduced to poverty, and the whole fabric of Southern aristocracy ripped to shreds. But he wanted in the same breath for the libraries to survive, for the gracious Georgian houses to remain intact, and for all that was truly genteel and cultured to be treasured as relics of a past age. One might rejoice that the Christians were no longer being thrown to the lions in Roman coliseums without crying for the great works of Roman art and architecture to be destroyed in their name.

"Yes," said Judge Arrows when he had pulled out a cigar and taken a seat in his favorite leather chair, "I find this war totally unnecessary. And in the beginning I said so. No one could question my loyalty to Virginia. So no one could call me a traitor."

"But you're not speaking out now?"

"No, I'm not. The situation has changed. It's not fluid anymore. Once a war is unleashed, there is no room for dissent. There's no room for argument or reason. The despot mentality takes over. And the despot mentality knows only that it must win at all costs— even if everything else is lost. Lincoln is not the only one to suspend the writ of *habeas corpus*. Jeff Davis is also throwing men into prison without bringing charges against them or bringing them to trial."

"Then you see no chance for ending hostilities?" asked Harrah.

"Not now. We have our fanatics and you have yours. There is no virtue in peace—only in war. Any appeal to common sense, any suggestion for conciliation is regarded as an act of treason or cowardice. The fanatics are doing their job well, just as the fanatics before them."

"Like Rhett and Yancey?"

"Yes. And John Brown and Garrison up North. Mind you, I don't blame Garrison for his stand on slavery. I blame him for his inflammatory rhetoric. Just as I blame the three R's in the South."

"The three R's?"

"Rhett, Ruffin, and Rant. Though in all fairness to Yancey, he doesn't rant. Why, in the eyes of these men even Jefferson Davis and Alexander Stephens are not secessionist enough. They chide Davis for shedding tears when he retired from the U. S. Senate. They call Stephens the reluctant Rebel. They hold Lee suspect because he has no truck with slavery. It's all too ridiculous. These men scream about independence and then try to suspend the liberties of all who deviate.''

A wry smile crossed Harrah's face. As he raised himself out of his seat, he roused himself from the spell Judge Arrows' eloquent even-handedness had cast him in. For a moment it seemed that reason still prevailed in these terrible times. But it only prevailed in the free atmosphere of the good judge's library. Outside the window things were pretty much the same as in the turbulent streets of Washington.

"By the way, do you remember Harley Colepaugh?''

How could Harrah forget one of the most bigoted guests Trescott House ever had?

"Of course.''

"Well, he's been arrested.''

"For what?''

"For diverting government beef and selling it for profit.''

That night Harrah could not sleep. The bed in the judge's guestroom was high enough off the floor and it carried a full complement of puffy pillows. So he could not fault its comfort. Nor could he blame his restlessness on the fact of his being in Richmond, hostile territory. Every place outside of Cape Island was hostile territory these days. No, the rattling on cobblestone streets of four-wheeled vehicles and the echoing through his window of soldiers' voices did not seriously disturb him. If anything, he welcomed the sounds as signs of life, much better than the muffled moan of cannon that he heard when he first crossed into Southern lines.

What troubled Harrah were fugitive thoughts of Madeleine Culpepper and the prospect that he would be seeing her the next day after a separation of ten long years.

Madeleine Culpepper. How the name excited him, even if by right she was now Madeleine Craddishaw! For ten years he had held his feelings for her in reserve, much as one stocks his best whiskey for another day. For ten years he had pretended that nothing final had taken place, that their parting was nothing more than a necessary hiatus, a gap that time would one day close. For ten years—

Rubbish! Harrah abruptly told himself as he climbed out of bed. For ten years he had cursed Madeleine for her ill-timed and ill-advised nobility, just as he had cursed himself for his obvious pigheadedness. For Madeleine had declared her unwillingness to deprive her children of their birthright and had returned home to Virginia, even though that birthright was tarnished by the stain of slavery and Virginia was all out of step with nineteenth century morality. And he, of course, had remained on Cape Island. For Harrah could not admit the possibility that one could live in the South and not immediately compromise his principles. Yet Judge Arrows was no slaveholder and no friend of slavery. And he remained in Richmond. Couldn't Harrah have done the same? Couldn't he have put his prejudices aside and worked towards the day when he could persuade Madeleine to return with him to the free air of Cape Island?

But even as he stood at the window looking out on the lamplit street, Harrah realized it was not the past that bothered him just now. The past was a newspaper yellow with age. What troubled Harrah was how he would handle the present. How, for example, would he react to a Madeleine ten years older than when he knew and loved her? What had then been a young mother in the prime of her beauty might now be a matron with a matronly figure. How would he react to that? Or even allowing for the changes of the years—certainly he had changed too—how would he react to a Madeleine who was another man's wife. However much they had remained kindred spirits in the occasional letters they had written each other, someone else had a claim on her body, her loyalty, her love. Someone else shared an intimacy that for one brief period of time he had known. The idea did not sit too well with him.

Yet he looked forward to seeing her, keenly aware of the sensation that gripped him, a sensation he had known when he had first come to love her. Harrah was all eagerness then, highly tuned, ready to dance with life itself. After ten years he was still ready to jump out of his skin for her.

The next morning, after confirming the address of the Craddishaw residence with Judge Arrows, he sent a message off to Mrs. Craddishaw. It was a brief note asking her to meet him outside of Morris, a store on Main Street which he understood had Worcester's pianos for sale.

At the designated time Madeleine appeared in a cape which covered a nurse's uniform. Though her face had lost some of its luster and she appeared thinner than when he had last fixed eyes on her, Madeleine was as good-looking a woman as he had ever come across.

"Aren't you going to kiss me?" she asked.

He leaned over and, undecided on the mouth or cheek, half-kissed her on the lips.

"You're out of practice," she said.

"Very much so, I'm afraid."

"However did you get here?" Madeleine asked.

"A certain judge—who shall remain nameless—a regular patron of Trescott House, made it possible. He was always inviting me to visit him. That, of course, was before the war. This year I contacted him. I asked if the offer was still open. He assured me that it was. I was even provided with a pass."

Madeleine Craddishaw was as much bemused by the idea as pleased.

"Well, the important thing is you're here." She looked at Harrah with the same intensity she had reserved for him a dozen years ago. "I think of you all the time, Nathaniel. I've never stopped thinking of you. Even when you stopped writing—"

"With the war on, that was no longer possible."

"I'm not blaming you—" Her emotions spilled over.

"I undertand that," he said, taking her hand. "And I realize I've put you in a difficult position by coming here. It won't be easy to account for a Yankee among your acquaintances."

"It may be harder to account for a former love." She grew serious. "My husband, of course, knows nothing about you. And I think it may be best not to introduce you to him. Or to any of my friends, for that matter. How long do you expect to be in Richmond?"

"Only for a few days." He squeezed her hand. "That is, if you can help me, Madeleine."

"Help you?"

"Yes," said Harrah. "You want this war to end, don't you? There's a chance, an outside chance, I can push things toward that end."

"Oh, if that were only possible. This war is such a horror! Such an intolerable waste! Every day I hear about someone's son being killed. Sunday morning the news came for one of the mothers while she was in church. Praying to God didn't help her any. I tremble that one day I'll hear of mine being dead."

"Yours?"

"Yes, that little boy on Cape Island is nineteen now. He's fighting in General Johnston's army. He's always in the thick of things. President Davis hates Johnston almost as much as Johnston hates him. So the general gets the worst assignments."

Harrah pulled a slip of paper from his pocket and handed it to Madeleine. "Do you know this man?"

She read the name and nodded.

"Can you get him to see me?"

"I don't know."

"It's most important."

"Then I'll have to find a way. Won't I, my dear?"

She met him at the Clifton Hotel, outside the dining room.

"I'm sorry it's such a drab place," she said, pointing out the peeling plaster and the faded walls. "But I thought we'd stand a better chance of not being seen here."

"Seen?"

"By friends or relatives. This is almost the last place they'd stop at."

He followed Madeleine into the dining room where a Negro waiter found them a place off to a corner. They sat down to a soiled tablecloth.

"If wine is what you have in mind," suggested Madeleine, "it may be hard to get."

"Why?"

"Jeff Davis closed the saloons and the gambling establishments. It's part of the austerity measures being taken. He's even had himself baptized. Somehow this is supposed to stop the advance of the Union Army."

She interrupted her conversation to address the waiter. "Coffee, please. And some biscuits."

When the waiter started for the kitchen, Madeleine turned towards Harrah and apologized. "I didn't mean to order for you. But I thought it best he hear my accent rather than yours—things being what they are."

She took his hand. "You see, I'm ever so discreet. And I've got good news. That man you wanted to see. He's agreed to see you."

"Splendid! But where?"

"At my place."

"I thought you said you were discreet," he chided her, welcoming the squeeze of her fingers.

"I am. But let me explain. By my place, I mean my very own. When we sold the plantation and moved to Richmond, I bought a small house north of here."

"Like 'our house' on Cape Island."

She nodded. "I had to have a place of my own. A place I could go to when I wanted privacy. In recent years I spend more and more time there. It's quite small and hidden away, but perfect for me. I read there or write letters or just walk around in my dressing gown. No need to talk or entertain or think about this horrid war.''

"When will I meet him?''

"At noon on Thursday.''

"Then I can see you tomorrow?'' He felt like a young suitor again, snatching time together.

"That's what I wanted to talk to you about,'' she said.

He looked downcast, expecting to be put off.

"Now don't interrupt till I finish,'' she continued. She braced herself for what she was going to say. "For the past few years I've felt like a prostitute. Yes, a prostitute. Oh, it isn't my husband's fault. It's mine. I admire the man. He's considerate of me. He's been a father to my children. But I don't love him. And, of course, I don't need his money.''

She looked at Harrah as though to remind him that she wanted no interruptions.

"So you might ask, what's at fault? The problem is not marriage. At least it wouldn't be a problem if I were married to you. You must know that! I gave myself freely to you and enjoyed every minute of it. In fact, I think about those days all the time. The problem is I am married to a man I do not love. And every time he comes near me I feel I'm compromising myself, my feelings. I feel I'm making a sacrifice of myself. Worse still, I feel like a trollop!''

Her face flushed although there was neither wine nor coffee on the table as yet.

"So I'll come right to the point. Unless you make love to me tomorrow so that I can feel like a woman again, a free spirit, I think I'll take to drink—Jefferson Davis or no Jeff Davis. What do you say to that?''

Harrah was too dumbfounded to reply. There now flooded into his mind little observations, trifles that Harrah had not had time to deal with until this moment. He had noticed a change in Madeleine's appearance when he had first seen her. He could not pretend that ten years had little or no effect on the woman. The eyes and the chin were not all that different, but a difference in their cast could not be denied. And there was a loss of tone in the neck of the once beautiful woman. Yet somehow at this second meeting these changes or differences did not seem so marked. And the overriding impression, despite any imperfections, was that Madeleine was still beautiful. If anything, a certain intelligence or maturity infused her beauty, making her all the more intriguing, all the more desirable. The years had laid bare the essence of her good looks, highlighting bone that flesh had once padded, exposing the lines of expression where flawlessness had prevailed.

"You're shocked?" she asked. "You needn't be. I know who you are, what you mean to me. I should not have to start from scratch again."

"No, my dear. I'm not shocked," said Harrah, as much moved as he was amused. "I'm flattered that you still think of me that way."

He cut short his reply to make way for the coffee and biscuits which the Negro waiter placed before them.

On Wednesday morning Harrah waited for Madeleine inside the St. Charles Hotel, a place with bare board floors and potted plants. As the crowd at the door thickened, he stepped out onto the sidewalk which was stained with tobacco juice and clogged with the bodies of sleeping soldiers. A number of the Rebels had traded in their kepis for soft felt hats which were slouched over their eyes. Others huddled in their short jackets whose buttonholes were stuffed with toothbrushes. Some curled up on blanket rolls or used their haversacks for pillows. Bags of "Long Jack" tobacco, coffee pots and frying pans hung from waist belts, and rifles were propped up against the walls.

A wave of pity for the young men swept over Harrah. Most were no more than youngsters, mountain boys or scrub farmers whose plight was little better than slaves. None were the rich scions of plantation owners who took rooms at the hotel or enjoyed officers' quarters. These had lively parties at night even as the city was beseiged, parties glittering with wine, women, and dancing while those who fought "the rich man's war" lay mutilated on wooden pallets in some church or storefront, tossing with pain.

No sooner did this thought occur to him than a young officer crossed his path. Though he had gained several inches in height by wearing his riding boots, Harrah recognized him instantly. A certain swagger of the shoulders, common among young male swimmers on Cape Island, "strutting their stuff," set him apart from the others, as did his strong curvature of the jaw and ridged adam's apple. And there was a bearing to the young man which immediately proclaimed that in a society of masters and those who did their bidding, this officer was decidedly one of the masters. His strong grasp of the sword hilt, his braided tunic, the plume in his hat—all spelled caste! And the smile he wore was not the smile of class-conscious benevolence. It was the smile of the cat that swallowed the canary and was looking for still more birds to swallow. As Harrah remembered it, humility had never been Francis Grandee's forte.

But as soon as he saw him, Harrah stepped back, letting the

shadows of the doorway all but envelop him. It would hardly do to resume old acquaintanceship in the Capital of the Confederacy. After all, he was a Yankee bent on a secret mission. And Francis Grandee was a Southerner down to the four-inch heel of his boots. No, acknowledgement would spoil everything. Besides, Harrah realized almost for the first time that while he had a preference for Southern women he had a prejudice against Southern men, especially suitors for his daughter's hand.

"There you are!" he heard Madeleine say. "You were so lost in thought you didn't hear me call."

"I'm sorry," said Harrah, glad to be awakened out of his gray musings.

"My carriage is at the corner," she indicated.

Harrah followed her down the squalid street which was in sharp contrast with her yellow gown and wine-colored cape. And he found time to admire her lady-like gait even as Madeleine hurried along.

Madeleine's driver, an ancient balding Negro, already knew their destination and set the carriage in motion as soon as the couple had climbed up and were seated.

During a thirty-minute ride through the city Harrah saw Negroes everywhere: draymen, hucksters, masons, sawyers, teamsters, stablemen, laborers of all descriptions. Clad in rough gray cloth, some with coats and capes and slouch hats, others with short blue jackets haphazardly buttoned, and kepis discarded by soldiers, these men were forever hauling things, repairing wagons, loading and unloading freight at the railroad depots, caulking and painting boats in the shipyard, digging along the riverbank, even in one side alley making pine coffins.

Where would Richmond be, he wondered, without this labor force? Who would procure the food and forage? Who would mine the coal and iron ore and niter? Who would fashion the heavy guns and shells, the fortifications, and the blockade runners? Who would stockpile the tons of supplies the Rebel army needed while the white man was off to war? The Confederate Negro, anyone could see, was every bit as important to the South as the Confederate soldier. Yet Lincoln, cloistered in the White House, was still refusing to proclaim his emancipation.

Madeleine continued to act as his guide. She noted the Mechanics Institute, an ungainly brick structure which housed the War Department. She pointed out the billowing smoke of the Tredegar Iron Works, whose mighty furnaces and forges roared day and night. And she drew his attention to the massive Chimborazo barracks and hospital sprawling high on a hill east of the city. Then abruptly her carriage left Richmond and spun into the countryside.

At a small Georgian brick house, sheltered by tall trees, heavy in leaf, the carriage pulled to a stop and Harrah helped Madeleine down. Flowering shrubs, jonquils, violets, hyacinths, and daffodils greeted the eye. And the sweet fragrance of magnolia blossoms tickled Harrah's nose.

"This is my place," she whispered. "My very own. My husband never visits here."

"Never?"

She nodded. "He knows better. Besides, he's too busy running errands for the likes of Jefferson Davis and Governor Letcher. You smile. But it's really not amusing. The South is being done in by its politicians. General Winder's men are all over the place. Detectives, he calls them. But all they do is issue passports and hide under beds."

Once they had entered the house and closed the door behind them, Madeleine sprang into his arms. "Oh, what a fool I've been!" she cried. "I never should have left Cape Island. Never should have gone to Virginia."

Harrah held her close to him, realizing he was as much a fool as anyone.

"I thought I was doing it for the children," she said. "Didn't want to deprive them of their heritage. Now they're gone. And with the war faltering as it is, there won't be much heritage to talk about."

"At least your generals manage to win a victory now and then."

"Oh, yes!" she said, pulling away. "We have our victories! And our self-deceptions! Every day there's talk in the newspapers of recognition by Britain or France. Of resistance to the war in the North. Of secret new pacts and strategies. But the truth is, the war's being fought on our soil, not yours, Nathaniel. And we have nothing but shortages. Shortages of men, horses, guns, food, medicines. In fact, all we have left is that indomitable Southern spirit, as stupid as it is determined. And, of course, belief in divine providence— which I understand Mr. Lincoln has, too."

She looked at him, surprised that she was revealing so much to someone who, however dear, still stood on the other side of things.

"But let's not talk. Let's hug one another and love one another. And for one delicious moment pretend that things are as they were." As she started for the bedroom she began to disrobe. And by the time she reached the door she had pulled her dress free of her breasts.

"You'll still want to touch them?" she asked, turning to face him.

"As much as ever."

"Good," she whispered as he reached for her. "I was afraid you wouldn't want me anymore."

"I'll always want you, Madeleine."

When Madeleine had finally found physical release, her body soft, warm, and moist, she rolled over on the bed and lay her head on her arm.

"I'm glad we made love," she said. "I feel so much better about myself, you've no idea. It's as if for the first time that I can remember I've given myself fully and freely. No holding back. No wishing I was elsewhere—or nowhere. Just with you."

She looked over at him, a wisp of hair with a faint trace of gray slipping loose over her temple. "A woman can't be happy without love, Nathaniel. It's not in her nature. She may be like a man in other ways but that will never change. Her feelings run deep and they can't be suppressed for long. They'll bubble up, they'll surface, like a swimmer gasping for breath." She reached for his arm as if to seize the moment and hold it captive. "I know we can't go back in time. I know that the years have passed us by. But somehow I feel that we set things straight today, that meeting together like this we righted a long wrong. Do you know what I mean?"

Harrah nodded and squeezed her to him. For him the moment had its magic and he delighted in it. But he had to think some more about what Madeleine had said before he could give it credence. Righted a long wrong? Could a long wrong ever be righted? He seriously doubted it. What they had done together was rather like setting the record straight, like telling one's private world that what one knew, one felt all along was indeed true—even if there was precious little one could do about it at the time. What they had experienced was vindication. A moment of sweet vindication. But the fact that something needed vindication merely pointed up how far down the wrong road the course had run.

When they were dressed once more, Madeleine brought out some wine and two glasses.

"I've kept this hidden for special occasions. I can think of no occasion more special than this."

Harrah smiled as she slowly poured the precious liquid.

"To you, my love," she said, holding up her glass. "To truth, beauty, and—"

"Peace," toasted Harrah.

"I'll settle for that. Oh, yes! I'd settle for that at once! I'm sick and tired of this asinine war. And the asinine men who are responsible for it! Yes, Nathaniel, let's drink to peace!"

After taking breakfast with his host, Judge Arrows, who discreetly did not ask him what he planned to do that day, Harrah again met Madeleine in front of the St. Charles Hotel. Madeleine did not speak of personal matters. Almost as if Harrah's lunchtime meeting dictated a less intimate relationsip, Madeleine spoke instead of the political situation and the general incompetence of Jefferson Davis's administration.

"Mind you, I realize that my husband is not without blame in all this. But despite the importance of his position, he is nothing but a courier at best and a glorified amanuensis at worst." She then detailed her condemnation. "With all the current talk about security, General Winder's brown paper passes can be had for one hundred dollars a piece. Worse still, the streets are filled with deserters whom President Davis persists in pardoning. And with all the government's austerity measures, there are gambling houses and brothels everywhere on Main Street. See the huge gilt letters over that door. They signify a gambling establishment. It little matters that Rittenhouse's orchestra will play there on weekends."

Harrah leaned over to see, then sat back again.

"Then there's the Conscript Bureau. It's called by some the 'Bureau of Exemptions.' Less than one in ten go to the army. Even with the purchase of substitutes, there are three thousand skulkers in Richmond alone. And those exempted spend most of their time in the illicit market or in houses of prostitution or in the Chickahominy Saloon."

"The illicit market? How widespread is it?"

"Very widespread. Even the commissaries speculate in army beef. If one had to depend on store stocks, one would quickly starve."

Madeleine took his hand. "I'm not suggesting the Craddishaws do without. But we pay handsomely for what we get. And at wedding parties—weddings are very popular in wartime, you know—we still see turkey, ham, and sausages on the table. Also stuffed eggs, oysters, terrapin, and Strasbourg pâtés. But the poor are not so fortunate. They make coffee from dried beans and peanuts, and use sorghum for sugar. And, of course, there's always 'Benjamin.'"

"Benjamin?"

"Hardtack soaked in water and liberally sprinkled with salt."

"As bad as all that?"

"Unless a ship runs the blockade. Or a trainload of supplies gets through. Or someone catches fish out of the James River. Then the Shockoe merchants ease up a bit."

"And the slaves?"

"I suspect they fare as well as the government clerks do. They're more resourceful. They'll eat eel and catfish and all sorts of roots. And there's still a quantity of dried Indian peas and rice to go round. Besides, not all of the blacks you see are slaves. At least one in ten are freed men and they do much of the skilled work around town. Though, talk is, they'll be conscripted soon, too."

"To do what?"

"Work on fortifications, on railroad freight cars, on boats, in the tanneries. But, most important, in the Tredegar foundries or rolling mills. Our own people won't soil their hands. So it's the Irish, the Welsh, imigrant Germans or Negroes, free and slave, who make up the bulk of Tredegar's labor force. Without Tredegar our military output would grind to a stop. If I sound unladylike about all this, the fault's not mine. That's all my husband talks about day and night. It's not the armies that win wars, he says. It's the men who put the weapons in their hands." She caught his gaze. "Does all this disturb you?"

"No," said Harrah, "it just makes me want to get on with my meeting."

"Yes, I know you're impatient. But the meeting will take place soon enough. After I've dropped you off at the house, I'll pick up your counterpart. It wasn't easy getting him to come, Nathaniel. The gentleman wanted to know who you were and by what authority you came. I had no trouble telling him about you, but I adroitly sidestepped the question of authority."

"You did well, Madeleine. Better than I had any right to expect."

When they stopped at the door of Madeleine's retreat, she accompanied Harrah inside, prettily sitting down next to him.

"I know how important this meeting is to you, Nathaniel. Important perhaps to all of us. But I must tell you, I'm still warm all over from yesterday."

Harrah leaned over and kissed her. "So am I."

A flush scorched her cheeks. "I didn't mention it before because I didn't want to turn your thoughts from the matter at hand. But I wanted you to know."

"And you must know how I feel," he said, taking her hand. She responded by squeezing him, then abruptly stood up.

"I must go now," she said. "After all we can't keep such a distinguished person waiting."

She stopped at the threshold to throw him a kiss, then quietly closed the door behind her.

After Madeleine left, Harrah waited in the drawing room for about a half hour. Then he heard a carriage pull up outside the house, and a few minutes later he saw the drawing room door open. He caught only a glimpse of Madeleine who quickly smiled at him and then disappeared. A slight misshapen man who resembled a well-preserved but shrunken corpse entered the room.

"Mr. Harrah," he said, "I understand you want to meet with me. Apparently you know who I am, so we'll dispense with introductions."

Harrah detected a sly air of self-amusement in the man, a trace of cynicism. But he in no way appeared unkind or overbearing.

"I want very much to meet with you, Sir. I believe we have a common interest."

"And what might that be?"

"Peace."

Harrah did not expect the word to have such profound impact upon the statesman. But as the former Georgia congressman pulled off his coat and squirreled into a seat, Harrah could tell that he had managed to capture his interest.

"Ah, peace. That much maligned word. I'm afraid it's a shade unpatriotic these days. You come from Cape Island, I understand."

"That's right. I own a guest house there."

"Mrs. Craddishaw speaks often of the place—fondly, I might add. I like the seacoast myself. But necessity dictates my being in Richmond." He broke off and studied Harrah, almost harshly, for a moment. "By what authority are you here, Mr. Harrah?"

"I'm here on my own."

"A rather risky business—just to talk peace."

"Would it be any less risky if I were here by delegation?"

"No, but your presence would carry more weight."

"Undeniably. But then I would be playing a partisan role. This way I can be the honest broker."

"How honest? You have your biases, I am sure."

"Only one. I am opposed to slavery."

"That's honest enough." Alexander Stephens sank back in his chair, looking even more misshapen as he relaxed. "What is it you want to know?"

"What are your conditions for peace?"

"Conditions? There's but one. A return to the Union only if the Constitution stays in place. Remember," he added, "this is not Jefferson Davis's position. This is mine. I'm only the Vice President."

"But what do you mean by the Constitution staying in place?"

"Free speech, press. Writ of Habeas Corpus. All the guarantees of the Constitution—with the Supreme Court the highest law in the land."

"I see," said Harrah, who in fact was only beginning to see. What he glimpsed was a man standing four-square on the Constitution. For what reason he was not sure. But he suspected it had something to do with legal justification. His suspicion was soon confirmed.

"This slavery business is, after all, a legal issue. It should be settled in the courts, not on the battlefield. Neither side can afford any more Shilohs. What a grisly business that battle has been. More than ten thousand casualties for either side. The North may count it a victory—particularly as we lost Albert Johnston. But considering Federal losses were even greater than ours, you can't afford many more victories like that."

"I can't disagree with you on that score," said Harrah quietly.

"But you do disagree about slavery?"

"It's too late to go back to where things were. Whether you like it or not, the war may have dealt slavery a death blow. Every day hundreds of Negroes cross over the lines. They see this war as a fight for freedom even if Lincoln maintains it's to preserve the Union."

"Nonsense," said Stephens. "Oh, you'll get some stragglers. Maybe more than a few. But by and large the slaves remain loyal to their masters. We're even thinking of conscripting them into the army."

"Are you really?" asked Harrah. "Are you seriously considering putting arms in their hands? You're not at all worried what they might do with them?"

The wizened face of the Vice President assumed an expression of pain.

"You don't mince words, do you, Mr. Harrah? You'll be the first to admit that war has its risks."

"Then let's find a suitable peace."

"All right," said Stephens, not without a certain condescension. "What do you propose we do with the Negro? Send him back to Africa? Colonize him somewhere?"

"What I propose matters little. But I understand Mr. Lincoln is willing to compensate the owners for their slaves."

"There isn't enough money to pay for that. Besides, your Congress wouldn't approve.

"Mr. Lincoln is not without influence. In any case," said

Harrah, "it would be cheaper than paying for the war."

Alexander Stephens struggled to his feet. "I am afraid, Mr. Harrah, we're off to a poor start. So we'd best break it off." But he managed to get in the last word. "A return to the Union and the Constitution. No more, no less. That's my position. Mine alone. Without that, there is no chance for peace. Not even with an honest broker."

Madeleine returned the moment Stephens was gone.

"Well, how did it go?" she asked, flushed with expectation.

"Not too well, I'm afraid. For one thing, he knew I wasn't authorized to speak for Washington. For another, he still thinks the South can return to the status quo. And that, of course, is impossible."

"I see." Her enthusiasm quickly dissipated.

"But his desire for peace seems genuine enough. That's a hopeful sign."

"Maybe. But he and Jefferson Davis don't get on too well. Stephens has openly criticized his policies. Even my husband thinks he's gone too far."

"In which case, he wouldn't be the man to talk to."

"Probably not," Madeleine reluctantly agreed. "On the other hand, he has his supporters. None of them too ardent about the war."

"They're not alone. There are plenty in Washington share that view. If we could somehow bring them together, we might be able to end this nightmare."

"If only that were so! Oh, how I wish the fighting would end! But I doubt it ever will."

"Why, Madeleine? Why do you say that?"

"Because of what I see when I meet the Davises. Even the war hasn't put a stop to dinner parties. And while Jeff Davis is gracious enough, I find him cold and unyielding. I sometimes think there's more at stake for him than secession and the Confederacy. He's a moody man, Nathaniel, given to brooding. I understand he suffers a great deal of physical pain. And he's blind in one eye. Of course, he's very stoic about it all. But that's part of the problem."

"What problem?" asked Harrah.

"He won't make accommodations. I don't think he wants peace, Nathaniel. At least not a peace that involves compromise. I don't know how to describe it. But I don't believe Jefferson Davis can bring himself to give ground."

Harrah was terribly dejected by all this. He had heard much the same thing before. Only then it was about Lincoln. The man's despondency, his brooding—although Lincoln's often caustic humor gave the lie to many of these stories. If a man's basic nature could play havoc with his judgment, how could one ever hope for a rational solution to the nation's problems?

"Are you telling me we're at the mercy of personal demons? That a mistaken sense of mission—feelings of pride or even vanity—will determine whether we have war or peace?"

"I'm telling you that there is more at stake than just the Union or the Confederacy here. Our leaders themselves may be the obstacles to peace. Whether they'll admit it or not, what they want is not necessarily what we want. Their fate is not inextricably tied to our fate. When they reject all alternatives but unconditional surrender, they reject the one hope we have for compromise."

Her eyes suddenly filled with tears.

"I'd like to see Jefferson Davis come out of this alive. I would, Nathaniel. But not if it will cost me my son!"

Harrah took her arm. "He'll be all right, Madeleine. In my heart, I believe that."

"I hope you're right," she whispered.

Even as he held her close to him, Harrah developed new respect for the Madeleine he had known. Although he had loved and admired her on Cape Island, he never suspected how deep her intellect ran. Her awareness of what was going on, her keen understanding of men and events—the shortcomings of the one, the dependent nature of the other—utterly amazed him. He had seen a glimpse of this in her letters before the war, but nothing to prepare him for what he was witnessing now. That hers was a perceptiveness heated by emotions did not in any way detract from its special quality. If anything, it added a biting edge to her observations.

"I won't see you again after today, will I, Nathaniel?" she asked when he released her.

"Why do you say that?"

"Because your mission is over. You no longer have any reason to stay. After all, it's been ten years since I saw you last. And—"

"And what?"

"I have the feeling you haven't quite forgiven me for getting married."

"I haven't quite forgiven myself for letting you go," said Harrah.

Madeleine clutched her chest and a wince of pain crossed her face.

"My heart breaks at the idea I won't be seeing you again. It breaks over what we did to each other. My children's Southern heritage, their legacy—it all seems so unimportant now. And—"

Harrah waited for her to go on.

"The irony is that once I married my husband I sold the plantation. So what stood between us no longer exists."

She detected a note of disavowal in his face.

"You don't go along with that? You think we're still on opposite sides? Well, maybe you're right. And if someone has to win, I'd rather it be the South. Not for the usual reasons, mind you."

"Why then?"

"Because I'm afraid what will happen to us if we lose. Like a revolution, a war gets out of hand. And the vanquished lose more than they bargained for, more than they ever imagined in the beginning. The prospect of losing frightens me, Nathaniel—almost as much as the prospect of winning. Can you understand that?"

"I think I can."

"Then kiss me goodbye and tell me you'll miss me."

"You know I will."

"And let me think we'll see each other again once the war is over."

But when Harrah kissed her he realized Madeleine's fears were well-grounded. They would never see each other again. The time for them to make a life together had passed. On Cape Island ten years ago the gate to happiness had been swung open. But neither he nor she would pass through. In Richmond during this second year of civil war all the gates were shut tight.

FIRST CAVALRY

In his march up the Shenandoah Valley with the First New Jersey Cavalry, Henry Sawyer got his first bellyful of the excesses of war. Arriving after other units of soldiers had just passed through, he saw that his predecessors had strewn utter devastation in their wake. In every direction furniture, of no use to anyone but their owners, lay shattered and mutilated. Beds were defiled, corn mattresses cut to pieces, mirrors broken, fragments of glass scattered about the road. In the houses themselves windows were ravaged, doors were unhinged, crockery was smashed, articles of clothing torn to shreds. Portaits, ripped from their frames, were slashed or perforated with bullet holes.

In one town rows of pews had been pulled out of a local church and left broken on the dusty road. The frame structures of several stores had been pulled apart, and barns still smoldered from fires set the night before. Books, glass doors of china cabinets, marble statues, musical instruments—all lay in front of a Georgian brick mansion, the spent objects of an orgy of pillage. And in the middle of a once beautiful garden, a grand piano lay hacked by an axe, its keys, like teeth, yanked from its mouth.

Sawyer was sick over what he saw. He could in no way justify the things his compatriots had done. War was a necessary evil. But the vandalism in evidence everywhere was totally unnecessary. He liked to think that no sober man could do these things, only rowdies, and to some degree he was correct. A Pennsylvania Regiment had gotten hold of a couple of barrels of old apple whiskey, and it was said not a man of them could ride the middle of the road. When his comrades in the First Jersey found a third barrel buried in the earth, they let out a whoop. They left their horses to fill their canteens. But Captain Broderick arrived with orders to destroy the contraband.

"Destroy it, Captain?" The men were disbelievers.

"Destroy it," said Broderick. "Smash it and let the stuff spill out."

"But Captain—"

"I'm just as thirsty as you are," said Broderick. "But we've had enough wanton destruction for one day. We're New Jerseyans, not Bucktails. Now get on with it!"

No one had the courage to defy the stern-faced captain, especially as he leaned across his saddle to watch his orders being carried out. Securing a pickaxe one of the men punched a hole in the whiskey barrel and sadly waited as the rich amber fluid poured down the side and into the ground.

Captain Broderick cast a look at Sawyer and, winking, addressed the mourners.

"Now climb back on your horses and move out."

By sundown Captain Broderick had secured lodging in one of the few farmhouses in the area that had escaped damage. A handful of officers, Sawyer among them, availed themselves of bedrooms upstairs while their troops fended for themselves in the huge barn. At the request of Captain Broderick, the lady of the house and her three pretty daughters prepared supper for the half-dozen officers under their roof.

"Where are the men of the house?" asked Captain Broderick zestfully eating his meal of eggs and cornbread.

"My husband's an officer in the Virginia Cavalry. And my sons are fighting near Fredericksburg." The lady of the house, still fairly young, made no attempt to hide anything from her interrogator though she moved in and out of the dining room with all the dispatch of a waitress.

The oldest of her daughters, emerging from the adjoining section of the house, announced in a shrill voice, "Look what the Yanks did to our drawing room. Mud all over the floor. A vase broken."

"Sorry, Madam," said Captain Broderick to her mother. "No harm intended."

"No harm? We've seen nothing but destruction since Union troops began passing through here. It's been a sorrowful time for Southern homesteads."

"No doubt it has been," ventured Sawyer. "But who's responsible for the state of things?"

"We are, I suppose?"

"It's your unholy rebellion," said Sawyer. "You complain about what's being done to Southern homes. But what about us? What kind of a life is it for wives and mothers to see their loved ones going off to war? It's your doing, this rebellion, not ours."

"You call it rebellion. But it's no different from 1776. We're fighting as much for freedom now as we fought then."

Captain Broderick put his fork down. "Freedom? For whom, Madam? Certainly not for the Negroes on this plantation!"

"Our negroes are perfectly content to stay on as slaves. Why, who'd provide for them if they were freed? Certainly not your Northern cities and towns! There isn't a man, woman, or child on this farm who'd leave if they had the chance!"

"Don't argue with them, Mother! Can't you see it's a waste of time?" This comment came from the youngest of the three daughters, a once beautiful girl whose face had been hardened by the war and its deprivation. "It's enough they've eaten our food. Don't let them devour our pride too."

Sawyer filled his cup with coffee and, rising from the table, went to his room. He had been in saddle since early morning and he looked forward to a soft bed with fresh sheets.

But he could not get the partisan talk out of his head. He understood where the women were coming from. Until now the war had been confined to the South. The North knew little or nothing of once fertile fields made barren, of once charming communities made into graveyards or ghost towns. He knew all this. Yet he could not, or would not, accept the blame for the war. These Southerners had brought it on themselves. For people who had created beasts of burden out of black men and women, they sure were high on the horse.

He was sitting on his bed, smoking a pipe, when he responded to a knock on the door. "Come in." Though he had his revolver nearby, Sawyer did not think he would need it.

The youngest of the three daughters poked her head into the room. Her eyes were sunken and dark, though her face and hair were flaxen. "I have some things to get in my drawer. You don't mind, do you?"

"Go right ahead. Get what you need."

She pulled several drawers open and removed some night clothes.

"I see you have some jellies and chocolates," she said, pointing to the open contents of his kit.

"You may have some," he said offhandedly.

"I'll pay you for them." Her brow formed a childlike arch. "Pay me?"

"Or give you something in return."

Sawyer put his pipe down to take a better look at the girl. She was no more than seventeen, and with her long blonde hair tied back reminded him of Willacassa. He pictured how sweet her face must have been before the war, flushed through with innocence and Southern gentility. And now so hard. If the war did nothing else, it was guilty of that.

"You don't have to give me anything in return. It's yours. Help yourself."

"I don't want any favors. Not from a Yankee. It'll be a fair exchange."

"What kind of exchange?"

"You can fondle me. Other men have. Fondle me—but no more."

Sawyer put on a dour face. "Go downstairs to your mother," he said, "before I spank you with the flat end of my sabre."

For the next few days Lieutenant Sawyer and the First New Jersey Cavalry were attached to General Bayard's Cavalry Brigade. Word had reached them that Stonewall Jackson had inflicted a terrible beating on Major-General Banks at Winchester. And Bayard's Brigade was one of the forces that had orders to thrust itself in the path of a feared assault by Jackson on the capital.

The brigade was travel-weary. Henry Sawyer's mount, like those of other horses in the regiment, had been marching without letup and was as played out as it was hungry. Wherever a crop of clover appeared along the road, Sawyer would stop for a few moments to let his horse feed, then catch up with the rest of the brigade. Intermittently it rained, sometimes quite heavily, and Sawyer donned his poncho although invariably the India rubber overheated him.

But nothing stopped the brigade's progress, not walls or fences or roads swarming with infantry and horse-drawn artillery. General Bayard and Colonel Wyndham forced their men and horses forward, tramping down the high grain and splashing through ditches and rivulets. In the distance, from the mountains surrounding the valley, they heard the continuous roar of cannon and howitzers. The booming sounds grew louder and there was a general run of excitement over the prospect of combat.

But instead of the enemy they encountered an army of runaway slaves. Like a swollen river they poured forth, men, women, and children, acclaiming the troops as liberators. And with their meager possessions, wrapped in red or blue bandannas, they swept the road before them.

"We'z free. De Lord has freed us! We crossin' the River Jordan! We jine ya in the fight 'gainst Massa. We slaves no more!"

Unable to push through the sea of bodies, the First Jersey came to a halt.

"Where are the Rebels?" asked Colonel Wyndham, determined at least to get some intelligence from the Negroes that might prove to be useful.

"Dey'z all 'round. Up dere in da mountains. Back dere at the river. Dey'z waitin' fo' ya. But dey'z waitin' widout us."

"How many are there?"

"Tousands!"

"Thousands! I didn't think their force was so large." Colonel Wyndham turned to Captain Broderick. "What do you think, Virgil? I'm not sure these Negroes can count."

"That may be so. But it sounds like a large number to me. Better to be on the safe side, Sir."

Behind the regimental leaders, the men became restless, their horses snorting and champing. If they were going into combat, they wanted to get on with it.

"Let's move ahead," ordered Colonel Wyndham.

"Easier said than done, Sir," said Captain Broderick. Neither he nor Lieutenant Sawyer could push their mounts through the surging crowd of Negroes.

Colonel Wyndham tried to make quick work of the problem. "Get these people to the rear!" he flashed.

The officers saluted, then tried to carry out the order, shouting instructions, waving sabres, making threats. But the road they were on was too narrow and the press of bodies more than they could handle.

In order to get the attention of the Negroes, someone drew a pistol and fired into the air. At first the sound of the shot had the desired effect. Everyone stood still to find out what was happening. But the shot frightened some of the dogs that had trailed along with the Negroes. And their yapping and snapping at skittish hooves agitated several of the horses. The cavalrymen did all they could to subdue their mounts. But their horses twisted and turned and bucked in all directions. It was no use. The spark of panic had been ignited. The horses reared and collided with one another. And like an explosion, the mass of Negroes rushed toward the rear, sweeping soldiers and their mounts in their path.

The men to the rear, mostly Negro servants, cooks, and other non-combatants of the regiment, thinking the surge of bodies heading in their direction was an attack, also panicked. In their haste to get out of the way, they created a stampede, pushing to a side everything before them, overturning supply wagons, knocking loose caissons and limbers, and disabling a regimental ambulance. Even the rear guard, composed of Broderick's company and part of Sawyer's skirmishers, was swept away in the rush. Cut off from their officers, they too believed they were being attacked. Turning about, they kicked their horses and raced madly for the nearest town.

Captain Broderick immediately took after them. Following his lead, Sawyer whipped his horse into action. Somehow, in whatever way possible, he had to regain control of his men. Fear was driving them. And they were fast fading out of reach. Sawyer's best chance was to head them off, to plough through the wheatfields around which the road turned. Plunging forward, he forged a path across the windblown stalks of grain. Pushing his mount, he reached a bend in the road and managed to cut off his contingent.

"What the hell's going on!" he shouted, waving his sabre and standing in his stirrups. "Can't you see what you're doing? What happened was an accident. Get back in formation before this turns into a rout!"

At first his skirmishers pretended not to see Sawyer. They tried to run their horses around his flank. But Sawyer kept blocking their path and repeating his warning. At last, shamed by his outburst, they gradually reined their horses in. Unable to face their leader, they steadied their mounts and stared down at the ground.

"Let's get moving," said Sawyer, winded from the chase but satisfied he was in charge once more.

Slowly his men turned their sweaty animals about and trailed back to Bayard's Brigade. At a distance Sawyer saw Captain Broderick's men returning from their unauthorized gallop. After a while order was restored and once more the Brigade went in reluctant search of Stonewall Jackson.

But Sawyer was unnerved. How easy it was for panic and confusion to reign! He had thought his men had crossed beyond that stage. All those months of training, all the small successes of their Valley campaign in May had instilled a new confidence in the First New Jersey. It had been a long time coming, but it had come. And now, because of a stupid accident, all that was dissipated. Panic was once again the order of the day. It was enough to make his blood turn cold. It was enough to make him wish he were a thousand miles away. It was enough to make him spit.

At noon on Friday, the sixth of June, the regiment took up a position on the hills near Harrisonburg. There Colonel Wyndham dispatched Captain Broderick's company as an advance group into the town. Riding smartly, Broderick's horsemen, carrying carbines, approached the outlying houses. They were last observed by the regiment dashing through the streets of the town, looking for pickets.

As Sawyer readied his skirmishers to follow Shelmire's squadron in, the First Jersey heard gunfire. Moments later Broderick's men emerged from the town, riding fast but with an orderliness that spoke highly of Captain Broderick's coolness under fire.

"A body of infantry opened up on us!" shouted Broderick when he drew his horse up beside Colonel Wyndham. "They fired from stone walls alongside the road."

"How many were there?"

"More than my men could handle, Sir. I thought it best to

retire.''

"You did well," said the colonel. Then the flamboyant Wyndham threw his arm up and signalled for a column of fours.

For his part Sawyer had his doubts about going in. Because he never knew Captain Broderick to turn back unless he was badly outnumbered, Sawyer figured the enemy to be in full strength. Even the runaway slaves had said as much a few days earlier. The First Jersey, on the other hand, was down from its full complement of eight hundred to about half that number. Apart from combat, the "flux" and inflammation of the lungs had taken their toll. And desertion by the bounty jumpers. But there was also a critical shortage of good horses, and this idled more men at the base camp than the regiment could afford.

But apparently Colonel Wyndham was not about to be intimidated. Trotting his horse briskly ahead, he led his regiment down and through the streets of Harrisonburg. After taking up a position beyond the town, the colonel sent Lieutenant Sawyer's skirmishers into the woods to ferret out information.

As Sawyer picked his way through the trees and the knotty grass and kept out of the path of the slanting shafts of sun, he stopped to listen. He was certain there were enemy troops in the area, all around them. At least a regiment of cavalry, with infantry to boot. Branches snapped, spurs jangled, the quiet snort of horses drifted on the air. But he had no way of making a count. A cool sweat pickled his skin. His eye twitched. His kepi matted his hair. Though he waved to keep his men crouching, he had the uncomfortable feeling his skirmishers were seen but were part of a strategic waiting game. At last he signalled his men to remount their horses and return to the edge of the road.

As he came out of the trees, Sawyer saw Captain Shelmire and his lead squadron moving towards the woods beyond.

Fearing a trap, he called out. "Captain Shelmire! Take care. The enemy's in force in the woods."

Shelmire turned in his saddle, waving in gratitude.

"Thank you, Sawyer. But I have my orders."

Lieutenant Sawyer then sped toward Colonel Wyndham whose columns were beginning to move forward with drawn sabres.

"There are too many in there, Colonel," he warned, drawing abreast of Wyndham. "Even with the Mounted Rifles to help us, we're badly outnumbered!"

"We've got to charge them anyway," countered the colonel, spotting a small body of Rebel cavalry at the wood's edge. "Go help Shelmire."

Moving forward, Wyndham turned and shouted to his men,

"Cavalry gallop! Cavalry, *charge!*" And the First Jersey plunged forward.

The first battalion reached the woods, driving the small squad of enemy cavalry before them. By design the second battalion veered to the left and began knocking down the fences that stood in their way.

Sawyer noticed that Shelmire's squadron had found an opening in the forest, leading to a small road. Following their captain, the squadron trotted boldly and confidently forward. Moments later a tremendous burst of fire poured from the woods. Enemy fire! Sawyer sped to Shelmire's aid. He arrived as three of the captain's men, Traughan, Parry, and Jones, toppled from their horses. At the same time a volley of fire from behind the fences hit the remainder of the regiment.

Shelmire's men drew pistols and fired back. But they were raked by a steady stream of bullets. Afraid of being outflanked by the Rebels, Shelmire retreated. But backing away in the open field, his men collided with the line being formed by another squadron of cavalry which was also taking fire from the woods.

The collision led to utter confusion. The regimental commanders were now scattered in all directions. A number of their men were unhorsed. The standard bearer lost his colors. There seemed no place to stake a position and rally the regiment. A few of the officers managed to gather their men about them and were fighting back. Sawyer and Lucas and Haines. But others had become separated and could not find their troops, much less stand up to the withering assault. In the midst of all this a squadron of Rebel horsemen came sweeping down.

Sawyer and Lucas tried to hold their ground, staying in place and firing their pistols at the charging Rebels. But their men scattered. Indeed, most of the regiment broke from the field and ran. Sawyer looked for the Mounted Rifles who were supposed to back up the Jersey, but they too had turned and fled. Still, there were small pockets of resistance though Rebel and Jersey horsemen became indistinguishable. Amid the confusion Sawyer spotted Captain Haines calling to his men, trying to rally them round him. Broderick, fighting savagely, was not far behind. As Haines pulled his men together and made ready to cross a stream, a squad of Rebels charged his flank. One of the officers fired broadside at him. Struck by the bullet, the slender Haines dropped from his horse and tumbled to the ground. Seeing his fellow officer fall, Captain Broderick reined in his horse and wheeled about. Taking aim, he fired his revolver. The shot hit the Rebel officer and emptied his saddle.

With the enemy pressing him, Broderick returned to where his comrade had fallen. He shouted, "Haines! Haines!" But the captain lay lifeless. Starting to dismount, he heard Sawyer shout and saw him frantically waving him on. Broderick returned to his saddle. And with the enemy close behind, the two officers galloped away.

Driving hard, they managed to catch up with their troops. Desperately they tried to check the rout, cursing and shouting themselves hoarse. But no one listened, no one broke stride. The fleeing men pressed forward, pushing their mounts to the utmost. They crashed through fences. They splashed through muddy water. They snapped tree branches as they bumped one another in the mad dash for refuge. And as bullets whistled overhead, they rode even harder, putting more distance between themselves and the enemy. All attempts to halt them, to regroup, to form a rallying point—desperate, frantic attempts by their officers—only resulted in greater havoc, greater confusion. Horses ran into each other, threw their riders, trampled on those that had fallen. Crazed with fear, men and horses swept on, leaving a trail of kepis, sabres, canteens, and pistols behind them. And they continued their wild gallop until stopped by utter exhaustion.

But their officers gave them no respite. Doggedly rounding them up, corraling them like cattle, with no colonel to lead them and no regimental colors in hand, Broderick and Shelmire and Lucas and Sawyer exhorted their men to give the enemy a taste of their own medicine.

"Show the bastards we're not cowards! Wipe the shame and humiliation from your faces! Empty your carbines at 'em. And take the sting out of this defeat!"

Sawyer was almost beside himself with rage.

"Damn it. Do something!"

Slowly, dispiritedly the men pulled out their carbines and took aim. It required only two volleys to slow the pursuit down. Just two volleys. After a while Bayard's Brigade appeared on the scene. Joined by fresh Pennsylvania Bucktails, spoiling to fight, they checked the Rebel attack. Cooling their carbines, the First Jersey quietly slipped away and retired into camp.

When Sawyer put his horse to feed, he could not face his men. He was afraid he would say things to them that no soldier should hear, afraid he would pass over the line from which there would be no turning back. Sawyer was in such a personal rage that he kicked everything in his way—slop bucket, water barrel, fence post—until his toe was sore from kicking.

He knew the other day when the runaway slaves had caused

a stampede that the First Jersey had yet to earn its spurs. He knew it just as sure as he knew panic was possible, given the unhappy combination of circumstances. Oh, one could argue that the regiment had been ambushed this time. Even seasoned campaigners would give ground before such a blazing ambuscade. After all, the First Cavalry, with all the action it had seen in Virginia, was not yet seasoned. All this was undoubtedly true. But somehow Sawyer had hoped the day was at hand, the day when the First Jersey would show its mettle. In sporadic instances Captain Broderick had carried off successful expeditions. Lucas had known small victories. Sawyer himself and his band of skirmishers had done all one could ask of them. Only a week ago—only a week ago the picture had been so different. Such hopes for the regiment, such high expectations! And now, appallingly, this!

Spreading his blanket out, Sawyer threw himself on the ground and rested his head on his saddle. Moments later he slept the sleep of the exhausted.

WILLACASSA'S WAR

Harrah stepped out of the Cape Island Post Office with several letters in hand, one from Lieutenant Henry W. Sawyer. Crossing the street, he could not help but notice how far removed from the war Cape Island was. Everything was in readiness for the summer season. Shops were stocking goods. Hotels were repainting their exteriors. Bathing houses were being moved into place on the beach. And the perennial talk about paving the streets, spurred by Joseph Leach's proposal that they dig to a little depth and fill the depression with a mixture of gravel and clay, came to naught.

There was an almost indecent normalcy about the place. A new Ice Cream Saloon had been opened up by Mrs. George W. Smith. The "Camp Casey Store" operated since November by R. D. Casey on Jackson Street near the Atlantic Hotel would supply provisions of all descriptions. And the farmers in the area predicted good potato and corn crops, also hay and strawberries, but pronounced the oat crop almost an entire failure, a fact which was sure to lead to higher prices for that commodity.

The only real reminder of the war, except for the Union flags flying from the hotels and an occasional man in uniform walking the streets, were the dispatches printed in the *Ocean Wave* or Forney's *War Press*, a weekly journal on the conflict carried in by the steamboats. By and large Cape Islanders were already inured to the war. The first son of Cape Island to fall had been Richard T. Tindall, age twenty. Young Tindall, who had made a profession of religion, uniting with the Cape Island Baptist Church a year before the war, had been among the first to join the Home Guard. Elected a second lieutenant, he could not form a company. And so he entered the ranks of the Seventh New Jersey Regiment as a second sergeant. In the Fall of 1861 he took cold, then died of typhoid fever.

Though there was nothing heroic about young Tindall's demise, his death gripped all of Cape Island. His funeral was well-attended. His mother, his step-father, his uncle, and his young bride, the former Annie Mecray were inconsolable in their grief. The war had come home. One of their own had perished.

A second death, that of John Shaw, a young married man from Cold Spring also aroused much feeling in the community though he too, like Tindall, did not die of war wounds, but rather succumbed to lung congestion.

Since then others had died. Young John Mecray, Stephen Bennett, Charles Silvers, Townsend T. Irelan—all killed in action in May. In fact, one fifth of the Jerseymen that went into combat with Hooker and Heintzelman's divisions in the battle of Williamsburg were either killed or wounded. But except for their immediate families, there was no outpouring of emotions, no cry of indignation. The war had hardened the sensibilities. Death was to be expected now. The pain of loss was softened by its replay.

Sitting on the verandah of Trescott House, overlooking the ocean, Harrah opened Henry Sawyer's letter. For the past few months now they had been corresponding. Harrah knew that Sawyer had friends in town closer to Harrah's age than his own: Joseph Leach, Samuel R. Magonagle, Captain Whilldin among others. He knew too that the tenor of his letters to these men was different from the ones he received. Harrah knew this because the others often shared snatches of their correspondence with him. Harrah understood why this was so. Unlike the man Henry W. Sawyer generally projected, strong, positive, patriotic, and steadfast, the man that emerged in his letters to Harrah was filled with doubt, dismay, and even anger—not so much at the war itself as the conduct of the war.

He might, for example, write to Leach or to the *Ocean Wave* itself that eleven New Jersey regiments were now in the field and that it behooved those of age in Cape Island who had not yet served to volunteer. But to Harrah he lamented that those who had volunteered were often in poor health, ill-trained, and as ignorant about caring for a horse as a blacksmith was about treating a sore tooth.

In the letter that Harrah had just opened and held against a stiff breeze, Sawyer described the Rebel ambush outside Harrisburg and his mortification at what had followed.

"It was bad enough that our men panicked. What made the whole thing so shameful was the absence of any kind of *esprit de corps*. Instead of looking out for his comrade-in-arms, it was every man for himself. One would be sorely tempted to call the men cowards. Yet only a few weeks earlier I had seen them courageously fording swollen streams, raiding at great risk enemy supply depots, and exchanging shot for shot with parties twice their number.

"I'm told that at Bull Run our troops acquited themselves quite well at first. Why in the end did they break and run? Was it fatigue and exhaustion? Do the Rebs have more determination, more staying power than we do? I'm at a loss to understand. I know only that I have trouble driving June 6 from my mind.

"I write all this in the knowledge that you will keep what I've said between us. But I must add that I'm determined more than ever I was to see the day when the First Jersey, indeed all of the

Union cavalry, will be on equal footing with the Confederacy as a fighting force.

"I pray that day will come soon. For I am rapidly losing patience with what I see as the one great impediment to this war—a lack of professionalism among our fighting men. In the First Jersey, at least our officers are soldiers through and through. It is my hope their courage and determination will trickle down to the men in the ranks."

Though he had his own misgivings about the war, Harrah did not share them with Henry Sawyer. The young man was in the field, apparently fighting for his life. There seemed little point in undermining either his confidence or his conviction that the war was just. He was content to be Henry's ear on this score, no more.

When he did write, Harrah confined himself to reporting on the changes that were taking place on Cape Island or on the new personalities in town. Sometimes he repeated what he had heard from Willacassa. And on this occasion he ended his letter with a promise that a package of pastries would be forthcoming from Rachel soon.

"The summer season is upon us once more. With Rachel in the kitchen it's like old times. The delicious scent of freshly baked bread wafts through the house and gets the juices flowing. Along with her forthcoming package, she sends her love."

But if Harrah was careful what he wrote to Henry Sawyer, he was nonetheless troubled by the conduct of the war itself. Before his visit to Richmond, Harrah firmly believed in the emancipation of the Negro on moral grounds. After what he had seen in and around the Confederate capital during his stay there, he became convinced that the abolition of slavery was also a practical necessity. If the war was not to be dragged out beyond all expectation, the South had to be relieved of its secret weapon, black labor. He discusssed this new view with Joseph Leach. Despite their on-again, off-again estrangement over Harrah's peace activities, Leach was anxious to find out firsthand what Harrah had observed on his brief trip South.

"None of this is for publication, mind you."

"Why not?" asked the fiery editor.

"Because mine was a peace mission. I don't want to be seen by those who were hospitable to me as some kind of spy."

"I can always attribute the report to an 'anonymous correspondent.'"

"I don't want that."

"Are you sure?"

"I'm certain."

"All right then. You have my word. I won't print any of it. But I reserve the right to editorialize."

"That's your privilege."

"Why is abolition suddenly a practical necessity? If anything," argued Leach, "the slaves give the Rebels more mouths to feed."

"That may be. But they're generally the last to be fed. The fact is, Joseph, that life in Richmond would come to a standstill if the Blacks weren't there. Forget the fortifications they're building and the boats and the other tasks they perform for the military. They do just about everything. They're the carpenters, the blacksmiths, the wheelwrights, the coopers, the tanners—"

"You mean there are no white men doing these things?"

"Of course there are. But more and more these men are being called to the colors. And the Blacks have to take their place. I'm not just talking about slaves, but the freedmen too. And then there are the teamsters and the railroad laborers and the ditchdiggers and the hundreds of other semi-skilled workers who pick up the slack. Not to mention the Blacks you don't see—in the hospitals in and around Richmond or in the Tredegar Iron Works. If Richmond, if Virginia had to rely on those effete young men who manage to buy exemptions to fill the gap or the well-intentioned wives of government clerks, the place would fall apart in three months!"

"So you're suggesting emancipation now—"

"Exactly. To shorten the war! Not just on moral grounds as you and I and others have been urging."

The wiry Leach stroked his graying beard.

"I don't know what to make of you, Nathaniel Harrah. One day I think you're nothing but a damn Copperhead. The next I see you as a partisan Union firebrand. You might just as well be wearing two hats or flaunting two flags. Just let me know which one you're planning to use."

"Well, it's a certainty Mr. Lincoln will see me as a firebrand. I've written him a letter urging the immediate abolition of slavery. I've listed the practical reasons for such actions. I'm sure he's aware of the moral ones."

"The President is a compassionate man."

"But also a crafty politician. Anyway, I doubt he'll get to read the letter. Probably end up on some bureaucrat's desk. It's the fate of letters these days. Maybe you can't guarantee me anonymity in your newspaper, Joseph. But I'm sure the government can. Only with them it comes under the heading of indifference."

"I might be able to help you," said Leach. "I'm not without influence in the Republican Party."

This was a much more conciliatory attitude by the editor than any Harrah had experienced lately. And he welcomed the change. Maybe they were closing the gap on their supposed differences.

"Good. Then just pass the word about my letter. Don't want it to end up in somebody's wastebasket." Harrah smiled. "It's the one marked 'personal and confidential.' And it has a Cape Island postmark."

Willacassa arrived in Washington late in July. She would have travelled there earlier but she wanted to be sure she had a place to stay. When she received word from her former landlady on Sixteenth Street that a room was indeed available, she packed her things, kissed her father and Rachel goodbye, and caught the first steamboat out of Cape Island.

Sixteenth Street had taken on the look of an armed camp. One of the houses, belonging to a Mrs. Greenhow, was being guarded day and night by rifled militia. Willacassa did not know whether Mrs. Greenhow, a self-confessed Confederate agent, was still confined in the house or whether she had been "deported" to the South, as some had said. She suspected that other political prisoners, mostly women, were being detained there. And as her own residence sat at the other end of the street, she made a point of avoiding the "secessionist" building and the notoriety that went with it.

As soon as she was settled in, Willacassa walked across Connecticut and Pennsylvania Avenues to the War Department, a small brick building on Seventeenth Street. She was stopped at the door by uniformed sentries, and it was only after much cajoling and insisting that someone agreed to seek out Captain Shiloh. When the soldier returned, he escorted Willacassa to a screened-in cubicle in the basement where at a crude table, on a narrow stool, Captain Shiloh was poring over some maps.

"Welcome to Camp Shiloh," the captain joked when he rose to greet Willacassa. "There's hot and cold running water and even a window or two. But it's all upstairs. One consolation though. It's cool down here. And for the months of July and August that's no small consideration."

Willacassa was amused but also a little dejected, not so much for herself as for the demeaning effect the cramped quarters might have on such a man as Captain Shiloh.

"Now don't be making a drawing of this place for *Harper's*," cautioned the captain. "Their readers will think it's the dungeon of Libby Prison rather than one of the lesser chambers of the awesome work quarters of the War Department. How are you,

Willacassa?''

"Wishing I was back on Cape Island. I miss the beaches and the clean ocean breezes.''

"I know. It's hot and sticky and dirty in Washington. And so terribly crowded with politicians and prostitutes and other seedy characters.''

Willacassa shook her head. "I had no idea there were so many convalescents and contrabands walking the streets. Where do they all come from?''

"They're beginning to straggle in from the Peninsula Campaign,'' said Shiloh. "Actually there's been more malaria and typhoid fever among the military than wounded. I almost think we have more to fear from rampant disease than from rampaging Rebels. How's *Harper's* been treating you these days?''

"A little like an orphan. Not enough to care. But not without some sense of responsibility. They throw a few assignments my way. But most of it is free-lance, so it's either feast or famine.''

"Speaking of famine,'' said the captain. "You haven't forgotten about Willard's, have you?''

"I was hoping *you* hadn't forgotten.''

"It's pretty crowded these days. But I think I can get a table for us. Where can I pick you up?''

"I'll meet you here,'' said Willacassa. "I live only a short distance away. You'll find me outside with the geese.''

Shiloh smiled. "At five?''

"Five will be fine.''

Willard's was as imposing as ever. The five-storey brick edifice with shuttered windows sat on the corner of Fourteenth Street. It reminded Willacassa of an urban fortress with flags flying aloft and military carriages parked outside. But it enjoyed landmark status for every politician, military officer, and newspaperman in town. Even from the huge dining room one could hear the incessant noise and laughter coming from the bar where battles were fought and re-fought and rumors floated about like Professor Lowe's silk observation balloons. Willard's in fact was the true Capitol of Washington. It was here the real debates and decision-making were carried on, fouling the air with purple language and blue cigar smoke. Not in the hallowed halls of Congress.

As soon as they were seated, Captain Shiloh ordered a bottle of French wine.

"You're as good as your word, Captain. By the way, what happened to Zeb Yount?''

"Took sick about a month ago. Just after we returned from our scouting assignment. Doctors said it was typhoid fever. Had a terrible time of it. They sent him home to western Virginia for a while."

"Poor Zeb. He's such a nice young man. And he thinks the world of you."

"That's why I like having him around. Since the Battle of Shiloh I'm not as popular as I might be. People have a way of associating me with the slaughter."

"Well, I like the name, despite what they say."

"Thank you. Shiloh's Hebrew, you know."

"Is it?"

"Yes, my father was a Jew. Actually, my given name is Samuel, not Frederic. My mother changed it because she wanted it to sound more Saxon. She was a Christian, you see. So they fought over me. My father wanted his only son to follow the Hebrew faith. 'What are Christians anyway?' he asked. 'They're only renegade Jews!' So I became a Jew. Oh, I didn't bother with the ritual. I didn't even go to the temple. But my name was enrolled with the tribe."

Willacassa smiled, but she did not comment. She could see that Captain Shiloh had not come to the end of his story.

"My mother, of course, had other ideas. Had my father outlived her, I probably would have remained a Jew. But when we moved from Cape May County to Indiana, he came down with prairie fever."

"I'm sorry."

"I am, too. The Hebrew religion is a lot easier to follow than Christianity. You believe in God and you get your just deserts. And that's it."

"And Christianity?"

"Well, I don't have to tell you. It's full of contradictions. The Hebrew of ancient times thought nothing of going to war. One bad turn deserved another. Christianity professes peace and brotherly love, and look where we are. Every day we send men out to kill—"

"Or be killed," added Willacassa quietly.

"Exactly. It goes against my Christian nature. Had I remained a Hebrew, I wouldn't have been plagued with so many doubts. I would have seen the injustice of slavery and been happy to punish the South for it. But I can't see these kids getting slaughtered—on either side. Yet every day someone's maimed or butchered out there. Like hogs they're butchered. Ours or theirs—it makes little difference. And it's the poor Southerner dying for the most part. Not the rich plantation owner."

" 'Rich man's war. Poor man's fight.' You implied that once before. And my father keeps saying the same thing."

"There's no doubt about it," said Shiloh. "Slavery has hurt

the poor white as much as the Negro. And from what I've seen, he's a decent sort. But he's the one in the ranks. He's the one doing the dying. And when the war's over, the mansions that denied him will still be standing."

Shiloh sampled the wine the waiter had poured.

"But enough of that. I should have been a preacher, instead of a lawyer. Certainly, instead of a soldier."

They dined again a week later, this time at Wormley's, a celebrated restaurant on I Street, owned and run by a mulatto. But on this occasion Willacassa insisted on paying.

"*Harper's* accepted a whole batch of my drawings. I want to celebrate. You're my one friend in town—except for a girl on Sixteenth Street who works nights. So I thought I'd ask you to dinner."

"I suspect there's more to it than that," ventured Captain Shiloh, not without a trace of humor.

Willacassa was embarrassed, dismayed even, but managed to say, "You do? What could you possibly suspect?"

"That it's the maps I work on in the War Department you're interested in. You can't tell me that Port Royal is only a passing concern of yours. Even with a blockade, a trip there is fraught with peril."

Willacassa had expected Shiloh to mention her trip to the Sea Islands when she first arrived in Washington. But the captain had somehow avoided the subject. Now that she had put the matter to rest she was surprised to find it suddenly resurrected.

"And how are your friends?" he asked.

"I didn't get to meet them. Their home had been put to the torch. They're no longer living in the area."

"I'm sorry. I had no idea."

She didn't know how much Captain Shiloh was making of all this. But it was important to downplay her visit. "Besides, my movements were restricted. Women are still regarded as a petty nuisance by the military."

"I know," said Shiloh. "I was only being mischievous." He looked down at the wine stains on the tablecloth. "I thought I'd stir you up a bit, intimate that Port Royal had something to do with your past..But I see that you aren't amused."

"To tell the truth, I'm not."

Captain Shiloh suddenly looked up. His was no longer a bantering mood. "Why are you so serious, Willacassa? I suspect you're the most serious young woman in Washington. Why don't you put rouge on your cheeks and go dancing like most of the girls in town?''

"Are you annoyed with me?" It was a subdued Willacassa who asked this question.

"Of course not."

"Then what?"

"I'm trying to find out who you are." His voice dropped but it was not unkind. "What I've seen so far—since you came to winter quarters—is too good to be true."

"Captain Shiloh—"

"Yes?"

Willacassa spoke haltingly. "What you said just now is no more than charity. The charity of a generous stranger. You hardly know me."

"But I thought—"

"We were friends? We are. I didn't intend what I said to be demeaning. I value our friendship. But there is still much about me you do not know."

"That's true," said Shiloh. "Forgive me. In times like these, people tend to make quick judgments. You don't mind my blaming the times, do you?"

"Not at all."

"Still, I meant what I said. You're much too serious. I know that the war is a serious business, but you must find some diversion. I'm sure there are any number of jaunty young officers out there who'd give up a promotion to dine with you or go dancing."

"I had my fill of 'hops' at Cape Island, Captain. And some of your officers are more interested in seduction than cold oysters. So I'll continue to draw a line instead of making a 'sketch' of myself."

Captain Shiloh smiled at the pun but did not pursue the matter any further.

When Willacassa slipped into bed that night she could not fall asleep. She had enjoyed her evening with Captain Shiloh, but he had hit a raw nerve—two raw nerves, in fact. Ever since the war broke out, Willacassa had in a special way regarded it as her war, the war that would set things straight, the war that would put an end to the monstrous evil of slavery once and for all. She did not foresee great bloodshed. She did not envision a long drawn out, protracted struggle. She did not expect a blurring of issues. Most of all, she never imagined she would set off for Washington for any reason other than to make a contribution to the war effort.

Yet from the beginning there was no denying that learning the whereabouts of Francis Grandee had become an obsession with her. She had sent him away, dismissing all talk of love, but no sooner was he gone than she felt compelled to know where he had taken himself, whether he was well or wounded, alive or dead. An obsession? Yes. But a private obsession—so at least she had imagined. Yet from one brief incident, her glancing at a map spread out on a camp table, Captain Shiloh had been able to deduce that Port Royal had something to do with someone in her past. And, of course, her trip had given that suspicion credence. Had she been so terribly obvious? Had she deceived no one but herself? The thought was unsettling, disturbing, and she almost resented Captain Shiloh for bringing the matter up.

At the same time, she recognized that the one person she wanted to keep from Captain Shiloh was Francis Grandee. That was the glaring truth. Willacassa simply did not want the captain to know anything about him. In fact, she dreaded his knowing. Yet if he did not know for sure, the captain certainly had an inkling. But why was it so important that Shiloh be kept in the dark? What was there about Francis Grandee that she wanted to hold separate from the man? She did not know. She suspected only that Captain Shiloh might not approve. But why she sought his approval and why he seemed such an important figure in her life these days escaped her. To be sure, he was a handsome man. And in his mid-thirties he showed a maturity that the eternal boy in Francis had always lacked. But it was not as if he were a rival of Francis Grandee for her affections. After all, Captain Shiloh still kept the photograph of his wife and two children on a shelf. Yet the question kept nagging at her. And it was not until she fell asleep and dreamt about mulattoes and piles of maps on the dining tables at Wormley's that she finally put the matter to rest.

News of another battle at Manassas filled the streets—as if one weren't enough. The Federals claimed a great victory this time, but all reports indicated that casualties were heavy. Why else were medical supplies and ambulances in such desperate need? Willacassa hurried to the War Department where she found Captain Shiloh on the verge of leaving.

"This summer's given us one defeat after another," said Shiloh, hastily packing his things. "Cross Keys, Port Republic, Slaughter Mountain, Bristoe Station, and now this."

"But they call it a great victory!"

"Nonsense. The casualty figures tell a different story. Ten thousand or more. Every available clerk and convalescent has been called to reinforce Pope. And I've got to get out there too. Fortunately my horse has been spared. So I should be able to reach the lines before long.''

"What shall I do?" asked Willacassa, aroused by Shiloh's alarm.

"Whatever you think best.''

"I've had some nursing experience.''

"Good. Then you might want to join the surgeons and the ambulances. I hear the medical corps out there has broken down.'' He took her arm. "But be careful. It's bad enough Zeb's out of action. I don't want to lose you too.''

Willacassa was moved by his concern. She stepped forward and kissed him on the cheek. "And you be careful too, Captain.''

Shiloh hesitated just long enough to glimpse the look in Willacassa's eyes. But he had no time to assess what he saw. He was gone before Willacassa had a chance to wave or add a parting word.

Unable to find a place among the ambulance wagons, Willacassa joined the throng at the Maryland Avenue Railroad Depot. The passenger trains were filled with troops who were hauling firearms through the open windows. And the freight cars were packed with male nurses on one side and boxes of medical supplies on the other. Several women had forced their way into the crowd, anxious to be of assistance. And Willacassa managed to get a helping hand up onto one of the freight cars. After a few false starts of the steam engine, the train pushed forward towards Alexandria.

It was a boisterous group of men who made up the nursing contingent, a rowdy hard-bitten lot who cursed and sang bawdy songs and tossed rolled bandages at each other. The train had been rattling along only ten minutes when they broke out a half-dozen bottles of whiskey that had originally been packed for the wounded.

"Can use some stimulant myself,'' one of the nurses shouted.

His companions roared approval and broke open their own bottles. With each swallow they grew more boisterous and their language turned increasingly coarse. One woman tried to keep a nurse from pawing her as their bodies were thrown together by the rocking freight car.

"Let me alone,'' she pleaded.

The nurse merely laughed and downed another drink. He then turned to Willacassa and clumsily tried to slip his arm around her waist.

"Back off, you oaf!" Rudely she shoved him away.

But the nurse grew bolder, lunging forward. "Come on, honey. That's no way to be.''

"Isn't it!'' Snatching a whiskey bottle out of its case, Willacassa swung it hard, crashing it on the male nurse's skull. Whiskey poured down the startled man's face and fragments of glass glistened in his hair.

"Are you satisfied?" she asked.

This provoked raucous laughter among the other nurses, half of whom were now stone drunk. But for the rest of the ride no one else was troubled.

At the hospital in Alexandria where Willacassa and the nurses, in various stages of intoxication, disembarked, the procession of wounded appeared endless. Some were straggling in by themselves. Others were carried in by comrades or hoisted in on pallets from wagons and ambulances. And yet as quickly as they were admitted, others were let go.

"Not serious enough, soldier. Have to save a bed for the badly wounded. Why don't you try the church down the street or Hadley's barn?"

"This one's done for. Better take him out the back."

One of the surgeons, his sleeves soaked with blood, studied the men and women who had come to help but were standing back along the wall for lack of direction.

"Which one of you can drive an ambulance? Appears some of the teamsters have run off to scavenge."

A lean man with a shock of gray hair stepped forward. "I've driven wagons all my life."

"Good. Then take someone with you and look along the road to Manassas. The ditches are strewn with men who can use a ride back."

Willacassa stepped forward. "I'll go too, if it's all right with you."

Neither the surgeon nor the gray-haired man who introduced himself as Mr. Mulliniks tried to dissuade her.

As they drove out of the streets of Alexandria against the heavy flow of limbers, wagons, and humanity crowding in, Willacassa thanked the man for letting her come along.

"A bloody mess, isn't it?" said Mulliniks. "Never expected so many wounded. Thousands, I hear. Now there's a shortage of bandages and medicines."

"There are some bandages in the wagon and some whiskey," said Willacassa, reassuringly. "I checked to see when we started."

"Good. We'll need it."

"Was your son at Manassas?" Willacassa did not know why, but the thought crossed her mind.

"My son was at Malvern Hill. He was among the Missing."

"I'm sorry."

"Don't know what happened to him. That's the worst part. May be dead or wounded somewhere, or taken prisoner. But I keep looking. Can't sit home and wait anymore. He's my youngest."

Mr. Mulliniks said all this with such an absence of pity that Willacassa found it difficult to deal with her own emotions. She too wondered what the boy's fate had been, unable to shake the sickening fear that the worst had happened. She felt deep guilt that she had no like loss, no son or little brother to place on the altar of sacrifice. But most of all she felt helpless to lessen the man's pain and the pain of all those passing corpselike on the road, men and boys who had seen the unutterable and were striving to put it behind them.

It was not long before they passed torn patches of wounded men who had flopped on the sides of the road, their equipment strewn about them. This apparently was all that was left, the remnant, the debris of what had once passed for a fighting force. Shattered in spirit and broken in body, they lay in the mud like the abandoned sheep of a storm-scattered flock.

Each time Willacassa saw Mr. Mulliniks look down at the fallen men, she expected him to draw the ambulance to a halt. But each time, after slowing up a bit, he pushed ahead again as though this was not quite what he was looking for. Willacassa was tempted to say something, to protest his failure to stop. But something in the man's determined visage, a face etched with anguish, prevented her from uttering a word. At last he pulled on his reins, brought the ambulance to a grinding stop, and pointed.

"There," he said, "in the open field. Three soldiers. They look like comrades. Let's pick them up."

He turned the ambulance off the road and bumped along a cowpath, shaking the wagon from side to side, until he reached the fallen trio. But as Mr. Mulliniks drew near, disappointment crossed his face. Shaking it off, he climbed down and pulled back the tail of the wagon.

The youngest of the three soldiers managed a wan smile as he tipped the visor of his kepi. "Jesse Breedlove, Ma'am. These are my comrades, Private Wilkins and Private Starns."

"Mighty glad you came for us," said Starns. "We're all pretty badly shot up. A minie ball ripped through my shoulder. Can't raise my arm. Wilkins here lost an eye where the handkerchief's at. And Jesse—"

"I'm fine," said Breedlove. "Just feel nothing in my legs."

"Can you boys make it to the ambulance?" asked Mulliniks. "If you can, I'll handle young Breedlove here myself."

Willacassa offered to help the man. But Mulliniks picked the boy up as he might an injured lamb. And though it was fast getting dark, Willacassa could see a pool of blood on the ground where the young soldier had lain.

Mulliniks carried the stricken boy to the ambulance, and his comrades who had climbed aboard moved aside for him.

Willacassa unrolled some bandages and wrapped the shoulder of Starns as best she could. Wilkins just pressed a wad to his eye. Meanwhile Mulliniks stanched the flow of blood at Breedlove's side, then opened a bottle of whiskey.

"You'd better take some of this, Son."

"I'm not a drinking man," Breedlove replied weakly.

"Best take some anyway."

He did, then leaned against Willacassa who sat down beside him.

"Glad you came, Ma'am," he whispered. "I'm feeling a mite sick." He swayed for an instant. "Fear I'm going to faint," he said. "Strange thing is, I feel nothing in my legs." He slumped back and soon fell asleep in Willacassa's arms.

When the ambulance reached the hospital, Mr. Mulliniks helped Starns and Wilkins down and led them inside.

"How's young Breedlove doing?" Mulliniks asked when he returned.

But the look on Willacassa's face told all. "He died in my arms a while back. Oh, my God!" she cried. "What are they here for? Why do they have to die? So young and so trusting!"

Mulliniks searched in the dead soldier's tunic for some form of identification and found a small bible.

"It's one of those Christian Commission's New Testaments with the address of his family on the flyleaf. I'll write his family," said Mulliniks softly. "At least they won't have to wait. They'll know right soon what happened to their boy."

For the next few days Willacassa did what she could to help the wounded. She obtained food without the necessary vouchers and made sandwiches for hundreds of hungry soldiers just sitting around. She got hold of tobacco for those too sick to eat and rolled cigarettes. She found a wagonload of brandy and cartons of condensed milk which she mixed and served as a punch. She wrote letters home for the dying. At night she was so exhausted she fell asleep on a bed of pine cones covered with an army blanket. And each morning she put on clothes so wet she could wring them out.

By the end of the week, though there were still makeshift tents along the hillside and depots where the wounded from the battlefield found refuge, things had improved somewhat. Wagons from Washington with "sanitary stores" inside were being unloaded. Barrels of potatoes and onions stood in each doorway. And temporary convalescent camps, set up to handle the "spillovers" from the hospitals, flew their flags.

The hospitals themselves were slowly getting back into order. Sheets were being changed, slop pails removed, and medical cabinets replenished. Chloroform, tourniquets, splints, and dressings which had been scarce before—in some places nonexistent—were now in evidence. Bread, soup, coffee and jars of preserves seemed to be common fare.

But the wounded lay everywhere—on beds, pallets, cots, stretchers, even piles of straw. And many of them still lay in dirty, ragged clothes, their faces covered with dried blood or caked mud. Though some lay uncomplaining, others groaned with pain from deep stomach wounds or raw, inflamed stumps.

One day someone tapped her lightly on the shoulder. Willacassa turned to see Captain Shiloh with a sheaf of papers under his arm.

"I thought I'd find you in one hospital or another," he said with that curious reserve of his.

Though she was happy to see him, Willacassa wanted to cry. Her clothes looked slept in and wrung out. And she was cross and tired when she wanted to be fresh and bright.

"What are you doing here, Captain?"

"It seems I'm odd man out. My new assignment is to bring in a count of the wounded. But I've been promised a return to the 25th once the job is done. Lieutenant Farnsworth has had his bellyful of battle."

"Well, if it's a count of the wounded you want, you've come to the right place," said Willacassa. "Just look about you."

"It's like standing chest high in a sea of anguish," observed Captain Shiloh.

Willacassa nodded, then followed silently as he began the task of checking what he saw against the records given him. Shiloh's face was set in cold anger by the sight of the wounded. Not once did he put a false front on things. Not once did he indulge in meaningless banter about what he observed, the trivia of hospital disorder or the callousness of the surgeons and male nurses. He simply jotted things down.

"Is everything all right, Captain?" It was the chief medical officer who addressed him, a smug man with an officious smile.

"Everything but the figures," replied Shiloh.

"You have some questions about them?"

"Only one. I've counted more wounded in the wards than you have listed here, let alone those in the tents outside and elsewhere."

"The figures I gave you are correct."

"I beg to differ with you. I find them suspect."

"Perhaps our definition of 'wounded' differs."

"I assume the men lying on those cots aren't here for their amusement."

The chief medical officer's face hardened and his eyes narrowed.

"And you're not going to tell me, Sir," continued Shiloh, "that the men carrying shell fragments are not wounded. Or that the amputees count as able-bodied men. Are you?"

"No need to alarm the public at large, Captain. I have it on good authority that the war department wants a conservative estimate of our losses."

"This is not a conservative estimate, Sir. It is an outright distortion."

"I don't take kindly to that remark."

Shiloh became heated. "And I don't take kindly to being taken for a fool!"

"Captain, you were sent here to collect data. I've given you the information you seek. I have no more to say on the subject." With that the chief medical officer turned on his heel and strode off.

Captain Shiloh had no comment on any of this for Willacassa who had stood nearby all the while. He merely continued his inspection of the wounded.

As Willacassa led him through the hospital tents and displaced churches, she wondered what it was that set Shiloh apart from the others. Most of the officers she had encountered were as strong for the war as they were for Irish whiskey. They mouthed the usual platitudes about preserving the Union, punishing the Rebels, and winning victories on the battlefield (if only they were allowed to fight their kind of war). If they showed impatience at all, it was with army rations, popular fellow officers, and the interminable delays that prevented them from getting new commands.

Captain Shiloh shared none of their enthusiasms. On the contrary, he seemed always to be implying that the war never should have taken place to begin with. Had President Buchanan shown some starch, South Carolina never would have seceded. Had Lincoln not miscalculated, Fort Sumter would have been reinforced. In any case, the price young men were expected to pay for the war was too high. "They don't know what it's all about," he said, waving his arm in the direction of the sick beds. "Someone beats a drum and they march to its tatoo. Someone spatters a little blood and everyone sees red. The poor kids never stood a chance.''

"But if the North wins, at least—''

"The South's going to win, no matter what,'' announced Shiloh.

"What do you mean?''

"Even if they don't win a military victory, they'll win.''

"How?''

"By dumping the burden of slavery on us. Once the slaves are freed—if they are freed—they'll leave the plantations and head North. Without jobs, without money, without land, they'll sweep through the North like a whirlwind. They'll put a strain on the cities and towns never known before. The South's sins—all those years of slavery—will become our punishment. And the Rebels will see emancipation as their emancipation.''

"Do you really believe that?''

"Wait and see,'' said Shiloh. "You can't let three million people loose on the land and not expect chaos.''

"Then you don't think they should be freed! But I thought—''

"Of course they should be freed—no matter what the cost,'' insisted Shiloh. "And the sooner the better. But I have no illusions who will pay the price of their freedom. One thing you can wager on, it won't be the South!''

Willacassa saw the smoldering anger in the man, but recognized the source of his frustration. He saw the war as legitimate only if slavery were the issue. And clearly at this juncture it was not. At the same time, unlike the abolitionists, Shiloh did not shy away from the terrible problems inherent in the prospect of sudden emancipation. Admittedly the President was in a difficult position. Yet, as the captain took a cup of tea on a barrel table outside, he criticized Lincoln for pussyfooting the issue.

"The only reason Lincoln isn't freeing the slaves is expediency. Do you think for a moment that half, that three-quarters of my company would fight this war if it was to free the Negro? Not a chance. Not a blessed chance!''

His glare quickly changed to ridicule.

"So Old Abe with that prairie sixth-sense of his—And I can say that because I come from a prairie state too—invents the myth that we are fighting to preserve the union.''

"That's hardly a myth,'' said Willacassa.

"Oh, isn't it?'' Shiloh became serious once more. "If slavery weren't the issue, would the South secede? Would South Carolina and Georgia and Mississippi and the others go their own way? Come now, Miss Harrah. Secession is inextricably tied to slavery. We can no more ignore this than we can ignore what happened at Fort

Sumter. But Lincoln plays it down because Kentucky, Maryland, and even your home state of New Jersey wouldn't like it."

Willacassa was upset. She could not control the tears that filled her eyes.

"What's the matter?" asked Shiloh.

"You're scolding me!"

"Scolding you?"

"Yes, you're acting as if I were somehow to blame."

"You?"

"Even my home state of New Jersey, you said. As if I were somehow responsible."

"That's silly."

"Is it? I can tell you're angry with me. You even started calling me Miss Harrah again."

"I'm sorry, Willacassa."

"That's a little better."

"I didn't mean to imply—"

"I understand that now."

"Then why—"

"I don't know. I guess I saw the anger in your eyes. I don't blame you for being angry. In many ways I share your anger. I just didn't want it to be directed at me."

Captain Shiloh threw up a hand. "Forgive me. I meant no harm. I should have realized what I was doing. Anger has a buckshot effect at times. It was inexcusable."

"That's all right. I'm better now. I don't know what came over me."

Shiloh seemed relieved. "I'll be more careful what I say in the future."

"No, I don't want that. I like what you have to say. I wouldn't want you to hold back on my account."

"As eloquent a defense of free speech as I've ever heard," said Shiloh with just a note of mischief in his voice. "When we're in Washington again, join me for a drink and we'll toast the First Amendment."

"I'd like that."

But the toast had to wait. No sooner did Willacassa arrive in the capital than Captain Shiloh was given orders to report to Frederick, Maryland. General Lee was pushing his army North.

CAPTAIN SHILOH

The war in the East since the first battle of Bull Run, in sharp contrast with the West, had been a largely uneventful one. Indeed, the dispatch "All quiet on the Potomac" pretty much told the story. Of course, there had been skirmishes and "campaigns" on the Peninsula. But by and large more soldiers perished from lung inflammation and typhoid fever than from gun-inflicted wounds.

But it seemed to Willacassa that the late Summer of '62 had been one continuous roar of smoke and death. The second battle at Manassas or Bull Run had taken an enormous toll of limbs and lives. That she had seen for herself. And within weeks Antietam had made Sharpsburg, Maryland, one massive blood-soaked graveyard.

And as she walked the quiet beach at Cape Island where she had returned to nurse what seemed to be a lingering summer cold she stopped daily at the post office. She did not admit to herself that she was looking for a letter from Captain Shiloh. She conceded only that if a letter arrived it could be from the captain. But the mail in the box was invariably for her father who would accept it with typical badinage.

"No letter from President Lincoln?"

"No, did you expect one?"

"Well, I did write to him," he smiled. "The least he could do was respond. Joseph Leach had a letter from him. I guess he writes only to Republicans."

But Willacassa was not amused. Harrah could see that his daughter was not totally herself. Apart from occasional fits of sneezing and watery eyes, she seemed to be restless and a bit cranky. He knew something was on her mind but could not even hazard a guess as to what it was.

But Willacassa knew what troubled her. She found herself wondering about Captain Shiloh and how he had fared. Though not much on maps, she knew that Frederick, Sharpsburg, and Antietam were in the same theater of war. She had no premonition of death or survival, nothing as dramatic as that. She was confident that, as far as such abilities went, he could take care of himself. But she was not so naive to think that he could escape unscathed on mere skill alone. A chance bullet, an exploding shell, a skittish horse—anyone of these things could be a man's undoing.

And so it was with an immense sense of relief that she received a letter from him in October. It was a short letter to be sure, dispatched from Washington, but a letter nonetheless.

"Dear Willacassa,

I just wanted you to know that despite the bad news out of Maryland I am all right. The regiment was badly cut up at Antietam. The slaughter was horrendous. The creek ran with blood for days. It is called a victory. But it seemed to me more like Armageddon.

We expect to set up winter quarters at last year's camp grounds. Jeb is back and would like to see you. In the hope that you can see your way to a second tour of duty, I have enclosed a pass.

Shiloh"

The letter pleased Willacassa. Oh, she could find things to quibble about, particularly the signature. (She would have preferred "Sam.") But on the whole it lifted her spirits. And the cold that had dogged her these past few weeks disappeared as if by magic. Still, she was not without conflict.

She had, just before receiving the letter, come across a set of newspapers from the South. They had apparently been brought in by a neutral steamboat and left at the Landing. Somehow her father had gotten hold of them and carried the lot to Trescott House. Though some copies were as much as a month old, Harrah enjoyed reading through them and comparing impressions.

"You read *The New York Times* or *The Herald*," he said, "and you get one version of the war. Then you read *The Charleston Mercury*, and you wonder which battle, which war they are talking about. I guess the truth lies somewhere between them."

When he left the room to tend to other matters, Willacassa quickly seized *The Mercury*. In no time at all she found what she was looking for. "Adjutant Tompkins of the Hampton Legion was wounded." So Wade Hampton was at the second battle of Manassas. And if he was there, Francis Grandee must have been there too. Oh, why hadn't she known that before?

After reading Shiloh's letter, she searched frantically through other issues of *The Charleston Mercury* for an account of the Battle of Sharpsburg, as they called Antietam. She saw the names of the Second and Seventh South Carolina Infantry and the Third Georgia Cavalry, but no mention of Wade Hampton's Legion. Then, South Carolina Cavalry was not there. She felt the cold sweat of relief. It would be hard to imagine both Captain Shiloh and Francis Grandee surviving such a bloodbath!

But why this coupling of names? Why did she mention them in the same breath? What nonsense was going through her head? Hadn't she dismissed Francis Grandee from her heart (and mind) over a year ago? Why did he keep cropping up? And why, of all people, was Captain Shiloh juxtaposed in her thoughts with

Francis? The captain was only her good friend, her guide, her mentor (at least where the war was concerned). Was it fair to think of him in any other way? Didn't that photograph he kept on his shelf establish the ground rules for their friendship? She would do well to remember that! The photograph stood for something. No, the photograph was everything!

Willacassa began her second "tour of duty" in the beginning of November. Though the weather was still mild, fallen leaves were everywhere and winter loomed in the sky. When she located Captain Shiloh's tent, she was tempted to burst in and announce her arrival. But instead she passed it by and carried her sketchpad to a row of log cabins with tent-like canvas roofs and barrel-top chimneys. She sketched these and the numerous "pup" tents that had sprung up nearby for the new recruits, the "pup" tents sporting such little wooden entrance signs as "Dog Kennel," "Hound House," and "Sons of Bitches Inside."

When she finally got up enough courage to visit the captain's tent, Willacassa found not the captain but the "convalescent," Zeb Yount, inside.

"How are you, Zeb?"

"Fine, Miss Harrah. Glad to see you again. The captain spoke of you only the other day."

"How are things in West Virginia?"

"Not too good. Particularly in the hills. Food's short. Horses been stolen and barns burned. And there's feudin' and fussin' between families. Not all the folks are standin' hard for the Union." He looked to change the subject. "How's the sketchin' goin'?"

"Good. Would you like to see what I did today?"

Zeb stood at her side while she flipped the line-scattered pages of her sketchpad.

"You're real talented, Miss Harrah. Wish I could draw like that. Those tents and cabins look like the real thing. Smoke and all!"

"Thank you, Zeb."

"No foolin', Miss Harrah. Those are mighty good likenesses."

"Thought for a moment you were talking to yourself, Zeb," said Captain Shiloh, stepping into the tent. "Now I see that you weren't. Good to see you again, Willacassa."

Captain Shiloh looked younger and even leaner in some ways than he had when Willacassa had first met him—in battle readiness, so to speak. But fine lines had crept into his face, particularly about the eyes. And there was desolate sadness in his smile. It was not as if he had taken on the look of a mourner. Yet he was definitely more subdued as though the horrors of recent battle were still vivid in his mind.

"Do you think you can make us some tea?" he asked Zeb.

"Better'n that," said the young sergeant. "I'll cook up some coffee. Lieutenant Farnsworth'll never miss it."

"Zeb—"

"Well, he lifted it right out of the quartermaster's wagon. The least he could do was spare us a pot."

"We'll have tea, Zeb."

"Whatever you say, Captain."

When Zeb was gone, Shiloh offered Willacassa a chair.

"And how are things at home?" he asked.

"You'd hardly know there was a war going on."

"They read the casualty lists over a cup of coffee, is that it?"

Willacassa recognized this attempt at irony as a sign of deep-rooted depression.

"How bad was it?" she asked Shiloh at last.

"How bad? It was absolutely devastating. I've never seen carnage like that. Life is cheap, Willacassa. Ever so cheap. The waste and brutality, the madness and stupidity of this war. It's just appalling."

She did not comment, feeling it was best to hear him out.

"You'd think the military learned something over the years. But they've learned nothing. We still attack in formation with companies marching side by side. We still attack in waves—so close together a shell or bullet that misses the front line ploughs into the second. Assault after assault, sacrifice after sacrifice, that's all they know. Yet only a little discretion, a little skill, a little common sense would make the difference, save hundreds of lives. In some places the slaughter was so bad you could walk across the bodies and never touch the ground."

He stopped to fight back the passions that threatened to engulf him.

"The raw recruits suffered the worst. A veteran will only follow an order he believes reasonable. He'll adjust to the terrain, get behind a ditch or a tree—no matter what anyone says. The green kids, too frightened to run and seek cover, follow blindly and are cut down like stalks of corn. Sometimes in a matter of minutes whole companies are wiped out."

Shiloh halted a moment. "Do you have any idea what five thousand corpses look like, stacked in piles or strewn along the field? Well, I haven't been able to sleep for thinking about it. If those torn bodies, those bloated corpses were laid in dooryards North and South— If Jeff Davis and Mr. Lincoln had to dig trenches to bury the dead— If they both had to look at the maggot-eaten faces of the fallen, they'd be doing a damn sight more to bring this carnage to an end."

He clasped his hands together and looked across the table at Willacassa. "I don't pretend to have the answer. I don't know what can be done. I know only something has to be done. We can't go on this way."

"Tea's on," announced Zeb Yount, carrying a tray of tin cups and setting it down on the camp table. He then reached into his pocket and handed Shiloh a dispatch.

Captain Shiloh read quickly. He seemed more like his usual self as he put the dispatch away. "Well, it looks like McClellan is out. General Burnside's the new commander of the Army of the Potomac."

"Does that surprise you?" asked Willacassa, welcoming the change in him.

"Not really. We all knew Mac's days were numbered. We didn't know the new chief would be Burnside. Now there's some talk of reorganizing the Corps into Grand Divisions."

"What does that mean?"

"It means that the 25th of Indiana may be brigaded with the 25th of New Jersey, among others. Should make you feel right at home."

Willacassa smiled. Any mention of New Jersey always brought a quickening of the pulse, a sudden longing for Cape Island.

"How do you feel about Burnside?"

"I don't think he's the soldier McClellan is. But he's a man of action. And that's what Washington wants. McClellan had a way of dragging his feet. He supplied himself so well with men and materiel that in the end he bogged himself down."

"And the Rebels?"

"They travel lighter, so they travel faster."

"It's as simple as that?"

Shiloh shrugged his shoulders. "Probably not. It's just my thought for the day."

"Why would you be brigaded with the 25th?" asked Willacassa.

"We had to be brigaded with someone. What was once two regiments is now virtually one."

Things soon were back to normal for Willacassa. In the late mornings and early afternoons, she worked on her sketches. She did not, however, limit herself to the daily routine of camp life. She visited the hospitals which still housed their share of convalescents and amputees. And on three occasions, with a pass from

Captain Shiloh, she rode out with a troop of engineers and their tool and chess wagons to watch them build trestles for damaged railroad crossings.

Shiloh had said that the engineers were probably the most efficient corps in the military, building pontoon bridges and trestles and railroad spurs almost overnight. And Willacassa tended to agree with him. But on her last outing a Confederate raiding party surprised the engineers at work.

Willacassa was in the midst of drawing the huge cross timbers of the railroad trestle, which in the broad perspective of distance dwarfed the men working on them, when the crack of rifle shots rang out. The pickets that the engineers had scattered at the foot of the trestle were taken by surprise. Before they could put their rifles to their shoulders two of them were hit. Another pair panicked and bolted, abandoning their rifles as they ran. Unfortunately they charged into the band of Rebel marauders instead of away from them and were cut down by a hail of bullets.

Making use of barrels of explosives, the Rebels managed to bring several of the mammoth trestle supports crashing down. But before they could finish the job, a party of engineers firing from war wagons routed them and rolled the offending Rebel powder kegs away.

Willacassa ran to the aid of the pickets that had bolted as no one had reached them yet. One was miraculously still alive and she signalled for help. The other, a young man of extraordinarily beautiful features, was dead. The engineers carried the wounded man away but left the other lying where he lay.

"No time to bury him now. Got to repair that trestle!"

A transfixed Willacassa remained at the dead youth's resting place. How beautiful he looked even in death! His magnificent brow, lashes, and cheekbones glistened with an inner radiance. In a few hours the singular beauty would fade. In a few hours death would creep into his features and mock them. Giving way to tears, Willacassa went back for pad and drawing pencil.

When she returned, sobbing and breathing with difficulty between sobs, she sat down on the yellow grass and proceeded to draw the handsome, tranquil face. She had read in Vasari's *Lives Of The Painters* that Luca Signorelli had painted a portrait of the body of his dead son who had been killed in Cortona. When reading about it, Willacassa did not at that time understand the artist's action. It seemed too cold-blooded, too calculating, too inhuman. But she understood it now. In a small way, by means of the sketch she was doing, she would still be able to contemplate the beauty of the fallen youth. In time there would be nothing left but the sketch. That's all. More than that the youth would not have. A poor legacy, but a legacy just the same.

Later Willacassa did what she could to help the wounded. But towards evening as the engineers waited for a hospital wagon she sat down to sketch two dead horses where they lay. What had started out as a routine assignment had become a day of harrowing encounter. And yet it had a grim fascination. Only by drawing was she able to quiet the turmoil in her breast. In the absence of an undertaker she was taking the lead in the mourning procession.

"It was a grisly experience," she later told Shiloh.

"I never should have let you go," said the captain, shaking his head in self-rebuke.

"No, I'm glad you did. I learned a good deal about behavior under fire. It's such a study in contrasts. Some are so brave and some so afraid."

"Sometimes it's a mixture of both, even with the best. There's General Hooker, for example. Oh, he's brave enough. But it's a bravery born of fear. He'd sooner take a bullet in the gut than admit he's afraid. Or even lose an arm. And Custer, one of Pleasonton's brigade commanders, is no different. What he lacks in intellect he makes up for with decision. It doesn't matter that it's the wrong decision. The important thing is not to hesitate. McClellan took the medal for hesitation. And no one wants to be stuck with the honor now."

"But your men say you're brave," said Willacassa with the faintest hint of a smile.

"Not brave, just foolish. If I were brave, I would have stayed at home and sat this war out. My wife didn't want me to go. Or the kids. But I felt it would be unmanly to let the others do the fighting. Besides—"

"Besides what?"

"Nothing. It's too complicated to explain."

Willacassa was not surprised. From the first Captain Shiloh struck her as a complicated man, the most complex man she had known since her father. But she did not regard this as a detriment. Rather she saw it as one of the intriguing aspects of what seemed to her a most unorthodox personality.

"Lieutenant Farnsworth tells me he's had some difficulty with some of your sketches," Captain Shiloh began almost off-handedly. "He's had this complaint before."

"Difficulty?"

"He finds your subjects too graphic, too unvarnished. Too realistic and unpleasant. Of course, I don't really care what he thinks."

"Well, if it's any comfort to him, *Harper's Magazine* finds much the same fault."

"Meaning?"

"Meaning the editors won't take them."

"Maybe it's because you're a woman."

"They think 'W. Harrah' is a man."

Captain Shiloh leaned back on his camp stool and loosened his collar. "I see."

"The trouble with the sketches is that they're too close to the bone. *Harper's* wants realism, but only the kind magazine readers can handle. If war is portrayed as too gruesome, their readers will be turned off. And the war effort may even falter. With a constant call for new recruits, it doesn't do well to stress corpses and the rotting carcasses of horses."

Captain Shiloh looked critically at her, but it was mock criticism, the devil playing advocate.

"Don't you know that you must put the best face on things— even in a war? Here," said Shiloh, handing her a sheet of paper. "Here's a list of casualties. Don't let the descriptions fool you. 'A ball in the left leg' doesn't tell you about gangrene setting in or that the leg will undoubtedly be removed. And it doesn't tell you about the men sent home with typhoid fever or sick lungs, men who will probably expire before the month is out."

"I'm sorry," said Willacassa.

"Sorry about what?"

"For going over ground you already know. Know all too well, I'm afraid."

"I'll tell Lieutenant Farnsworth you have my permission to sketch anything you choose," said Shiloh, suddenly rising from his camp stool and rebuttoning his collar. He put on his cap. "Any problems with your editors, of course, you will have to deal with yourself."

"Thank you, Captain."

She left not knowing whether he had followed her out of the tent or whether he had stayed behind to gather up some papers or maps for a meeting with his superior officer.

What Willacassa did know was that suddenly there was some distance between them. Nothing she could point to, but something palpable nevertheless. She attributed a good part of this to the depression that had apparently taken hold of Shiloh since Antietam, a depression that had the effect of turning him inward.

Willacassa could deal with this. Such a reaction was natural, something to be expected of someone who had seen the worst of things. What she could not deal with was the impact it was having on her. She could not bear to see the Captain dejected. She could not bear seeing him as anything but the alert, vibrant man she had come to know. It hurt her. It played havoc with her feelings. It left her weak and ailing.

And then one day she saw Shiloh laughing. The company cook had been chasing a chicken. And just when he was about to grab hold of it, he tripped and fell into the horse's trough.

Even Willacassa had to laugh. Things were all right again.

Willacassa hated to go to the sutler's tent. It was always being besieged by hungry soldiers and in off hours by regimental officers who came looking for such necessities of life as oranges, dried apples, cheese, crackers, candles, comforters, boots, gloves, buttons, toothbrushes, razors, pencils, and stationery, and for such unnecessaries as whiskey, tobacco, yeast powder, patent medicines, and pornographic pictures.

"Don't come near, Miss," the sutler would call to Willacassa when he was showing some of his wares around. "These aren't things would interest you." And Willacassa would step back and wait until the crowd around the sutler's tent subsided.

The sutler had no more license to sell these unsavory drawings than he had license to sell whiskey, but he sold them just the same, the whiskey bottles packaged in hollowed-out loaves of bread. And the very officers one might protest to, if one had the inclination, were his best customers.

But more than his tent, Willacassa hated J. M. Cutliffe, the regimental sutler. Cutliffe was an odious man who had greed written all over his face, though he was not without decent features, his eyes and nose forming a T-bone from which the tender loins of the cheeks had been removed, giving his face, even with its whiskers, an altogether skeletal appearance. His prices appeared to be uniformly marked, yet Willacassa could not help feeling that with nervously shifting eyes he sized every man up either as someone who could be taken or someone not easily skinflinted, and proceeded accordingly.

There appeared to be no decent fiber in the make-up of the sutler, though he looked manly enough to be in arms himself. He showed no compassion for those who had little or no money. If anything, he sneered contempt. What he displayed first and foremost was a keen understanding of a soldier's needs, particularly the soldier who felt there might be no tomorrow, and a well-developed instinct for self-aggrandizement.

When Willacassa finally approached his counter, she asked for needle and thread, a newspaper, soap, and a tin washbasin.

"How much?" she asked.

"Thirty cents for the soap. Fifty cents for the needle and thread. Dollar and a half for the tin basin. And ten cents for the newspaper."

This was roughly four times the going rate in a Washington shop or a general store in a nearby town.

Willacassa gave him the money and carried her things back to her tent.

"Can't something be done about it?" asked Willacassa when she related to Shiloh what she had encountered.

"About what? The pictures or the sutler himself?"

"Both. I went back and told Mr. Cutliffe I would complain to you. Especially about the pictures."

Captain Shiloh rose from his camp stool and walked to the other side of the table.

"I can see where they would be offensive, Willacassa. But the military's had a serious morale problem since Antietam. Not only in this regiment, throughout the Army of the Potomac. I don't know whether it's Burnside's doing or Hooker's, but the situation is much improved."

"And you attribute this improvement to pornographic pictures?"

"No. I attribute it to a more liberal attitude toward a soldier's needs. Leaves and furloughs are granted on a more equitable basis. Our officers look the other way when liquor is sold—"

"They also look the other way when filthy pictures are distributed."

"Exactly."

"And you think this is all right? You think boys can be boys—so long as they go to war and die like men. Is that it?"

"Something like that."

"Then you endorse this type of thing?"

"Endorse? I endorse nothing. Anymore than I endorse prostitutes on the streets of Washington. These boys may survive the war. But syphilis will do them in as certainly as poor army rations." He looked to see how his remarks were being received but found no encouragement. "As for pornographic pictures, they're sickening, disgusting—whatever word you want to use for them. But I have no authority to put an end to their distribution. And if I did, I'm not sure I'd use it."

"Why not?"

"Because I don't want to impose my standards on anyone else. Any more than I want them to impose theirs on mine."

Willacassa sparked outrage. "You're afraid to do anything

about it. Isn't that it? You set standards for everything else—uniform dress, care of weapons—why not the goods to be sold in the sutler's tent?''

"The government has set standards, rigid standards. But—"

"But obviously they're honored in the breach.''

"Obviously. And I've got better things to worry about than the sutler's tent. If you're so troubled by all this, why don't you speak to General Hooker himself?''

Willacassa looked shamefaced. "Because my presence may be honored in the breach too.''

Twenty-four hours later Willacassa was sorry she had given Captain Shiloh such a difficult time. He did indeed have better things to worry about. And she had such a deep and abiding respect for the man that it seemed the better part of foolishness to quarrel with him over the least little thing that offended her sensibilities.

At the same time she was determined to strike back at the sutler. For there was something so offensive about the man and what he stood for that his mere presence was a personal affront. And it seemed that the best way to get back at him was through the good offices of Captain Shiloh. But wasn't she exploiting the captain in this regard, taking advantage of their growing friendship? Wasn't she using all the wiles of a wife, mistress, or daughter to involve him in her dispute? Yes, she had selected Shiloh as her champion. She wanted him to do battle for her. And she did not need a soothsayer to tell her she was wrong. She made up her mind to apologize to the man at the first opportunity.

She returned to her work feeling better about things.

"Miss Harrah?''

"Yes?'' Putting her sketchbook aside, she turned to face a corporal she had never seen before.

"Captain Shiloh would like to see you in his tent.''

When she was ushered into the captain's tent, she found Shiloh sitting grim-faced in a camp chair.

"You may go now, Corporal,'' he said to her escort, not once looking at him.

"Yes, Sir.'' The corporal saluted and left.

After staring a long time at the tent opening, Captain Shiloh at last turned his attention to Willacassa.

"Will you sit down, Miss Harrah?''

So it was Miss Harrah now, not Willacassa. She sat down, wondering what had brought about the change.

"I'm afraid I have some questions to ask you,'' he began.

"Afraid?''

"You may not like them."

"I really can't imagine what you're talking about."

"Let me say that I only ask them because it is my duty to do so."

"Ask what, Captain?" Willacassa was becoming impatient with him.

Shiloh leaned forward, disbelief and pain shading his blue eyes. "Are you a member of the Knights of the Golden Circle?"

"What?"

Shiloh withdrew the question. "Never mind," he said. "Are you acquainted with a Mrs. Rose O'Neal Greenhow?"

"Acquainted, no. But I have heard of her."

Captain Shiloh's stern expression eased a bit. "Do you know John B. Floyd?"

"The name's familiar."

"He was Secretary of War under President Buchanan."

"If he stayed at Cape Island, I might have met him."

"Mr. Floyd is now in the South. I don't know if he ever visited Cape Island."

"Then I don't know him," said Willacassa. "Why are you asking these questions?"

"It has come to my attention—that is, it has been charged—"

"What has been charged?"

"That you are—how shall I put it? That you are an agent of the South."

Willacassa stared at Captain Shiloh in such utter and total disbelief that all at once he leaned back and allowed himself the luxury of a smile. Her reaction, far from distressing him, seemed to reassure the officer.

"I'm sorry I had to ask these questions, Willacassa. But when a charge is made, I have to investigate it. I didn't think there was any substance to it. Now I know there wasn't."

"Who—who made the charge?" She was so overwrought she could barely talk.

"Mr. Cutliffe, the sutler."

"Mr. Cutliffe? That dreadful man! Why would he spread such a slander?" Willacassa was so outraged and infuriated by the idea that a crimson patch appeared on her neck and spread beneath her collar.

Captain Shiloh rose and came round the table to calm her.

"I want you to know that this was a most unpleasant business for me."

Willacassa did not respond to the captain's comment, nor to the gesture of an outstretched hand.

"I want to confront him!" she demanded. "I want him to make these charges to my face!"

"That won't be necessary," said Shiloh. "I'm satisfied they were completely groundless."

"I want to see him anyway. I have that right! I want to get to the bottom of this!"

"There's nothing to be gained by that, only more unpleasantness for you. I'll give the man a talking to myself."

"Please, Captain. Let me see him. I have to face this thing on my own." Hers was not so much a plea as an insistence on her due.

"Of course," said Shiloh. "Whatever you wish."

The captain strode over to the tent flap and called for his orderly. "Will you please have Mr. Cutliffe report to me?" He then pointed to a small kettle sitting on a field stove outside. "And bring bring me two cups of tea. I'll take the tea before you go."

Captain Shiloh carried the cups into the tent and handed one to Willacassa.

"Don't mind the tin. It keeps the tea hot."

Willacassa shook her head, then sipped. "I've drunk out of tin cups before."

"A bit too sweet, isn't it?" observed Shiloh as he returned to his seat.

"I like it that way." Though she was calmer now, Willacassa did not want to lose the hostile edge she was reserving for Cutliffe. It was as if having committed herself to battle, she was keeping her sabre drawn.

Captain Shiloh was not surprised by the depth of feeling aroused by the sutler's charges. He had come to regard Willacassa as a deeply sensitive young woman with strong convictions. But he now saw a new side to her, a tenacity that a mere desire for justice on her part did not adequately explain.

Willacassa had just put her cup down when Cutliffe was shown into the tent. The sutler was in a particularly vexatious mood.

"This is my busiest hour, Captain. Couldn't you have made it another time? I stand to lose a great deal of money."

"You may lose a great deal more," suggested Shiloh. "Please tell Miss Harrah what you told me the other day."

"I thought that was told in confidence, Captain," said Cutliffe, not once turning his T-bone face to look at Willacassa.

"No such promise was ever made."

"Well, that was my understanding. Otherwise I'd never mention it."

"It was your patriotic duty to confide in me, wasn't that the way you put it?" said Shiloh.

The sutler shifted uneasily and asked permission to sit down. "Help yourself," said Shiloh, indicating a camp chair.

After he had squeezed into the chair, Cutliffe turned toward Willacassa. "It's not that I've got anything personal against you," he said. "I'm not even angry about your interference in my business. Though why you insist on butting in where you have no call, I don't know. But I heard stories about you and I thought it best to bring them to the attention of Captain Shiloh. If the stories are true, it makes no sense giving you the run of the place."

"What stories?" asked Willacassa, her face taut with anger.

"Stories about the pictures you draw, for one."

"My sketches?"

"Pretty good likenesses, I'd say. Could be of use to the enemy—this being a military camp and all."

"There are sketch artists and sketches in every camp in the army," interjected Captain Shiloh. "I can't see of what use they could possibly be to the enemy. But this wasn't what you charged the other day. Let's get back to Mrs. Greenhow."

"Oh, that lady. Well, the newspapers were full of stories about her aidin' the enemy. Linked her with the Knights of the Golden Circle and other groups sympathizin' with the South. They said she lived on 16th Street in Washington. Then the other week, in the bag of mail dumped in my hut, I saw this letter from 16th Street—"

"Mr. Cutliffe, Miss Harrah's mail should never have gotten into your hands!" Captain Shiloh fired this broadside with such suddenness that even Willacassa was startled. But she managed outwardly to calm herself even as she grew angrier.

"Yes, I did live on 16th Street," she admitted quietly. "And I still correspond with a girl I know there. But I never knew Mrs. Greenhow personally."

"I find that hard to believe," muttered Cutliffe.

"I don't care what you believe! Are you suggesting that everyone on 16th Street is a Southern spy? If that is the case, Mr. Lincoln had better close the street down and place a quarantine on every house."

"Just seemed more than a coincidence," remarked Cutliffe. "That's all." He was now anxious to get back to his tent.

"Then you have no direct knowledge that Miss Harrah is implicated in any way?" asked Shiloh.

"Direct knowledge? I never said I had any, Captain."

"That's not the way it sounded at the time."

The sutler surrendered his chair. "Got to go," he said. "With your permission I'll head back to the tent. Been missed too long already."

"You may be missed longer than you think," advised Shiloh.

"What do you mean?"

"For one thing, you'll no longer do business with my company."

"You have no authority to say that."

"Maybe not. But if I see you anywhere near my men, I'll dump your wares on the ground and have them confiscated."

"I'm appointed by the regimental commander," countered Cutliffe, not too troubled by Shiloh's threat. "Only the regimental commander can suspend my license."

"Then I'll write to the regimental commander—just to make it official. But what I said still stands. Good day, Mr. Cutliffe."

When he was gone, Captain Shiloh came round to where Willacassa was sitting.

"I'm afraid I was remiss," he said. "I should have checked Cutliffe's story out before calling you in. It's just that—"

"You wanted me to have an opportunity to deny it—before you went any further?"

"Something like that." Captain Shiloh removed his cap. "It's clear now that Cutliffe wanted to get back at you for blowing the whistle on his illicit activities. In fact, he wanted you out of the way. And so he branded you a spy. And I was stupid enough to fall into his trap."

Willacassa was not totally forgiving, but she managed a smile. "You weren't stupid, Captain. Just prudent. In your place, I may have done the same thing. May I go now?"

"Of course."

He cleared the tent flap for her, though he really wanted more time to explain himself. Without any further exchange, Willacassa passed in front of him and stepped outside.

The humiliation Willacassa suffered in Captain Shiloh's tent did not immediately take its toll of her. She returned to her room outside the camp with little more than indignation gnawing inside. If anything, the incident increased her desire for food—she had skipped lunch—and she prepared an omelette for herself in the farmer's kitchen. But after she had eaten her little meal at the sturdy oak table and heated herself a cup of coffee on the black stove, she found that she had fallen into a deep depression.

That Cutliffe had accused her—of all things—of being a spy did not really bother her. She dismissed the man as a troublemaker, the more so because she had made trouble for him. And, on the face of it, the charge he had levelled was too ludicrous to get upset about.

What troubled her, she suspected, was Captain Shiloh's response to the charge. Yet Captain Shiloh had every reason to be suspicious. The map incident involving Port Royal, which she could not dismiss too lightly even though Captain Shiloh had made light of it all along, and her trip to the Sea Islands "to see friends" had enough substance about them to raise eyebrows if not suspicions. Captain Shiloh had no way of knowing that her interest in Port Royal was innocent enough, innocent of the war, that is, if not innocent romantically. But no suspicions had been aroused. Still, he had dutifully conducted an investigation of the sutler's outrageous charges. That he should have doubted her for an instant, to satisfy either his obligation as a Union officer or some other fancied patriotic or high-minded purpose upset her deeply. It shattered her feeling of absolute trust in the man, a feeling she could not deny she had developed.

Willacassa realized that such a lofty opinion of Captain Shiloh, his judgment and his character, made it extremely difficult to deal with the man in an ordinary way. Every little thing, every human foible would now be called into play. It would be virtually impossible for Captain Shiloh to perform his duties and obligations and still enjoy her confidence. But without absolute trust in the man Willacassa could not function. And this discovery unnerved her almost as much as her disappointment in his behavior.

But what depressed Willacassa even more was that the incident had caused a rift between them, a break in their developing friendship. This friendship had quietly deepened with each encounter, even though there was no sign from Captain Shiloh that this was so. And now that it was in peril, Willacassa recognized that its importance to her took precedence over any friendship she had known. Oh, she had held good friends in the past—Eliot Irons, Reverend Moses Williamson, Joseph Leach, Harriet Tubman, Harriet and Henry Sawyer, though the last was a light-hearted friendship. But none had dug so deeply the vein of admiration that Captain Shiloh had struck. It was in its way a startling phenomenon how easily, almost unobstrusively the Union officer had gained entry into the inner sanctum of her heart chamber, igniting a steady, even flame of special feeling and regard.

But now the rift. And she recognized, to her sorrow, that because of the way it came about she could not heal it. However unwittingly, the captain had brought the issue to a head. It remained for the captain to repair the damage done. And Willacassa had her doubts Sam Shiloh could do this. For one thing, her presence in camp had been a continuing problem for him. It was at great criticism from his fellow officers that she, a woman, was allowed free access in the camp though male artists roamed at will. For another, Captain Shiloh was responsible for the security of his men. It seemed the wiser course for him to end all contact with her, innocent of Cutliffe's charges or not.

And so for the next few days Willacassa worked as far from Shiloh's tent as possible. At the end of each day, instead of dropping by to show the captain her work or to chat with him, she left camp without so much as a glance backward.

"You don't like me anymore," she heard him say one day. Shiloh was standing just behind her in the small frame bank the government had set up a few miles from camp.

"I didn't expect to see you here." And in fact she was so surprised to find him standing in a place other than at camp that she did not know quite how to hide her fluster.

"We were paid yesterday," said Shiloh. "But with money being snatched out of our tents lately, I've been depositing what spare cash I can."

"Who is snatching it?"

"Some of our own recruits, I'm ashamed to say."

"Your own?"

He nodded. "The sad truth is a few of our boys enlist for the bounties. Then they jump with whatever else they've squirreled away in their rucksacks. We're none the wiser for the experience. But they're a lot richer."

Captain Shiloh watched Willacassa step closer to the teller's window. "You still haven't answered my question," he said. "What I meant to say is, I haven't seen you lately."

"Maybe now that I've done with my sketches I'll jump camp too. Can't chance having them impounded."

"Then you admit you've been avoiding me?"

"I admit nothing of the kind."

"You're still angry about the Cutliffe incident?"

"Shouldn't I be?"

"I suppose so. But it couldn't be helped. I had to check the charges out, no matter how ridiculous they seemed."

"And you did."

"But obviously not to your satisfaction."

Willacassa did not answer Captain Shiloh, ostensibly because she had reached the window.

"Can you cash this draft for me?" she asked the man behind the copper bars.

"Do you have an account here?" The teller was a tall angular man with a green visor.

"No," she replied.

"Then I'm afraid I cannot."

"But I have an account," interjected Captain Shiloh. "The lady's with me." He did not once look at Willacassa.

"Then there should be no problem. May I see your account number, Sir?"

Captain Shiloh slipped his bankbook under the window guard, enabling the teller to note the account number. Then the teller doled out the money to Willacassa.

"That was very kind of you, Captain," said Willacassa when Shiloh finally turned to look at her.

"It was the least I could do," replied Shiloh. "I know I can never make amends. But a down payment is still in order."

Willacassa smiled in spite of herself.

"A down payment, is that what you call it?"

"Until I can think of something better." He tipped his cap and let her pass.

About a mile outside of camp, sheltered by a grove of pines but very close to the road, another encampment had sprung up. The traffic in and around the encampment was as thick and bustling as the crowds that pressed the sutlers' tents when they opened for business. The encampment had no permanent structures as such, only tents, wagons, outhouses, and a dance floor covered with a canopy. And this was as it should be, for the encampment was meant for a transient population, so transient that one's stay was measured by the half or quarter hour.

The men, mostly young, that frequented this encampment were Union soldiers. Though they usually arrived in regulation dress, allowing for differences in regimental uniform, they invariably left in a state of dishevelment or half undress.

Willacassa came upon the encampment quite by accident. Her horse coming unshoed, she asked if there was someone about who could help her.

"Not right now, Miss. But if you're riding into the military camp, one of the wagons going back may make some room for you."

The man who said this wore civilian clothes. From the way he smoked his cigar, Willacassa guessed he was not without authority in the area.

"Thank you. But what about my horse?"

"It can tag along."

He seemed anxious to turn Willacassa's attention from the tents. For as soon as one man emerged from one, another eagerly moved in to take his place. But Willacassa looked past the cigar smoker. And only when she saw the heavily rouged face of a girl poke her head outside a flap, wearing nothing more across her chest than an open blouse, did she realize where she was.

"I think you'd best wait here," said the man in civilian clothes, pointing to where the horses were tied. "I'll find someone to help you in short order."

"Never mind," said Willacassa. "I'll walk back to camp. And I'll take my horse with me."

Back on the road again Willacassa shook her head. All those fine young men who had paraded down Pennsylvania Avenue in '61, had they been sent off to war or to whore? In their spanking new uniforms, in the bloom of innocence, did they have any notion, did they have any idea harlots would be camped not a mile from their quarters?

Who was responsible for this curious juxtaposition of things? And why was it permitted? Or was Willacassa hopelessly naive? Was the camp follower part and party of military life, something everyone knew about but discreetly kept quiet?

Willacassa confronted Captain Shiloh with her discovery. Now that the Cutliffe incident was behind them, she felt she could speak freely again. "We're not just talking about filthy pictures this time. Don't tell me you didn't know about it," she chided him. "That would be difficult to believe. The place is only a mile from camp."

The captain responded quietly. "I knew about it."

"But you have no authority to take any action."

Shiloh dismissed the taunt. "I'm a brigade captain. Not the commander. Besides, I haven't been inside the place. I've only heard about it."

"I want to do some sketches there," announced Willacassa.

"Sketches! What for?"

"With all the pictures of camp life being printed in the magazines, the reader might get a distorted view of things. Apparently our soldiers are doing more than just writing letters home."

"They're fighting—and dying."

"And whoring."

"You don't mince words, do you?"

"Why should I? That's the plain fact, isn't it?"

"I don't know. I have your word for it."

"Do I have your permission?" asked Willacassa again.

"To do what?"

"To sketch the place. I'm only asking because it involves the military. I don't want to be accused of spying again."

142

"I can't let you go."

"Why not?"

"Because it's not a fit place for a lady."

"Then accompany me there." She hesitated when she saw the expression on the captain's face. "I don't mean openly. I'd like to catch them unawares."

"I can't do that."

"Then I'll go myself."

"All right, Miss Harrah. I'll accompany you there—if only to see why you're so interested in the place. Armies have always had their camp followers. It's nothing new. It's as old as the Romans, probably older."

"Where there are men, women will follow, is that it?"

"Where there's money to be made, women will follow."

"And what about the men that arrange these things?" asked Willacassa angrily. "Men that make money off the women?"

Captain Shiloh backed off. "I guess your point's well taken. Can you meet me later? I won't be free until five."

"Here?"

"No, just outside the camp, where the old tavern used to be. The one that's all boarded up."

They met at the agreed-upon time and place, and left the boarded-up old tavern for the notorious encampment. Neither of them had much to say. Willacassa was already regretting she had asked Captain Shiloh along, for she could see he was a most reluctant companion. Shiloh obviously had second thoughts and wanted to put the expedition behind him.

At the approach to the road leading to the encampment, Shiloh directed his mount into the woods and Willacassa's horse followed. After a while at the sound of strident voices Shiloh dismounted and tied his horse to a tree. Willacassa did the same, then followed as the captain made his way closer to the encampment, brushing the boughs of pine trees to a side in order to do this.

They found themselves at the top of a sloping escarpment and lay on the ground so as not to be seen. But apparently they had arrived in time to witness a change in shifts. A long open wagon with a fringed canopy and rows of seats had just pulled in. And as a score of ladies in loose blouses and ruffled skirts jumped off, looking freshly painted and primed, a dozen weary females in various stages of disarray climbed aboard. A standby crowd of men in blue uniforms lustily cheered the coming and going.

No sooner did the fresh crew of girls disembark than they gathered on a wooden platform to show off their wares. First they walked slowly in a circle, nodding to their admirers and acknowledging their plaudits. Then at a signal by one of their overseers they removed or pulled apart their blouses and paraded bare-breasted before the young recruits whose shrill whistles shattered the peaceful dusk. To both Willacassa and Shiloh they looked like pale African women at a Southern slave market.

But that was as far as the comparison went. As soon as the women had seized the attention of their audience, individual prostitutes with hands, legs, and buttocks made lewd gestures or swung their breasts from side to side. Then in what sounded like billingsgate they tried to entice prospective customers into their respective tents.

These tents measured little more than the length of a bed, and provided for no more than a quick roll before the young patrons were thrust out the back end of the tent, some with no time to put on their trousers or recover their billfolds. In contrast, a totally naked women emerged from one tent, chased by a half-naked recruit with a pistol in his hand. The prostitute screamed for help while the soldier shouted a volley of obscenities at her. And it wasn't until the soldier was restrained by two burly men in bowler hats that the peace of the place was restored.

All this was observed by Willacassa and Shiloh with strained silence. Willacassa furiously fashioned her quick sketches, flipping the pages in her sketchpad. Shiloh meanwhile rested on his elbows wondering why he ever allowed Willacassa to witness such goings-on.

"Are you finished?" he asked at last. "I think we've seen enough."

"Just one moment." She put the finishing touches to a drawing, then got up and dusted herself off.

"Not a pretty sight, is it?" remarked Shiloh.

"No, it isn't." She started back to the horses. "What I can't understand is why women subject themselves to that kind of thing."

"Women? They're not your usual run of women. They're either mental deficients or the sweepings of city streets. Probably lured into the business before they were thirteen."

"Mental deficients? I never thought of it that way."

"Mental deficients or emotional deficients. It's all the same thing."

Mounting his horse, Shiloh said no more about the matter and returned with Willacassa to "Camp Hoosier."

When Willacassa received a letter from *Harper's Magazine* addressed as usual to "W. Harrah," she quickly tore it open. Short of funds, she had been hoping for a bank draft that would enable her to buy some new clothes. As she read the letter her hopes were firmly dashed.

"Dear Mr. Harrah,

You cannot possibly believe that *Harper's* would use your latest packet of drawings. Not since Hogarth's *Rake's Progress* have I seen such a scalding indictment of the pleasures of the moment.

Even in peacetime *Harper's*, a family magazine, would not publish such pictures, however accurate they pretend to be. At a time when our nation is in the throes of a civil war, what some of our young soldiers are purported to be doing during the lull between battles can in no way do justice to the sacrifices they are making and can only cast doubts on the noble mission of the Army of the Potomac.

Heretofore, your illustrations of life in the army gained much favor here. We are still willing to consider more of the same. We trust that what we received the other day was a momentary aberration that will not be repeated.

Until we receive instructions from you as to what to do with 'Betty Yank's Contribution to the War,' we shall hold the drawings here where, I must confess, they have provided some titillation and amusement for the younger members of our staff.

Sincerely,
H. Clough"

When she had come to the end of the letter, Willacassa grew so angry she could shout obscenities. Of all the hypocritical nonsense! If *Harper's* wanted to hide its head in the sand, more's the pity. Why, at the very beginning of the war, at a hospital in Washington, she heard that one out of every twelve soldiers had evidence of venereal disease! She suspected it was no different with the Rebels. Even the Richmond newspapers complained that decent people couldn't walk the sidewalks because soldiers and their trollops had overrun the place. And there had been several scandalous reports—a few definitely confirmed—of women who had disguised themselves as men in order to gain entry into the camps without having to share their earnings with madams or pimps.

In fact, it was no less a Jerseyman than Colonel Judson Kilpatrick, a self-assured little gamecock with blonde sideburns, who camped a special "girlfriend" in a regulation tent next to his own so as to save himself the trouble of having to bed her down at her place of business.

Yet *Harper's* could pretend that makeshift brothels and camp followers didn't exist. Or, if they did exist, pretend that the magazine's readers showed no interest in the tawdry aspects of military life.

After she had managed to stifle her rage, Willacassa shared the letter with Captain Shiloh.

The captain was not at all surprised by the magazine's reaction. But he could read the anger in Willacassa's eyes. "What are you going to do now?"

"I'm tempted to have nothing more to do with them. I'm tempted to write them that W. Harrah is not a man as they have assumed. And that as a woman I resent the suggestion that what would shock their readers titillates their staff."

She slumped into a camp chair and crumpled the letter.

"What prevents me from doing so is that I need this job. And I don't think *Frank Leslie's Magazine* would see my sketches any differently."

"That makes good sense."

"Oh, I'm ever so reasonable," snapped Willacassa. "But what do I do with my rage?"

"You take it out on some oysters the new sutler wheeled into camp. I've been hiding a bucket of them under the table. They're nicely iced, too. I was just about to start eating them when you walked in."

What Shiloh said quickly cooled Willacassa down. And the idea of their sitting together and eating oysters when she had more pressing matters in mind caused Willacassa to laugh, then giggle.

"Well, if you won't eat them, Zeb Yount will. And he doesn't half like them."

"All right," agreed Willacassa when she had recovered her composure. "But next time I'm angry, let me enjoy it."

"There may not be a next time," said Shiloh. "At least for a while. The regiment's moving out. I'm not at liberty to tell you where. But you'll know soon enough."

So that's what the oysters were all about. A kind of last decent supper. Willacassa covered Shiloh's hand with her own. "Be careful, Captain." She could say no more.

UP AGAINST A WALL

The day dawned pale and blustery. Strong winds blew snow across the tents and blanketed the fields. And as the damp cold numbed his fingers Captain Shiloh knew that he was just one more actor in yet another colossal blunder by the Army of the Potomac.

First there were weeks of delay waiting for pontoons to cross the Rappahannock, a delay that enabled Lee to strengthen his positions. Next the Federals launched a heavy artillery bombardment that tore up the streets and houses of Fredericksburg but did not dislodge the Rebel sharpshooters. (It took a group of volunteers, who were ferried across the river, to engage in bitter house-to-house combat before the sharpshooters withdrew.) Then General Burnside forced a crossing of the Rappahannock so that the Federals stood with their backs to the river and their eyes fixed on a wall of fortified heights beyond.

Now with the fog lifting, thousands of blue-jackets with parade-ground precision marched out across the open plain, bugles blaring, drums rolling, and horse-drawn artillery rattling at the side. It was a magnificent sight, Shiloh imagined—at least for the enemy on the heights. Regimental flags whipping in the breeze. Officers' horses prancing up and down the line. Rifles and bayonets gleaming in the pale winter sun. Shiloh gritted his teeth. Didn't the Federals ever learn? What passed for a parade, splendid in its beauty, was an engraved invitation to wholesale slaughter.

Within minutes the slaughter came. Wave upon wave of Union troops advanced against the fortified wall at the base of the hill. And as they advanced, Rebel guns pounded from the heights. Smoke seared the air. Shells ripped huge holes in the Federal lines. Cannon exploded before they could be fired. Limbers and horses were blown skyward. Still, masses of men rushed forward. And as Rebel guns poured volley after volley, hundreds of the charging troops toppled headlong. To Shiloh, the batteries at the top of the heights stood a screeching Lorelei. And at the wall below lay a river of bloody, broken bodies.

The decimated Union brigades were forced to regroup. Battered companies of men were quickly pieced together. Again and again they charged the stone wall. Into blistering fusillades they hurled themselves. But each time their charge fell short. Each time they gave way before shell bursts and withering gunfire. Forced to retreat they left a trail of corpses in their wake.

A colonel galloped forward to order still another charge. But this time, his eyes burning with smoke and rage, Captain Shiloh refused.

"We've been crippled by losses, Sir. You can't ask these men to try it again! Not these men!"

The Colonel sped away. In his place a scarlet-faced man appeared. The general had trouble getting his foot out of the stirrup. Shiloh attributed his difficulty to a hidden wound.

"What's going on here, Captain?"

"My men have been cut to pieces, Sir. They can't put together another charge." He pointed to the remnants of three companies sprawled on the ground, leaning on their rifles.

"They'll have to move out."

"To what? That damn wall!"

"Those heights must be taken."

"No one's going to take those heights! Not now, not ever."

"This is no time for debate, Captain."

"It's no debate, Sir. And it's no battle. It's mindless slaughter!"

"Soldiers are expected to die when the time comes."

"Soldiers? Human sacrifices, you mean!"

The general pulled a pistol on Shiloh and waved it in the air. "I'm fast running out of patience, Captain. Get your men the hell out of here or be shot for mutiny!"

Though he saw the general's arm waver, Shiloh had no doubt he'd carry out the threat. Out of sheer frustration, if nothing else. Yet the danger to his life had a calming effect. Shiloh now spoke in measured words as though before an appeals court, but the passion was still there.

"Sir, you've had five assaults on that wall already. I can't count the number of casualties—from the 25th alone. And you want us to hit that wall again?"

"You've heard the order, Captain."

"There's no way in hell we can take that wall! Before we ever reach it, we'll be mowed down. It was bad enough when we had an open field. But we'll be climbing over our own dead bodies if we go that route again."

"I'm not here to argue with you, Captain. I want you to move your men out! That's what the order calls for."

"Whose order?"

"General Burnside's."

"I want to see it." Shiloh thought there was only a slim chance he'd be indulged. But the general pulled out a folded piece of paper.

Shiloh read quickly. "There's no order here to take the wall. The wording is deliberately ambiguous."

"I see no am—ambiguity."

"With a view to taking the enemy position, it says. What

position?''

"The stone wall. It's perfectly clear to me.'' The general reeled for a moment and Shiloh wondered what was troubling the man. And then it dawned on the captain that his superior officer had been drinking. The flush on his neck and cheeks was the flush of whiskey, not the flush of argument.

"In short, you don't know what the order is,'' said Shiloh, turning away in disgust. "You don't have the foggiest notion.''

"Where are you going, Captain!''

"Back to my company.''

"And you'll proceed with the attack?''

"I will not!''

"Captain Shiloh! Any man—any man who refuses to take part in the attack will be shot! I'll have no cowards in this regiment.''

Shiloh wheeled around. "Cowards? Why, damn it, these are the bravest men I know! And for serving blindly under the likes of you—the stupidest. All right, we'll attack the wall again. We'll be good little soldiers. But if we come out of it and you were wrong, I'll have your hide on the end of a bayonet.''

"Captain!''

"I mean that, General. So, go ahead. Drink the rest of your whiskey now. Because Lord pity you if you were too drunk to know what you were doing!''

As the general grabbed at his sleeve, Shiloh pulled back and wrenched away.

"Remember! You'll have the dead to answer for! No matter how badly shot up I am, I'll come looking for you when it's all over.''

She found him among the wounded. A bandage was wrapped around his head, and an angry gash, stained purple, scored his left leg.

"How bad is it?'' asked Willacassa, pointing to the leg.

"Not as bad as it looks,'' said a disgusted Shiloh. "Someone poured iodine on it and I jumped out of my skin. But the bullet only grazed the bone.''

"And the head?''

"Just a flesh wound.''

He tried to sit up but only half succeeded, dizziness overtaking him. "Get me out of here, Willacassa. Get hold of Zeb and help me to my tent. They need these beds for the others. I'm not seriously wounded. These others are. I'm only in the way.''

Willacassa did not argue with him. She knew better. And when she found Zeb among the packing cases, digging out small vials and bottles of medicine, she communicated the captain's wish.

In his tent Shiloh lay on his cot as Zeb prepared to bandage his leg. Then as an afterthought Zeb produced the jar of yellow salve he had brought with him.

"Surgeon said this'll help heal the wound. Want me to put it on?"

"I'll do it," volunteered Willacassa.

She washed her hands in a basin of water, then gently applied the salve to the wound.

"Does it hurt?" she asked, not without a sense of pleasure at being close to him.

"No," said Shiloh. "It has a cooling effect."

"Good. I'll wrap the wound loosely to give it a chance to heal." She glanced up at him. "If you're thinking of wearing your boot on top of this, forget the idea. The wound needs time to form a scab."

"My boot's been cut to pieces," said Shiloh. "But I'll be up and about as soon as I get a new one. Zeb, see if you can come up with another pair at the quartermaster's shed. Size 12. And stop at headquarters. I'm expecting a reply to my message."

"Why are you so determined to push yourself?" Willacassa asked when Zeb Yount was gone. "You need some rest."

"I've brought charges against one of my superior officers. I want to be on hand to substantiate them."

"Charges?"

"Never mind. It's a military matter." Feeling faint for a moment, he lay back on his cot. "It was awful, Willacassa. All those kids and fine young men butchered, just butchered. I'll never forget it. And I'll never forgive them."

He closed his eyes and slept for a time, so Willacassa had to be content with speculating on whom "them" might be.

Later as he slept and as she watched Shiloh, Willacassa became acutely aware that a transformation had taken place. She had crossed an emotional river. It was more than Shiloh lying wounded (though apparently he was now in no great physical danger). It was rather the realization that her fate was inextricably tied to his. No longer did she stand on the opposite shore, on the opposite side of where her feelings ran. She was now caught in the mainstream of his life and if anything happened to the man she could not simply drift away. The fact was, he had come to mean too much to her, too much to pretend that he counted no more than a chance acquaintance or associate. Suddenly he was everything: friend, supporter, mentor, the only man she could bring herself to love again. And far from being frightened by the thought, she found comfort in it. It did not matter there were obstacles, perhaps insurmountable obstacles—his wife, the children, the war. She loved him, and she felt good loving him. Whatever had counted against such feelings in the past counted for nothing now.

Shiloh opened his eyes and as he met Willacassa's fervent gaze he somehow understood what she was thinking. He knew too that he had to make an instant decision. To ignore the reality of her presence or to give way before the onslaught of his feelings. He held his hand out for balance while he raised himself up. And Willacassa, thinking it an invitation to love, instantly seized it.

"Oh, Sam!" she said, covering his hand with kisses.

Shiloh saw the mistake. He saw its impact too. But he did nothing to discourage it. Instead he cradled her head and drew Willacassa towards him. "I was a fool to think I could see you and talk to you and not fall in love with you. It was bound to happen sooner or later."

"You're not sorry, Sam. Are you?"

"No. But—But this is quite a fix for you."

"That's not true! All I want is to be with you. When I'm near you I feel alive and trusting and wise. I've never felt quite that way before. When you're away, I feel empty, wasted. I can't wait for time to pass."

Shiloh lay back and as Willacassa rested her head on his chest he stroked her hair.

"I feel we've known each other all along," he said. "I don't understand why I feel that way, but I do. Even that first day when you stood in the path of those falling trees, I felt I knew you."

"It was the same way with me. Not at first. Much later. But the feeling was definitely there. And now it's as though my life has begun all over again. You have the same kindness, the same quiet strength of my father."

Shiloh smiled. "But you're father would never approve of this."

"Well, we can't let that trouble us, can we?" She lifted her head to see his reaction. But all she caught was a sad, thoughtful, almost fatalistic expression of the eyes.

When Zeb returned with a new pair of boots, Willacassa retired to the farthermost corner of the tent where she pretended to secure a flap from the icy wind. Zeb set the boots down, then, pulling a dispatch from his pocket, handed it to Shiloh.

Shiloh ran his eyes across the contents, then let the dispatch drop slowly to the ground.

"Anything wrong, Captain?"

"Everything, Zeb."

"Anything I can do?"

"Yes, pack my things. As soon as Captain Farnsworth arrives—"

"Captain Farnsworth?"

"That's right. It's 'Captain' now. I'm moving out again."

"But that's not fair!"

"Fair or not, those are my orders."

"Can I go too this time? I'd like to accompany you, Captain."

"I don't know. With all the influence I've got, I doubt I could arrange it."

Willacassa did not at first gauge the full import of what Shiloh was saying. But when she saw the look of bitterness and dejection that consumed his face, her stomach began to churn and she expected the worst.

"What's wrong?" she asked when Zeb Yount had stepped out again. Drawing near, she regretted what Shiloh was going to say before he said it.

"My charges were dismissed out of hand. 'The general carried out his orders without hesitation,'" he mimicked. "And I would do well to do the same. It was unfortunate that the 25th took such heavy losses. But other regiments suffered as badly, and there were no complaints. It would be best for all concerned if I were transferred West for a time. 'Captain' Farnsworth would temporarily be assigned to my command."

Shiloh paused for a moment and looked sharply at Willacassa. "Translated, it means they want me out of the way. And there's a veiled threat that if I want to play lawyer they will bring charges against me."

He set his feet on the ground and slowly, painfully, began pulling the new boots on.

"The worst of it, the terrible part is, he'll get off scot-free. Drunk as a sot, our general will in no way pay for what happened."

"I'll go with you, of course," whispered Willacassa, touching the captain's arm.

Shiloh did not immediately respond.

"There's no way I'll remain here," pursued Willacassa, alarmed by his silence.

"I'd best go alone."

"But why? We've only just—"

"Discovered each other? I know. But seeing you here—in the natural course of things—is one thing. Having you disrupt your life, for all intents and purposes—"

"I don't care what people think."

"But I care. I don't want people saying anything to hurt you.

I'd hate myself if that happened."

"Then—"

"Then what about us?"

She reluctantly nodded.

"Nothing can change what has happened. We'll simply have to wait, that's all. They can't keep me out there indefinitely. Meanwhile I'll write and—"

"I don't want letters, Sam! I want you!" Willacassa surprised even herself with her outburst. But she managed to calm herself. "If it's your wife you're concerned about, I've already told you—"

"It's not my wife—though I am concerned about her. It's you. I want you to be sure before—"

"Before I throw my life away? Until now I had no life to throw away. Don't you understand? I sleepwalked. I lay dormant. I didn't know what it meant to feel alive."

Shiloh took her in his arms. "I'm going to say it once, Willacassa. Then I won't mention it again. I love you. Nothing is going to change that. Not time, not this war, nothing! But I won't have you traipsing about the country like some camp follower—"

She started to protest.

"Wait! Let me finish. I'll be back, Willacassa. If you still want me then, I'll be yours. But it will be here in the East. Nowhere else. It'll be on your terrain, not mine. I'll extend myself for you. I'll not have you extending yourself for me. Not in my position. Do you understand?"

She closed her eyes in assent.

"Now go—before I make a fool of myself."

"But your leg?"

"Don't worry about my leg. It feels good, almost as good as new."

She fell into another embrace, then pulled herself away.

"Where can I reach you?" he asked as she stood at the tent opening.

"At my Sixteenth Street address. At least until June. I may spend the summer on Cape Island."

"Wish I could be there with you," said Shiloh.

"So do I, my love." She threw him a kiss, then left while she was still in control of her emotions.

BRANDY STATION

His horse's reins wrapped around his fist, Henry Sawyer awoke with the taste of battle in his mouth. He fumbled for his cap. It was still in the pitch of night, a heavy haze all but obscuring the moon and putting out the stars. General Gregg's Division lay quiet and unseen, having bivouacked without fires or the clank of cooking utensils.

The day before, a scout had made his report on Rebel movements. On June 5, somewhere between Culpeper and Rappahannock, not too far from Brandy Station, Jeb Stuart had put on a review for the ladies. Dashing Jeb, always good for a show, had marched his troops in a cavalcade of splendor, his horsemen surging back and forth with glistening sabres. What pomp! What glory! Spectators in open carriages, on verandahs of nearby houses, even on a halted railroad car cheered and applauded. After the spectacular display, Stuart was bedecked with flowers. And his lady friends arranged a ball for him to celebrate the occasion, with all the commanders and officers in attendance. Then on June 8 Stuart paraded his men again, this time for Lee and Longstreet and the other Confederate bigwigs. This latest review was not so much a demonstration of dash and panoply as a mammoth show of military strength. Horsedrawn cannon, caissons, and wagons trailed the troops. Guns were poised and sabres flashed. By evening the ladies had gone their respective ways and the men were in bivouac, storing in equipment, preparing to move out.

Henry Sawyer knew that the report spelled battle. If rumors were correct, it would be a large operation with all of Pleasonton's men called into play. And large operations inevitably meant heavy casualties. There was one consolation, however; the heavier the casualties on the Rebel side, the sooner the war would be over. Just what General Pleasonton would do with this news, Sawyer did not know. But he suspected that a surprise was being planned. Surprise, after all, was the mainspring of battle.

And if surprise came at the expense of Jeb Stuart, all the better. Henry Sawyer, like the rest of the First New Jersey Cavalry, had his belly full of unfavorable comparisons. Maybe he didn't have Day and Martin polish on his boots. Maybe his uniform was worn at the seat and threadbare at the sleeves. Maybe he wasn't the showman Jeb Stuart was. But every fighting muscle in his body was stretched for action. After all, Henry Sawyer was Captain Sawyer now, having been promoted in October. In command of Company K, he had none of the hesitancy that marked the new recruit or the unseasoned horse soldier. From Culpeper Courthouse to Aldie Gap to Fredericksburg, he had been in skirmish after skirmish, at least once being seriously wounded. And he had no doubt that the First New Jersey Cavalry could hold its own with any of Jeb Stuart's highly touted popinjays. Given a chance, couldn't Jersey sabres cut as deeply as Virginian? Couldn't their pistols shoot as deadly accurate? Not in vain did Henry patronize the shooting galleries of Cape Island these past ten years. Experience would tell. So long as his horse stayed under him, he would make the day a memorable one for the Union.

After swallowing some cold tea, Sawyer met briefly in General Pleasonton's tent with a few other company and brigade commanders. Most of the big boys were there. General David Gregg, with the piercing eyes and patrician beard; the flamboyant Colonel Percy Wyndham, soldier of fortune and son of a British peer; the Frenchman, Colonel Duffie and that other foreigner, Colonel Cesnola; Colonel J. Irvin Gregg; and Colonel Judson Kilpatrick—"Kill-cavalry" his men called him—with his scrawny sidewhiskers, his long nose, and sharp tongue.

Brigadier General Alfred Pleasonton's eyes were deep-set and sad but brooked no nonsense. His instructions were brief but cogent.

"We'll move out just before dawn. Should be fog then, and this will give us excellent cover. The enemy is placed as follows. Stuart himself is camped on Fleetwood Hill, his headquarters. They say he actually sleeps in a bed. Fitz Lee's brigade is north of the Hazel River, near Oak Shade Church. 'Rooney' Lee's brigade at Welford's Station. General Jones is bivouacked along the road to Brandy Station. He's stationed pickets about a mile and a half above the railroad bridge crossing the Rappahannock."

General Pleasonton paused just long enough to point out that in front of Jones's brigade four batteries of horse artillery were carelessly exposed, and this would be one of their targets.

"There are also pickets—Robertson's men, I believe—at Kelly's Ford." Pleasonton tapped his sabre on the map sprawled out on the camp table. "And in a five mile spread between the Barbour Farm and Stevensburg at least two brigades are deployed. Robertson's and Wade Hampton's."

He issued envelopes to his company commanders. "These are your orders. I put them in writing so there would be no misunderstanding."

"My readin' ain't all that good," feigned Sawyer. His little remark and the laughter that followed relieved the tension that the meeting had created.

At very early dawn General Pleasonton brought up three cavalry divisions with infantry supports, some ten thousand men, to the edge of the Rappahannock River.

"All right, Gentlemen, we make our move."

Under heavy fog, in two columns, the Union crossed the Rappahannock, the right column at Beverley Ford, north of the Orange and Alexandria Railroad, the other at Kelly's Ford about five-and-a-half miles lower down the stream.

Henry Sawyer's company was attached to the column assembled at Kelly's Ford. His men crossed the Rappahannock without difficulty though there were reports three men and several horses drowned in the swollen river a day or two before. On the other side of the Rappahannock, the Union column was again divided, the smaller force advancing on Culpeper and the larger, under General Gregg, moving in a wide evasive sweep towards Brandy Station.

Sawyer pushed forward among the larger column of men, noticing for the first time that the fog was lifting. Almost at once some of Robertson's pickets were spotted. But General Gregg's men made quick work of them and forged ahead with its two cavalry divisions. At the Willis Madden House, General Gregg, halting briefly, sent Duffie's Second Division, Cesnola's and Irvin Gregg's brigades, off on the left fork to Stevensburg. He took the Third Division, Wyndham's and Kilpatrick's brigades, with him northwest on the road to Brandy Station.

Although all this was prearranged, Sawyer had the distinct feeling that his company, part of Colonel Wyndham's brigade, would soon be in the thick of things. If Buford and Duffie were the pincers, Gregg's division logically would meet Stuart head on.

Pressing forward some five miles, Sawyer's company arrived at Brandy Station in the vanguard of the Third Division. With the flamboyant Colonel Wyndham leading the way, the regiment crossed the tracks of the Orange and Alexandria Railroad.

"What's that?" Sawyer asked of a scout, pointing to the gentle rise that commanded the whole of the region.

"Fleetwood Hill, Sir."

"Fleetwood Hill?" Sawyer checked his map. "That's our prime target."

He had scarcely uttered the words when a battery on the hill opened fire. Colonel Wyndham's arm shot up. The Union column halted and dismounted. Quickly it deployed itself into small parties. Scurrying about, the men brought their horse artillery into action.

"Not much more than a howitzer up here," shouted a liaison

officer. Not so flamboyant now, Colonel Wyndam nodded, then ordered Lieutenant-Colonel Broderick to ready the First Jersey for a charge.

The thirty-five-year-old Broderick, in the prime of health and vigor, responded to the order with an enthusiastic salute. At a signal the First Jersey drew its sabres. Moving splendidly forward in a column of squadrons, the blue horsemen advanced in a steady trot. As they passed over the hard, narrow ground near the railroad, Lieutenant Hobensack led the left squadron of the first battalions down a steep embankment and up a nine-foot rise. The right squadron followed Broderick who was advancing rapidly up the hill towards Stuart's headquarters.

Sawyer spurred his horse on. If there was one thing he loved in battle, it was a charge. There had been charges enough in past encounters to sober his thoughts. Bullets pierced the air, horses stumbled, men fell. But the charge itself was always an exhilarating moment. Sweat pickled the skin, smoke tickled the nostrils, glare dazzled the eyes. Nothing, not even the touch of a woman rivalled the tingle of anticipation, the joy of the thrust forward.

As he leaned across his saddle, Sawyer watched his men and fellow officers strive upward. Gaining momentum, they swept the ground beneath them. Their hard-galloping horses leaped ravines without breaking stride. Even a random volley from the enemy's guns did not slow the charge down.

Sawyer clutched his sabre. He could now see the enemy up close. With a piercing cheer, Broderick's men broke into the ranks of the Rebels. Then Sawyer's company leaped over the guns. Piecemeal they struck down the defenders. In a matter of minutes they destroyed the brigade in front of them. The surviving gray-jackets ran down the opposite slope of the hill in utter confusion.

But where was Stuart? His headquarters were now in Union hands. And his regiments were scattered in flight, wildly chased in all directions—a sight to gladden a horsesoldier's heart. Yet the cavalry leader was nowhere to be seen. And where was Stuart's bed? A search among the tents ensued. But no time to look further, no time to gloat. Over the crest of a hill Sawyer saw units of a Virginia regiment racing towards them. How well they rode! How fast they covered ground! And in the best cavalry tradition they were performing a classic maneuver. Like a wedge, the Rebels were going to strike, to split them in half. With speed and daring, they made up for a lack of manpower.

Several companies rode to intercept them. K Company peeled off to blunt the Rebel attack, Sawyer firing both his pistols. Then he and his men drew sabres. They braced for impact. Like a wave on a ship's bow, the Virginians' wedge broke apart. The attack smashed, their batterymen and screaming drivers tried to limber up. But their horses panicked, leaving them exposed to capture.

Another Rebel regiment suddenly appeared, a body in full strength, dashing at a mad gallop across the field. No time now for the First Jersey to take prisoners. They met head-on, horses and men and steel. The clamor was tremendous. Riders fired at close range, sabring as they went. Impossible to see the nearest combatant. Once again the Rebels fell back. This time the hill was secured.

Sawyer's company took a small breather. The men emptied canteens and reloaded pistols. One cavalryman pulled out a pipe. But before he could light up, he saw Wade Hampton's graycoats sweeping the field below. Riding in magnificent order, they whirled artillery alongside, their wheels spinning madly. K Company mounted up. With Sawyer in the lead, his men rode to head off the Rebels. Looking the field over, Sawyer saw that more than Wade Hampton's legion was involved. Across the whole breadth of the open plain, troops of cavalry were furiously galloping towards one another. He could not believe how large the number of men! At least a brigade on each side! Waving his sabre, Sawyer dashed forward and met the enemy head-on. The clash of steel and horses split the air. Smoke mixed with gunfire. In hand-to-hand combat, figures thrust, slashed, fired, and tumbled from wounded horses. Bodies lay strewn, trampled underfoot; riderless mounts raced in all directions. Caps, carbines, and sabres dented the grass.

First seizing ground, then grudgingly relinquishing it, then snatching it again, the Union cavalry gave a good account of itself. Three times a New Jersey guidon was lost, and three times doggedly recovered. Sawyer's blood was high. He'd show Jeb Stuart's dandies that Northern cavalry could match them. Not just ride, but outmaneuver them! Across the open ground the battle continued, taking a heavy toll. Still, the Union riders, in squadron order, charged. And Confederate sabres caught silvered snatches of the sun. The glint of steel almost blinded Sawyer. But when he wheeled about and scanned the field he spotted Colonel Broderick. His comrade-in-arms was fighting on foot. How vulnerable he looked without a horse! Yet how savagely he fought! Swinging his sabre, he managed to keep his antagonists at bay.

Sawyer spurred his mount and sped to his rescue. But he let up when James Ward, the bugler, reached Broderick and turned his horse over to him. While the young bugler ran clear, Broderick broke away and headed for the railway station. Turning back,

Sawyer heard the whistle of bullets. He himself took aim. But in the thick smoke of combat his pistol misfired. As the enemy crowded round him, he was forced to slash his way through with his sabre.

How long the seesaw battle went on, Sawyer could not tell. But the First Cavalry had to abandon the ridge of Fleetwood Hill to reinforce troops at the railway station. Sawyer found his other pistol and began his charge. He led his men by the length of four horses. But the soldiers at the station were already giving way before a fresh Virginia regiment. At the station Colonel Broderick looked to the First Maryland for help. When they failed to come, Broderick shouted obscenities at them. Nothing worked. Instead of moving forward, the bastards wavered, then broke. And the First Jersey was left to fend for itself.

The whole field was now covered with small squads of fighting men. Charged front and rear, Broderick was hard pressed. A knot of men was closing in on him. The horse he was riding, Wood's horse, was not strong enough to break through. Forced to fight, Broderick took on his adversaries one by one. He struck the first man so hard he was thrown ten feet from his saddle. But the rider's horse still blocked his path. Swerving to a side, Broderick escaped a second Rebel's blow. The thrust of another was warded off as Broderick struck him across the forehead with his blade. But in the act he lost his sabre. In desperation he pulled a pistol from his boot and fired into the oncoming crowd. Then the young colonel put spurs to his horse and almost broke free. But at the last second his mount stumbled over an animal that had collapsed just in front of him, and Broderick himself fell from a shot.

Sawyer pulled his horse up to help him. There was no thinking by him now, only knee-jerk reaction. You were fired at and you fired back. You were near cut by a sabre and you crossed swords. Any attempt to think hobbled the reflexes. The crowd that had blocked Broderick now turned on him. Two Rebels fired at close range but missed. Before one of them could cock his revolver again, Sawyer charged the man. His sabre caught him in the neck, cutting the jugular. As his blood gushed out in a black stream, the gray rider gave a horrible yell and fell over the side of his horse. The other rider dashed away.

Sawyer took the opportunity to reload his pistols and stuffed them in his holsters. He looked to see if his men—at least what was left of them—were ready for another go at it. His cap was pulled down low over his head. His boots chafed his legs but he welcomed their pinch. He put his hand on the stock of his carbine to reassure himself it was there. Then he thrust forward to where he saw Broderick fall. He followed the railroad tracks and had gone about fifty feet when he was fired upon with a volley. Several men nearby toppled from their mounts. Pressing on, Sawyer reached the spot where Colonel Broderick had fallen. He grimaced as a bullet ripped through his thigh. No great pain, only a sharp sting. He shrugged it off. Then a second bullet struck his right cheek, passing out of his neck. The hurt here was sharp and he winced, but still he kept his saddle. Pointing his sabre, he charged a small battery that was being turned towards him. He was almost upon it when at the crack of a shot closeup his horse sprang into the air and fell forward. Sawyer hit the ground with such force that an enveloping darkness was all he could sense.

When Henry Sawyer recovered consciousness, he found Lieutenant-Colonel Broderick lying nearby. He crawled up to him and rolled him over. The brave lieutenant-colonel was dead. A short distance away he recognized Major Shelmire. He too was dead, lying across the body of a Rebel. In fact, all around him were men of his own company and other Union cavalry. All were killed or wounded. Not a man was left standing.

Unable to move any farther, Sawyer lay on his back at the side of Colonel Broderick. Cannon-puff clouds darkened the sky. For the first time that day he thought of his wife and children. How would they know he was alive? The same clouds, didn't they darken the sky over Cape Island? Surely they could read its message. He was alive, badly wounded but alive. Would they know that? Would they know by looking?

Two Rebel soldiers brought a stretcher. They carried him to a nearby ditch where they washed the blood from his face with water.

"Now at least we can see what you've got. It's a bad one, Yank. Pretty bad. But I think you'll live. I'd call you Captain—Hey, wait a minute, your thigh's bleedin' too. And your neck. It's a mess, I'd say. We're taking you to the rear."

CAPE ISLAND '63

The Emancipation Proclamation had come and gone. It was now six months since it had become official, and as far as Harrah could see it had brought about little or no change. What should have been a moral bombshell had tossed up a few mounds of dirt. Yes, there had been feisty editorials, praising it as the greatest document since the Declaration of Independence or condemning it as the work of the Devil. But any real impact had yet to be felt.

What dismayed Harrah was that it had been so long acomin'. And when it arrived, like a mud-splattered stagecoach, its passengers battered and weary, one could not recognize at the reststop what was proclaimed from what had existed before.

"But it's a first step," argued Joseph Leach. "And first steps are all important."

"Exactly. All the more reason for doing it up properly. This kowtowing to 'loyal' slaveholders has no place in the scheme of things. But that's an old story with cautious, slow-moving, placating Abe."

"I'm sure there were other matters to be considered," volunteered Captain Whilldin, who was Joseph Leach's constant companion these days, outbound steamers being limited more or less to transport service.

"Such as?"

"The border states for one. Kentucky and Missouri would not fight for the Union if slavery were the issue."

"Then why should they fight now?"

"Because," said Leach, "the president went to great pains to differentiate. Only those slaves in rebellious states were to be freed. He said nothing about the border states."

"That's just the point," argued Harrah, becoming just a little heated. "It's only the slaveholders in the Rebel states who are being punished. In states loyal to the Union, slaveholders are being rewarded. No abolition there."

"Come now," eased Whilldin. "One step at a time."

"And just suppose," said Harrah, "that the war had come to an end before January 1, the day emancipation went into effect. What would have happened then?"

"What do you mean?"

"Suppose the South had returned to the fold before January 1—"

"But they didn't," interjected Whilldin.

"But if they had, the South would no longer have to free its slaves. Because it would no longer be in rebellion. Isn't that the height of cynicism?"

"What would you have done?" asked Leach, not without a hint of condescension.

"I'd have freed them all unconditionally. Without compensation for the slaveholders. Lincoln has this obsession with compensation. As though we owe the slaveholders, instead of their owing for two hundred fifty years of bondage."

"You're forgetting one thing," said Leach.

"And what's that?"

"Political reality. It's this Mr. Lincoln has to deal with. Not a moral imperative."

"I disagree," said Harrah. "When a country as backward as the Russian Empire has freed their serfs, all their serfs—not only has freed them but given them land—then it's time to regard the abolition of slavery as a moral imperative."

"But the Russian serf is white, not black," said Whilldin.

"What we're talking about is slavery, not color. The fact is, apart from the United States, the only two countries that still practice slavery are Brazil and Cuba. I don't take pride in that. Do you?"

"Of course not. I'm only trying to understand what the president had in mind."

"I don't know what he had in mind. I know only what he's done. And that's not nearly enough to salve the conscience of a country that's supposed to be free."

Brant was one of those nearby farmers who grew a couple of small crops on a few acres of sandy soil. Harrah did not buy much from him. A few bushels of corn and some tomatoes, little more. Occasionally they exchanged a few words. But this time he could see he had a lot on his mind.

"My son is no soldier. He's deathly afraid of firearms. He could no more kill someone than he could crush a butterfly."

"They'll mark him a coward, you know."

"I'll take that chance. He's strong in other ways. He works his tail off on the farm."

Brant just kept shaking his head in protest.

"It just isn't fair, Mr. Harrah. I don't have the three hundred dollars to buy his way out. If they take him, they should take them all. Not allow the rich to get a substitute to fight for them. They talk about equality like it was peach pie. But they don't tell you that the big boys get the big slices and the rest of us only the crumbs. You're right to question the war. What kind of a war is it when the rich get off scot-free and the poor do the dying?''

''I'm not questioning the war, Mr. Brant. I just want the killing stopped. I don't like it when we're told we're fighting to preserve the Union if all that means preserving slavery too. Why, in Virginia before the war selling slaves was big business, its biggest business—even bigger than agriculture. I hate to think that if Virginia stayed put, remained in the Union, the slave trade would go on as before.''

''But Lincoln wants to free the slaves. Didn't he say so in that Proclamation?''

''Only in the secessionist states. To me, that smacks more of expediency than principle. If he wanted to free the slaves he could do it without prolonging the war. He could set up state governments loyal to the Union for all the secession states, and pass a constitutional amendment. He could declare the Confederate governments null and void. Then your civil war would be confined to the South—between the blacks who'd have something to fight for, their freedom, and the slave owners. The rest of the South—those who can't or don't want to own slaves would stay out of it. If necessary, we could pay them bounties to stay out of it. Just as we pay bounties to drag our boys into the war.''

''It won't work, Mr. Harrah.''

''Why?''

''Because the generals would have nothing to do. Besides, it's easier to fight than to think of ways not to. Thinkin' takes more work than loadin' a gun.''

Brant was right. Thinking took a lot of work. And as he drove home it seemed to Harrah he was thinking a great deal these days. His son Jonathan kept coming to mind. In some ways Harrah felt guilty that other men's sons were fighting, and his son was not. Oh, there was an element of danger in running the blockade, as Jonathan was doing, and even ''neutral'' ships were fair game for coastal sweepers. Some were boarded and others fired upon. But it was not quite the same as shouldering a rifle or standing firm against an enemy charge. Other men might see Jonathan as a ''skulker.'' And after a fashion Harrah himself saw the young man as a shirker, if not a shirker, a crass opportunist.

Yet Harrah did not entirely blame him. He himself saw no merit in the war, indeed saw it as a grotesque mummery, the mummers engaging in a ridiculous, hypocritical, ceremonial performance that left a pile of bodies in its wake and created more problems than it solved. What Harrah regretted was that Jonathan lacked any real conviction for what he did. Harrah could understand a conscientious objector, someone who opposed the war for pacific or religious reasons. He could even appreciate opposition to the war on political or constitutional grounds. After all, there could only be "union" by mutual consent, just as there could be no "confederacy" of master-slave except by mutual consent, a consent, of course, that did not exist. But his son harbored no such noble sentiment. And it was Harrah's recognition of this failing in his offspring that he blamed himself for.

He also blamed himself, as he drew near Trescott House and his thoughts turned to Willacassa, for what he perceived to be a shortcoming in his daughter. Willacassa had arrived at Cape Island only a few weeks ago. Though she lightened up the house with her radiant female presence, she seemed at times to fall into periods of irritability and an unaccountable sadness. Though Harrah did not see the swing in her moods as significant, he regarded Willacassa's failure to marry as an inexplicable shortcoming, his shortcoming if not hers. After all, the girl was twenty-five, and as pretty as any young woman on the island. There were girls at her age with three children clinging to their skirts! Jumping Jehoshaphat, it was one thing to be independent and talented and committed to a cause (whatever that cause might be)! It was quite another never to talk of beaus or "hops" or the prospect of marriage!

Harrah saw himself as at least partly responsible for this unhappy state of affairs. Had he provided a surrogate for her when her mother died. Had he provided a "year-round" environment for her in her growing years instead of the one Cape Island afforded—Cape Island which came alive ten weeks in the year and hibernated for the next forty-two—she might have turned out differently.

"Would you like to go for a ride?" asked Harrah when he had set his bushels down in Rachel's kitchen.

"A ride?"

"Yes, I have a new buggy to show you."

"Not just now," said Willacassa. "I've got work to do."

"Later, then."

"Yes, maybe later."

But when Harrah looked in at the kitchen at noon, Rachel informed him that his daughter had gone for a walk.

And indeed Willacassa did go for a walk. At first she resented the signs and signature of summer at Cape Island. At the water's edge it was bathing as usual. In the ice cream saloons and confectioner's shops large crowds of patrons gathered. In the big hotels and the cottages, shiny with new paint, porches were decked with rocking chairs and recent summer visitors. And in the parlor of Trescott House itself the latest issues of *Arthur's Home Magazine* and *Peterson's National* (for ladies) lay on the coffee table.

With a war going on as badly as it was, it seemed that a more somber note should prevail. Instead of an announcement in the *Ocean Wave* of a "hop" at Congress Hall or an advertisement by Thomas Salts of Cold Spring that he repaired watches or a filler revealing that the watchman and lamplighter were getting $1.50 a night or an item indicating that more cottages were rented this season than the summer before, it seemed to Willacassa that the war and nothing but the war should be on the minds of Cape Islanders and their guests.

But as she walked the streets of the bustling resort to see what changes had taken place she found herself thinking less and less of the war and more about "trivial" things. The Ellsworth House, opened last year on the corner of Washington and Ocean Streets, was just a short walk from her father's place and the imposing Columbia House across the street. Its proprietor boasted a first class bar and good stabling. But at $1 a day or $5 a week it was hardly competition for the Trescott House where $5 a night was considered a good buy. No, her father need not worry about losing his clientele, at least with Rachel in the kitchen.

If there was a threat to Harrah's business it came from such people as John P. Sloan, a clothing dealer from Philadelphia, who had erected a beautiful cottage in the gothic style on Lafayette Street. At one time "cottages" of that sort were unheard of on Cape Island and their owners guested instead at luxury hotels like Trescott House. Now the trend was shifting. In spite of the war—or because of it, her father suggested, with all the money being made in manufacturing—the wealthy were building their own. It appeared that the North had its special version of the Southern planter.

And Willacassa wondered if such preoccupations should after all be the run of things, and all the killing and maiming and blood-shed considered out of place. Certainly there was as much to be said for seeing a sign, "Samuel R. Ludlam, housepainter and glazier," as having a young Ludlam sent home in a pine coffin.

As she walked back by way of the strand, Willacassa took note of the sloop of war, *Saratoga*, cruising off the Cape. It had been plying the coastal waters for two weeks now, protecting the shore and the vessels going to and from Philadelphia. Evidently the war was not as far away as she had imagined. There were, of course, the usual dispatches on page two of the *Ocean Wave*. She was reminded of this as a copy of the newspaper, blown about the beach, wrapped itself tenaciously around her leg. Pulling it off, she saw at one and the same time that the 25th Regiment of New Jersey Volunteers had been disbanded in June after a career of less than ten months and that Doctor Hoofland's non-alcoholic German bitters (for 75 cents a bottle or a half dozen for 4 dollars) would effectually cure nine-tenths of the diseases "induced in soldiers by exposure and privations incident to camp life."

And now it was this thought that troubled her. Would the war and the reminders of war never end? Would the need for a Dorothea Dix to issue a card thanking the ladies of New Jersey for their aid and assistance to the wounded in Washington and Fortress Monroe never cease? Would the casualty lists never fade from print? Would the editorials and speeches crying for victory, or at least a resounding defeat for the enemy, never give way to more mundane things such as cattle feeding on the graveyard at Cold Spring? Would the whole twisted outlook on life, life seen as no more than a sacrifice of the young on the bloody altar of war, never twist back and become sane again?

She had, Willacassa realized, come full circle. And she smiled at her apparent shift in attitude. Here she was lamenting Cape Island's preoccupation with the war, limited as its contact was, just as a little while ago she was castigating the island for shunning the drama of the battlefield to play once more its summer role as queen of the resorts.

Always critical, she thought, always dissatisfied that Cape Island was not a mirror of the rest of the country. The only mirror people wanted it to be was the mirror one stood in front of before plunging into a summer's day.

She met Harriet Sawyer at Enoch Edmond's Cape Island Store, and asked after Henry.

"No definite news yet. I've heard he's been wounded. I believe he's been taken prisoner. But I've had no letter from him. Oh, Willacassa, I don't know what I'm going to do! I've had my hands full with the children. I've been sick myself. I don't know how it's going to end."

"Harriet, I've known Henry for a long time. He's strong and resourceful. And he loves you. I can understand your concern. But I am sure you will hear from him soon."

"He never should have volunteered, Willacassa. That's where the trouble lies. It's one thing to fight for your country. It's another to leave and let your wife and your children fend for themselves."

Harriet's lament left its mark on Willacassa. For weeks she had been feeling a knife-edged pity for herself. The man she loved was hundreds of miles away, banished to some obscure military camp, while she had nothing but an occasional letter to show for his absence. It had been a lonely, trying time, capped by the uncertainty of whether she would ever see Shiloh again. She walked the dusty streets of Cape Island. She salvaged conch shells along the ocean's edge. She read innumerable books and newspapers. Yet time stood choked in its hourglass, and the bells that tolled in her father's clock only mocked her with their plaintive ring. The only good she saw in all this was that she no longer thought of Francis Grandee. Francis Grandee was Cape Island of summers past. Which regiment he served in, what battle he had fought in, was no longer of vital interest to her.

But perhaps her pity was misplaced. To let wife and children fend for themselves, Harriet had said. Was that what Sam Shiloh was doing? Was that what Willacassa, by capturing his affections, expected him to do? She thought not. She believed that she was making no claim on Shiloh beyond her claim on his love. But someone else—her father, for example, or Joseph Leach or Reverend Williamson—might see things in a different light.

Suddenly Willacassa became aware of a crowd that had gathered on the oceanside. She thought at first to pass it by. Then seeing an ambulance wagon drawing up, she changed her mind and walked towards the busy scene.

"What happened?" she asked of an elderly bystander.

"Young lady ventured too far into the breakers."

"And?"

"She drowned. They brought her in but couldn't revive her."

"How dreadful!"

"Catherine Thornton's her name. Was staying at the Centre House. Only here a few days. Did you know her?"

"No," said Willacassa. "Was there nothing they could do?"

"Nothing. Took too much water. They say her fiancee's in the navy. On that sloop out there."

"The *Saratoga*?"

The man nodded. "But could be a story someone made up. There are all kinds of stories 'bout the war. More likely she just ventured too far out. Those breakers 'll do you in. Never should have ventured out. But they never listen."

LOTTERY OF DEATH

Libby Prison was by no means an officers' rest home. Sleeping quarters were crowded and infested with lice. Blankets were scarce. There was little or no straw on the floor where some officers slept. Food rations were short: dry bread, coffee, and a half pound of boiled beef, sometimes with rice, sometimes with beans or soup, was the rule. And there was but one water closet in the huge room, which competed with the cooking odors in fouling the air of the place.

But for a man on the mend, Henry Sawyer felt he could do worse. He might just as easily have been sent to Belle Isle on the James River, where reportedly there was a scarcity of tents and the ground was littered with animal droppings. The place was also terrorized by bounty jumpers from city slums who preyed on and robbed their fellow prisoners with an indiscriminateness surpassed only by their savagery.

"They're still exchanging prisoners, aren't they?" he asked of Lieutenant Porter who was sitting on the next bed.

" 'Fraid not, Captain. As of May 25th only noncommissioned officers and enlisted men."

"Too bad," mused Sawyer. Though he found little solace in the news, he still preferred Libby Prison to Salisbury or any of the other camps farther south.

Feeling hungry, he put his feet down and looked to see how many men were at the stove.

"Think I'll make myself some breakfast."

"Too bad one of the privates can't do it for you."

"I'm quite capable of cooking it myself. My wound's doing nicely."

"It's not that. Most of the officers consider it degrading to do their own cooking," explained Lieutenant Porter.

"But they do it!"

"Of course. Otherwise they'd go hungry."

"My sentiments exactly."

As he stood near the cooking stove, watching the others clumsily stirring their breakfast in a black iron pot, Henry Sawyer reflected that the Cape Island hostelries could teach them a thing or two. In a resort town at least, the preparation of food had a high priority. Even the casual onlooker learned to undercook beef or turn a potato. How he longed to be sitting in the kitchen of the Columbia House or to be watching taciturn Rachel go through her routine at Trescott House with Willacassa looking over her shoulder! Not to mention the kitchen of his own home where Harriet would be frying a couple of eggs and some slivers of bacon in a scrubbed iron pan.

As he waited his turn, Sawyer heard from someone that the other prison rooms were filled to overflowing and that the prospect was things would get worse, not better.

"Is it they're taking so many prisoners?"

"That's part of it. But with the parole system things are getting out of hand."

"What do you mean, Sir?"

The man Captain Sawyer was addressing was a colonel and though a general camaraderie existed among the officers, protocol was still in order.

"The problem is two-fold, Captain. On the one hand you have the bounty jumpers. They practically deliver themselves to the enemy knowing they'll be paroled. When they're sent back North, they insist on being assigned to state camps. They'll sit this war out if it drags on to doomsday—with the bounty in their pockets."

"And the others?"

"They're your stragglers. They'll fall into the hands of the Rebs only to get a little rest from soldiering. A number of them'll surrender for the sake of getting home. It's an epidemic in places. An intolerable abuse of the parole system. It's worse than desertion!"

"Well, if I get out of here," declared Sawyer, "it's back into action for me. I don't want parole. I don't want to waste my time sitting in another camp—even if it's in the North. I want exchange. It's the only way to get this war over with."

"You may have to settle for parole," commented a Captain Forsby, "until there are enough of us to exchange. Right now there are more of us than them. At least according to the Richmond papers."

He sat down to his meal of cornbread and coffee, which he balanced on his lap, taking care to wrap his blanket around him. "Pretty nippy this morning for end of June."

Across the floor another officer was busy picking lice from his clothes. When he had gathered enough of the little creatures together, he tossed them into the fire of the stove.

"Didn't give me a moment's rest last night. Sure could do with a bath."

"Why don't you send a letter to General Winder asking for some tubs," came a wry comment. "He's right susceptible to suggestions."

"I will, Johnson. And when they arrive like the shirts and socks and blankets we asked for, I'll stick your head in one of them.''

The morning of July 6 began obscure and gray, as did all the mornings at Libby Prison. Though still conscious of his wounds, Henry Sawyer skipped breakfast and took his walk through the former tobacco warehouse of Libby & Son, which still stored the pungent fragrance of the leaf, if not the leaf itself. In his easy, affable way, Captain Sawyer exchanged pleasantries with his fellow officers, most of whom were huddled over the cast-iron stove on which they cooked their scanty rations. Sawyer's barrack measured 103 feet by 42 feet, as did the other three rooms of the warehouse, and if Henry hadn't counted it off a hundred times in the past month he had not done it once.

When he had gone full circle and returned to his cot which opened on a wide window overlooking the sentries' pitched tents below, he saw the warden enter the barrack, accompanied by some aides. Taking a position at the center of the room where he could be heard by all present, Captain Turner asked that all officers of the rank of captain join him at the far end of the room to hear a communication he had just received.

The captains, some seventy of them, did not know the meaning of this unusual request, but at least half of them anticipated an order for exchange of prisoners as they gathered at the far end. Officer exchanges had been suspended for the time being. But so long as there were Rebels to trade, a captive who held body and mind together could look forward to eventual release.

"What do you think, Henry? Will you be back on Cape Island before the summer is over?"

"I'll settle for a Washington soup kitchen. Anything but this." Sawyer looked to the warden for some enlightenment.

"Gentlemen," began Captain Turner, more in the solemn tones of a Baptist minister than a jailor, "it is my painful duty to communicate to you an order I received from General Winder, Provost Marshal of Richmond, which I will now read."

Captain Turner cleared his throat. " 'In retaliation for the execution of two Confederate officers, Captain William F. Corbin and Captain T. J. McGraw, by General Burnside at Sandusky, Ohio, on May 15, I am ordering Captain Turner to select by lot two Federal captains for immediate execution.' "

The prisoners were flabbergasted.

"Execution? You can't be serious, Sir."

But the expression on the warden's face proved them wrong. Captain Turner gave the men time for the stunning news to sink in. For a few minutes the officers exchanged incredulous glances.

Then Captain Turner resumed.

"As ordered, the selections will be by lot. It now remains for you, Gentlemen, to choose someone to draw the ballots as your names are called."

A brief and awkward silence greeted this directive.

"You mean now?"

The warden nodded.

"But that's impossible!" exclaimed one of the prisoners.

"I'm afraid not. One of you, gentlemen, will have to do the choosing. Which one will it be?"

Not a man stepped forward. No one made a gesture to help things along. After all, there was reality and unreality as far as the seventy officers who had been gathered together were concerned. And what was taking place in a corner of the huge room of the converted warehouse had all the earmarks of unreality. Sawyer himself was used to unreality. Time and again he had experienced it in battle. One moment a man was vigorously alive. The next his body lay still and lifeless on the cold, hard ground. Reality had changed clothes with unreality. And Sawyer had difficulty keeping up with it. But he played the game. What was life one moment was death the next. It was merely a matter of adjustment. It did not matter that there was a yawning time gap before the unreality sank in. And now this grim business of a lottery. What could be more unrealistic? Yet there was Captain Turner standing among them. His pronouncement had no semblance of reality about it. It was too absurd; there was no logic to it. But it had been made nonetheless. And if one were to survive the moment, one had to pretend that it was reality after all.

"Come now," rebuked the warden. "Someone must do the choosing. You must understand that. There's no way of getting around it."

Still no one was inclined to break the deadlock—until Henry Sawyer spoke up.

"May I make a suggestion, Captain Turner?"

"Feel free to do so."

"Apparently we have no choice in the matter. Could Chaplain Brown, then, of the 6th Maryland draw the ballots? I think the officers would feel better about it if one of their own did the drawing. One who is not involved."

Captain Turner made a sweeping survey of the other officers. "Is that your wish?" Finding general agreement, at least among those whose emotions had thawed out sufficiently to respond, he signalled approval.

"Let's proceed, then."

Chaplain Brown, a prisoner housed in one of the rooms below, was sent for. When he appeared with a bible in hand and bewilderment on his face, Captain Turner explained the situation to him. "Do you understand, Chaplain?"

"I do, Sir."

"Then let the roll call begin." The warden signalled to one of the aides who tersely began reading the first name listed in a small cardboard notebook.

"Captain Elias Matthews."

The grim reading of the name threw the cold water of reality on what until then had been a common feeling of disbelief. Someone among the ranks shuddered.

With an apologetic glance at Matthews, the chaplain drew. "Blank," he pronounced with a shrug of relief.

The aide proceeded with the reading of names.

"Captain Jacob Lawrence."

A heavy silence followed, but the next lot drawn was blank as well.

And so it went until nearly half the roll had been called with neither of the written ballots being selected.

"Captain Henry W. Sawyer."

At the sound of his name Henry stiffened and stood erect. He fastened his eyes on the chaplain's hand as it reached into the box for a ballot. The chaplain blanched as he unfolded the paper, but recovered in time to hand the ballot over to Captain Turner.

"Execution," whispered the warden.

A silence almost shroud-like followed. Sawyer inhaled deeply. Then with no apparent emotion he remarked, "Someone had to be drawn. I guess I can stand it as well as anyone."

But when the roll call resumed it was clear Henry had stopped listening. The second fateful ballot was drawn and announced, and he did not hear it.

Henry's mind had drifted off into thoughts of Cape Island. He saw the boats on the summer waters, steamboats, sailboats, skiffs. And the endless rolling in of the waves. How wet the breezes felt against his cheek! How tart and cool! And the children playing on the strand were his children, shouting and carefree, running towards Harriet, then running towards him. But never, not once, did they see him. Not once did they acknowledge his waving hand.

Captain John Flinn of the 51st Indiana was white and very depressed when his name was sounded and the word "Execution" read. It was only at the urging of Captain Turner that Flinn stepped forward to join Captain Sawyer.

"I'm sorry, Gentlemen," said the warden. "But you will have

to be separated from your comrades. My orders leave no option. The execution will take place at once. Please prepare yourselves.''

"A letter," interrupted Sawyer. "May I write a letter to my wife?" He did not falter. In fact, he seemed as steady and calm as any doomed man the warden had ever seen.

"You may, but do it quickly," replied Captain Turner. "We really must get on with it.''

Breaking out of his trance, Captain Flinn managed at last to speak. "I'd—I'd like to see a priest, Sir."

The warden nodded. "A Roman Catholic bishop has just finished visiting the prison. I'll send him to you."

The prospect did not relieve Flinn's despair but it did give him something to cling to.

Half an hour later Sawyer had written his letter and was joined by Flinn on the way to the gallows. The Cape Islander proceeded with unfaltering courage. There was no bravado, no affectation of recklessness on his part, just steady, calm resolve. A summer's day. His last day would be a summer's day.

"You're a brave man, Sawyer. I take my cap off to you," said the warden, walking by his side.

"I come from a state of brave men, Captain. I want no one in South Jersey to be ashamed of my conduct here."

Flinn too was now ready to meet his fate. The bishop had given him his last rites and he was at peace with himself.

"Captain Turner," interceded the bishop who was accompanying Captain Flinn on the way to the scaffold. "These men are innocent. They've committed no crime. Why must they die?"

"The two Confederate captains were innocent too."

"But as you explained it, they were caught recruiting behind Union lines. They were spies. A little charity, Captain. Can't you delay the execution until I see General Winder?"

The warden halted his progress. "Do you know what General Burnside said when a sister of one of the victims begged the general to spare his life?"

The bishop shook his head.

"General Burnside said that he had quit handling rebellion with kid gloves."

"All I'm asking for is a delay. Ten days, no more. It would give the men time to see their spouses and to get their affairs in order. And I could appeal to General Winder."

Captain Turner had no reason to grant the request. He was under orders to provide for retaliation and as a non-Catholic he was in no way bound to defer to the cleric. But he could see no reason to deny the request either. The important thing had been decided. An execution would take place, and the men to be executed had been selected. "The Lottery of Death," someone had whispered. The lottery had been effected. Death could wait its turn.

"All right, ten days. But I'm afraid it will only prolong the agony."

When Henry Sawyer finally convinced himself that he was not being led to the gallows and that thanks to the Catholic bishop he and Captain Flinn had a ten-day stay of execution, he asked for his letter to be returned. It occurred to him, almost as straw grasping, that in writing his wife a farewell he had an opportunity to expand the nature of his original letter which he had written in extreme haste. In fact, he revised the letter several times, wiping his brow of the cold sweat that had formed there, until he was satisfied that it expressed what he wanted to say. For it would be his last word, his last opportunity to convey his feelings; there would be no other.

"My Dear Harriet.

"My prospects look dark.

"This morning all the captains now prisoners at the Libby Military Prison drew lots for two to be executed. It fell to my lot, myself and Captain Flinn of the Fifty-first Indiana Infantry. We will be executed in retaliation for two captains executed by Burnside.

"The Provost-General, J. H. Winder, assured me that the Secretary of War of the Southern Confederacy will permit you and the children to visit me before the execution. You will also be permitted to bring an attendant. Captain Whilldin or Uncle W. W. Ware or Mr. Harrah had better come with you. You will proceed to Washington. My government will give you transportation to Fortress Monroe, and you will get here by a flag of truce, and return the same way. You will be allowed to return home without molestation. Bring along a shirt for me.

"My situation is hard to bear, and I cannot think of dying without seeing you and the dear children. I am resigned to whatever is in store for me, with the consolation that I die without having committed any crime. I have had no trial, no jury, nor am I charged with a crime, but it fell to my lot.

"My dear wife, the fortune of war has put me in this position. I have done nothing to deserve this penalty. But if I must die, a sacrifice to my country, with God's will I submit to my fate. On no account will I be a disgrace to you or the children. You may point with pride and say, 'I give my husband for my country.' Only let me see you once more, and I will die becoming an officer and a man. But, for God's sake, do not disappoint me.

"Oh, Harriet, it is so hard to leave you. I wish the ball that passed through my head at Brandy Station had done its work. But it was not to be. My mind is somewhat befuddled, for this business has come so suddenly on me.

"Write as soon as you get this, and go to Captain Whilldin. He will advise you what to do. Leave the letter open and I will receive it. Direct my name and rank, by way of Fortress Monroe.

"Farewell, and hope it is all for the best. God will provide for you and the children; never fear. I remain yours until death.

Henry
H. W. Sawyer
Captain
First New Jersey Cavalry"

When he had finished writing his letter, Captain Sawyer was escorted to a vault in the cellar of the prison where he was joined by a distraught Captain Flinn. The dungeon was barely six feet wide and had no opening for light or air except a hole about six inches square cut in the cell door.

At first Sawyer was scarcely aware of his surroundings. His vision turned inward as he tried to grasp the import of the shattering day's events, as he tried to understand what had happened and how to deal with this new, terminal element in his life. He was too preoccupied with the twisted thread of his lot to worry about the place he was in or the manner of existence he would experience during his short stay there.

Sawyer accepted the quixotic nature of chance. As a soldier, a cavalryman, he could appreciate being shot off his horse and narrowly escaping death. He did not know whether the ball that had struck him had been a wild shot or one deliberately aimed. It did not really matter. With bullets flying in every direction and shells whistling in the air, the chances of being hit were never small.

But the prospect of having one's name drawn out of a box of some seventy-four officers' names—this wasn't chance. This was fate. A wretched, unthinking, unspeakable fate, a fate that dangled no reason and no justification at its side.

Still, when he measured it all out and came up short, he saw the whole thing as at least a test of his valor. Until now Captain

Sawyer had conducted himself with honor. As a soldier, an officer, he had done everything asked of him and more. Even at the onset of the war, he had enlisted freely. No bounty or bonus had to be held out to Henry W. Sawyer. He had volunteered. And in all his undertakings he had acquited himself as befit a Cape Islander, a husband, and a father. But now was the real test. After all, valor was the soldier's coin. And if it was to enjoy real currency it had to come to the fore even when the ultimate mission was death. This notion somehow gave Henry, in what time was left to him, purpose, if not reason.

When Sawyer finally noticed Captain Flinn at the other end of their tiny dungeon, the Indianan's head was pressed against the damp wall. "Why, why me?" Flinn kept asking. It was a piercing, plaintive cry of protest, emanating from a wound of deep anguish and resentment. And Henry Sawyer had no criticism of the man for the lament. Why him, indeed? Why not any one of the other seventy-two capains? And if someone else, why should it be that one? It was a round-robin of questions, this searching for reasons, questions that had no answer. It spoke only of the unspeakable, the inexplicable. And it did no one any good, least of all Captain Flinn who looked as though he were presiding at his own wake.

By day's end and in the desolate hours of early morning Sawyer's attention was drawn to his new quarters. Though he was tired and longed for sleep he soon discovered that either he or Captain Flinn would have to stand watch or neither of them would get any rest. Rats were swarming all over the place or gnawing at their straw mattresses and even their bodies.

"I'll stand guard, John. I'll use my belt to beat them off. In a couple of hours you can take over."

Captain Flinn nodded his appreciation. Then, without undressing, he lay on his side, his hair curling with sweat and his handsome beard pointing sadly at his chest.

By morning, hunger made both men feel nearer to life than death, as their stomachs growled with digestive juices. The sentry at the door, who challenged them each half hour and demanded a reply from the inmates, awake or asleep, at last slipped some corn bread and water through the six-inch hole.

"Don't eat too fast, Yank. There's no more where that came from," he said.

Sawyer gave Flinn his half share, then looked at a row of boxes the Indiana Captain had fashioned on a piece of paper.

"What's that?" he asked, motioning with the cup in his hand.

"A calendar," said Flinn. "But instead of weeks and months, it has only days. Ten days. And this is day two."

MISSION OF MERCY

Rachel came into his office one day with a cup of coffee and a plate of blueberry muffins.

"Why, thank you, Rachel. You read my mind."

Rachel did not leave straightway but stood with her hands folded.

"I've something to say, Mr. Harrah."

"Nothing unpleasant, I hope."

"Mr. Planks and I are getting married."

"Married? Mr. Planks? I—"

"He's the gentleman's been helping me out when you've been away."

"Oh, yes. Of course."

Harrah stood up and extended his hand to the woman. "Why, Rachel, this is altogether splendid news. I'm terribly pleased for you."

She wiped her hands on her apron, then accepted Harrah's congratulations.

"He's a widower. Has a cottage on Decatur Street. Wants me to move in with him as soon as the season's over. You've no objection to my getting married, do you, Mr. Harrah?"

"If it means I'm going to lose you for next season, I'll simply close the place down."

"That's just it. Mr. Planks wants me to give up Trescott House. And I told him I can't do that."

"Why, Rachel, you've been here since the start of things. I couldn't imagine the place without you."

"Nor could I, Mr. Harrah. So I was thinking."

"Yes?"

"If you could let us have one of the larger rooms here, you could rent out my room. And Mr. Planks could rent his cottage next summer. If you don't mind having us as guests, that is. Then I could continue in the kitchen."

"That sounds like an excellent idea. But how would Mr. Planks feel about the arrangement?"

"I think he'd like being one of the swells at Trescott House. Not that his cottage isn't comfortable. It's just that he never mixed with the rich before. He was a lantern maker before he retired."

Harrah thought he detected a tremble in her voice.

"I just couldn't leave Trescott House, Mr. Harrah." Her eyes welled up as she said this—such uncharacteristic behavior for

Rachel. "You and Willacassa—and in the old days Cassandra, bless her sacred soul—were all the family I ever had. And Jonathan, too, poor boy. So I didn't think to marry or worry about it. But Mr. Planks has changed all that. Only, I don't want too much of a change. So long as you need me, I want to keep cooking at Trescott House."

Sweet, dear, plain-faced Rachel! How beautiful she looked to Harrah at that moment. The tears that tracked slowly down her cheeks spawned a spiritual awakening in him, an awakening to the treasure his family had enjoyed all these years—and taken for granted. And to think he was on the brink of losing it!

"Tell Mr. Planks I'd be happy to give you away, if you'd do me the honor, Rachel."

"I'd be most proud, Mr. Harrah."

"I can't believe it," exclaimed Willacassa after hearing the news. "How happy she is! And what a darling, Mr. Planks! And his cottage is absolutely charming. All those years and I always passed it by. Little did I know its occupant would be marrying our own dear Rachel!"

"He's a true-blue gentleman," remarked Harrah. "He extends every courtesy to Rachel. Takes her arm, brings her flowers, pays her compliments. He has to be the most attentive man on Cape Island."

"Does he have any children?"

"Not that I know of. Rachel will be all the family he has. All that he needs apparently. The two are inseparable. Even when she's in the throes of preparing dinner, he's there to help her. Fetches bowls and pots and cooking spoons. Carries in the coal for the stove. Boils the water. Have you seen the lantern he made for her? He fashioned it out of an old sextant."

"Yes. A very clever piece of workmanship."

"Poor Rachel. We all gave up on her. Too soon, it would seem."

"Just as you've given up on me?"

Harrah took his daughter to task with a disapproving glance.

"Nobody's given up on you, Willacassa. There isn't an available bachelor on Cape Island wouldn't marry you this instant. You know that! You're as pretty and splendid a woman as I've ever known. That you're not married is your own doing. Your decision, no one else's."

"And the idea doesn't trouble you?"

"Trouble me?"

"Every man wants grandchildren."

"I'm in no hurry. Time enough for that. Besides, I can't see myself a grandfather just yet."

Rachel's wedding took place in the Baptist Church on Franklin and Lafayette Streets, only yards away from the spot where Willacassa had almost been spirited away to Philadelphia for violating the Fugitive Slave Act. But Willacassa had little thought for that unhappy time. Her heart and soul were preoccupied with Rachel's happiness, not her own. And when she entered the white frame church with her father, she was so overcome with love for the loyal, motherly Rachel that her eyes spilled over with tears.

"How much alone she must have been all these years, Daddy! It was as if she existed only for us. A nanny, a cook, and a dear soul to love and care for us. Nothing more. We all took Rachel for granted. It was as if she had no life of her own unless it was at Trescott House."

Harrah put his arm around his daughter.

"Well, all that's changed, my dear. She's even asserting herself now. She insisted that Mr. Planks be baptized. As they have no baptismal pool in the church, she took him to Schellenger's Landing and had him immersed in Cape Island Creek."

Inside the Church they found Joseph Leach, Captain Whilldin, and the happy couple. Joseph Leach wore his preacher's suit, which was also his Justice-of-the-Peace garb. The wiry editor of the *Ocean Wave*, himself an ordained minister and a deacon of the church, had put down his pen for the moment in order to marry the couple.

After a quick exchange of greetings, he asked the small party to assemble before the altar. Then he began the wedding ceremony with Harrah giving the bride away. The bridegroom looked elderly but handsome in his gray hair and starched white collar which pinched his neck. And when it came time to present the ring he produced one with a small Cape May diamond inserted in the wedding band. Mr. Planks had planned a much more pretentious stone, but Rachel wanted what was native to the place.

"Where are you going on your honeymoon, Rachel?" asked Captain Whilldin when the ceremony was over.

"Honeymoon? When you live in a town such as Cape Island, you don't need a honeymoon. Besides, I've got Mr. Planks's cottage to fix up."

"It needs a woman's touch," confirmed the smiling bridegroom.

"More'n that," said Rachel. "It needs a decent kitchen. I'll have the carpenters in tomorrow."

When the wedding party had assembled at a corner table for a small reception, Captain Whilldin took the happy couple aside. "I know what you said about your husband's cottage, Mrs. Planks. But I think a honeymoon's in order. My steamboat, the *George Washington*, stops at both Frenchtown and Baltimore. You're welcome to join us."

Willacassa could not help overhearing. "Why don't you, Rachel? A boatride would be just the thing!"

Mr. Planks wavered, but Rachel held fast. "First things first," she said.

Just then the church door was flung open and a distraught Harriet Sawyer appeared, a letter in hand.

"I'm sorry to barge in like this, but—"

"Why, Harriet!" exclaimed Captain Whilldin, breaking away from the others. "What's the matter? What happened?"

Harriet Sawyer showed him the letter.

Captain Whilldin read at arm's length. "Confound it! What kind of nonsense is this? They can't do that. It isn't civilized!" He passed the letter on to Harrah.

Harriet Sawyer gave way to tears. "Apparently they are doing it." She fell into the arms of Willacassa while Mr. and Mrs. Planks and Joseph Leach stood helplessly by.

"Now, now, Harriet," soothed Captain Whilldin. "Don't take on. We'll find a way to stop this."

"But how?"

"How? We'll bring it to the attention of the authorities. There's no way they'll let this take place."

"If only I could believe that!"

Meanwhile Harrah finished reading the letter. "This is July 13th, isn't it?" he asked.

"Yes."

"Then we have only three days until the scheduled execution."

Captain Whilldin stood resolute. "The three of us are going by stage to Washington," he said, looking at Harrah. "I'll telegraph ahead. With a little luck we'll arrive there tomorrow evening." He turned to Harriet Sawyer. "Do you have someone to look after the children?"

"I will," volunteered Willacassa.

"Good! Then pack Henry's shirt, Harriet. And meet us at the stage depot."

A somewhat relieved Harriet Sawyer turned to Mr. and Mrs. Planks before leaving.

"I'm so sorry, Rachel. First I couldn't attend the wedding because of the children. And now this."

"Never mind," said Rachel, clutching Mr. Planks by the arm. "My husband and I understand. It's your husband needs looking after now."

Mrs. Sawyer had not yet arrived, but Captain Whilldin was already at the stage depot when Harrah pulled up.

"Well, Harrah, what do you make of this?"

"It's a sick turn of events."

"Sick?"

"Yes, I feel nothing but shame and mortification. When will men get over their blood lust? Of all things, a lottery!"

"Well, it has a certain objectivity," mused Whilldin. "In one sense, it seems eminently fair."

"How can it be fair? No one of the captains committed a crime. War is one thing, but a game of blind chance?"

"I suppose it does add spice to the slaughter," observed Whilldin, feeling that he had been misunderstood. "Ah, there she is," he said suddenly, twisting to see Harriet's carriage turn the corner.

Harriet Sawyer had never been what one would call a pretty woman, though she was attractive enough with muted coloring and a flawless complexion. But the stresses of the moment and the urgency of her mission lent her personality a vitality of concern that was both appealing and compelling.

"Do you think we'll make it, Captain Whilldin?"

"Don't fret. We'll make it, Harriet."

She turned to greet the owner of Trescott House.

"Mr. Harrah, I'm so glad you're coming."

"Just want to help Henry any way I can."

The three of them mounted the stage that was now harnessed with horses and ready to strike out for Washington. And in a few moments, they were on the road, driving faster than any of them had ever ridden before.

Throughout the long, desolate ride, Captain Whilldin kept up a chatter of conversation pieces all designed to take Harriet's mind off the probable fate of her husband and to keep it fixed on the strategies of their mission to the capital. For Captain Whilldin had already telegraphed some influential friends there with the object of securing an immediate audience with Secretary Stanton and then, hopefully, with the president himself.

"Mr. Naismith and his wife know Mr. Stanton through her sister. The two families have attended the theater together and are as close as two ropes on a windlass. With any luck at all, we should be seeing Mr. Stanton tomorrow evening. Do you know Stanton,

Mr. Harrah?''

"Only what I read in the newspapers."

As Captain Whilldin reeled off his list of important acquaintances, in no immodest way, merely to encourage Harriet Sawyer who was becoming more despondent as the journey dragged on, Harrah had the uneasy feeling he was just going along for the ride. He even drifted into a kind of despair himself. This lottery of death—it had to be one of the more cruel and bizarre facts of an unexpectedly cruel war. How did one adjust to such an outrage? How did a man reconcile all this with a belief in the sanctity of life? It was bad enough that the slaughter had become commonplace. Was a new ingredient to be added to the indiscriminate spilling of blood?

When at last the stagecoach reached Washington, Harrah looked at his watch. They had made good time. He took comfort in that. At least this aspect of the journey had been succesful.

The President stood at a window overlooking the Potomac. When he turned to greet his visitors, Harrah saw a tall, gaunt man with skin drawn about the eyes like someone in mourning. Prominent cheekbones and deep creaselines gave him a raw-boned look, which was not unappealing. But his beard partially covered a multitude of sins, not the least of which was a gangly neck and a narrowly constructed chin. His black lawyer's tie and dark, unpressed suit added to the undertaker's mien. And his voice which was hushed though high-pitched did nothing to dispel the impression.

"Come in, Gentlemen. Come in. And by all means be seated." Indicating two chairs, he himself sank stiffly into his own chair behind the presidential desk.

Captain Whilldin took the foremost seat and leaned forward, "We're here, Mr. President, to seek help in the notorious affair of Captain Sawyer. I believe you've already met with the Captain's wife."

The President, who seemed for a moment to be lost in reverie, as though he hadn't yet made the transition from his previous interview, suddenly perked up.

"Yes, I spoke to Mrs. Sawyer only a little while ago. You'll have to forgive me, Gentlemen. But I thought it best to see her alone."

"Of course. And we thank you, Mr. President, for granting her an audience—especially at this late hour."

"Mrs. Sawyer is not without friends in Washington and they prevailed upon me to see her," smiled Mr. Lincoln sadly.

"And, Mr. President—"

"What have I decided?"

"Yes, Mr. President."

The former lawyer leaned back to study the two appellants. It was clear he was in a terrible state of fatigue. The past few days had been critical ones for the Union forces. With Lee in full retreat and an end to the siege at Vicksburg announced, he could claim the tide had turned. But 23,000 casualties at Gettysburg alone staggered the imagination. And the body count at Vicksburg was by no means complete.

"I've decided," he said at last, "that we cannot permit Captain Sawyer and Captain Flinn to be executed. The two officers we shot were Southern spies. These men are prisoners of battle. Equating one with the other can in no sense be justified."

Captain Whilldin breathed an audible sigh of relief. But Harrah was not yet satisfied that any concrete measures had been taken to halt the executions.

"July 16th is the scheduled date, Sir," he interjected. "That leaves very little time."

"I'm aware of that, Mr. Harrah. That's why I've ordered Secretary of War, Mr. Stanton, to collect hostages of our own. You are familiar with General 'Rooney' Lee?"

"No, Sir," said Harrah.

"Well, William Henry Fitzhugh Lee, or 'Rooney' as he is known to his father, is Robert E. Lee's son. As a prisoner of war, he and another officer, no lower in rank than captain, will be held in close confinement. Word has been sent to the Confederacy that if Sawyer, Flinn, or any other Union captives not guilty of crimes punishable by death should be executed, Lee and this other Confederate officer will die in retaliation. The good book makes much of an eye for an eye. I haven't always subscribed to the notion. But I think maybe the Hebrews had something. At least the idea seems appropriate in this instance."

"And you think the South will back down?" asked Captain Whilldin.

"I think the South will see things in a different light once the message is received."

Captain Whilldin stood up and, taking this as a signal, Harrah rose, too.

"I thank you, Mr. President. All of South Jersey thanks you."

"You're from Cape Island, aren't you?"

"Yes, both Mr. Harrah and I."

"My wife and I were there some time ago. Stayed only one night, but thought it a charming, romantic place—something like land's end. Hope to visit again some day when the Rebels have had enough of war and we can return to domestic tranquillity.''

As Harrah followed Captain Whilldin to the door, he heard his name called.

"Mr. Harrah, can you stay a moment? I would like to talk to you about your letter of June 9.''

His letter of June 9? Harrah had all but given up on it. At this late date he had not expected to hear of it again. He indicated to Captain Whilldin that he would join him later.

"Why, certainly, Mr. President," Harrah said and he took the seat offered him.

"Your letter was turned over to my Secretary, Mr. Hay. We receive quite a bit of mail from men described as Copperheads. And yours was singled out as one of them." Mr. Lincoln leaned forward. "I read the letter and I must say I'm not convinced that every man seeking peace is a Copperhead.''

"Thank you, Mr. President. All I want is an end to hostilities. I don't pretend this will resolve the issues that divide us. But at least it will halt the bloodshed.''

As Harrah looked at the melancholy, sorrowful eyes of the tired president, he saw nothing of the prairie lawyer he had heard so much about. Nor did he see the raw-boned man of the Middle West who had a quip or a joke to match any situation and who used this skill to extricate himself from the awkwardness of a question that had no satisfactory answer or whose honest answer would expose him to honest criticism. Instead Harrah found in the almost wizened face, softened only by the bearded chin, a man in pain, a man whose night of torment saw no end, only more misery, more frustration, more destruction, more sacrifice.

"Mr. Harrah, I'm no stranger to death. But I don't treat it lightly. I've anguished about this war—the wounded and the dead—from the beginning. There isn't a night I'm not haunted by the spector of young and innocent men slaughtering one another on the field of battle. It is an unrelenting nightmare, made no less painful by the knowledge that maybe some good will come out of all this bloodshed. I tell myself that there are other alternatives, other solutions—much like yours. In fact, I can say with some justice that you have read—or at least anticipated my mind to an astonishing degree.

"You will recall that I suggested the adoption of a constitutional amendment in December. It provided not only for gradual emancipation all across the land but for full compensation for the slave owners. But Congress wouldn't buy it. You suggest I try again. You suggest that the slave owners *not* be compensated. You suggest instead that we pay bounties to those young men in the South who take themselves out of the war. And that we make the most of the natural animosity between the rich and the poor in the Secessionist States, labeling the Rebel cause a 'rich man's war.' In short, we divide and conquer—a kind of psychology in reverse, given the Rebels' propensity to divide this land. Have I stated your case correctly?''

"You have, Mr. President. Except that I want to stop the killing. All these proposals are designed to stop the killing, at least of our boys. If the South wants to fight among themselves rather than go along with emancipation, that's their choice.''

The president rose from his chair, rather stiffly Harrah thought, and grimacing from the effort, walked slowly toward the window. He seemed to look out on the lawn below.

"We both want to stop the killing, Mr. Harrah. Every day I go to the war office to deal with the reality of our casualty lists. Just as I have got to deal with the reality of raising more troops, knowing that hundreds, maybe thousands of these raw recruits will never return. I am telling you all this because I want to convince you of my sincere desire for peace. If I can convince you, Mr. Harrah, I can convince those of my critics who have treated me less than kindly in the pulpit or in the newspapers.''

"May I speak freely, Mr. President?''

"Please do.''

Harrah shifted in his seat. He did not want to alienate the president. He appeared such a decent, kind human being. His concern struck Harrah as real concern, his pain as anything but feigned. At the same time Harrah realized that this was his one and, probably, only opportunity to speak his mind to someone in a position to do something about the war. Standing opposite him was someone, all six feet four inches of the man, who had more naked power than any potentate in Europe. Harrah did not want to miss his chance to make his point.

"You say, Mr. President, that you tried certain approaches and that they didn't work. I imagine that there would be opposition to a constitutional amendment even in the North. The threat to labor by a freed black man is, I'm sure, a very real threat. And prejudice against the Negro in the North is also very real. I can see where your efforts met with serious opposition, enough to make you withdraw.

"On the other hand, your generals have not always been successful in the field. But this did not prevent you from trying to find a general who could bring victory to the Union. And at last in Gettysburg a victory was won. May I respectfully suggest that if you pursued as vigorous a course to push through a constitutional amendment at this time you might be equally successful?"

The president returned to his seat once more and stretched his large bony hands across the top of his desk. Although he seemed to have taken umbrage at Harrah's suggestion that he hadn't done all he could to bring about a speedier end to the war, he appeared determined to maintain his equanimity.

"Mr. Harrah, I've been criticized for a lot of things before. And maybe some of the criticisms were just. But I'm not sure I merit criticism in this regard. Yes, at the beginning of the war I felt that any efforts at securing peace would be rebuffed because we were not dealing from a position of strength. The Rebels were whipping us all along the line. Carried away by the euphoria of victory, they weren't about to sit down and talk peace—except on their terms. Now the tide has turned. We've had a few victories and they the setbacks. The time would seem more propitious for peace overtures. But I suspect the Rebels too will be unwilling to deal from a position of weakness. This does not mean that I will try any the less to secure a just and lasting peace. I have tried in the past and will continue to try."

He looked rather sorrowful, almost like the mourned at a funeral, rather than a mourner.

"Despite what they make of me in the newspapers, I am after all no absolute ruler. I have Congress to deal with and men of all shades of political persuasion. I sometimes think it is easier to split rails with a dull axe than it is to pound sense into the heads of some of our people's representatives. But I do keep trying. And I keep my eyes open for opportunities to push through legislation that will help bring the war to a speedier conclusion. It is not an easy task. And I'd pray even harder to the Good Lord if I didn't think they were prayin' just as hard down South."

The president rose once more but with the same stiffness of limb that characterized his first effort.

"And now I'm afraid I'll have to cut short our little discussion as I have a meeting with some generals on the agenda. A few of them are addicted to cigars and if I don't get there soon there'll be no penetrating the screen of smoke. Thank you for coming to Washington in Captain Sawyer's behalf. On that score I can assure you there will be speedy action."

Harrah took the cue and looked for his hat. "We're grateful for what you're doing for Henry, Mr. President. All of Cape Island is grateful. There is no finer man in your service. And—and if I appeared to have spoken out of turn a moment ago, please forgive me. I have no doubt you want the war's end as much as I do."

He hesitated as though deliberating whether to leave things at that or venture out. "If by chance—If by chance I am able to bring back some proposals from the other side, would you consider them?"

"Proposals?"

"Peace proposals."

This did not seem to sit well with Lincoln. For a moment Harrah detected anger over what appeared to be meddling in the President's domain. But the anger or displeasure was brought under control.

"I will consider them. And I will not ask how you went about securing them. But understand this clearly, Mr. Harrah. I cannot sanction such a mission. In light of what I said, I don't think I have to spell out the reasons."

"I understand, Mr. President. Thank you for giving me so much of your time."

Mr. Lincoln closed his eyes and nodded, but said no more.

THE PEACEMAKER

Jonathan made port again. The young man's ship had put in at Cape Island to take on fresh meat and water, and its crew was given a few days' leave. It did not matter that the island was half deserted. The sailors took over the beaches of Cape Island by day and slept aboard ship by night. All except Jonathan, who shared his father's bedroom.

Harrah could see that his son had grown in confidence. Always given to puff, Jonathan could now wait to sing his own praises. Emptying his sack of gifts on the floor, he singled out the ones he had brought for Harrah.

"The humidor is Spanish. Just right for those big cigars your patrons smoke. And the gold watch, Swiss. But my favorite is this British sea captain's cap." He plopped it on his father's head and waited for the reaction.

"Not bad," observed Harrah, poking at the mirror. "But it will hardly do for a landlubber."

"Maybe not. But it could attract some house guests. Things are rather dead around here. Aren't they, Dad?"

"The season's over, you know."

"But I hear it was a poor summer."

"I've known better."

"Here," said Jonathan, pulling out a roll of pound notes. "Maybe this will help."

"I don't want any money just now."

"Why?" asked Jonathan. "Because I run the blockade? I'm on a British ship. It's all legal—well, almost."

Harrah could see that his son was terribly disappointed. And he had no desire further to offend his sensibilities.

"No, Jonathan. I have a favor to ask instead."

"A favor?" Jonathan was clearly puzzled but somewhat mollified.

"The ship you're on—"

"The *Birmingham*?"

"Yes. Does it take on passengers?"

"It can be arranged."

"You said you were stopping at New Orleans."

"That's right."

"I want you to secure passage for me on the ship. Would this be any trouble for you?"

"I don't see why. The captain likes me. And if I tell him you're my father—"

"I don't want him to know that," said Harrah. "Simply tell him I'm a friend of the family. Call me—" He hesitated. "Call me Nathaniel Hall."

Excitement colored Jonathan's face. "Why all the secrecy? Are you on some kind of mission?"

"Mission? Yes, a mission of mercy."

Jonathan had no trouble securing passage for his father. Harrah—that is, Nathaniel Hall—climbed aboard the *Birmingham* and was shown his berth by one of the ship's officers. Nothing so large as a stateroom; rather, he suspected, the quarters of one of the petty officers who had been moved out for the occasion; just a bunkbed and a table no bigger than a shelf. But Harrah spent all his time on deck, leaning on a railing and squinting past the sun at the tossing waves and whitecaps of the sea.

As often as Jonathan could get away from his tasks, he was joined by his son.

"Just finished my watch, Mr. Hall. Thought I'd join you for a spell." Jonathan took singular delight in playing the role assigned.

"Glad to have your company, Jonathan."

"Didn't know you smoked," said the young man, pointing at his father's pipe whose gray wisps were blowing with the wind.

"I don't generally. But this seemed like a good time to fill a bowl."

Jonathan leaned closer to his father and without looking at him asked, "What is this mission of mercy? Has it anything to do with the war?"

"I'm not at liberty to say."

Far from being offended, Jonathan enjoyed the mystery. "But you will tell me about it sometime?"

"Sometime—if there's anything to tell."

The fact was, Harrah's mission was entirely speculative. For better than a year now New Orleans had flown the Federal flag. On April 24, 1862, Captain David Glasgow Farragut's fleet had run under the guns of Fort Jackson and Fort St. Philip at the mouth of the Mississippi and steamed its way through burning rafts and the Confederate blockade to New Orleans. The next day the premier depot of Southern trade fell into Union hands.

At the outset of the occupation the citizens of New Orleans were rabidly Rebel in sympathy. But since the departure of the widely unpopular General Ben Butler several months back, the city had returned to a relative state of normalcy. Northerner and Southerner alike now walked the streets, each with his own prejudices and each, if not exactly tolerant of the other, tolerating a kind of co-existence.

As soon as he had landed, Harrah bade goodbye to his son. "I'll miss you, my boy. And thank you for everything."

"Goodbye, Father." Jonathan was overcome by emotion and could not wipe away the tears fast enough. "I'll make you proud of me yet." He fell into his father's embrace.

"I'm proud of you now, my son."

When Jonathan had returned to his ship and waved his last sad goodbye, Harrah sank back in his carriage and tried to turn his attention to Dr. Edmonde Zachary. At the nearest hotel he dispatched a messenger with a letter of introduction given him by Madeleine Craddishaw.

He had heard of Dr. Zachary almost by chance. At meetings of peace movements his name came up, but never in a partisan way. Rather it came up in connection with some diplomatic overture. Harrah gathered that Dr. Zachary had at times served as a mediator. On other occasions he seemed to have played an unofficial role in some unexplained mission. In any case, no one could claim him as theirs. If he was American by birth, no one was quite sure where his birthplace had been. Certainly he was identified with neither North nor South. All that was known of him was that he owned a house in New Orleans, that his wife was a Creole, not of mixed racial blood, but of pure Spanish-French ancestry, and that if he practiced medicine it was not while he sojourned in the great Mississippi port.

But it appeared that Dr. Zachary was not without influence. He at least had the ear of those in the highest Confederate circles. And he travelled regularly to France and England where it was whispered he had been instumental in getting promises of aid and recognition if the Confederacy would only disavow slavery.

Of course, none of this could be substantiated. Rumor played upon rumor. There was even talk that he had a quadroon mistress who was in part responsible for his enlightened point of view. But one thing was unmistakable. His name commanded respect, even a kind of awe, especially among those who succeeded only in alienating people to their cause when they had nothing but the best intentions.

For his part, Harrah could claim no such credentials. He was aware of the Federal Government's displeasure with citizens who engaged in private diplomacy. President Lincoln himself had been less than encouraging when Harrah suggested that he might attempt a peace overture on his own.

This policy of the government was puzzling to Harrah. It was not as if Washington with its sprawling bureaus of organized incompetence had made any progress toward meaningful diplomacy. Despite their holier-than-thou attitude, government leaders had been no more effective in their peace efforts than John Brown had been in leading an insurrection. And any new attempt by Washington to negotiate peace could only result in vacillation and failure. From all indications, official Washington stood only for official weakness.

But Dr. Zachary enjoyed some reputation and some sanction in Richmond, even if Harrah did not in his own bailiwick. And actions by private negotiators could undoubtedly help both sides save face. So, authorized or not, Harrah felt the attempt should be made.

"Mrs. Craddishaw is a remarkable woman," said Dr. Zachary when his carriage picked Harrah up outside his hotel.

"Yes, indeed," agreed Harrah.

"And an outspoken one too."

Harrah nodded. "We need more of her kind. Are there any in New Orleans who see conciliation with the North as possible?"

"The Federal government had a splendid opportunity to make capital in New Orleans," volunteered Dr. Zachary. "There were pockets of known sympathizers here. But General Butler changed all that. They called him 'the beast,' you know."

"Was he?"

"The man was a fool, that much I can assure you. That edict of his, labeling women sympathetic to the South as prostitutes, turned the whole city against him. It was bad enough he confiscated some of the homes and turned them into brothels—or at least his men did. When he started arresting everyone in sight—including the mayor—and speculating in cotton, he incurred the wrath of even the most ardent Unionists. There were even rumors that he was selling seized muskets and powder to the Confederates for personal gain. With fools like that, you can turn the greatest victory into defeat."

"But he's gone now," observed Harrah.

"Yes, he's gone, withdrawn. But his legacy lingers on." Even now Dr. Zachary shook his head in disbelief.

Strange, thought Harrah. In the North Butler was regarded as a kind of hero. Not just the military governor of New Orleans, but Washington's able emissary. In New Orleans he was seen as the reincarnation of vulgarity and stupidity. Apparently there was no middle road.

Dr. Zachary rode, as it appeared, aimlessly about the town. He said almost nothing, pointing now and then to some elaborate wrought-iron grillwork and quietly uttering such words as "charming," "delightful," "extravagant." From time to time his carriage seemed to stop and Harrah thought they would disembark, but the doctor would signal the driver on.

He eschewed such places as the regal and monumental Cabildo with its mansard roof and dormer windows, the redbrick Pontalba buildings at Jackson Square, the Ursuline Convent on Chartres Street (an ideal meeting place), and the colossal French Opera House on Bourbon and Toulouse Streets, settling instead for an unpretentious house at 632 Dumaine Street, with a second-story porch facade and two shuttered dormers at the top.

After making a brief excursion into the Creole-style courtyard to make sure they were alone, Dr. Zachary showed Harrah a small room off the front gallery. It was a stark but charming place with bright windows, white walls, and a panelled fireplace. Dr. Zachary scraped across the hardwood floor and sat down at a small table with a teapot and a vase of flowers on it. He offered Harrah the other straw-seated hardback chair. A portrait of the Marquis de Lafayette looked down at them from the white-plastered chimney wall.

Dr. Zachary came right to the point, "Are you here with Mr. Lincoln's blessing, Mr. Harrah?"

"I have to be candid. I am here on my own. As you no doubt know, I do not enjoy free passage in the South. I feel therefore that I should do the hard part first."

"Which is?"

"Get some kind of understanding. The basis for an agreement to end hostilities. And then do what I can to bring this proposal to those in power in the North."

"Then you have important contacts?"

"The contacts will be made—once I have something to offer."

Dr. Zachary reflected on the character of the man he was dealing with. Even Harrah could detect his concern. Apparently the doctor was still not satisfied he could speak freely.

"I don't want you to think my meeting you is a reflection of weakness on our side."

"I'm aware that both sides are in a strong bargaining position," said Harrah.

"How's that?"

"The South is winning battles. The North is building a mighty fighting machine."

"Then you think time is on their side?"

"Time is on no one's side, least of all the soldier in the field. If we can save but one life—"

Dr. Zachary sat down and poured himself a glass of wine.

"Would you care for some sherry?"

Sherry was not Harrah's favorite drink, but he nodded in the affirmative. As soon as Dr. Zachary filled his glass, Harrah brought it to his lip.

"The crux of the problem, of course, is states' rights," continued Dr. Zachary. "If each of the Confederate states can be guaranteed its sovereignty, we might be able to start discussions."

Deciding it would be best not to comment on this, Harrah took another sip of wine.

"You disagree, Mr. Harrah? Are we going to get tangled up in the slavery issue even before we get started?"

"What I want to know, Dr. Zachary, is not what the ultimate resolution of the issues will be. That must be worked out between the parties themselves—face to face. What I have to know is what it will take to bring about a cease fire."

"But a cease fire can only be successful when there is the expectation of a solution," replied Dr. Zachary. "Actually there are several proposals I believe the South is prepared to offer. Without a basis for solution, we are only indulging in an exercise in futility."

"Agreed," said Harrah. "But we must find common ground first. Otherwise we'll get caught up in the mischief of confrontation. Remember, too, that we're dealing with a rapidly changing situation. An almost volatile state of affairs. What is a viable solution one moment becomes an impossible idea the next."

"What do you suggest then?"

"An immediate cease-fire—where the sides stand. And sixty days to work things out."

"Sixty days?"

"With a promise not to recruit or add military hardware during that time."

"What makes you think there'll be an agreement after sixty days? There were attempts before the war to come up with a solution. Obviously they failed."

"At that time," said Harrah, "men had no idea how terrible this war would be. Now with Shiloh and Antietam and Gettysburg—the dead and mutilated on both sides—we know what to expect if an agreement is not reached. Having seen the rot and smelled the stench of war, I don't think anyone would want to stare that hell in the face again. Not anyone with a trace of pity or humanity."

Not only was Dr. Zachary deeply moved by what he said, so much so that he had to stand and face the wall, Harrah himself was unsettled and had to break off at the end.

"The problem, Mr. Harrah," Dr. Zachary resumed at last, "is that we have men on both sides who fear peace more than they fear war. War, terrible as it appears, is predictable. Destruction, arson, pillage, rape—it has all been seen a score of times. It has a familiarity, a certainty that, horrible as it is, we have learned to live with. Peace—the changes that peace will engender—is more frightening to some. How will their station in society be affected by it? What great social changes will be unleashed by it? Things can never be the same once we take stock of the devastation and try to reconstruct the edifice that has been torn asunder.

"You know, I am sure, that things are not solid in the South. Your newspapers and magazines have carried stories about desertions, conspiracies, Union sentiment, hostility between the rich and the poor. There is some truth to this. East Tennessee, Northern Alabama, Western Carolina, parts of Mississippi and Georgia have been a hotbed of resistance to the Confederacy. Marauders, draft dodgers, deserters roam the land at will. There aren't enough state militia to contain them.

"Yes, the government in Richmond and the government in Washington can agree to a sixty-day cease-fire. But will the guerrilla bands stop their activity? Will your night lantern groups refrain from sabotage? Will a cease-fire prevent looting and violence by runaway Negroes? Will starving Texans in Galveston halt their food riots?

"No, the war, the battle cry, is the great unifier. The war sustains authority and at least a semblance of order. Without it, the South would fall apart, state by state, county by county. And I'm sure much the same problem exists in the North and the West. Weren't there draft riots in New York City? Didn't Copperheads in Illinois attack a Union troop and slaughter soldiers in their beds?

"The only peace the South will buy is a peace that assures them a return to the good old days, with a constitution guaranteeing slavery in the cotton fields and a supreme court guaranteeing the slave as a property right. For anything less, the war in the South will have been fought in vain, a futile, bloody sacrifice."

"Then there is no hope for a cease-fire?"

"Not yet, anyway. These are gloomy times, Mr. Harrah."

"Yes, but we are looking for better. We must look for better."

"When our youth are bled white and the earth is soaked with blood and it can hold no more—then maybe someone will listen to reason. Not before."

At Harrah's downcast look, Dr. Zachary hesitated. "However—if something should develop, if an opportunity should present itself, something that would best be explored through

194

unofficial channels, I will contact you."

"How?"

"Through an intermediary. You've heard of Kendall Gillingham?"

"The Congressman?"

"The ex-Congressman. Though he's bitterly anti-war, he's from the Midwest and still enjoys freedom of movement."

Looking at his pocket watch, Dr. Zachary rose and returned to the street by way of the courtyard. A moment later a landau with its top thrown back rattled to a stop.

With a handsome smile, Dr. Zachary greeted its occupant, a very pretty Creole of mixed blood. Turning, Dr. Zachary saw the look of consternation on Harrah's face.

"You're wondering," he said, "why all the secrecy when my mistress is a party to this meeting of ours. The fact is, she was displaced by your arrival. Don't think ill of me, Mr. Harrah. Even with a war on, dreadful as it is, a man must have his little pleasures."

Harrah made no comment. As the pretty quadroon was helped down from the landau, her perfume wafted seductively in the air. Adjusting her hoop skirt and bodice, she paused just long enough to flash her lovely white teeth at him. Harrah nodded, tipping the brim of his hat ever so slightly, then climbed up and took the seat she had vacated.

CONTRABANDS

By Thanksgiving Willacassa had become exceedingly restless. The summer season at Cape Island had long since passed. Her father had taken his mysterious trip "abroad" and would say little or nothing about it. And word from Shiloh was haphazard at best.

The letters he wrote, though filled with interesting anecdotes, said very little about the War in the West and never raised the possibility of his coming East soon. Shiloh's chief problem seemed to be combating boredom. He had volunteered for any number of special assignments, some quite dangerous, but each time he was turned down. "We need you here," he was told, "but not once was I given to understand why."

Then one day Willacassa received a letter from him describing a camp for contrabands that had sprung up outside of Vicksburg. Shiloh was particularly moving when he detailed the conditions the contrabands lived under, so moving that Willacassa almost felt guilty for their plight though she had nothing to do with it.

"What most of them want," wrote Shiloh, "is rudimentary learning. They see in education a kind of Moses, their passport out of the terrible wilderness of slavery—if not for themselves, for their children. It is a longing they have that is almost pathetic in its poignancy. But except for a few Northern missionaries who have passed through, setting up an occasional classroom in a shed, a barn, or an abandoned church, precious little has been done for them."

Willacassa wanted to send a telegram in immediate reply but she soon discovered there was no way it could be received in Mississippi. She then dashed off a letter to Shiloh, in much the same language she had composed for the telegram.

"Dear Captain,

Have decided to offer my services. 'Teacher' will arrive as soon as transportation permits, hopefully after this letter is received.

Love,
Willacassa"

But Willacassa found travel in the third year of war to be a most unpredictable and arduous venture. Her journey began promisingly enough when she caught a train of the Baltimore and Ohio Railroad at Baltimore's Calvert Station. Though sidetracked on several occasions to make way for a train speeding in the opposite direction, she eventually found herself on the Indiana Central, which left a trail of smoke that could suffocate an entire city. Arriving at Indianapolis, she found the water tower so frozen and the railroad yard so windswept and desolate that she was tempted to put up for the night. But as she had no way of knowing how frigid the weather would be the next day Willacassa switched instead to a Jefferson Railroad train headed for Louisville. No sooner was she seated than she was dislodged, along with other civilian passengers, to make way for reinforcements and the delivery of provisions, ammunition, and even forage for the horses. Standing outside in the bitter cold, she flashed her correspondent's pass to at least four U. S. Military Railroad officers before one of them allowed her to climb aboard again, if she could find the room. In Louisville, she finally forsook the railroads and boarded a steamer which carried her the rest of the way to Mississippi.

"It was awful," she told Shiloh, "but at least I'm here."

"I dropped the bait," he said when she fell into his arms, "and you snatched it hook and sinker. I knew that if I mentioned the camp you'd come running. And you did. You see, I got tired of being noble. I knew I'd go mad if I didn't see you again."

"I'm so glad you want me."

"But I wasn't fair, was I?"

"Nonsense. I would have come sooner or later anyway. But where is the camp?"

"I'll take you there in the morning. Though I'd better prepare you. It's primitive, worse than a prison camp. The filth and the stench are unbearable. Except for a few convalescent soldiers, the contrabands have no one to look after them."

"It doesn't matter. I want to help!"

"Good. I've set up a schoolroom for you. It's an abandoned house just outside the camp. You'll see that too in the morning. But tonight, I want tonight to be ours."

She clenched his fingers. "It will be, Sam. It will be."

They took dinner in what passed for an officers' club, an old broken down saloon that had been converted by three black army cooks into a restaurant. Later Shiloh escorted Willacassa to a frame residence, a building needing paint, that had once been a private school for the daughters of wealthy landowners and now housed some local citizens burned out by the war.

"They think we're married," said Shiloh. "Do you have any objections to that?"

Willacassa shook her head.

"You should have, you know."

"Objections? Why should I when I have everything I want."

"Everything?"

"I have Sam Shiloh, haven't I? That's all I want. I knew that when I was alone on Cape Island. And I know that even more now."

After that declaration, there was little more to be said. They spent the night together in a second-floor bedroom.

The contraband camp stood on a levee that overlooked a small stream where Willacassa and Shiloh saw black women washing clothes. No houses stood on the high ground, only tents or makeshift huts, chinked with mud. Most of the contrabands were women and children, the able-bodied men having been assigned by the military to tasks as stevedores, teamsters, woodsmen, stablemen, army cooks, nurses, orderlies, or servants. There were a few black men in uniform who patrolled the camp. Some proudly wore buttons with the letters "U S" on them. But they were an auxiliary force at best whose main job was to protect the camp against Confederate guerrillas.

The condition of the camp was appalling. Everywhere Willacassa saw piles of refuse spilling over the few barrels that had been set down to contain the garbage. Cats and mangy dogs roamed the camp with impunity. Some of the women and children were in patches and rags, with little but small fires to protect them from the raw winter chill. And the crowding and congestion was so widespread that Shiloh and Willacassa had difficulty moving among the contrabands who gathered in knots and enclaves based on kinship or place of origin.

"Where do I start?" asked Willacassa, depressed by what she saw and angry at the same time. "Couldn't the military do more than this?"

"The army's here to fight a war. They weren't prepared for the outpouring of men and women that infiltrated their lines."

"But they've got to do something!"

"They are. They're getting these people out of the way. War takes precedence over humanity, you know."

Willacassa recognized Shiloh's characteristically ironic view of things but found herself becoming impatient with it just now.

"It's inexcusable!" she burst out.

Shiloh took her arm. "You're right, Willacassa. It's inexcusable. It's also inhumane and stupid and insensitive. But if you're to do some good, you're going to have to steel yourself to the wretched conditions here. The thing to do is start recruiting students. How old do you want them to be?"

"Somewhere between eleven and fifteen, I should think. At that age they want to learn. The younger ones want only fun and games."

"You'll recruit mostly girls this way. Boys of that age fancy themselves young bucks and regard school as unmanly."

"I'll take that chance. Besides, when I went to school the girls were always the better students. The boys were busy playing pranks and pulling up dresses."

Willacassa did all the recruiting herself. She wanted no protection from Shiloh who offered to accompany her and only reluctantly let her go among the contrabands herself. Walking from one end of the camp to the other, on ground so soggy that she sank ankle-deep in the dark mud, Willacassa managed to persuade the black women to permit some twenty of their daughters and younger sisters to attend her school. She also managed to talk four boys into attending class by assuring them that they would drive the wagon to and from the school and cut the wood for the stove, altogether manly tasks that would put them in good stead with their peers.

Willacassa found the schoolroom that Shiloh had set up for her to be a practical if somewhat crude affair. A half dozen rough benches were laid out in rows. Placed on each bench and set apart were four piles of school supplies. Where he got the chalk and slate boards from, Willacassa did not know. But her desk appeared to have been requisitioned from the private school that now served as her residence. It had a black-leather top with a built-in pencil box and three smart drawers that slid open without much pull. And the potbelly stove that had been connected to the back wall of the room heated up quickly and also boiled water for the herb tea that the students drank between lessons.

Willacassa did not have much success at teaching the alphabet until one talented girl sketched a word to match each letter, such as teacher for T and barrel for B. Later Willacassa read simple stories and made up flash cards for key words in the stories to help the students recognize the words. After a few weeks some of the brighter girls were reading short sentences and printing some fifty short common words.

But there was also a problem of attrition. Those girls who could not form the words and had trouble remembering the letters of the alphabet stopped coming to school. But others who through word of mouth had heard about Willacassa's classroom quickly took their places.

"I've got three groups going at one time," she told Shiloh. "Beginning, middle, and advanced. And the advanced are helping the beginners. It's all very exciting."

But the best part of Willacassa's day was what happened after school. Three or four girls always remained behind. (The boys made a second trip with the wagon to pick them up.) And they talked freely about their lives on the plantations.

Scootie, a short, energetic fourteen-year old, told how she spent much of the day sleeping in the corn rows instead of working in the fields. Jerusha, a tall, lean young woman with mischievous eyes, delighted in tricking her overseer by putting stones in the cotton before weighing time. But Mandy, a husky, rotund female who looked older than her years, described the whipping she got for refusing to go to bed with a "breedin' nigger."

"Ah may be fat. But ah ain't no cow. No bull man's gonna give me babies. Ah'll pick ma own man when time comes. Dat's what I said. And dat's when ah got whupped. Still have de welts on ma bottom."

"Breedin' Negro?"

"Yeah. He da one Massa pick fo' stud. Big an' strong, so de kids be big an' strong. Massa make mo' money dat way."

"How awful!"

"Not all Massas mean," said Scootie. "Ma Massa treat us good. He keep sayin' you won't go off when dem Yankees come? An' we smile an' say, 'No, Massa. We lak it heah. We lak de plantation.' But soon as blue coats come up de hill, we scoot off."

"See dat chalk," said Mandy. "If ah tried to write, Massa'd break dem fingers. If ah even lookin' at a book, ah be put in a hot box. But now we lookin' at books all da time. Massa'd have one big stroke if'n he knew."

"'Course, tings ain't too good in camp. But gettin' betta. Army rations startin' to come. Some clothin' too. Pretty soon we be really free."

Pretty soon, thought Willacassa. And then what?

"I don't know what they're going to do, what'll become of them," she confessed to Shiloh. "They're free, but they're not free. They're certainly ill-equipped to make their way in the world outside."

"Well," said Shiloh, "they've got a lot of hate to deal with, a lot of fear."

"It's more than that. They walked off the plantation. They turned their backs on that life. But at least they knew what to expect there. They don't know what to expect in their new, strange world. If the contraband camps are any indication, they have a way to go before they improve their lot."

"Trouble is," said Shiloh. "Nobody's ready for them. It took weeks, months before the military set up this camp. Even if the war should end tomorrow and they're all freed, we haven't the least idea what to do with them. Oh, some will go back to work for their old masters, those who treated them right. And some will hire out for wages. But those who knew nothing but picking cotton will find it hard to eke out a livelihood.''

"Yet a lot of these girls—and even the boys— are bright and willing. If given the chance, they'll make something of themselves.''

"And people like you are giving them that chance, Willacassa.''

"Not really. We're scratching the surface, that's all. What we need is a massive effort, the kind of effort we put into the war. Without that, it'll take a hundred years before we see any results.''

"Well, you won't get that," said Shiloh. "Until the war is over, no one's going to worry about the contrabands. No use pretending otherwise. So long as the South can't have them, we'll put up with them. That's all the military worries about. What happens to them afterwards is of no immediate concern.''

"Oh, I feel such pity for them, Sam.''

"They don't want pity, Willacassa. What they want is a start, enough of a start to help them help themselves. And you're giving them that.''

"But—''

"We can't go on being paternal. That's what ole massa did. They've had enough of that. Oh, there'll be preachers aplenty after the war, teaching them this and teaching them that, but mainly teaching them the Lord's word. And maybe their own preachers will be doing the same thing. But until they learn how to fend for themselves—and some are already doing that—they won't be truly free.''

Willacassa looked at Shiloh with a mixture of awe and hostility.

"Talk about preaching! You do a pretty good job yourself!''

"That's not preaching, Willacassa. It's argument. The bedrock of my profession.''

"I still think it's preaching.''

Shiloh took her arm. "Maybe it's the rumblings of an empty stomach. What say we get something to eat?''

Willacassa laughed, totally disarmed by him, then joined Shiloh for dinner in what passed for the officer's club.

On a raw day in November a troop of Union soldiers descended on the Pettigrew plantation and proceeded to strip the place clean. Chickens, cows, horses, mules—anything they could lay their hands on. Even the hams in the smokehouses and the corn in the crib. They left nothing for the slaves to eat even though the owners had long since departed and had taken with them such provisions as they could haul away in their carts and wagons.

"But we'll starve if yo' take the livestock," protested Mandy's mother.

"Get out of my way, old woman!"

The soldiers pushed the slave aside and began chasing two hogs that had broken loose from the barnyard. When they caught them, they cut the hams off the living animals and left them writhing and groaning on the ground. Mandy's mother killed the hogs to put them out of their misery.

Mandy's mother liked to think the soldiers had been drinking lest they wouldn't be so cruel. But there was no sign this was so. And then the soldiers dragged several slave women off to their camp and raped them. One was later found in a shallow grave mutilated by razors.

This was one of the stories Mandy told Willacassa when the girl had learned to trust her. And Willacassa in turn narrated it to Shiloh.

"Your Union soldiers are often no better than the Rebs," she noted. "At least when it comes to the contrabands. Oh, Sam, how could they be such butchers!"

"I make no brief for these men," said Shiloh. "There are sick, despicable people on both sides. I'm sure Mandy's told you equally gruesome stories about the plantation owners and their overseers."

Willacassa nodded. "She has. But those stories don't surprise me. I was led to believe our side was more humane."

"And many of our soldiers are. I was with a group that shared their meat, bread, and coffee with hungry slaves. And I've seen officers help scattered families make contact with their loved ones. It isn't all one-sided."

"I realize that," sighed Willacassa, "It's just the more I get to know these people the more I find how deep-seated is their hatred. I wonder if they'll ever come to trust white men again."

"It'll take time, Willacassa. It's like a red-hot poker. Once burned by it, a person handles the thing quite gingerly for a while."

"But what do you do with the seared flesh?"

"Try to let it heal. Oh, I know it's easier said than done. Yet it's the only course to take."

"But It's been so hard for them. Nothing but pain and more pain."

"Yes, it's been hard. And the worst is yet to come. Once the war's over, the real agony begins. Even if the slaves are freed, their ordeal will not be over. They'll be cast adrift in a society that has no place for them— other than what they've been allowed to do before. It's going to make for a lot of chaos and a lot more suffering. Great expectations on the one hand. Profound disappointment on the other."

" 'But at least we're free!' Scootie keeps saying. I guess that counts for something."

"It counts for a great deal. But they'll pay a price. We'll all pay a price."

Shiloh now fell into a passive quiet, and Willacassa knew something was troubling him. Disquieted when anything unsaid was between them, she drew near to him.

"Is something wrong, Sam?"

"Wrong? No. It's just that I've been transferred back East again.

"Back to the 25th?"

He nodded. And for the first time that Willacassa could remember, Shiloh was tentative. "You will come too?" he asked.

Willacassa had assumed at first that the question begged reassurance, that Shiloh was asking her whether she loved him enough to follow him across the country again.

"Of course I will." But no sooner had she said this than she hesitated. "Though not right away."

What Shiloh feared had suddenly confronted him. "I was afraid you were going to say that."

"It isn't that I don't want to go. You must know that. I just can't leave my work in the middle of things. You said yourself these people need all the help they can get."

"Did I say that? I suppose I did. But I didn't mean that you had to do it all yourself. There'll be others to pick up the standard."

"Of course there'll be others. And when they arrive I'll join you."

"That might be a year or more."

"Nothing like that! In any case, I'll join you this summer. The army's told Mandy they'll be needed in the fields for planting and harvesting then. Otherwise there'll be nothing for anyone to eat."

Shiloh was appeased but not comforted.

"Just a few months and we'll be together again."

When she was left alone later—for there were reports of Confederate guerrilla activity in the area and Shiloh had drawn night duty—Willacassa reassessed her position. Had she offended Shiloh? Had she been too quick to say she was staying behind? She was not sure. The one thing she did not want to do was hurt him. For she loved the man beyond anything she ever imagined possible. Her stay in Mississippi from the day of her arrival had been one continous celebration of life and love. But her work with the contrabands had been so demanding that she found no time to reflect on her happiness with Shiloh.

Yet this happiness was the spring water of her life, constantly replenished by the moments she spent with him. It did not matter whether they were in an intimacy of talk or in communion at the dinner table or in one another's arms. Always she was happy with him. Always she discovered more in him than she had ever expected to find. The very best in a man was revealed in Sam Shiloh. Strength, yes. Strength of intellect and an unrivalled integrity. But strength of tenderness too. He was not afraid to show his feelings for her, though he couched them with subtle humor and a uniqueness of language peculiarly his own.

"I like your outfit," he would say when she wore the coarse army fatigues he had gotten for her on the days she cleaned and overhauled her classroom.

She laughed. "They're marvelous youngsters but they're forever tracking in mud."

"That's not surprising. There's nothing but mud in camp."

"I know. But I want the schoolroom to be appealing. I found some sprigs and a vase. Can't wait until the flowers are blooming again."

"And I can't wait until I see you tonight. I'll make sure my boots are clean before I set foot on your carpet. I'm mad about you, you see. But I'll not be mud about you."

Willacassa smiled. Shiloh was unmistakably Shiloh. Still she feared that he would mistake her determination to stay on as a repudiation of her love for him. She did not know how to convey the intensity of her feelings and at the same time meet what she considered to be a prime commitment. She knew only that she had a compelling duty to continue the work she was doing, at least for now. There was no way she would turn her back on this. Scootie, Jerusha, Mandy and the others had become an essential part of her life. Their dogged attempts to learn, to unravel the mysteries of the printed page, to scratch out letters that froze an utterance until the slate was wiped clean—all this had filled her with surging emotions and a vibrant sense of achievement. She had never quite experienced these feelings before, not even when she had put together a sketch from life with a few bold strokes of the pen.

But there was no sense of self-importance here. Not for a moment did Willacassa pretend that she had accomplished anything someone else might not have done. She recognized that she had no special powers, no special gift for teaching. She was in no way superior to anyone else in this regard. What little she had achieved she had done because she had taken the trouble to do it. She had established her little school smack in the middle of a starving student body. It was no wonder they had made a feast of their opportunity.

The night before Shiloh was scheduled to leave, they sat outside the camp listening to the mournful singing of the contrabands. It was a warm, cloudy night. The sky was darker than usual with no fires lighting up the levee as on cooler evenings. Everything sat in darkness. Only the pure sound of voices rose up in the night air, the deep resonant voices of the older men and the incredibly lyrical, heartfelt tremelos of the women, young and old. It was a spontaneous, responsive singing, full of purple sorrow and deep melancholy. And the emotional effect on those listening was so profound as to evoke a magical, religious ecstasy, filled with the cry of anguish and the joy of hope and redemption.

"As Scootie says, her people's singing comes gushing up from the heart. It's got a yearning and a passion," said Willacassa, "we whites will never know."

"I'm not so sure," said Shiloh, squeezing her hand. "Now that I'm about to lose you, I have an idea what passion and yearning are all about."

"You're not going to lose me, Sam. You know why I'm staying behind. It has nothing to do with my love for you."

"I know because you tell me that. But I can't convince myself that it is true."

"It is true, my love." She turned to kiss him. "And it won't be too long before we're together again. Just as soon as I'm able, I'll be going back East."

"Only to return once more."

"I'll return just long enough for someone to replace me. There should be a whole slew of teachers and ministers on the way by then."

"Well, it's my own fault," admitted Shiloh. "If I hadn't written you—"

"If you hadn't written me, I wouldn't have come. And if I hadn't come—"

"You're right, Willacassa. If you hadn't come, I would never have known how precious you are to me."

Shiloh spoke no more of it until the hour he left.

"Remember," he said, mounting his horse. "Come summer—"

Willacassa handed him a love note. "There's no way I'll forget."

He leaned over and kissed her goodbye.

BACK FROM THE DEAD

It was early in March but Henry Sawyer could not remember what day it was. He had long ago given up remembering the day of the week. And dates had even less meaning for him. One gray day blended with another at Libby Prison, just as the faces did in time, the pale, bland faces of the inmates and the sun-tanned faces of the guards.

It seemed the better part of a year since he fell at Brandy Station. But he could still feel the pain of that occasion in his bones, and the headaches that went with it. On raw days his head and thigh wounds drew like strings on a bow. That was hard to forget. But remembering what day it was only produced confusion and irritation in the man.

He was told to get his things together. He was moving out. Moving out? Was he being transferred? Where was he going? Never mind, he was told. He would find out soon enough.

Not long after, but still before dawn, he was joined by Captain Flinn of that Indiana regiment of volunteers whose number he could not remember either. They were marched to the prison doors, ever so quietly however. Then, lo and behold, the doors were opened.

Only when the prison doors were shoved aside did Sawyer feel the darkness lift.

"You're being exchanged," volunteered one of the guards, but no more was said.

The two prisoners, scarcely believing what they had heard, followed their escorts. They were turned over to Confederate officers who led them to a waiting carriage, Sawyer walking with his usual soldierly bearing, Flinn, his head down, a man broken in health and spirit.

So the rumors were true. For days now Sawyer had heard via the grapevine that he would be exchanged, he for "Rooney" Lee, and Flinn for another officer of rank. Imagine, "Rooney" Lee, General Robert E. Lee's own flesh and blood! It was enough to make a man who had almost given up on himself feel important.

"Is it really 'Rooney' Lee?" he asked of one of the Confederate officers accompanying him.

"The prisoner you're being exchanged for?"

"Yes."

"It's General Lee all right. Can't say I'm happy though."

"Why?"

"Would have liked to see you shot. After all that fuss in the newspapers, doesn't seem right to let you go."

It was well outside of Richmond that the official exchange took place. The carriage that Captains Sawyer and Flinn were seated in had its shades drawn. Not once in the semi-darkness did their Confederate escorts exchange words with their prisoners. The carriage waited for about a half hour before another carriage, also with shades drawn, pulled up on the other side of the road.

"You may step out now, gentlemen." The door of the carriage was pushed open and Captain Sawyer stepped down. Then he turned to assist Captain Flinn. When both men were free of the carriage, a man in dark civilian clothes approached them. He carried a sheaf of papers under his arm.

"Will you sign here?" He indicated where he wanted the Confederate escorts to scrawl their signatures. Then Sawyer heard the scratching of pens on paper.

As soon as the documents were signed, the dark-suited civilian returned to his carriage and opened its door. Two Union soldiers alighted and they made way for two Confederate prisoners to step down. One of them, tall, regal, and about twenty-seven years of age, Sawyer recognized as "Rooney" Lee.

"Are you satisfied that the prisoners are the ones listed in the exchange papers?" The civilian posed the question to one of the Confederate escorts who had followed him.

"I am satisfied."

"And you?" he asked, indicating the Federal officers.

Before replying, one of the officers strode across the road and addressed Sawyer's comrade-in-detention. "Are you Captain Flinn, sir?"

"I am."

"Will you be able to travel?"

"Where are you taking me?"

"To Washington, sir."

"I'd much prefer Indiana."

"In due time, sir. In due time."

"I'm ready, then."

Sawyer was somewhat disappointed. He had half expected he too would be addressed. But when the two men were led to their new carriage, one of the Union officers did turn to him and say, "Captain Sawyer, I'm from South Jersey myself. Dennisville. Glad you're back with us once more."

"Glad to be back."

At this very instant Captain Flinn and Sawyer crossed the paths of the two Confederate officers who had also been held as prisoners. Sawyer stopped. The exchange might be no more than a routine exercise for the military, but for him it was a matter of some importance. He raised his arm and saluted. His counterpart also stopped. In the spirit of reconciliation, General Rooney Lee returned his salute and even broke into a benign smile. "A fair exchange, I would say."

"Thank you," replied Sawyer. "Hope to see you again on Cape Island one summer."

"Cape Island?" Then a flash of recognition lit up the young general's face. "Of course. Hughes Street. We spent a couple of summers there. I would very much like that. Yes, indeed. Good luck, Captain."

At the Methodist Church on Friday night, April 30, Cape Island honored its war hero. Before a large audience which included Nathaniel Harrah, Captain Whilldin, Joseph Leach, Harriet Sawyer and the children, Captain Henry Washington Sawyer was presented with a handsome saddle and bridle.

"To a brave and dedicated soldier who just happened to be a Cape Islander," said Mr. Magonagle, the new publisher of the *Ocean Wave.*

This was greeted by a spontaneous standing ovation and thunderous applause. Then the choir broke into "We'll Rally Round The Flag, Boys." And when they came to the words, "shouting the battle cry of freedom," those present again rose to their feet and broke into a resounding tribute.

Sawyer, deeply moved, brushed a tear from his cheek. His voice faltered when he turned to speak.

"First, I want to thank you all, especially Mr. J. F. Cake who was the prime mover in obtaining for me so beautiful a set of cavalry equipment. I trust I will do it honor before too long. Some of you have asked that I recount the whole terrible episode that brought me here. Though I feel the newspapers have given a fair account of it, I will retell it—later in the evening.

"But at this time I want to pay tribute to those gallant men who fell at Brandy Station and were not fortunate enough to survive the day. Men like Lieutenant-Colonel Broderick and Major Shelmire, two of the bravest officers I have ever known. These men never wavered in their determination to bring the rebellion to an end. They never questioned an order or refused to obey one. They were always in the thick of things. And except for some bad luck they'd be standing today and I'd be buried at Brandy Station. No man who fights as hard as they did should die in vain. And it is my belief that neither Lieutenant-Colonel Broderick nor Major Shelmire died in vain. They died to preserve the Union.

"I have to confess that early in this war, like many of our Cape Islanders, I was not in favor of President Lincoln or later his emancipation of the Negro slaves. It's not that I wanted to perpetuate this abominable institution. I simply did not feel that the Negro was ready for freedom.

"I have had a good deal of time to think about these things in Libby Prison during my long stay there. Prison too is a kind of servitude. And its hardships are not the hardships of choice. If nothing else, it teaches a bitter lesson on what freedom really is. And so I am now of the mind that no man should be enslaved or imprisoned without just cause, whatever the problems his freedom would entail. And I can no more justify perpetuating the bondage of the Negro slave than I could see perpetuating my own bondage as a prisoner of war.

"However humble his origins, however different he may seem from the rest of us, the Negro is after all a man. And as a man he deserves the same consideration and regard that we reserve for our neighbors. I recognize that there will be a long, hard road ahead of him. And I don't pretend to know what reforms should be brought about to make this road less arduous. But Mr. Lincoln's Emancipation Proclamation seems like a good starting point for bringing the matter to an end.

"By the same token I am now convinced that Mr. Lincoln should be re-elected to office come November. I say this not because he was instrumental in my release, although that would be reason enough. I say this because he is the one man who can bring this unhappy war to a successful conclusion. And with the war's end, I hope to see an end to evil in the land.

"As for your heartfelt support, never will I forget this evening. The handsome tribute you have paid me warms this soldier's heart, this neighbor's heart. Cape Island has been my home for many years now. And I hope to live out my days here. I am too much overcome to say any more at this time. I trust you will forgive me. All I can say is thank you and God Bless you."

"That was a fine speech," said Joseph Leach when Sawyer stepped down.

"That was no speech, Mr. Leach. That was the contraband of war."

Henry Sawyer sat with his legs up on the porch railing of Trescott House, a cup of coffee in his powerful hand. Harrah and he had decided the day before to greet the dawn from the wide verandah facing the ocean. Pulling their rocking chairs forward, they dug into a pile of biscuits which they had plucked from a bowl

209

in Rachel's kitchen.

"I'd forgotten how beautiful Cape Island can be. At Libby I often thought about it and imagined that time and distance had cast a rosy hue. But now that I'm here I realize that, if anything, my memory of the place failed me. It's even more spectacular than I ever imagined. The strand, the sea, and the sky—and a beautiful sunrise! What more can a man ask?"

Harrah held his cup up in the way of a salute and nodded agreement. "I know what you mean. I've been away for only a few weeks at a stretch. But each time I come home I find the place more beautiful than before."

"And how's Willacassa?" Sawyer asked.

"Well, I expect. She doesn't write often. And when she does write, her letters are so full of impressions and experiences that she says nothing of herself."

"A fine young woman, that girl. Do you think she'll marry soon?"

"It's hard to say. She's twenty-six. Yet no talk of marriage. It's as if that Francis Grandee affair took all the starch out of her."

"What about Eliot Irons? He seemed like a proper suitor."

Harrah looked surprised. "Didn't you know? We lost him just after Bull Run. Wasn't his wound killed him, but pneumonia."

"I'm sorry. I didn't know." Sawyer sadly shook his head. "So many fine young men have been lost. I wonder how many more."

"Thousands I'm afraid. The bloodletting never stops."

"Is that why you're in the peace movement?" Sawyer was not being critical. But Harrah knew that he had little patience with that sort of thing.

"I suppose you've heard the talk around the town."

Sawyer looked down at the deck-painted boards of the porch floor. "I've heard."

"I imagine I've been accused of being a Copperhead. Or even a traitor."

"Not quite that bad."

"Well, I'm no Copperhead. My sympathies are emphatically not with the South. And I'm no traitor, either. But I confess to wanting the war ended."

"Were you a party to the New Jersey Resolutions of 1863?"

"I was in favor of setting up commissioners—on both sides—to see if some formula could be found. But I was opposed to many sections of the proposal, including those on slavery. There can be no compromise on that issue. And so I didn't support it."

"I'm glad. There were plenty of us who regarded it as a stab in the back. Some field officers drafted a response to the resolution and sent it on to Trenton.''

"I read about that. It's natural to stand up for what you're fighting for. But I see no harm in looking for peace.''

"Quickest way to get it is to win the damn war!'' Sawyer set his feet down as if to punctuate his remark.

"At this stage of the game, you may be right, Henry. Still, it seems a shame to let the killing go on.''

"You're right about the killing. I've seen a lot of it and it sticks in the craw.'' A grimace accompanied Sawyer's comment. "I've seen men blinded and their heads blown off. I've seen their entrails hanging out or seen them horribly emasculated. I've seen limbs piled up in hospital wagons like lumber—a bloody mess. Yes, it's sickening, a nightmare in broad daylight. And what's been done to homes and livestock isn't too pretty either. But what's the alternative? Let 'em secede? If the Confederate States secede, what's to stop the other states from seceding? Then where will this country be? We've got to keep fighting, that's all.''

Harrah knew that he was being outflanked. But he held his ground.

"The war will end one day anyway. You admit that?''

Sawyer reluctantly nodded.

"Then why not end it now? Are we always to be the victims of vain and stubborn men? Will another fifty thousand deaths prove anything?''

"The war will end when we stick it to them,'' said Sawyer grimly. "Not before.''

A gaunt Henry Sawyer visited Joseph Leach at his home. Though he had taken a strong stand on the war with Harrah, he was not entirely satisfied with himself. He had too much time on his hands. He had too much weight on his mind. He knew only that the former editor and publisher of the *Ocean Wave*, who by virtue of a Republican Party appointment had become the postmaster of Cape Island, was a kindred spirit. The war had made comrades of them, each in his own way, Henry Sawyer firing pistols on the battlefield, Joseph Leach launching salvos in the press.

"You're a hero, Henry. A bona fide hero. Do you know that?''

"I don't feel like a hero.'' Nor was his face, which was drawn and wan, the face of a hero, however rugged it remained.

"After what you've been through, you've reason to be proud.''

"After what I've been through,'' said Sawyer, "I've reason to re-examine all that I believed in.''

"Re-examine? Not your faith certainly.''

"No, that's been confirmed. Anyone who's been plucked from

the jaws of death as I have cannot find his faith wanting. It's other things I've come to doubt. I've met 'Rooney' Lee, you know.''

"The officer they exchanged for you?''

Sawyer nodded. "When I met him I recognized him as one of the Lees who used to vacation in a house on Hughes Street. And I remember him as a quite decent fellow. If the exchange didn't go through, two former Cape Islanders would have been shot. Not just a Yank and a Reb.''

Leach surrendered a faint smile at the irony.

"You don't think that strange?''

"Yes, I do, Henry. But, more important, I think it no small accomplishment to be exchanged for Robert E. Lee's son.''

Leach could see that Sawyer was thoughtful and troubled at the same time, a man of conflicting ideas as well as a veteran of conflict.

"I'm reporting back to my company, Mr. Leach.''

"To fight again?''

Sawyer nodded.

"But you've done enough fighting, don't you think? And Harriet could do with having a husband at home for a while.''

"The war won't be over until we drive the rebels into the ground. All that time spent in Libby Prison did nothing to bring the end closer.''

"Some people think the end is near already.''

"Then they don't know the enemy, Mr. Leach. These rebels are a stubborn lot. And—''

"And what?''

"And I'm afraid if I stay at home I'll become a changed man.''

"Changed? In what way?''

"I'll let myself soften. I'll let myelf feel the spray and the breeze of Cape Island. I'll forget what it's like to put a sabre to a man or shoot his brains out. If I forget that, I'll never be able to go back. And the war will drag on.''

"Is that what you're afraid of?''

Sawyer nodded. "I was never more afraid in my life. If I allow myself to change, to become a Cape Islander again, I'll never be able to ride a horse into battle. I'll never be able to lead a charge. I've got to keep going while the blood is up. I can't let men like 'Rooney' Lee soften me, even though I knew him in a way. Even though if it weren't for him I wouldn't be alive today.''

"There would have been other prisoners to exchange.''

"Someone other than Robert E. Lee's son wouldn't have turned the trick. Not for a moment. I owe my life to him. And I don't like the feeling. The feeling that I came so close to dying—but for him."

"You're still feeling the effects of confinement, Henry. It'll take time to overcome that."

"I don't know what I'm feeling. All I know is it was simpler before. They were rebels, traitors, and we had to go get them. Even that popinjay, Jeb Stuart. Now, at least some of them—are people. It's easier to put a sabre to a traitor than to someone I once knew on Cape Island. Do you understand what I'm saying?"

"Yes, Henry," said a sober Joseph Leach who always had trouble keeping his enthusiasms in check. "Maybe for the first time I understand what a terrible war this is."

"Say hello to Granville for me when you see him. I remember when he visited us in camp. It was a sight for sore eyes."

"He's a soldier now too, you know. He was a reporter then."

"He never stopped being a reporter. I've read his letters in the *Ocean Wave*. A good job he's done, telling things as they are. If you're looking for a hero, Joseph, try your own son. Or any mother's son on Cape Island, whether he served in the 25th Vols or some other regiment or lies in a desolate grave on a distant Southern hillside."

Joseph Leach put his hand on Sawyer's rugged shoulder. "There'll come a time when you put all this behind you. And you'll return to Cape Island to pick up the good life. Maybe even manage a big hotel, or build one. It'll all come one day. You'll see. One day the long nightmare will be over."

Sawyer nodded as he pulled a seegar from his tunic pocket and bit off the end.

"They're spelling it c i g a r in the newspapers now, Mr. Leach. But I still prefer seegar." So saying, he put a match to it.

COPPERHEAD

It had to be close to midnight when Harrah heard a knocking at the front door. He put on his trousers and a robe, and made his way downstairs. As the knocking was irritatingly persistent, if not loud, he thought for a moment of going for a derringer that he kept in his office. But in the end he changed his mind. Though he was certain everyone on Cape Island was asleep at this hour, he allowed for someone being in trouble.

"Yes?" he asked as he opened the door and made out the figure of a rather tall man partly hidden in the shadows thrown by a distant streetlamp.

"Mr. Harrah, my name is Gillingham. May I come in?"

"Gillingham?" Harrah did not recall the name.

"Yes, I was told by Dr. Zachary that you shared our concerns. Unfortunately I am not the bearer of good tidings. In fact, I'm here on my own account. I'd be obliged if you let me in. I know it's quite late."

Harrah swung the door wide.

"Of course, Mr. Gillingham. Come in. I'm sorry I didn't recognize the name at first."

Gillingham stepped inside, and in the light of the vestibule Harrah saw a troubled man, with a tired, drawn face and thick strands of brown hair tumbling from a high forehead over pale blue eyes. Harrah was struck by the eyes. They were—if such a thing existed—a visionary's eyes, steady, piercing, with an inner brilliancy that blinded all opposition. Correct in their view or mistaken, they were the eyes of total conviction, of unfaltering belief in what they projected.

"What brings you to Cape Island?" asked Harrah. Despite what Gillingham had said, Harrah was still looking for word from Dr. Zachary.

"May I sit down?"

Harrah was shamefaced. "Forgive me. I don't know what's the matter with me. First, I don't invite you in. Then I fail to offer you a seat. Let's go into the drawing room. May I get you some whiskey? You look as if you can stand a drink."

"Thank you. A drink, by all means."

Harrah poured a small glass out of his best bottle and offered it to the man.

Trembling as he took the whiskey, Gillingham downed it at a gulp.

"I'm afraid I'm a little out of sorts," he said. "I've been riding

214

some ten hours. All shook up. I took the liberty of putting my horse in your stable. The poor beast all but collapsed.''

Gillingham sank into the couch.

"The truth is—and I do want to be fair to you—I'm on my way out of the country."

Harrah was surprised by what the man said but not particularly disturbed by the revelation. Discerning no appreciable reaction in his host, Gillingham leaned forward.

"You see, Mr. Harrah, I'm *personna non gratis* in the North. It's my anti-war activities. They don't sit well with the men in Washington. Having been harassed and then detained by them, I now find that they want me for questioning. As you know, writs of habeas corpus have been suspended. Rather than rot in jail for months on end without ever being charged or brought to trial, I decided to find refuge elsewhere."

"In the South?"

"No, that would be regarded as an act of treason. And I'm no traitor. I'm hoping to find passage to Canada. Others have gone that route."

"And what will you do there?"

"Continue to work for the Peace Movement. Write letters. Disseminate pamphlets. Try to maintain contact with men like Dr. Zachary. Even with Gettysburg behind us, I feel that thousands of lives can yet be saved. I don't know what your feelings are at this time. But if you can help me, I'd be eternally grateful."

Harrah did not reply at first.

"I realize I'm putting you in a difficult position. But you must understand what's at stake here. The very freedom we're supposedly fighting for. Dissent, you see, is regarded as disloyalty. The war is used as an excuse to control all thought, to silence all opposition."

"There is the press," said Harrah. "Seems to me they've been pretty outspoken."

"Oh, the press can hackle some feathers and get away with it. They're too powerful to be completely put down."

"I suppose that's something to be grateful for."

"Grateful? There's freedom of the press, all right, if you're rich enough to own one. Besides, they only argue about the conduct of the war. For the most part, they don't put down the war itself."

Harrah only half-listened. To be honest, he was not too comfortable with the situation. Gillingham's predicament was but a magnification of what his own predicament could be had he been more outspoken in public and less circumspect. Harrah recognized that his own style had always been to work quietly, under cover of secrecy if need be. He believed in the efficacy of action, not words. Yet here he was, contemplating doing something, and he was not sure he approved of what he was going to do. At the same time he was disappointed that Gillingham's role was not that of intermediary. As an intermediary for Dr. Zachary, he would have been more than welcome. As a man on the run, Gillingham made of his presence a nuisance and a danger.

"It's getting late," Harrah said at last, downing a glass of whiskey he had poured for himself. "There's a small bedroom you can use on the second floor. But I suggest you put the lamp out before too long."

Gillingham understood.

When Harrah stopped at the "Union Now And Forever" provisions store for his groceries, Aaron Garretson tallied up the bill. "Five dollars and thirty-cents. That's more than you've bought in quite some time. You must have company."

Harrah blanched, then recovered himself. "Yes, Robert E. Lee and Jeff Davis have taken a room for a week."

Aaron Garretson laughed. "All you need is Grant and Lincoln staying across the street at the Columbia House and Ocean Street'd be the Great Divide."

Harrah stowed the groceries in his buggy and headed for the small bridge back of the creek. Two black trash collectors hailed him as he rolled past them. From the landing a steamboat whistle marked the hour at ten-thirty.

Back of the salt marshed behind the creek, Harrah pulled up at the new railroad depot. For years Joseph Leach had championed a Millville to Cape Island Railroad. On June 22 trains began running from Millville to Dennisville and from Cape Island to the Court House. Now with stretches of track laid all the way down the line, a train could make it to Camden in five hours.

Harrah studied the train schedule posted outside the station house. Then he turned the buggy around and under a graying sky chucked his horse back toward Trescott House.

"There's no boat going to New York till Wednesday," he announced once he was back home again.

Gillingham clicked his fingers in disappointment.

"But there's a train goes daily to Camden. You need only take the ferry and you're in Philadelphia."

"Too risky," said Gillingham, becoming increasingly edgy and irritable. "Philadelphia is rife with Federal agents. I'd stand a better chance in New York. After the draft riots Washington has been loosening the reins there."

Gillingham looked directly into Harrah's eyes, his own eyes brilliantly clear though the skin around them was pinched with pain. "I hate to do this to you, Mr. Harrah. But as you can see I'm desperate. If you can bear with me another few days, I'd just as soon take the boat to New York."

"Just as you wish."

And so for the next few days they talked and played chess or read the latest magazines off the steamboat from Philadelphia. Sometimes Harrah would leave him alone in the house to stroll the windswept beach.

Though Harrah had readily engaged Gillingham in conversation while they were locked in the house together, he found himself avoiding further discussion of the Peace Movement. It was as if he were afraid to discover that the men had serious differences despite their general agreement that the war should be ended. He did not know how Gillingham felt about the South or slavery in general. Many of the Peace Movement advocates revealed themselves in their speeches as strongly pro-Southern in sentiment, true Copperheads. And not a few made pronouncements that were virulently anti-Negro. Harrah knew that if he had heard what he regarded as tainted argument from Gillingham he would bridle and perhaps regret that he had given the man refuge. And that he did not want to do.

Harrah wanted instead to keep foremost in his mind the reason he was helping the man. He bitterly opposed the Lincoln Administration's efforts to seize war powers and trample on the basic freedom his countrymen enjoyed. He bitterly opposed the suspension of the writ of habeas corpus. He bitterly opposed the attempt by the government to drive its critics out of the country or, worse still, to throw them into prison in order to silence them. He bitterly resented the failure by the government to distinguish between honest criticism and acts of treason. Yet he was afraid that if he learned that Gillingham did not exactly share Harrah's point of view on why the war should be brought to an immediate end, he might slide back in his defense of the man. It was one thing to denounce government-imposed conformity. It was not so easy to denounce a standard of conformity of one's own. And so he kept reminding himself as he watched the waves toss on the breakers and the gulls circling in search of fish that what he was doing for Gillingham he was doing on broad principle. He was not going to let this principle be swept away by private misgivings or personal judgements.

Harrah managed to walk this mental tightrope until Wednesday morning when he fried some eggs and thick slices of salted ham. After taking breakfast, Gillingham pulled his horse from the stable and made ready to leave.

"I won't write to you," he said, mounting up and leaning forward in his saddle. "Don't want to put you on the spot. I'll remember what you did, though. And maybe when the war's over I'll find a way to thank you."

"Let's hope it ends soon," said Harrah. He waved goodbye, not without a profound sense of relief, then returned to Trescott House.

It was not a day later when Harrah found two Union soldiers camped on his doorstep. The burly one, wearing a sergeant's stripes, rose to address him.

"Are you Mr. Harrah?"

"I am."

"We're looking for Kendall Gillingham. I understand he's gone now, taken a boat somewhere. But we've reason to believe he stopped here."

"He did," said Harrah.

"And you let him stay?"

"I had no reason not to."

"Did you know he was a fugitive from justice?"

"What was he charged with?"

"Nothing yet. He's wanted for questioning."

"Then he wasn't a fugitive from justice."

"What do you mean?"

"Was he charged with any crimes?"

"No."

"Until you charge a man with a crime, you can't legally hold him," said Harrah. "I'm sure you know that."

The two soldiers looked at each other. "But we have this paper." They showed it to him.

Harrah read the document. "Nothing here about a crime being committed. Are you sure this is legal?"

"Look, Mister," said the burly sergeant, snatching the paper out of Harrah's hands. "We were told to arrest Kendall Gillingham. We know he stayed here, then took a steamboat, probably to New York. What we want is information."

"I know no more than you do. But I suspect that what you are doing is illegal."

The sergeant did not take the remark kindly. "Don't be telling me what's legal or illegal. I have my orders and I mean to carry them out. You'd better watch your step, my friend, or we'll be taking you in."

Harrah's neck reddened. "Let's understand one thing. I don't have to watch my step. Not in my own house. And not on Cape Island. Is that clear? What's more, even if we are at war, this is still a free country. I think you'd do well to remember that!"

The sergeant turned abruptly away. "Come on, George. We're wasting our time here. Let's get to the telegraph office."

Mounting their horses, the two soldiers disappeared in the dust of Ocean Street.

FURLOUGH

When spring planting began, Willacassa knew it would not be long before her students were called by the army into the fields. But the call did not come until June.

The army apparently had its own sense of priorities. It had early pulled most of the able-bodied men from the camp to work as laborers for the military. The remainder—women, children, the elderly, and those a bit less than able-bodied—they hired out to private entrepreneurs who leased the plantations that had fallen into Union control. The one thing the military did not want was to have an idle population on its hands.

Some of the negotiations for the labor force dragged on interminably, and even Mandy spoke of wages and written contracts, tickled by the novelty of it all. But as things worked out, many plantation hands under "the new system" toiled for little more than room and board. There were "deductions" for clothing, deductions for medical treatment, deductions for days lost because of illness or "orneriness." It seemed that the old slave system was still in effect, except that it had taken on a few new wrinkles.

In time even her students, twenty girls and five boys, were hired out—to return in the fall. Dashing off a letter to Shiloh, Willacassa took leave of Mississippi. Only this time she travelled by boat to New Orleans—the whole of the river was now patrolled by Union gunboats—and from there to Cape Island.

Willacassa remained on Cape Island just long enough to help her father and Rachel prepare for the new season. But it was long enough for her to draw certain conclusions as the Fourth of July was ushered in. Willacassa in her walks witnessed a shoddiness of taste and an ostentation of dress among the new arrivals that crossed the border of vulgarity. The war-enriched manufacturers, merchants, contractors, jewelers, job lotters, speculators, and undertakers had invaded Cape Island with a vengeance. The men wore diamond stickpins and gold cuff links and silk hats and cassimere shirts. The women wore fur pieces (even in summer) and camel's hair shawls and white lace gloves, and girdled their throats with diamond necklaces. They talked loudly about expensive new carriages, Persian carpets, aubusson tapestry, German clocks, Chinese screens, sterling silverware, and crystal chandeliers. All the while they stuffed their faces with patie de fois, truffles, terrapin, goose, pickles, melons, and French bon bons.

Yet for all their wealth and new-found worldliness, it was Beadles Dime Books, half of which were romances, that they plucked off the bookstalls and tables of the newsdealers' shops and made into ''best sellers.''

Money, Willacassa could see, was no object. These people hired their own hands, brought their own clergymen with them, and almost every night threw lavish banquets and grotesque parties. In their extravagance they made even the old Southern aristocracy of the antebellum years look poor and penny-pinching by comparison. And not once did they give thought to the war, or at least its victims, except to hope that the tide of wealth and profits never ebbed and that when the war ended, as inevitably it must, they would be recognized as the new upper class, the new rich, the new aristocracy.

Willacassa shared none of this with her father. She dismissed the new breed as unworthy of comment, hoping that when the war was over things would be different. Instead she talked about her experiences in Mississippi. And Harrah, who was delighted to have Willacassa home again, listened with rapt interest to her stories about the contrabands and her little school, interrupting now and then to gain more information about the military and its role in the scheme of things.

Of Captain Shiloh, Willacassa said nothing. There was, after all, nothing she could tell Harrah that her father would sanction. She was in love with a married man. She had even cohabited with him. She saw little or no prospect of her ever being his wife. As the classic ''other woman'' in a man's life, she had no excuse or apology to offer, not even the war.

Nor did she tell her father that her relationship with *Harper's Weekly* had been terminated. Somehow the editors had discovered that ''W. Harrah,'' their sketch artist, for whom they had secured a correspondent's pass, was a woman. How they had found out, Willacassa did not know. She suspected that fellow sketch artists, from whom she kept her distance, had in the spirit of unbridled competition informed on her. In any case, the letter she received from one of the assistant editors pretty much told the story.

''Dear 'Miss' Harrah,

Harper's Weekly was distressed to learn that 'W. Harrah,' for whom credentials had been secured from Washington, was not of the masculine gender. While it is not our practice to hire only male sketch artists, we have as a matter of policy never considered sending a woman into military camps where someone of her sex might be exposed to outrages too indelicate to mention. After all, a military camp is a male bailiwick, not always peopled by gentlemen and courteous, well-bred West Pointers.

While we were inclined to consider other assignments for you, more in line with a woman's background and breeding, we have decided against such an offer. This was a most reluctant decision on our part as you are obviously a woman of exceptional artistic gifts. But *Harper's Weekly* felt that it could not reward deception, however well-intended, with the stamp of quality that the magazine represents."

Willacassa was not as distressed by this as she might have been a couple of years earlier. She had published a number of her sketches. She had earned a little money. And given the reception of her "Betty Yank" drawings, she had suspected her days with *Harper's Weekly* were coming to an end. Besides, she was not hurting for income. She always had her ability as a portrait artist to fall back on. When photographers with their wagons were not around, she did quite well in military camps. What bothered Willacassa about the whole business was the fatuous, condescending attitude of those responsible for the letter. "W. Harrah" was still W. Harrah. How did being found out change anything? The sketches she had done had in no way been altered by the discovery. W. Harrah might now be Miss Harrah. But her sketches—with the exception of "Betty Yank"—did not wear skirts. And "Betty Yank" didn't wear much of anything.

Willacassa arrived in Washington after Jubal Early's raid on the suburbs of the capital. At first Willacassa had difficulty locating Captain Shiloh's regiment. But as her war correspondent's pass had never been rescinded by *Harper's*, she was advised that Shiloh's company was temporarily stationed at Fort Reno, which guarded the Rockville Road.

Arriving at Fort Reno in a quartermaster's wagon, she was immediately impressed by the engineering of the outpost. Trenches, revetments, and sharpened tree limbs, pointing toward the enemy, provided the first line of defense. Strong earthworks, supported by sandbags, gabions, and logs walled the fort itself. And along the parapets, center-pintle guns, mounted *en barbette*, poked their noses over the masonry.

Fort Reno was only one of numerous forts and blockhouses that ringed Washington. And it looked as if it had taken some hits in recent days.

When Captain Shiloh met her inside the fort, he seemed surprised.

"You never received my letter?" she asked.

He shook his head. But then he smiled and led her under the

gorge wall where he locked her in a warm embrace.

"How I missed you, Willacassa! You'll never know how much!"

"I'm glad. For a moment there I thought you were disappointed to see me."

"Disappointed? Never! Surprised, shocked even. Had Jubal Early appeared, I couldn't have been more surprised."

Shiloh stepped back a bit. "You see," he explained, "we were called up to strengthen Washington's defenses. That raid by Early really had the capital in a panic. Prior to that, we were dug in before Petersburg. The last letter I got from you was at winter quarters."

Shiloh drew her close to him again. "But that's neither here nor there. Your coming was a Godsend. I put in for a furlough a year ago. I'm due to get one any day now. And I want to spend it with you."

"But what about your children?" Willacassa did not mention his wife.

"I'll see them next time. I did manage to spend a few days with them when I went West. But this time I want to be with you. Unless—unless you have other plans."

She squeezed his hand as hard as she could. "I have no other plans."

"Good. Then find a place for us to spend the furlough. I may get as much as a month. Farnsworth—you remember him—is leaving to run for office at the end of August. It's amazing the connections he's got. Until now we've been co-commanders of J Company. Once he leaves for Indiana, I'll have sole command again."

"Where shall I look?" asked Willacassa.

"Anywhere—so long as it's away from the war. Away from everyone."

"But don't you have any ideas?"

"No. I'll leave that entirely to you, my love. You know this part of the woods better than I do."

Willacassa found a place for the furlough on Long Beach Island. A Captain Bond who had purchased Joseph Horner's Guest House some ten years earlier had advertised in a Washington newspaper. And Willacassa knew enough about such advertisements from her experience on Cape Island to know that it was nowhere near as pretentious as the captain made it sound. In fact, she expected that if would be suitably private with the ocean on one side, the bay not far behind it, and nothing but swamps and empty beaches north and south.

"Sounds perfect," said Shiloh. "We leave on Friday. I've got a whole month and I can't think of a better place to spend it."

"It'd be best going overland," said Willacassa. "I've worked out a route by train and stage to Manahawkin. From there we can take a ferry to the island."

"Does the proprietor know we're coming?"

"I've written him. But we could very well arrive before the letter does."

Shiloh drew her to him.

"It'll be rather like a honeymoon. Won't it, my love?"

"I expect it will.,"

"Captain and Mrs. Shiloh?"

She nodded. "I thought it best to put it that way."

The island was not as isolated as Willacassa had hoped. Actually there turned out to be several places to choose from. The "Club House" proved not as exclusive as one might expect, just room and board for fishermen at five dollars a week. The Harvey Cedars Hotel counted more loose boards than clientele. And the Mansion of Health was neither a mansion nor particularly sound, its steps wheezing whenever someone set foot on them. There was also an Ashley House. But that was some eight or nine miles to the north, near Barnegat Light. So the couple dropped their bags at Long Beach House, reminded the owner of Willacassa's letter, and paid for a room facing the ocean.

Long Beach House had some twenty guests, a mixed bag of people from New York and Philadelphia. Most were regular patrons who were quite familiar with the area and walked the ocean's edge or fished off the rocks on the beach itself. Unlike Shiloh, there were no soldiers or officers staying at the place. So Shiloh quickly disposed of his uniform and dressed like a "salt." Willacassa did likewise, wearing a light peacoat and ducks during their morning walks.

The meals at the house were substantial, sometimes chicken, sometimes the "catch of the day," usually bluefish, weakfish, or tile. They washed all this down with cider, beer, or a good white wine. And there was always a pile of oysters in the backyard, to which Shiloh helped himself.

After a few days Willacassa arranged for their evening meal to be taken in their room. She carried the food upstairs herself, balancing the fried flounder and clams and rolls on a tray, while Shiloh selected a bottle from Captain Bond's ample stock of wine. Then by candlelight, with the shades drawn, they dined at a small round table that the oil lamp used to sit on, the lamp having been removed and tucked away in a corner of the room.

"The guests are fine people. But I just wanted a little privacy," she said.

"In our own private chamber?"

"Exactly."

"You'll get no complaint from this quarter." He leaned over to kiss her as she put her wine glass down.

"Are you flirting with me, Captain?"

"Just reconnoitering."

" 'Flirting' is the term used on Cape Island."

"Well, this is Long Beach Island. And only the gulls and horseshoe crabs 'flirt.' The natives would blush at the word."

"Blush? Did you hear some of the language the fishermen used?"

"I thought it best not to mention it."

"Then I won't mention it either. But it was raw just the same."

He grew serious. "I love you, Willacassa. Surely you must know how much."

She cast her eyes down, not out of modesty as much as a need to suppress her feelings.

"I know," she whispered.

"I wouldn't be here if I didn't."

"I know that too."

Shiloh drew her towards him.

"I can't justify what I'm doing. At least to the rest of the world. And maybe I can't justify it to you."

"You don't have to justify anything to me, Sam. I'm here of my own free will."

"But I want you to know—"

She put her fingers on his lips. "I know all I have to know. I love you, Sam. I see nothing wrong with that. I'm here with you. I see nothing wrong with that, either. I'm sure my father would not understand. Or Reverend Williamson. Or your wife. But I'm here nonetheless." She smiled wanly. "And the strange thing is I don't feel I'm doing anything wrong. Maybe it's not right in the eyes of the law. Or the church. But in your eyes I see nothing to be ashamed of. In your eyes I see only love."

"I didn't mean to raise any ethical questions, Willacassa. I wanted only to assure you—"

She kissed him on the lips. "You talk too much, Captain Shiloh. You have a way with words. But at a time like this—I like your silences better."

Shiloh acceded to her wishes. Blowing out the candles, he did not say any more that night. He found he did not have to.

But the question came up again several days later. And in the interim Willacassa gave the matter a good deal of thought. Willacassa did not have to convince herself that she loved Captain Shiloh. She knew her true feelings on this score. Apart from her physical attraction for the man, she had intense admiration for the person he was. In fact, her admiration was almost a passion with her. She had such an overwhelming desire to be with him, to listen to his irreverent but ardent discussion of men and events, to lose herself in his manly presence that she felt her time wasted when she did not spend it with him.

As a girl she had fallen madly in love with Francis Grandee. Ever the dashing young Southerner, Francis seemed ideally suited to such a place as Cape Island, and Cape Island was as much a part of Willacassa as the strand and the ocean. But she never saw Francis as a person of strong convictions. He was a boy she had fallen in love with who might one day become a man. And her visit to South Carolina had proved that this "one day" might be a long time coming.

As for Eliot Irons, even at his best he never inspired her with confidence—poor Eliot who now lay in a damp grave near Alexandria. Eliot had learning enough and conviction. And in his way he had been as much the abolitionist as William Lloyd Garrison. He had even been a conductor in the Underground Railroad. But he never demonstrated to Willacassa the strength that she looked for in a man of conviction, the kind of strength she saw in Shiloh. And so she had early ruled out Eliot Irons as a prospective suitor.

Willacassa realized that she could only hitch her emotional wagon to a man of strength and intellect. (She could not love a weak man or a man of middling intelligence.) And when these qualities were joined by spirit and compassion, she could race the course of love as wildly as any woman. Shiloh was not a god; and she did not want a god. Nor was he the self-proclaimed minister of a supreme being. He was simply master of himself, as no man she knew, and that in itself was enough.

But on a more prosaic level, she had some difficulty dealing with her situation. Though she had never met Captain Shiloh's wife, she could not pretend the woman didn't exist—or his children. They were a fact of life. She knew, however, enough about "affairs" from her experience on Cape Island to put one myth to rest. A woman never took a man away from his wife. He had already left his wife by the time he found another woman to his liking. And though Willacassa did not pretend to understand what was lacking in their relationship, she was convinced that Captain Shiloh and his wife were in trouble long before Willacassa fell in love with the man.

"Oh, by all standards she's a good wife," he said when they were walking on the beach. "Attends church. Keeps a good home. Gets the boys to eat their breakfast. A good-looking woman, some will say. Clean and proper." He took a path leading through the dunes. "Then what's the problem, you're asking. Frankly I don't know."

"Do you love her?"

Shiloh squinted against the brilliant afternoon sky. "I've pondered about that—even before I knew you. Do I love her? By all odds, by all reckoning, I should. She's a decent person. Well-intentioned. And she's the mother of my sons. But in all honesty I cannot say I do."

"Oh, Sam. How awful!"

"Awful?"

"Yes, why do people fall out of love?"

"Why? Maybe they weren't in love from the start. Just thought they were." He did not quite understand Willacassa's reaction, at least its intensity. But he did not dwell on it. "Anyway, that's neither here nor there. The fact is, I feel free now. No longer in bondage."

"The bondage of matrimony?"

"No, the bondage of institutionalized emotion. I don't mean to shock you, Willacassa. Or disillusion you. But your Captain Shiloh, who preaches restraint in all things, has allowed himself unbridled license. The license to leave his family and go to war. The license to fall in love."

No, he did not shock her. How could he? If nothing else, the war and slavery proved this wasn't the best of all possible worlds. And it was doubtful all marriages were made in heaven. So when by some strange twist of fate two people found in one another the kind of happiness that was so elusive in life, should it be sacrificed on the altar of conventional morality? Not if she could help it. The chance of such a coming together as theirs was too slim to fritter away.

"When the war is over—and it will be one day—I'm not returning home," said Shiloh that evening.

"Time to talk about it then."

"It's best we talk about it now. Unless of course—"

"Unless what?"

"Unless I don't make it through the war. That's always a possibility."

Willacassa took his hand. "Nonsense! What's that you always say? As long as they aim you're safe."

Shiloh broke into a smile. "That's true enough. But seriously—"

"I think you're getting much too serious, Captain. We can't celebrate our private party and be serious at the same time."

"Will you wait for me?"

Willacassa could no longer keep up the pretense.

"If you mean, do I love you? Yes. I do, Sam. But I'll not burden you with any promises. Besides, the end of the war may be a long way off."

"But we'll continue to see each other?"

"Of course we will. And I ask nothing more. I know the situation you're in. I don't want you to do anything on my account you'd later come to regret."

"I'm not going back," he said quietly.

"Of course you are. You'll want to see your children, won't you? And you will, the next furlough you get."

"We'll deal with that when the time comes. Meanwhile—"

"Meanwhile let's get a breath of ocean air. Not a long walk this time. Just as far as the old shipwreck." Willacassa was already putting on her peacoat, so there was no denying her.

But on the beach Shiloh was unusually silent and pensive.

"What is it, Sam?"

"What is what?"

"You're lost in thought. What's troubling you?"

Shiloh kicked a clamshell into the incoming tide. He looked at the gathering clouds.

"I want to set this thing straight," he said. "I don't like drifting in the shallow water of uncertainty."

Willacassa walked quietly for a while, then took his hand. "There's no uncertainty about my feelings for you. Isn't that enough?"

"For me, yes. But what about you?"

"The last few days have told me what I want to know. I'm sure that you love me. That's all the certainty I need."

"Even for the long run?"

She stopped for a moment and faced him, finding Shiloh in his seaman's clothes a more vulnerable person than the captain she knew.

"Look, Sam. There's enough to concern yourself with in this war without having to worry about me. I've never been happier in my life than I am now. Everything seems so complete, so full. And it's all your doing. I can't ask for more. Not now. Not ten years from now."

"And the future?"

"The future will take care of itself."

"You have that on good authority?"

"The best. Rachel's always said that."

"Rachel?"

"My father's cook on Cape Island."

"I see. I guess that settles the matter."

"I'm afraid so," she laughed.

Reaching the shipwreck, they turned into the wind and retraced their footprints on the wet beach.

The last day at Long Beach Island broke cloudy and mist-like. Both Willacassa and Shiloh sensed it would be a difficult time when they found they could not do justice to Captain Bond's generous breakfast. Shiloh ate his eggs, leaving the bacon and the fried potatoes. And Willacassa swallowed a cupful of coffee before they set out on the beach for their early morning walk.

It was a hazy morning, casting a coat of damp gray on everything, sea, sky, sand, and the isolated ramshackle dwellings that sprawled on the dunes. Even the boats in the distance were gray. And gray pretty much set the mood.

"Have you any regrets about the furlough?" asked Willacassa. "I imagine your wife would have welcomed a chance to see you."

"I told you. I wanted to spend it with you."

"But I'm sure she misses you. And you'd probably be happy to see her."

"Happy?" Shiloh smile was a painful one. "My dear Willacassa. A man enlists for three reasons. He's caught up with patriotic fervor. He's drunk. Or he's not happy with his wife." He paused just long enough to unbutton his collar as it was getting warm. "I wasn't caught up with patriotic fervor. And I wasn't drunk."

"Is she that bad?" Willacassa dared to ask.

"That's just it. She's not bad. Nor are the kids bad. They're quite lovable in fact. And I miss them more than I ever imagined I would. What's bad was the feeling I was only half existing."

He drew her towards him and kissed her. "You do understand, don't you?"

A surge of conflicting emotions swept over her and prevented her from replying.

"I didn't mean for anything to happen this way," said Shiloh. "And I didn't mean to cause you any pain."

At this moment Willacassa realized she was not the woman she fancied herself, a woman wise in the ways of the world. Rather she was a young girl, passionate with anticipation, caught up in the paradox of life. "You've caused me no pain."

"It's still not too late to turn back," he said.

She lost herself in his embrace. "I'm afraid it is. At least for me."

"It's this war," added Shiloh. "If it weren't for the war, I wouldn't be here. And you'd be back on Cape Island, wasting no thought on a married Hoosier who practiced law but did not practice his religion."

"I want only to make you happy, Sam."

"You have made me happy."

"Then I'm satisfied. I love you, Sam. I love you so much I can't contain it."

"And I love you Willacassa. But you deserve more than Long Beach Island, beautiful as it is."

"I don't know what my deserts are," said Willacassa, stopping to turn over a horseshoe crab. "And I don't know what the future holds. I know only that I wouldn't trade this time we've had together for the world. It's been the high-water mark of my life."

"And mine."

"And if this life were to end tomorrow, I'd have no regrets. Oh, I don't want it to end. I want it to go on and on! But I regret nothing."

Shiloh stopped and put his hands on her shoulders, gently squeezing her.

"Listen, Willacassa. I have no regrets either. And I won't make any promises—until the war is over. It's been a bloody and brutal war. And except for the contrabands, I doubt much good will come out of it. But at least the war has brought us together. It'll never make up for the killing and the bloodshed. Nothing will. But at least there is that. And I'm grateful."

They turned around. Out of the gray sky a lonely gull began to circle, conducting its periodic search for breakfast. Swooping down, it spotted a string of mussels intertwined among the debris and seaweed lying on the beach. The gull continued to circle, nervously triumphant. Its frenzied, screeching cries pierced the air. But they in no way distracted the two solitary figures trekking the long sandy path back to the guest house.

LETTERS FROM AN IRONCLAD

They gathered in the parlor of Trescott House to talk, Captain Whilldin, Joseph Leach, and Harrah. They did not doubt for a moment that they would disagree. But so much had happened in recent months that they had to test the political waters.

"I tell you Mr. Lincoln will have a hard time getting re-elected," predicted Captain Whilldin, balancing a cup of coffee on his knee. "It's not just Frémont and the Radical Republicans. But 'Little Mac' himself will get the Democratic Party nomination, and he's a very popular man."

"Yes," agreed Joseph Leach, glancing contemptuously at his former newspaper, the *Ocean Wave*, then casting it aside, "but I can't see how General McClellan can rebuke the President for his conduct of the war when he was largely responsible for its early failures."

"Makes no difference. The country is tired of war. Tired of casualties. The push for peace is strong. Looks like you're in the swim of things for a change, Nathaniel."

"I still think Lincoln will be re-elected," countered Leach who had just contributed twenty-five dollars to his campaign. "Running under the National Union Party with pro-Union Democrats like Andrew Johnson gives him broader appeal than he had before. And there's talk Frémont may withdraw in favor of Lincoln."

"Really?" Captain Whilldin cast a doubtful eye. "I heard no such talk. In the end the military situation will determine the victor. If the Union generals win battles, Lincoln will win the election. If not, look for a change. A miscalculation in the field could prove to be the President's downfall. Just as a miscalculation in '61 brought on the war."

"You mean Fort Sumter?" asked Leach.

Captain Whilldin nodded.

"Both sides miscalculated," said Harrah at last, "long before the war. What some in the South really wanted—even twenty years ago—was an end to the tariff. The tariff was always a red flag for the plantation owner. But the North would not give ground. And the Southern States could not muster enough support for the issue. So Calhoun found an issue they could unite on—slavery. Only he called it 'States Rights.' Fort Sumter was just an excuse to splatter some blood. Once blood was spilled, the North would see the South meant business."

"But Lincoln meant business too," pointed out Leach. "Buchanan might have backed off once the firing began, but not

Lincoln.''

"Of course not. The Northern industrialists who backed him for the presidency needed cotton. They also needed the Southern market for its manufactured goods. And it was easier to get cotton while the South was in the Union than out of it.''

"I don't think that's fair,'' protested Leach, his color rising. "What would you have him do? Let them secede!''

"Sooner than spill all that blood.''

"This is what I object to, Nathaniel. Your partisan interpretation of things! Always your appeal has been an emotional one. Stop the bleeding! Stop the killing! Stop the war! I'm not convinced to this day you know what the war is all about. I want to stop the killing as much as you do. But I can appreciate the overriding imperatives that made the war necessary.''

"Overriding imperatives! Which one? The abolition of slavery? Or the preservation of the Union? It's my contention neither one was an overriding imperative for Lincoln. Cotton was the overriding imperative. He made show of force for cotton and the Southern market. Calling up the militia, he had now to gather popular support for this show of force.''

"Nonsense!''

"Let him go on,'' urged Captain Whilldin. But Harrah did not wait for Joseph Leach's sufferance.

"As I see it,'' he continued, "Lincoln had two alternatives. One was to justify the war on moral grounds, as a means to end slavery. This, of course, was not politically expedient. For there were those up North who sympathized with the South on the slavery issue. And once you freed the slaves, what about the cotton? The other was to argue the need to preserve the Union. It did not matter that there was nothing in the Constitution to prevent the South from seceding.''

"Are you sure of that?'' challenged Leach.

"Well, you tell me! Where in the Constitution is there a prohibition against secession?''

"Never mind, Joseph,'' Captain Whilldin broke in. "Go on, Nathaniel.''

"So Lincoln charted the second course and insisted we were fighting to preserve the Union. This idea stirred up patriotism in the North and kept a hold on the Border States. But the support Lincoln counted on from those in the South who were not secessionists never really materialized—except in West Virginia. And it also created a dilemma for him. For it cost Lincoln the early support of the abolitionists. And it ultimately fostered a feeling in the South that somehow the slavery issue would muddle through—win the war or lose. It wasn't until the Emancipation Proclamation that Lincoln regained his equalibrium and his moral integrity and perhaps even a military advantage. Now, ironically, he's running on the Thirteenth Amendment.''

"What matters how a man changes?'' suggested Leach. "So long as he comes out all right in the end.''

"What matters,'' said Harrah, "is the more than two hundred thousand men on each side who will never see the change. And the count keeps going up. I'm not faulting Lincoln any more than the Secessionists. But he's got a lot to account for, too.''

"I think Lincoln's a great man,'' maintained Leach. "And a great president—despite what you say.''

"I believe he was a great man,'' said Harrah, "during the Lincoln-Douglas debates. He reached his peak then. His moral conviction matched his oratorical eloquence. But he has gone downhill ever since. His support of the Thirteenth Amendment is most welcome. Only, it's a little late in the day.''

"Then you won't vote for him?''

"I plan to vote for Frémont. If Frémont steps down, I'll reconsider. I'm no great admirer of McClellan either—even if he is for peace.''

"But I thought you were against the war—all wars,'' chided Leach.

"I'm not against all wars. I'm against wars where the issues are fuzzy—not at all what they seem. If a man must put his life on the line, there has to be a compelling, an unassailable reason. Besides, I can't see this war dragging on much longer. Sherman has taken Atlanta. And Richmond is under siege. The Rebels will be hardpressed to keep their armies together.''

Harrah too was hardpressed as he walked to the post office the next morning. Even as he had argued with Leach about the war, he was acutely aware that Joseph Leach's offspring had at least served in the army. His son had not. Instead Jonathan had turned the war to his own advantage, making a handsome profit running the blockade. Though there was danger in this, there was no honor. The shirttails of disgrace limply hung out.

To their credit, neither Joseph Leach nor Captain Whilldin made any reference to Jonathan's activities. It was enough for Joseph Leach that his eldest son, Granville, had enlisted in the 25th New Jersey in the summer of '62 and had fought gallantly until the regiment was disbanded a year later. Granville had stood foursquare behind his belief in the war. No one could deny that. Jonathan, however wrong the war might be from Harrah's point of view, had precariously maintained a questionable "neutrality''.

But at the post office, almost as a response to what he was thinking, Harrah found a battered pair of letters.

"Dear Dad,

"I don't know when this letter will reach you—or where. The last time I landed at Cape May, Trescott House was shut down. I know it was the off season, but I never thought of Cape Island without you being there. I did not leave a note because I thought I would be back in a week or two. As things turned out, my ship was boarded by Federal officers and I was pressed into service. It was either that or being charged with trafficking with the enemy.

"Before the week was out, I was assigned to one of those experimental ironclad ships being built by the navy. The hope is they can stop the ironclad blockade runner the South has launched so successfully.

"We haven't seen action yet, and at this point I don't care if I do. Actually it makes little difference to me if I live or die. You can't imagine how hot and how stifling it gets below. I don't know how the firemen and the coalheavers stand it. The sun beats down on the water and on the armor plates. The heat given off is horrendous. We can't open the hatches when the sea is rough because the ocean would come pouring in. As a result, the wardroom is a steam bath and we are forever building devices overhead to keep the leaks out. Moreover, the place is filthy. The galley when it's used spreads its grease throughout the ship. And as cooking only adds to the heat, I'd just as soon do without and eat cheese and dry crackers.

"Sometimes when the weather permits and the sea is calm I go up on deck and sit on the shady side of the ship. Some of the men will bask in the sun. But after being cooked in the oven below I can't see being baked some more on deck.

"There is some question about the seaworthiness of our ship in battle. One of the engineers told me that he didn't think we could outrun anybody but another ironclad. In all likelihood, when the time comes, we'll be towed into position by other ships. In that way we'll be able to put our firepower to good use.

"I'm not at liberty to tell you the name of our ship at this time, but I can tell you that I man one of the guns. This gets me on deck a good deal of the time. I've been tried at a number of stations, and I have to admit I like this one best. Manning the big guns reminds me of those shooting galleries on Cape Island, except that the targets are bigger. It's a little like firing at the Columbia House or Congress Hall. How can you miss?

"I'm not at liberty to go ashore either. Since I've virtually been pressed into service, the ship's officers are afraid I'll take off once on land. I have been promised leave soon, however, but in the company of petty officers. Pretty dull stuff, but better than sitting in this pot all the time.

"There's talk of our moving off the base to encounter the Confederate ships somewhere. I imagine it'll be off the coast to stop the blockade runners. But I haven't the faintest idea where. Though I don't particularly relish going into combat, almost anything would be an improvement over staying where we are—a hot, sultry part of the world with nothing to look forward to but more heat, more perspiration, more filth.

"How I miss Cape Island! How I miss the stiff breezes along the beach! How I miss Rachel's cooking and those pretty summer visitors at the "Hops!"

"But, most of all, I miss you, Dad—even Willacassa. I never knew how much until now."

"Love,
Jonathan"

"Dear Dad,

"I no sooner posted my letter to you when we received sailing orders. We raised anchor and in the next few days made port at such places as Key West and Dry Tortugas. We had a spell of good weather and in anticipation of shore leave I got my white ducks out and ironed them. At the last minute I was given gun inspection duty with no time to change. My ducks are now covered with rust and grease.

"A few days later we put in at the Navy Yard harbor in Pensacola. We filled our time with drills and clearing the decks for action. Or else we whitewashed the hold and took in coal. But no matter what we did to clean up the ship, it remained at best a filthpot. I looked longingly at the decks of the other ships in harbor. They were sparkling and clean and spacious compared to our tub. The crews and their officers moved freely about their decks while we crowded around the turret or hung over the iron railings.

"With shore leave cancelled, the men figured we'd be shoving off soon. After a few false starts we heaved up anchor and steamed out into the Gulf. From the direction we were taking we guessed we were heading for Mobile Bay. We guessed right. But for two weeks the flotilla under Rear Admiral Farragut sat outside the bay waiting for the rest of the fleet to assemble.

"From where we lay we could see Fort Morgan rising above the ground, enclosed by a thick wall of sand. Cannons were mounted on the fortress walls themselves and on the wall of sand. But even as we watched, Rebel steamers were sailing back and forth

235

in full view of our ships. And lurking in the background was the *Tennessee*, the Confederate ramrod that had been the scourge of our navy.

"We heard—and this proved to be true—that several lines of floating torpedoes were strung across the channel. Made from beer barrels, they were calked watertight, filled with gunpowder and friction fuses, and moored in the path of our ships. These torpedoes were supposed to explode on contact. And though our officers assured us that most of them would malfunction, we weren't anxious to test them out.

"On August 4 one of our ironclads exchanged fire with Fort Gaines on the other side of the channel. But the gunners on both sides were miserable shots and little damage was done. The next morning the full fleet got under weigh. The four ironclads chugged along on the right of the other warships, facing Fort Morgan. Firing had scarcely gotten under way when the *Tecumseh*, not a ship's length from us, hit a torpedo and blew up. She sank in a matter of minutes, losing ninety-two men.

"But we had no time to mourn the loss. The exchange of fire was extremely heavy as we sailed past Fort Morgan to engage the four ships that made up the Rebel fleet. We could see our own vessels, the *Hartford* and the *Brooklyn*, take a pounding. But our fleet managed to sink the *Morgan* and capture the *Selma*. And then they tried to ram the *Tennessee* which was of the same monster class as the *Merrimac*. After banging into her, the *Monongahela* and the *Lackawanna*, two big sloops, were more chewed up than the *Tennessee*. And the *Hartford*, Farragut's ship was severely mauled when it drew alongside and shot it out with the *Tennessee*. It wasn't until one of our ironclads, the double-turret, four gunned *Chickasaw*, began to pump her guns into the *Tennessee* that the ramrod's iron plates started to break off. When her smokestack collapsed, our ship came in for the kill. My own 15-incher began a racking fire that all but crippled her. I was ready to let loose again when the Captain shouted, "Hold your fire. The *Tennessee's* surrendered!"

"I joined the men that boarded the ship and stripped her colors. I have to tell you that proud as I was to be on the winning side, I turned sick at the sight of the *Tennessee's* deck. I never saw such butchery. Bits and pieces of flesh were scattered everywhere. The scuppers ran with blood. So thick was the going because of the mangled fragments of limbs and torsos that I slipped every time I took a step. I was glad to be back aboard our own ironclad again, hot and filthy as it was from the smoking guns and turret.

"A few weeks later when after a savage bombardment we took

Fort Morgan I saw how deadly our marksmanship had been. There wasn't a wall of the fort that didn't have a hole in it. There wasn't a structure that hadn't collapsed. The fortress was pierced through and through like a five-sided swiss cheese.

"I guess it was on the strength of this that my captain recommended me for a medal. Imagine, me getting a medal! If they did it properly, it'd be Cape Island's shooting galleries got one. But I'll take it. Although for my part, I'd gladly trade it in for a discharge.

> "Your son—and sometime hero,
> Jonathan"

FREEDMAN'S CALL

The last months of 1864 were the most painful and exuberant of Willacassa's life. She had seen in Mississippi startling, radical changes in the deplorable existence of the contrabands, if not exactly a revolution.

The contraband camp, a sinkhole of filth, crowding, and disease, had gradually died out. About one in four, mostly the old and the new-born, had perished from epidemics of fever and smallpox. The rest had been marched or carried in old cotton wagons to a newly established freedman's village several miles away where tents and a few log cabins were erected next to existing structures of a town abandoned a year earlier during an advance by Union forces.

Around the village a stockade had been built by contraband laborers who did the ax-cutting and the heavy work while white supervisors stood back, smoked, and watched them. As was the practice with the contraband camp, black military men stood guard against Confederate raiding parties and small bands of guerrillas.

Clothing, medicine, rations, basic household utensils were all provided by the army. And work details were set up by the white superintendent of the village—in the words of Mandy—"to see no one gets into mischief." But there was mischief enough nonetheless. Many of the men worked as servants for the army officers when they would have preferred to work their own land. And those that worked the land now labored for white overseers, some of whom were no better and no less demanding than the old plantation bosses. The war might unwittingly be grinding up the institution of slavery but a new kind of bondage was slowly being forged.

"Without land," insisted Mandy, "a man could only be half free." She fell into her old dialect to make her point. "De niggers still sweat, an de overseer still fills his belly off'n dat sweat."

And things were not much better with some of the younger women. Scootie had been taken on as a cook and a part-time laundress. But at least she took her books with her. Jerusha, on the other hand, had been taken in as a white officer's concubine and might have contracted a venereal disease. Camp followers knew no distinction of color.

But then came the dozen women of the American Missionary Association to set up a freedman's school in the village itself. What a welcome sight they were! Clean, upstanding, three or four bespectacled, and two of the women black as coal. And they came well-armed—with readers, bibles, notebooks, pencils, and even slateboards in their leather bags. There was a no-nonsense attitude about them that scattered opposition. And if the male white superintendent thought he had the last word in the affairs of the village, he'd better think again.

"There'll be no coercive labor here," they announced. "There will instead develop an appreciation of the necessity and nobility of work."

"Then you will get no one to work!"

"Oh, yes we will! There is dignity in work. It is bag and baggage of the Protestant ethic. In New England, labor is the product of self-discipline and self-reliance. The urge to work comes from within, not without. Indolence is nothing but wanton wickedness and degradation."

"We'll see."

"Yes, you will see."

And see they did. In fact, the white superintendent and his aides were astonished by what they saw. Employing Mandy to make it a baker's dozen, the freedom school faculty quickly got its rooms in order and hoisted up a school bell. In no time at all, blacks in uniform, blacks in plantation rough, blacks in rags left their tents and sheds and cabins and crowded into the school where they flipped the pages of their books and copied in an unsteady hand their blackboard assignments.

"You're sure you won't join us? You don't have to be a member of our church, you know."

Willacassa smiled and shook her head.

"I'm just an amateur," she said. "Now that you're here, my job is done. And I'm free to return home and do the things I do best."

"But look how well you did for Mandy."

"No one could do for Mandy. Once you put a book in her hands, she was bound to learn—with or without a teacher."

"But our duty—your duty—is to see the Negro through!"

"Perhaps it's just to give them a start and they'll see themselves through. See, already you've got three of their own on your faculty. That's the noblest part of what you're doing."

The headmistress basked in the warmth of the compliment.

"Now if your church can get them some land," added Willacassa, not wishing the good lady to get too fat with complacency, "they'll know what real freedom is."

"We're already working on that," said the headmistress. "And if Congress would see its duty, too—"

"Oh, Congress will see its duty. It just won't like what it sees."

Suddenly Mandy, who had been standing by quietly and

listening to all this, stepped forward and threw her ample arms around Willacassa's neck. "I can't stand it anymore," she said. "I don't want you to go!"

"But I must, Mandy."

"Then I'll say goodbye, Miss Harrah. But be quick about it. 'Cause I'm going to cry. I'll miss you. We'll all miss you. We all love you."

Willacassa was so moved by Mandy's ingenuous outburst that all attempts at speech were choked off. She leaned forward and kissed the girl, squeezing her shoulder, then quickly departed.

She found Captain Shiloh in winter quarters. He was lying on his cot, having had a long bout with fever. Shiloh had traded in his tent for a chinked log hut, but despite the heat of the fieldstone fireplace he was still chilled. Nevertheless he managed a smile and sat up to embrace her. Swinging the latch of the door closed, Willacassa climbed into bed beside him.

"Where's Zeb?" she asked.

"Sergeant Yount is delivering some reports to headquarters."

"So it's Sergeant now?"

"About time, don't you think?"

She cuddled up close to him. "Are you warmer now?"

"Much warmer. Beginning to heat up, in fact."

"Now don't get any ideas, Captain!"

"You climb in beside me and tell me not to get any ideas. I may be sick but I'm not unconscious."

"I still have my clothes on," she cautioned.

"That can be remedied."

"Under the covers? It would take a bit of doing."

"I think I can manage it."

"Is that what I get for being considerate of you?"

"That's what happens when you put yourself in a compromising position."

"Then I'll beat a hasty retreat."

She tried to slip out of bed but Shiloh stopped her. "I'm afraid you're surrounded," he said, throwing his arms around her and drawing her to him.

"Forced to surrender, I see."

"Unconditionally."

"Hasn't it always been unconditional?"

Shiloh kissed her face, flushed with the excitement of the moment, then fondled her breasts.

"Yes, my dear. But that will change soon." Struggling with the covers, he helped her disrobe.

They lay in each other's arms for the better part of a half hour before Willacassa began to dress again.

"Can't have Zeb barging in here and seeing us like this," she said.

"He won't barge in. Besides, the door's locked."

"Nevertheless—"

As soon as Willacassa was dressed, she stood in front of a small square wall-mirror on the chinked cabin wall and combed her hair.

"You're even more beautiful than I remembered you," said Shiloh, admiring her pretty shoulders and long hair.

"I think you're prejudiced, but that's all right."

"Will I see you later? There's much I want to talk about," said Shiloh. "As soon as I take a bath, I'll be my old self again."

"There's nothing wrong with you that I can see," she teased. "I think this lying in bed is nothing but playacting."

"It's you," he said, sitting up and leaning back against the wall. "You're the cure. I can't get over the difference in the way I feel."

"You don't expect me to believe that. You have your own brand of eyewash, Captain Shiloh."

He half-smiled. "Seriously, there is much I want to talk to you about. I've been doing a lot of thinking these past few months. And I've made some decisions I want to share with you. The war should be over soon. The South can't go on much longer. And I want—"

"We'll talk about all that when I get back," Willacassa gently interrupted. "You see, I've got to go to Cape Island. I haven't seen my father in some time."

"Cape Island? But I—"

"I'll be back, my dear. It's just that I've had this terrible premonition of something happening. My father is not yet sixty and he's in good health. Still—"

"I understand." Shiloh's was a reluctant assent.

"But as I was so near here I thought I'd stop and see you before going on."

"And I'm glad you did. These long stretches without you are getting harder to bear."

She returned to Shiloh's cot and sat down beside him.

"I don't think you have the faintest idea how much I love you, Sam. I think about that sometimes—how fortunate I am to know you."

Shiloh took her hand. "My precious, I'm the fortunate one. I came into this war looking for—I know not what. Maybe it was idealism. Maybe a romantic escape. Certainly not happiness. Then I met you. I never imagined that in the midst of all this I'd find

El Dorado.''

Willacassa looked at Shiloh's honest blue eyes and the several days' growth of beard on his pale, fever-parched face, and her heart overflowed with love.

"Let me go," she whispered at last, "or I'll never leave."

Shiloh acquiesced with a brief, tired closing of his eyelids.

"It'll be a couple of months, no more. Maybe less. If I don't go, I'll never forgive myself.''

She leaned over and kissed him softly on the lips. Her heart pounding, she found herself unable to bid him a decent goodbye.

Willacassa not only found her father well but found him in the teeth of a land-for-freedom campaign. Of course he was delighted to see her. Of course he would not let on, but she could see a tear forming in the corner of his eye. Of course he wanted to hear all about the freedman's village and her plans for the future. But there was this bill before Congress and unless enough support for it could be mustered in the next week it would fall calamitously short of passage.

The leather-top coffee table in the parlor and the magnificent armchairs were covered with petitions. Lists of voters in towns as far north as Dennisville and the Court House were pinned to his office walls. Batches of letters tied in neat bundles sat on his desk. And in the evening he met with Captain Whilldin, Reverend Williamson, and Joseph Leach—yes, Joseph Leach, his severest critic these past few years—arguing, talking strategy, or exchanging articles cut out of *The Liberator*, *Commonwealth*, *Independent*, *The New York Times*, *The Tribune*, or reading pamphlets and flyers by Wendell Phillips, Frederick Douglass, or George Julian, an Indiana congressman.

"Yes," Harrah argued, seemingly unaware that his daughter was sitting in one of the huge armchairs, listening attentively to him, "George Julian was right. Unless we adopt an equitable homestead policy, unless we break up Rebel plantations into small farms for the freedman, we'll fall back on the old system of land monopoly. Only this time we'll be selling off the plantations in large tracts to speculators and the black man will be no better off than under slavery itself.''

Reverend Williamson nodded in agreement, but Joseph Leach took exception.

"I hold second place to no one in the matter of emancipation, Nathaniel. But I agree with the President that we must go slow. Otherwise there will be seething resentment and in the South seeds planted for another rebellion.''

"If the President had his way," insisted Harrah, "the South would be back in the Union the day after the war ends—with no reparations, no payment of war debts, no change in the status quo. The Negro would be free, but he'd have no land he could call his own and no bread on the table. And the former white slaveowner would have the vote."

"How's that?" asked Captain Whilldin.

"How? It's the ten-percent rule. As I understand it, if ten percent of the voters in a Rebel state swear allegiance to the Union, the state is back in the fold and it's business as usual. The state then determines who will vote and who will not. And those who take a loyalty oath will get their confiscated property back. Under such a setup the old aristocracy will soon have the upper hand again. And the Negro will be back in harness. He won't be any better off with his new-found freedom than he was with pre-war bondage. Nor will the poor white, for that matter. He rarely had the vote before. Nor is he about to get it now. A handful of men will own the land once more and the rest will work it."

"Well," insisted Leach, "you can't just seize a man's land even if he was on the wrong side of the war."

"No, not if the man works the land," conceded Harrah. "But if someone else has worked the land—under compulsion—then he too has a stake in it. I'm not saying take all of the slavers' land. Leave them as much as they themselves can work. Thirty, forty acres. After all, how much land does a man need?"

"And the rest?"

"The rest you allot to the freedmen and Union soldiers and Southern whites who did not espouse slavery or secession."

"As the American Anti-Slavery Society suggested?"

"Exactly," said Harrah. "Look, the black man has earned a right to the land. He's been working it for years with nothing to show but lash marks on his back. If he's to remain a homeless, landless class of people, he'll never be free. He'll forever be a burden to society and to himself. The time for land reform is now. Not twenty, fifty or a hundred years down the road."

"What's wrong with colonization?" asked Captain Whilldin. "Even Lincoln favors that."

"Nothing—if the Negro wants colonization," replied Harrah. "But if the Negro was good enough to live side by side with the white man when he was a slave, he should be good enough to live side by side as a freedman."

"You know, of course," volunteered Reverend Williamson, "that in certain coastal areas General Sherman has set aside land for *exclusive* Negro settlement. Georgia, Florida, and South Carolina come to mind. Despite the *Commonwealth's* opposition to this, I don't hear the Negroes complaining. The only whites allowed in the area are authorized military personnel."

"You must remember," countered Harrah, "some Negroes don't trust the whites. And for good reason. My understanding of the order is that it was designed to keep out speculators and unscrupulous traders, whites who might take advantage of the freedmen. But white teachers are allowed there and members of freedmen's aid societies and white missionaries. I'm not saying the Negro can't decide to live by himself. I'm saying it's his choice to make. And if he chooses to live among the whites, that's his decision too."

"Well," said Joseph Leach, "all this points up one thing, Nathaniel. No one can call you a Copperhead anymore. If anything, you'll be accused of being a Black Republican. You don't have a mulatto mistress, like Thaddeus Stevens, do you?"

"My only mistress is simple justice," replied Harrah, smiling. "You're familiar with the wench, I assume."

"By the way, Willacassa," Leach said, looking her way. "I hope all this talk hasn't offended you."

"About black mistresses?"

The wiry Joseph Leach nodded.

'Not in the least, Mr. Leach. I've been among the military these past four years. Very little offends me now. It's Reverend Williamson you'd better worry about."

"Hardly," said Reverend Williamson, shifting in his chair. "My sermon this week is 'The harlotry of war: the profit makers.'"

They all laughed, Captain Whilldin most of all. "I'm afraid," he said, "the war has had a liberating influence. Time was, only salts of the sea spoke of such things. Now—"

"Why, Wilmon! There will still be things that only a seaman can speak of. Don't despair, my friend!"

The next morning at breakfast Willacassa revealed to her father her surprise at his militant stance.

"I thought you were the peacemaker, Father. Always the peacemaker. War was taboo. This new pugnacity of yours seems somewhat out of character."

"Obviously I failed as peacemaker. I can't pretend otherwise. This is the fourth year of war and bloodshed—though mercifully it may come to an end soon. But I haven't changed my view that the war was wrong. If all the blood spilled and all the dying is to count for something"—here his voice cracked a bit—"we must give the freedman at least half a chance."

"I don't disagree with you for a moment. It's just that—"

"You're not used to seeing me carry the torch?"

"Exactly."

"Well," said Harrah, "I've become impatient with patience. The situation is fluid now. This is the time to act. If we wait, it'll all turn hard and fast again. And we'll be fortunate just to chip away at the past."

With Harrah's new attitude came a new vigor, and Willacassa welcomed the change. Harrah no longer walked through the house, he strode through it. He took the stairs two steps at a time. He mounted his horse before his foot was secure in the stirrup. Time, time was suddenly a critical factor. And the economy of time was uppermost in his mind.

"Freedom is one thing," said Harrah at another gathering of the men. "But without the ballot it'll be freedom without teeth. The Negro must have the vote to chew on and the teeth to chew it with."

"You sound like Dr. Kennedy," smiled Captain Whilldin. "Watch out he doesn't get you in his chair."

"The Negro will get the vote," said Reverend Williamson. "Give him time. He's just got his freedom. He'll have to learn to read some and write before he can vote."

"That hasn't prevented some white men from voting."

"What the Reverend says is true, Nathaniel. Education is the thing we'll have to focus on," interjected Leach. "Education gets first priority. With education the vote will follow."

"Give him the vote and he'll get the schoolhouse," argued Harrah. "There's the Irish. Did anyone take them seriously until they got the ballot? No, they were the butt of every politician's joke. But once they started to vote, every ward healer in the big cities went after them, flattered them, made provision for their welfare. Now they count for something. It's the same with the Negro. Without the vote, he's still a man in boy's clothing. With the vote, he'll come of age."

"And what about women?" interjected Willacassa, warming up to the discussion although she was still sitting off to a side. "Are we no better than emancipated slaves? Shouldn't we have the right to vote too?"

"It's still a man's world," sighed Captain Whilldin. "There's enough going on, Willacassa, without changing that too just now."

"Hold on!" said Joseph Leach, springing to his feet. "I think Willacassa has a point. If the Negro is entitled to the vote, literate or not, why shouldn't women have that right? They read as well as men, maybe better."

"And they're every bit as intelligent," flushed Willacassa.

"Maybe more so," observed Reverend Williamson, leaning back and spreading his fingers tip to tip. "But as a practical matter, we have to do this one step at a time. There's enough heated opposition to Negro suffrage in Congress without adding women's suffrage to the fire. Let's get the Negro his vote first, then we'll go from there."

Willacassa was not entirely satisfied by this. "Obviously I can speak only for this woman, no one else. And I readily admit that whatever inequities we have suffered, whatever discrimination, it cannot compare to what the Negro slave has gone through. But as my father said, without the vote no one takes you seriously. That's the sad truth of it. So go ahead with Negro suffrage, those of you who are in the thick of things. But remember, once that fight is won, we'll be waiting in the wings."

"You've won your battle, I see," said Willacassa some weeks later.

"Which battle?" asked Harrah.

"The Freedman's Bureau bill. That section about land."

"Oh, some freedmen will get land. 'Not more than forty acres' is the wording. But it's at a rental—with an option after three years to purchase. And some vague promise as to title."

"You don't sound too enthusiastic."

"It's not definite enough," said Harrah. "Any lawyer could punch holes in it. And the vast majority of freedmen will get nothing. Yet the railroads have been given 67 million acres of land, not counting track. What for? If that land were given to the freedman, each family would have its forty acres and a mule."

"But most of that land is in the West. Shouldn't land in the South be confiscated?"

"Exactly. But it won't. The big landowners will find a way to keep their land. They always do. It doesn't matter whether they're on the winning or losing side."

"Then you don't see much hope for the freedman?"

"When you have four million people about to be cut loose in the land, with no real worry or plan for the future, we'll need more than hope. Maybe Mr. Lincoln has a plan. But right now it's only Congress working in their behalf. And once the war is over and the South is back in the Union that may change."

APRIL IS THE CRUELEST MONTH

Willacassa had intended to return to Virginia the first week of April. But the sudden illness of Rachel's husband, Mr. Planks, who was stricken with a fever, kept her on Cape Island. Rachel was her usual taciturn self throughout the whole ordeal, preparing broths and mixing teas at home as skillfully as she cooked things up in the kitchen of Trescott House. But Willacassa could see that she welcomed her support. Fortunately the old gentleman fashioned a recovery as rapid as the onset of the fever. And Willacassa made preparations to leave.

Her departure was spurred on by Robert E. Lee's surrender at Appomatox Court House. At long last the war was dragging to its end. And Willacassa wanted to be with Captain Shiloh when the final moment arrived. Not just to share in the celebration—as if one could celebrate a war's end. No, it was more than that. Decisions had to be made. Momentous decisions. Decisions that would have an impact on days and years to come. Shiloh himself had said as much. And she had her own ideas about the future.

Oh, she wasn't going to make demands on him. Shiloh was encumbered enough already. Better to cherish their life together, the few precious moments they managed to share. That was the trick. To have their time together, but not make him pay dearly for it. If that was self-sacrifice on her part, it was also self-fulfillment. The one balanced out the other.

Still, she believed that a new understanding had to be reached between them. They were no longer sometime lovers. Shiloh could not forever use the war as an excuse to be away from home. He had somehow to fashion a workable arrangement, one that would provide for his family and also recognize her place in his life, how much she had come to mean to him.

At the same time Willacassa knew intuitively that her thoughts on the matter would remain private thoughts. Talk was not necessary to confirm what she already knew. And talk would do nothing to elevate the truth. What understanding developed between them would grow out of their behavior toward one another. That was how it all started. That was how it would continue, moving through their lives like a Cape Island steamboat plying the ocean waters.

The camp was in a state of mourning when Willacassa arrived. News of President Lincoln's assassination had swept the compound. Flags were at half mast. Tents, caissons, and wagons were draped in black. Soldiers wore charcoal armbands and snatches of ribbon in their caps. The saddles of officers' horses wept with widow's weeds.

Even Zeb Yount greeted her with a mourner's look. This was natural enough. A soldier should mourn his commander-in-chief. But his grief seemed excessive. It carried sorrow too far. Could Willacassa be mistaken? Hadn't Zeb's smile always worn the look of sadness about it? It was stupid to think otherwise. Stupid, stupid, stupid!

But the look persisted. And when he took her hand—young Zeb who always kept at a respectful distance—she had a fleeting sense of doom. Had she stumbled upon a grim truth? She could see by the pain in his eyes that she had. Zeb was not in mourning for the President. No, Zeb was in mourning for someone else . . . .

When Willacassa opened her eyes she was lying on a cot, his cot, the cot that Captain Shiloh would rest upon no more. She tried to raise her head, by raising it to dispel the hard fact and the pain and the emptiness that suddenly choked her life. But she succeeded only for a moment. Slowly she fell back. "It can't be," she whimpered. "It can't be." Then she lapsed into the dizzying, swirling, spasmodic world where tears and emotions and screeching injustice collided, and only exhaustion and numbing despair put mind and body to rest.

She slept for hours, awoke briefly, and suffered Zeb to place a cold compress on her head. But unable to stifle the piercing pain in her chest, she slept some more. A troop of images paraded before her. Winter quarters, the battlefield after Manassas, makeshift hospitals. But she dismissed them with a scream. Then she saw Shiloh, clearly as before. He was leaning across his horse, warning her to stand away from the falling trees. But the trees kept falling, their branches stirring up the dust. All the mighty young trees falling—until she could see him no more.

"Do you want to sit up?" asked Zeb when she awoke once more.

She nodded and, letting him assist her, leaned back against the cabin wall.

Zeb propped up her pillow, then threw a coat across her legs. As he leaned forward, she saw the hurt on his face. And suddenly Willacassa hated herself for her selfishness. Zeb was suffering too. She had not wanted to distress the young man. But by indulging her own anguish, she was clearly disregarding his pain.

"Tell me what happened," she said when she found a brief respite from the dull ache in her chest.

Zeb Yount handed her a cup of tea. Blinking his eyes and moistening his lips, he cleared his throat of a choking mist. In a husky voice, no longer boyish but prevented by a drawl from being fully a man's, he told his story.

"We were in the vicinity of Culpeper, scourin' the countryside for decent horses. Our troops had horses enough. Besides, we were infantry and only the officers and their aides were mounted. We knew the Rebs were huntin' for animals. And it seemed the more good horses we took from the farms, the fewer their cavalry would have to draw from.

"At one farmhouse, a dilapidated run-down place, one of our men brought out an old mare, spavined and swaybacked like a quarter moon.

"Don't take our horse. It's the only horse we have. And we need it for plowing,' the old lady begged, her dress so ragged I wanted to cover her with my jacket.

"'Orders is to take every available horse,' said the soldier whose name I won't mention. The truth is we had orders to take any horse the enemy could put to use. There was no way this old horse could pull a caisson or carry a cavalryman. And if she could, she'd never get him where she was goin'.

"'You can't use that old horse,' she pleaded. 'It's sick and it's swayback. It's only good for plowin'. If we can't plow, we can't eat.'

"The soldier paid her no mind, just kept walkin' down the road with the mare hobblin' after him.

"The old woman kept on trudgin' behind. 'Please,' she said, 'if you have any heart left for the sufferin', you'll let us keep our horse. Can't hurt you in any way.'

"A boy no more'n fourteen came runnin' after her. 'Come on, Grandma,' he said, taking her arm. 'He's not goin' to let her go. You're just wastin' your time!'

"I saw him flash a look at us. And there was such hate in the eyes I knew he'd strike us all dead, every damn Yank in the bunch—if he could.

"At last the old woman give up and, with her scrawny shoulders shakin' from weepin', turned back towards the farmhouse.

"When we got back to our field quarters, I reported what had happened to the captain. You know how Captain Shiloh was about such things. Even in the midst of war, little things like that got at him.

"He called the soldier in and sort of suggested he return the horse to its owner.

" 'I can't do that, Captain.'

" 'Why not?'

" ''Cause we'd lose face. Like we don't mean what we say or do. Besides, the order was—'

" 'I know what the order was, Soldier.' So sayin', he rose from his table and cut across the field to where the commandeered horses were grazin'. I followed close by. Captain Shiloh had no trouble singlin' out the horse in question.

" 'This is the mare, I take it. A sorrier looking animal I haven't seen!' He grabbed the rope round its neck and led the beast to where his own horse was tied. Then, after climbin' onto his saddle, with the mare in tow, he started down the road to Culpeper.

" 'Where is the place?' he asked me as I followed close behind.

" 'I'll show you, Captain. It's an old farmhouse. Straight down the road. No more than a mile and a half.'

"He trotted off slowly so that the mare could keep pace with him. I kept thinkin' as I lagged behind what a fine man Captain Shiloh was. Here with the war draggin' on, with the Rebs hurtin' real bad, he finds time for Christian charity. I couldn't wait to see the old lady's face when he rode up with the mare. Yankee or Reb, it would make no difference. A little human kindness would bridge the gap.

"He couldn't have been more than thirty feet from the farmhouse, his shadow thrown across the barnyard by a blazin' sun, when I heard a shot ring out.

"It was only then I realized how foolhardy it was to come ridin' in there so short-handed—even though the countryside was secured.

"I sprinted to where he fell and jumped off my horse. But he was already dead when I got there. A bullet hole in his tunic and a circle of blood—that's all I could see. That's all was necessary to see.

"The old lady came running out, horror-struck and hysterical. 'My grandson didn't mean to do it. He's just a boy. Just a foolish boy! Is the officer dead?' She was trembling like an aspen tree.

"I nodded, unable to talk.

" 'What shall I do with the horse?' she asked, almost apologetic.

" 'Take it,' I said, somehow choking the words out. 'That's what he brung it for.' ''

He was standing in the road, looking at her, although his body was pointed in a different direction. His clothes were a beggar's rags, torn and shabby. Except for his tattered Rebel jacket, there was no trace of the soldier in him. Thin and drawn, if not emaciated, he appeared not only shorter but smaller than she remembered him. His face was covered with stubble and road grime. Only his eyes, startlingly drained of color, stared out unsullied and defiant.

"Willacassa, don't you remember me? It's Francis Grandee."

Francis Grandee? How could it be? Francis Grandee had been handsome beyond measure, spoiled beyond reckoning, reckless and self-indulgent as only a young man ignorant of his fallibility could be. Francis Grandee had been the one grand illusion of her life: lord of the strand, prince of the surf—equally at home on horseback or the dance floor. Wearing the mantle of Southern suzerainty, the Francis Grandee she remembered had come in search of the holy grail, Cape Island in summer, and had come away with Willacassa's heart.

She peered intently at him. Yes, Francis it was. But there was no trace of the Grandee about him. The pathetic-looking young man who stared back at her was devoid of all grandeur. Missing was the vanity and insufferable arrogance the Grandees had carried with them to Cape Island. Missing was the Norman nobility, the Southern cloak of superiority. What had once been the pride of South Carolina had been dismantled by the years and tattered. All that was left of Francis spelled rags and humiliation.

"I never thought I'd see you again," he said.

"The war had to end someday." Willacassa was not quite sure what she meant by this, but she said it nonetheless.

"The war was one thing," he said. "But Pea Patch Island was an endless hell." He drew a step or two nearer to her, his cracked shoes creaking as he walked.

"Pea Patch Island?" Willacassa had heard of the place. But all she could think of was the creaking of the cracked shoes.

"Yes. I was a prisoner there since Gettysburg. Can't begin to tell you how terrible it was. All of us confined in the old fortress. As foul and damp and stinking a place as I've ever known. Food scarce. Medical supplies non-existent. More often than not, forced to strip the corpses for something to wear."

He paused as though he were waiting for a comment from Willacassa. But she said nothing, and her silence only compelled him to go on. "And there were corpses aplenty. I myself saw hundreds of prisoners die. Some from the flux, some from the river that flooded the island, others of malnutrition. Even the crusts of hardtack we'd fight so hard for were indigestible. I wish I had a dollar for every body I rowed ashore to bury at Finn's Point."

He waited for Willacassa to say something, to indicate in some way that he was moving her. But she made no comment, her face rigid and inscrutable.

"And the brutality of the place! We got whipped for disobeying orders, whipped for draggin' our feet, whipped for being too sick to work. We were treated like animals, nothing human, like—"

"Niggers?"

Pale and gaunt as he was, Francis Grandee blanched. "You'll never let go, will you, Willacassa?" In despair he shook his head. "I've suffered for my mistakes. We've all suffered, paid a heavy price. But you'll never forgive us for what was done. You'll never forget what is past. Will you?"

He drew a step closer, his arm stretched out in a supplicant's gesture. "Do you know what kept me alive on Pea Pack? Do you know what kept me going all those long days and nights? Thoughts of you, Willacassa. I never would have survived if it weren't for that. I thought of you all the time. I thought once this war was over, feelings would be different. I thought we could put these things behind us. Yes, even wed one day. You see, I'm still in love with you, Willacassa." He removed his soiled hat. "What does a person have to do? What can I do? What can I say to convince you I've changed? That I'm a different man?"

Even Willacassa sensed that she was a woman without pity just now, a woman hardened to pain. But she could not bring herself to act differently. The grindstone of war, the millrace of blood had taken their toll. She was too numb, too dead inside to draw on softer feelings. And she could not plumb the depth of these feelings even if she wanted to.

"I guess the charitable thing to say is that you've suffered enough, Francis. And maybe you have. We've all suffered in this war. But to suggest that one day I'd marry you. That we put aside four years of bedlam and go back to romping on the beach—it's too ridiculous to contemplate. I'm not that romantic, Francis. Not anymore."

"But Willacassa—" Francis could barely comprehend her. He had suffered so much. The war, Pea Pack Island, the confiscation of his lands, the destruction of his ancestral home. Pure justice dictated that his suffering should have its reward. Could he have waited all this time for nothing? Come up empty-handed? It was inconceivable, ungodly, so unfair!

"Besides—" she said.

"Besides what?"

"Never mind. Some things are better left unsaid."

"I know. I know," anticipated Grandee. "It's my present condition. The abject state I'm in. I know I don't resemble the prosperous young man who first came to Cape Island. But all that will change. I'll get my land back. I'll swear allegiance to the Union. I'll win amnesty, if that's what it takes. And if that fails, I'll drive them off the land—those who've taken possession. And then I'll build a new and bigger plantation."

His eyes darted back and forth in excited afterthought.

"But don't worry. I'll give the Negroes their due. Slavery is dead. I recognize that. Still, they'll have to work for someone, won't they? And most will go back to their old masters. In any case, I'll make you proud of me again. You'll see. I'll make you forget that I stood like a beggar before you. Just give me time, Willacassa. A little time. And it'll be back to the old way of life again."

Staring at Francis Grandee, partly out of disbelief, partly out of morbid fascination, Willacassa could make neither head nor tail of the fickleness of fate. At the beginning of the war, for a whole year, she had hoped to encounter this man, despite everything, despite their vast differences. She had been prepared to wait if need be until chance or injury or the war's end brought him to her. And then, who knew what passions, what embraces awaited her! Only now could she admit openly to these feelings. But somehow, somewhere things had changed. A new perception had taken hold of her. And now it little mattered if Francis Grandee was alive or dead, friend or foe—the Francis who had been revealed to her in South Carolina or a changed man, as he insisted. The startling truth was that he counted for nothing in her life. No more than a tarnished memory. No more than a bent, cracked photograph.

"Goodbye, Francis."

Without another word, she turned her back on him and, leaving him standing in the road, walked away.

So much the war had accomplished. Eliot Irons was dead, buried somewhere in a soldier's grave in Virginia. And Francis reduced to this. She supposed that one day the struggle between the states would be hailed as a valiant chapter in American history. And the men who fought the war would lament the glory days, or at least their role in the debacle—once they put the pain behind them and dimmed their memories with whiskey! But Willacassa knew better. It was a stupid war, an insufferable war, a tribute to man's vanities and his blunders. Any man who claimed otherwise was a fool.

And then there was this other matter. It was still too painful, too soon for Willacassa to be thinking of Sam Shiloh. And so she avoided thinking about him. But she could not avoid thinking about his baby. Oh, she had entertained some doubts at first. She had not been sure of the signs. But what little doubt there was had been put to rest. He was gone, poor Sam—the one man she could truly say she had loved. But Willacassa was not left totally alone. If any good was to come out of this war, it would be Captain Shiloh's child. Yes, with a little luck and a midwife she might never be alone again.

"What's wrong, Willacassa?" Harrah had entered her room after knocking, and found his daughter sitting in her high-backed Shaker rocker, staring out at the sea.

"Nothing's wrong."

"But you don't eat anything, Willacassa. You don't leave your room. All you do all day is sit in that chair and look out the window. I haven't seen you like this since—"

"Since I broke up with Francis Grandee?"

"Yes, since that time."

Willacassa did not turn to look at Harrah, but she did run her fingers across the old sheet-iron betty lamp that stood on a wine table nearby.

"I don't think you'd want to know what's wrong," she said quietly.

"That's a strange thing to say. Not want to know? I love you, girl. I'm your father. What could I possibly not want to know?"

Willacassa did not reply. But Harrah could see that if he hadn't made any headway in his plea, it hadn't been rebuffed either. At least his daughter wasn't sobbing this time. He had heard her during the night. A heartrending, painful run of emotions that was retched from the depths of her soul and exposed her naked, vulnerable female being.

"Please, Willacassa, let me help you."

When she showed no sign of response, Harrah started for the door and muttered something about being downstairs if she needed him.

"Wait, Father!" Willacassa called when he had all but closed the door. "If you really want to know—if you don't mind being terribly disappointed in your daughter—I'll tell you."

Harrah reentered the room, standing, almost framing the doorway.

"You'd better sit down," she said, only half looking at him this time.

Harrah took the remaining chair, a brown Hitchcock, and, sitting on its edge, leaned slightly forward.

"While I was doing sketches for *Harper's*, I became attached, so to speak, to a particular outfit in the army." Willacassa's voice at this time was clear and free from strain."

"Was this the outfit from Indiana?"

"Yes, I suppose I wrote to you about it. Anyway, I spent a lot of time there and I became friendly with one of the company commanders, a Captain Shiloh. At first he just answered questions and provided access to the camp. But in time I came to depend on him and developed a high regard for his outspoken views. In that he was unlike many of the other military officers around. Most of them were martinets, popinjays even, strutting around like so many cocks in a barnyard. Captain Shiloh was one of the few men I met who saw the war with all its blemishes. He was one of those officers who died a little every time a young soldier was shot, killed, or torn up by shrapnel. He was, I suppose, the first man I met who did not march in step with the others, who understood the follies of our time and our leaders.

"He used to say we were dealing with two wars. The war they told us about and the war that actually took place. And they were as different from each other as the blue and the gray. He was afraid we'd believe the myths we created and never know the truth about the war. He didn't want that to happen."

Willacassa shot a glance at her father as though she recognized something for the first time.

"I suppose, Father, that in this regard he was very much like you. I hadn't really thought about it until now. Except that Captain Shiloh wasn't as reserved as you are, as tolerant."

As she said this, Willacassa suddenly lowered her eyes and stared at the wideboard floors.

"You're thinking that all this really isn't telling you anything, that I'm somehow avoiding what I was going to talk about." She sighed deeply. "But I suspect you know what I was going to say already."

She turned to look out the window once more, where a curlew made a wide circle in the sky.

"What started out as friendship, each of us pursuing his own profession, ended up a love affair." Willacassa interrupted herself to say, "Love affair is such a terrible word, I don't know why I used it. Yet in a sense it is the only word I could use. You see, I didn't mention that Captain Shiloh was married. And I didn't mention that he had children. I didn't mention these things because they made no difference to me.

"Oh, you're probably saying to yourself, 'How could you, Willacassa!' How could I indeed? But the truth is, I did fall in love with this man. And not once during the whole time we were together did I feel immoral or that what I was doing was wrong. All I felt was happiness. Pure, contagious happiness. And a sense of worth I never knew with Francis.

"I won't say that I didn't think about what would happen when the war was over. I won't say that the thought of his wife never crossed my mind. I won't say any of these things because that would be dishonest. I will only say that I had no regrets, was never filled with remorse. If I had to do it over again, I would."

"I think I understand," said Harrah quietly.

"No, you don't understand, Father!" For the first time Willacassa let her emotions spill over. "Two weeks ago—two weeks ago I learned that Captain Shiloh was killed. It was one of those pointless killings that wars are famous for. He had gone to return a farm horse that some Federal soldiers never should have taken. It was this act of kindness that proved to be his undoing. He was shot leading the horse back to its owner."

"I'm sorry," said Harrah, "I had no idea." But he could see that his daughter was not yet finished.

"I suppose some could say that I was punished for what I did, that we were both punished. But I don't subscribe to such nonsense. What happened was an accident of war. That's all his death was. Certainly his children didn't deserve to be punished. It was an accident in a war that should never have happened."

Willacassa paused as her voice broke off. And Harrah could see that she was preparing herself, preparing him for something more.

"I'm going to have his baby," she said at last. "That's what I wanted to tell you and had the hardest time doing."

"So that's the whole sad story," concluded Willacassa, rising from the rocker. "Not quite what you expected from your daughter, is it?"

Harrah got up from the chair Willacassa had sat him in and put his arms around his daughter, holding her for a long time. When he had his emotions in tow once more, he kissed her on the cheek and took a step backward.

"No one can say that you aren't your own woman," he commented.

Willacassa looked critically at him still waiting for an answer.

"Is it quite what I expected? I don't know," said her father. "I guess I had hoped you would marry the man you fell in love with. But that's neither here nor there."

"The question now is what you're going to do with me?" said Willacassa slowly, almost imploringly.

"Do with you. I'm going to take care of you."

"Until I have my child?"

"Of course."

"And then what? What will I do then?"

Harrah stepped forward and embraced his daughter once more, chucking her under the chin.

"What will you do? You'll work here at Trescott House—with me. Only as a full partner this time."

"A full partner?" Willacassa could not conceal her astonishment.

"I've been thinking about it a good deal, Willacassa. Even before this. And the idea looms better and better. You know the workings of the place. You know them inside out. As I get older I have less patience with all the details of keeping the house up. And there's no denying the guests have always taken to you. It doesn't hurt to have a pretty woman around."

Willacassa luxuriated in the relief, the pleasure of the moment, then patted her tummy. "Even if I start to bloom?"

"That's nobody's business but your own. If you want people to know the truth, that's all right with me. If you want them to think you're a war widow, that's all right too." Harrah paused only long enough to collect his thoughts. "Though I must say, I think of you that way—as a widow, I mean. It makes little difference that there were complications. I never met your Captain Shiloh, but he must have been a decent man. And I'll not condemn him for having been married. A man rarely marries the woman who best suits him. It takes him a long time to find out what he wants. By then it's often too late."

Willacassa leaned against her father's shoulder and cried softly, tears of relief and rejoicing. How she appreciated the man! How good it was to have him close to her! All these years she had taken him for granted. Just as she had taken Rachel and Trescott House for granted. The precious things in life—were they always to be regarded that way, like the roll of the ocean or the beauty of Cape Island?

"But what about Jonathan?" she asked when the thought belatedly occurred to her. "Shouldn't he have a stake in Trescott House too?"

"Of course, if that's what he wants." Harrah stepped back. "But I suspect Jonathan has bigger things in mind. Don't be surprised if he opens up a hotel of his own one day."

"A hotel? Where would he get the money?"

"I don't know. I'm sure he'll think of something. Jonathan always finds a way."

Willacassa became reflective for a moment.

"You're right, Father," she said at last.

"About what? About Jonathan?"

Willacassa shook her head. "About what you said before. I

don't care about the social niceties. They mean nothing to me. But for the child's sake, I'll pass myself off as widow.''

SPOILS OF WAR

The war was at last over. General Kirby Smith, who proved he was a bigger fool than anyone had thought by continuing to hold out, finally surrendered his last-ditch Confederate army at the end of May. And now only small guerrilla bands offered scattered resistance in the West.

For Cape Islanders the summer of 1865 promised to be its most successful season in five years. To be sure, those from the Deep South would not soon again take lodging in the big hotels. Even those from nearby Virginia would be scarce. A pity, too, because Southern women in particular had lent a special elegance and vivaciousness to the watering place. Without them, things would be dull. Their beauty, their flirtatiousness, their exhilarating conversation and laughter would be missed.

In their place and in place of their escorts, crowds of nouveaux riches would flock to Cape Island. These were people who had made their money in the war. And in fact, once summer was officially on, gunmakers and gunsellers, clothing manufacturers, storekeepers and provisioners, harness makers, Northern politicians, railroad men, merchants of every description poured into Cape Island and put a strain on its resources.

Columbia House and Congress Hall were at full strength, as was the United States Hotel and the Atlantic, the Delaware and the Centre House, and the dozen others of somewhat smaller capacity. Even the new La Pierre Hotel on Ocean Street had its one hundred guests.

The streets and sidewalks, dusty as ever, more like a frontier town than a thriving resort, were crowded with hacks, carriages, promenading visitors, and pickpockets. Some said the pickpockets were from New York, but from the way they pronounced their o's Harrah suspected that at least some of them came from the Market Street Wharf in Philadelphia.

A variety of entertainment was provided for the visitors. Boat races in the surf and horse races on the strand, target and pigeon shooting, quoits, tenpins, and a pastime called "baseball" were popular diversions. And, of course, there were concerts by Beck's Philadelphia Band and Simon Hassler's Military Ensemble. No lack of activity or celebration anywhere.

Still, Harrah detected an underlying sadness in the frivolity, a sense of gloom in the wake of so much recent pain and death. It was as if the early morning dips and the wending about the shops and the hops and the sumptuous seafood dinners at the big hotels and the cavorting about in carriages and four-wheeled rockaways could not quite dispel the pall that the war had cast on every phase of life these past four years. The butchery, the slaughter, the unbelievable destruction as reported in the newspapers and magazines or by eyewitnesses had an impact even on such a remote place as Cape Island. To pretend these things never happened or that the war was indeed all over only resurrected ghastly images just when Harrah thought they had been put to rest.

How could a country put more than six hundred thousand deaths so quickly behind it? And who knew how many mutilations and amputations? Not to mention the rampant destruction of whole cities and the devastation of the countryside? Did the vultures that came to feed on the bodies at Gettysburg ever leave that "hallowed" ground? Two years later they were still finding carcasses there and threatening to make their visit permanent.

Worse still, the South in a rash of self-deception persisted in referring to the horrid war as a glorious "lost cause." And those in the North, except for an embattled President Johnson, were prepared to exact a terrible price for the insurrection. Didn't they ever learn?

"Do you know anyone who has at least fifty acres of firm land to sell?"

It was S. R. Magonigle who asked Harrah that question when they met outside Aaron Garretson's "The Union Now and Forever" Grocery and Provision Store. Samuel Magonigle who had been Cape Island's mayor and the publisher (successor to Joseph Leach) of the *Ocean Wave* for the past two years, also dabbled in real estate, although it seemed of late he made most of his money as Cape Island's agent for The Travelers Insurance Company of Hartford and the Mutual Benefit Life Insurance Company of Newark.

"No, except for the Jonas Miller property near the Turnpike."

"Miller's breaking it up into lots. Some five hundred, I understand," said Magonigle. "So that's out."

"Why fifty acres?" asked Harrah.

"A state commission is looking for a site for a Disabled Soldiers' Home."

"I see."

A Disabled Soldiers' Home. Another legacy of the war, like the military graves at Cold Spring's churchyard or the Ladies' Aid Society for Orphans and Widows.

"If I hear of anything, I'll let you know," said Harrah, starting back to Trescott House.

Harrah appreciated the fact that most of the Cape Islanders who had volunteered for the war were now back home. Many had been discharged when the 25th New Jersey was disbanded in June 1863. But of the first thirteen young men who volunteered from Cape Island, four— Stephen Pierson, Townsend T. Irelan, John Mecray, and Charles Silvers—never made it past '62. And James Flavegar (who had no relatives to mourn him) was struck down in '63. A sixth, Owen Clark, had his leg amputated at Gettysburg. Not a very favorable survival rate!

And, of course, there were others: John Shaw and Thomas Hand and Albert Edmunds from Cold Spring; John Woolson of Fishing Creek; John B. Robinson of Dennisville; and from other parts of Cape May, Stephen Bennett, William G. Eldridge, David Hand, Hugh Edmonds, David Hildreth. After a while Harrah had lost track.

Nor could Harrah forget the brief letter he had received from Madeleine Craddishaw in April.

"I received word this morning that my son was killed in the lines at Petersburg, the day we put the torch to Richmond and abandoned the city.

"I curse the Yankees. I curse the war. I'd curse God himself but I no longer believe in one."

That was all. A cry of unassuaged pain—no more. And Harrah was helpless to do anything about it.

At the end of September, on a raw and damp morning, Willacassa drove her buggy to Cold Spring. She got out at the "Red Brick" church and wandered among the gravestones. There was no Sam Shiloh buried here, but somehow the cemetery made her feel close to him.

As she walked slowly around the back of the church to the northside of the graveyard, she came upon Henry Sawyer. The war hero was standing a silent vigil over a child's grave. He looked up when he became aware of another presence.

"Willacassa." That was all he said at first. Then breaking the spell of the quiet morning, he added, "I didn't know he—your husband—was buried at Cold Spring."

"He's not. But somehow I feel closer to him when I'm here."

"I understand."

Henry Sawyer patted down the soggy earth with his foot. "Tommy is buried here," he said hoarsely. "Last time I saw him was in August '64. Just before I rejoined my command. He died at the end of September that year. He was just nine and a half years old."

"He was a beautiful boy."

"That he was."

Sawyer spoke with a hitch in his voice, like a rusty wheel. "I sometimes think he would have survived—the other, too—if I hadn't gone off to war. At the time it seemed the right thing to do. But it was hard on Harriet."

Willacassa felt it best to say nothing, to wait for Sawyer to go on. After a long silence he turned away from the tiny gravestone and walked back across the scrubby grass toward the main path. Then, realizing he had gone without her, he stopped to wait for Willacassa.

"I fought hard for my country," he said. "I was wounded in four different encounters. And I don't regret any of that. Nor do I regret having to spend that time in Libby Prison under a death sentence. Men do these things when they have to. It's the manly thing to go off to war. But—"

He paused when he saw how intently Willacassa was looking at him, a pregnant archangel against the background of the red-brick church.

"I was going to say it seems a mite irresponsible. Does that surprise you?"

She shook her head.

"If I had stayed home, Willacassa. If I had put my family first, there's a good chance Tommy'd still be here. I guess he was as much a casualty of the war as Captain Broderick and Major Shelmire, officers I knew. Or even your husband. I'm sorry, but I didn't know his name."

"Shiloh."

"Captain Shiloh, was it?"

"Yes. Captain."

Sawyer stuffed his hands into his pockets and walked with a slight limp.

"I've had these thoughts lately. Troublesome thoughts, Willacassa. I don't know what to do with them. I didn't think much about the war while it was being fought. But I think about it all the time now. It's as if I see it all clearly for the first time—now that the last shot has been fired."

"It's been a long war. Especially for you, Henry. You were one of the first to go and the last to come back. You saw more than most."

"And I don't like what I saw."

The once youthful, exuberant Henry Sawyer had matured into a pensive, restrained man. Willacassa was not yet quite used to the change, but she wanted to understand what Henry was experiencing. She realized that a cemetery brought out the sad, the morbid side of feelings. But these too had to be dealt with and not dismissed as mere playthings of mood.

Sawyer smiled, the saddest smile she had seen on a person for some time.

"The war," he said. "It seems for nought. Oh, the slaves have been freed, and I have no quarrel with that. I suppose the likes of John Brown would say we paid in blood for what we did to the Blacks. But who paid? Not the slaveowners for the most part. Most of the Rebs who had their skulls split open or a bullet in their guts did not look like slaveholders to me. They looked like dirt farmers or mechanics or just plain kids who had the life snuffed out of them for no good reason. And what about our boys?"

For a moment Henry Sawyer had to fight the spill of tears as a rush of memories surged back.

"They died for the Union, they say. That's a pretty high price for a shotgun marriage. We should have let the Reb States go. Had nothing to do with them. Declared them pariahs for having slaves this day and age. Or even fought them over slavery from the first. Called a spade a spade. Not pretend it was Secession that bothered us.

"But we didn't. Instead we gave them a cause to fight and die for. And the bitterness over it all will last a hundred years."

As Willacassa returned home she could not put what Henry Sawyer had said out of her mind. It was no surprise when her father uttered such sentiments. From the first he had regarded the war as a blunder, as a string of follies that led to needless bloodletting. But when Captain Sawyer, a bonafide hero who epitomized the Union's fighting man, began to have doubts about the war, it was time to reconsider her own feelings on the conflict.

For in the beginning, in a strange way, Willacassa had regarded the Civil War as her war. The struggle, of course, began with the importation of slaves into America and the development of that most degrading of institutions which the South called "peculiar." But on that day at Higbee's Beach when as a little girl she had come upon the agonized bodies of slaves, slaves who had been dumped overboard to enable the captain of the *Carolina* to escape detection—on that day Willacassa laid claim to a personal stake in the abolition of slavery, by fair means or foul. The wretched institution had to go. The mentality that made it flourish had to be exposed. The slave market with its shameless parade of black flesh had to cease. The pitiless exploitation by a self-appointed privileged group over another group of human beings had to end.

And over the years she not only saw a terrible conflict coming, she welcomed it. For it appeared that only with blood could the shameful stigma of servitude be washed away. Willacassa had assumed in her naive way it would be the blood of the guilty that would be spilled. But time proved her wrong. So many innocents perished in the slaughter that the idea of just retribution perished too. The slaughter was just that. No way to justify or dignify it by any other name. It was senseless, unmitigated slaughter—a monument, rows of monuments, to man's unredeemed stupidity. If in the end some good came of it—almost out of desperation, out of a fumbling ineptitude—it was of small comfort to those who died and had no business dying.

So there was guilt here, a deeply-felt guilt. Not guilt over her opposition to slavery. No, there could be no guilt in that regard. But guilt over the belief that an easy solution had been at hand. People were oh-so-quick to send men off to war. War was inevitably the first solution, the first resort instead of the last. And these same people who with such unseemly haste sent men off to war had no more notion of where the war was heading or what its impact would be than they had when they impetuously placed bets on a cockfight or a barroom brawl.

Even Mr. Lincoln at its onset hadn't the foggiest notion where the war would lead. If he had a policy or a plan, he kept it a deep, dark secret. After the firing on Fort Sumter fugitive slaves were still being returned to their owners! A year and a half into the war Lincoln was still formulating rationales for justifying the conflict and for convincing friend and foe alike that slavery was not the issue but the ungluing of the Union. And as late as 1863 he was inviting the South to return to the fold and to the state of affairs that existed before the war.

What Willacassa had hoped for in the war was a moral crusade, something that would remove the stain of infamy from Southern soil. A triumph not only for the human condition, but for America itself. A blow struck against unforgivable selfishness and obscene class privilege. A coming of age for a country that prided itself on self-congratulatory adolescent rantings about freedom, equality, and opportunity when four million of its people were in bondage.

But what she saw during four years of war was indiscriminate and wanton destruction, destruction that rivalled the Crusades in their bloody marches through Asia Minor. And, oh, the cost in human life! More than six hundred thousand young men—and who knew how many others—had suffered the ultimate agony. Six hundred thousand men who would never have another chance to see a sunrise, to study the world about them, to love a woman and see their children grow, to shape the path and character of their lives, to enjoy the fruits of their labor in this bountiful land.

Willacassa's grief gnawed at her. Even the consolation of emancipation was small consolation. For the abolition of slavery was more a result of accident than design in the war, an act of expediency at best. The hatred was still there. The blind prejudice. The unjustified disdain. And the obstacles placed in the path of the freedman gave the lie to any real chance for freedom.

This, then, was the legacy of the war, Willacassa's war. This was what the mourning was all about. This was the dirge of the dead and the dying.

"Where have you been?" asked Harrah.

"To bury the dead."

"The dead?"

"Dead notions. Ideas that have had their time. Strange things like that," said Willacassa.

"I shouldn't have asked," said Harrah.

"No, Daddy. I'm glad you did."

Willacassa heard the clock strike four bells and awoke from a restless sleep. As it was the offseason for Cape Island, her father had set up a temporary bedroom for her and the baby in the ground-floor parlor.

"No point walking up three flights of stairs with a newborn infant," Harrah had said. "By summer we'll have a little cottage built just back of Trescott House. Of course, you'll have to give up that airy perch you had and that unobstructed view of the sea. But your baby will have no complaints so long as she can build sand castles and dig up clam shells. That's all right with you, isn't it, Willacassa?"

Of course it was all right. He knew it was all right. But he had asked anyway.

Willacassa threw on her cape, then leaned over the crib to look at her baby. She could barely make her out in the early morning shadows except to see her outline in the blanket. Nor did she want to light the lamp as the gray light of dawn could be seen out the window. Better to take the child to her first sunrise.

Gently picking the baby up, Willacassa wrapped the blanket snugly about her. Holding her close, she slipped out the back door and on to the beach.

It was cool on the beach, with a wind blowing, but not so cool as to turn back. Barefoot, Willacassa carried the infant to the water's edge. Stepping ankle-deep in the rising tide, she looked out over the ocean. The morning sky was russet with the sun's rays, beckoning to her. With outstretched arms, Willacassa held her baby over the water.

"Here she is, Sam. Isn't she pretty? It'll only be a symbolic baptism—" Her voice broke and she could not go on for a few moments, her whole body quivering with emotion. Then she pulled herself together, tossing back her long blonde hair and staring defiantly at the sky.

"I was thinking of calling her Fredericka. But I remembered you weren't too fond of your Christian name. So I'll call her Samantha. But not Shiloh, Sam. The name has taken on a new meaning since the war. And we've had enough of blood and battle. It'll be Harrah, after all—for my father. Samantha Harrah. I know you'll understand."

Willacassa stepped back, overcome with agitation. But she fought through the throbbing pain, determined to lift the burden from her heart.

"I'll miss you, Sam. Oh, how I'll miss you!" Tears were falling freely now as celebrant waves lapped at her legs. "But I'm going to live this life for both of us. And I'll give it no quarter!"

She raised her face to the sky once more, a now brilliant sky whose broad, far-flung horizon spanned a new day. "I'm done with dying, my love. And I'm back on Cape Island to stay. Do you hear? I'm back on Cape Island. And it'll take more than a war to drag me off again."